"The château's owner was the mistress of the cult," Elaine said with relish. "She killed her newborn babies and boiled them down for the fat to make candles for the witches' ceremonies."

"How horrible!" Bridget said rapturously.

"They burned human sacrifices in wicker baskets on the meadow . . ."

"Burning people and killing babies!" Kei looked aghast and continued, "Elaine, everyone says you're a witch. Is it true?"

"Don't be silly," Bridget answered. "Elaine fools around with the ouija board and tells the cards, that's all. Why are you trying to frighten Kei out of her wits, Elaine?"

Elaine smirked. "Such an idea would never enter my head—I want her to feel welcome here."

Bridget continued, "Everyone in the village thinks all old women are witches."

Elaine seemed to swell slightly, and a flush mottled her neck. "Give me time, my dear, and I'll show you whether or not I'm a witch . . ."

THE WITCHING

BY FRITZEN RAVENSWOOD

ZEBRA BOOKS

KENSINGTON PUBLISHING CORP.

ZEBRA BOOKS

are published by

KENSINGTON PUBLISHING CORP.
475 Park Avenue South
New York, N.Y. 10016

Third printing: May, 1989

Printed in the United States of America

To the model for Simon,

with gratitude and apology

PROLOGUE

Her flesh shuddered back from the rough stone. Cold. Cold and dark, except for the candle flame, blue at its heart, the yellow blade of light dancing in a pool of transparent oil—the distilled fat from stillborn and aborted children. A greasy ribbon of smoke folded and unfolded slowly upward from its tip. *Concentrate on the candle, on the brown and red stripes—the devil's colors. Concentrate on the candle and blot out the pain.*

This was the way she'd learned to shut out reality since she'd taken that first step on Midsummer's Eve, so easily, excited by her daring, triumphant that he could never laugh at her again if he knew. Proudly she'd accepted the fine iron chain they'd put around her neck. Not knowing that they would draw her along, patiently and persuasively, through one horror after another, letting her realize gradually for herself that if she protested she'd become another body discarded and festering in the rank weeds beside the canal.

The pungent oil from his body prickled along her back when he left her. The sonorous chanting stopped as he stood behind the altar, and ragged voices, unsynchronized, called out from the blackness, "Behold the Hornèd God, your Master!"

She was one of them now. She tilted her head up from the stone slab. As they put his robe around him, she could see a dark, glistening line of hair snaking up his belly in the light from the candle, but not his face, hidden in the shadows of his hood. Never his face.

They helped her upright and steadied her as her knees buckled. Now they would take her measure with the thick silk cord of crimson that would bind her to him forever. The cord slid around her waist and away again as they marked the distance with a knot. From the shoulder to the tip of the longest finger. Then a knot. From the base of the feet to the top of the head. Another knot. Around the head. And a knot.

His hands reached across the altar for the heavy red cord. Took it. Placed it with others in a black brassbound box. Closed the lid. Now she belonged to him. And still he did not speak.

Silently, he pushed the coven's Book of Shadows across the stone toward her and held out a pen. She hesitated a moment, then took it and resignedly wrote down her secret name, Alecto, in a wavering script on the brittle, browning paper at the foot of a centuries-long list of those who had chosen to be vassals of Satan, agents of evil—names that could never be erased.

As they helped her into her robe, a voice whispered in her ear, "You have the sacrifice?" She knelt and picked up the container from the chill, damp grass and put it on the stone slab.

"Your athame," the voice said. She felt the handle of her ceremonial knife, the black-handled athame, come into her hand. She stood there, rocking slightly on her heels, staring up at the vault of the ruined roof and the blackness beyond. *I cannot open it. I cannot look at the thing inside.* Almost inaudibly, bare feet slithered across the grass as the robed figures gathered closer to watch the ritual.

The voice was impatient. "You know what to do," it said.

The lid rattled as she opened the container and turned it on its side to roll the contents onto the altar. She could not touch the thing. It was a monster—distorted, waxy flesh rejected before its time by the womb that carried it. A turgid, queasy tide washed back and forth in her stomach. After the sacrifice, they would take it away and render it down to make more candles. But first she had to slice open the dead throat. *I can't! Oh, Simon, I'm so sorry, so sorry! I didn't know it would be like this!* She had only wanted him to take her seriously, not to laugh at her any more, and now . . . Now a hand came down over hers and guided it, did the work for her, pressing down the knifeblade.

He reached across the altar again, this time pointing his own athame at her. His knuckles shone in the candlelight, crisscrossed with black from the ritual oil with which they'd anointed him.

"This is your charge," he said, and at last she knew him, knew his voice. "Bring us the talisman of the old cult. The drawing-back ceremony was successful. We entered her dreams and called her back. She is here now, bringing the talisman with her. Your charge is to take it from her and give it to us. We will dispose of her later. With the talisman of Sélène, our power will expand and grow, and nothing will be impossible to us."

Carefully, he scraped at the sacrifice with the blade of his athame. He set a golden chalice on the altar stone, poured it full of wine, stirred it with the bloody knife, and held out the cup to her.

CHAPTER ONE

Wearing dark glasses and standing beside a pillar that he could duck behind to compose himself if she turned out to be too utterly ugly, Simon watched three middle-aged women get off the train. She was, her résumé said, forty-five.

Two of the women were met, immediately enfolded in family bosoms, and hurried away. The remaining one, a horse-faced person who — although he couldn't be sure from this distance — looked as if she would have warts with hairs in them, lifted her head like an animal sniffing the wind, obviously looking for someone. Simon sighed and stepped forward.

Opening her mouth in an ecstatic smile, the woman rushed toward him with open arms. Simon fell back in alarm, but she charged along the platform and passed him. By the baggage cart she seized a squatty, sharp-nosed woman, whose hat popped off and rolled down the platform. Both women ran after it, but the horsey one outdistanced the other, picked the hat up, and began beating the dust out of it by whipping it against her thigh. "Mon chapeau, mon chapeau!" the short woman piped in protest, making snatches at it. Her friend jammed the hat on the little woman's head and yanked it down until her brows beetled before marching her off, half blind, to the taxi stand.

Relieved, Simon turned back to the train. A tall, leggy woman with tousled beige and silver hair had materialized on the platform. In spite of the heat, she wore an elegant beige mohair coat and, pulling at her short leather gloves, looked about her impatiently, as if annoyed because her chauffeur was late. Clearly not a secretary, Simon thought.

Nevertheless, she raised a hand to him in recognition. Keeping her eyes on Simon, she hitched the long strap of her smart suitcase over her shoulder, posed her right foot against her left in fashion model style, and waited for him to come to her. Simon's first reaction was surprise. Then irritation. Damned cheeky for a new employee, if that's what she was, he thought angrily. She was all wrong!

"Is this all of your luggage?" he said between his teeth.

"I travel light," she said with an imperious nod. "My trunk will be along later."

Taking her arm, Simon dragged her along to the car, shoved her in, slammed the door, and threw her bag into the back seat. The tires squealed as he pulled out of the parking lot and, he noted with satisfaction, her head snapped back sharply when he swiveled into traffic.

12

Never employ anyone sight unseen, regardless of references! He *knew* better, he thought with fury. Everything was going to be ghastly. Her clothes alone gave that away. A sober suit and shoes with sensible heels would have been right and proper, promising efficiency and unobtrusiveness, and that designer's coat had no relationship to the plain, slightly threadbare one she should have been wearing. Too much money and vanity there for her to have a comforting attitude of respect and dedication. Secretaries should be as solid and sexless as their typewriters. Not running around in spike heels and pants that fit like a coating of suntan oil. How could Jeremy do this to him?

What Simon had wanted was to have his pages of scrawled, crossed-over script magically transformed into neat stacks of perfect typing, with a minimum of fuss and conversation. Oh, a secretary should correct the spelling, of course, since his was hopeless. Or add a comma, at most. But no tinkering! She probably wouldn't have dared to alter his art criticism. He was too well known an authority in the field for that. But autobiographies were different, and this—this *person*, by the very line of her jaw and the tilt of her high cheekbones, threatened massive rewrites and wrangles over grammar. She might even have the nerve to accuse him of exaggerating about his—er—well, he'd have to use a delicate touch on his romantic history.

He looked at her out of the corner of his eye as he drove. She was also looking at *him* out of the corner of *her* eye, which rattled him so much that he missed his turning and had to make a humiliating tour around the block to get back on course.

Under the coat she wore a blouse the color of tobacco—and no bra. A gap between buttons made that clear. On the instant, his driving became wretched. He was already going faster than normal, and now his coordination was thrown off. He was, in fact, scaring himself badly.

She rummaged in a handbag roughly the size of a bathmat and flinched as he nearly collided with the car in front. "I assume you *are* Simon Eagleton and not just a look-alike who's kidnapping me for the white slave trade," she said, sticking a cigarette in her mouth and snapping open a gold lighter while keeping her eyes on the road. "It's hard to tell from your pictures in the magazines. You take a rotten photo."

The gap between buttons shifted and widened as Simon nodded, peeking at her.

"My God!" she exclaimed at the sudden lurch and sway. "Do you *always* drive like this?"

"Always," he said grimly, his hands clammy on the wheel. No admissions of ineptitude. Establish authority immediately, or she'll take the reins in her hands. Simon was further infuriated to realize that, by saying this, he had committed himself to a pattern he'd have to maintain now until he could get rid of her. How long he could manage to carry on this way, ripping around the countryside like a maniac, he couldn't calculate. Not long, if he wanted to keep on living.

14

Thank God, they were soon out of town, where he could tear along the smooth blacktop at a screaming speed without being quite so terrified. As they neared the château, chickens from a neighboring farm took it into their silly heads to migrate en masse to the other side of the road. With horror, Simon saw that it was either brake suddenly and risk skidding into the ditch or plow on through.

Feathers exploded across the windshield. The secretary clapped her hands over her eyes. Doggedly, he sped on until they passed the turn at the bottom of the hill, where the car was hidden from the farmer, who — when last seen in the rearview mirror — was jumping up and down and waving his arms, surrounded by scattered corpses.

"See here," Simon said resolutely, determined to stop all this nonsense, "I really don't drive like this. I think I've been showing off. Juvenile of me."

But he spoke to unhearing ears. The new secretary had her head out the window and was otherwise occupied.

Hilaire, gardener and man *à tout faire,* was waiting at the front door of the château, chewing a moribund cigar, when the Mercedes skimmed over the crumbling little bridge that spanned the miniature moat. His jaw dropped at the sight of the red asterisks and white feathers decorating the car as it scrunched up beside him and stopped with a jounce.

15

"You should have warned me that you drove racing cars on the side," said the secretary, wiping her mouth with a handkerchief and looking ashen. "You must have nerves of steel!"

For a split second, Simon fancied swaggering around in a macho role, but that would have taken more dramatic ability than he possessed, and lying about oneself demanded constant attention to worrisome details. He'd better clear this up immediately.

"I don't really . . . " he began but was interrupted by the crunching of Hilaire's heavy, mud-crusted boots on the gravel of the parking area.

"I beg your pardon?" said the secretary, putting away her handkerchief.

"I don't . . . "

Hilaire flung open the back door of the Mercedes and yanked the suitcase out onto the ground with a noisy rattle of pebbles.

"What did you•say?" asked the secretary.

"I never . . . " Hilaire slammed the door shut with a loud, solid whump, and Simon snapped, "Oh, never mind!" out of patience. He dug in his pocket for some bills and handed them to Hilaire with sotto voce instructions to reimburse the chicken farmer.

"Tiens, tiens!" Hilaire said reprovingly, rolling his bloodhound eyes. He said something about getting the garden hose and tromped off, shaking his head.

Annoyingly—and everything she had done so far was annoying—Ms. Ronald did not exclaim in delight at the château, and Simon had been looking forward to being very off-hand about it. Clearly, she wasn't going to give him a chance to be modest about it.

It was not one of the great châteaux, being only about three hundred years old, but it was the size of an American courthouse and undeniably picturesque, with towers at the four corners, from whose conical roofs flew brave little tin banners.

Ms. Ronald's eye fell on the sculpture by the front door, a giant marshmallow in spongy white stone atop a black marble base, and her nostrils flared. Simon felt his temper getting out of hand. Who was she to question his taste in art? Silently she studied the tall gray walls of the château, fronted with windows that opened outwards behind curlicued iron railings, and then at the ducks bobbing and circling in the moat. He'd expected a secretary to go all a-twitter at the sight, but she simply stared at the mound of glossy-leaved ivy that hid the air-conditioning unit that kept the third floor at the right temperature for storing canvases and made no comment. She turned to glance at the shelter stacked with split wood ready for the fireplaces and beyond to the wrought-iron gate that opened into the high road leading to the village of Fay-sur-Loire. Not a word. Simon seethed. Any normal woman would have been at least a little awed, but Ms. Ronald looked as if she might whip out a rating sheet and give the château bad marks as a tourist site.

The two mastiffs were jumping at the foyer

17

doors, their noses making smears on the glass. Determined to get a reaction out of her, Simon said, "Ms. Ronald, I'd like you to meet two very important members of the household, Mitzi and Bayard," and opened one of the doors. The dogs burst out and joyously knocked her flat on the ground, scattering the contents of her handbag on the gravel. A compact rolled down the bank of the moat and plunked into the water. Mitzi planted pieplate-sized paws on the lady's chest and gave her face a thorough washing down.

Promptly ashamed of his glee at seeing her bowled over, Simon called the dogs off and helped Ms. Ronald up, settling her coat about her shoulders while she scrubbed at her face with her handkerchief and shot him a vicious look. The dogs raced away along the path to the back property and disappeared. Simon helped her collect the things that had spilled from her bag, but he thought it better not to mention the drowned compact.

When she snapped her bag shut, she looked up at him with her long hazel eyes narrowed and her jaw squared and said, "I've gone through a lot of trouble and come a long way—*at* my own expense!—to get this job. But—" She was enunciating her words very precisely, as if she were biting each one in two. "—*But* I didn't count on your being some kind of sadistic madman. You could have killed me with your crazy driving. And you wiped out a whole flock of chickens without a backward glance. You're the kind of person who chains his secretary to her desk and lays on a blacksnake whip at teatime. For all I know, you could have your old secretary walled up in the basement. I quit, as of now!"

Just as Simon was thinking how uncommonly attractive her eyes were and how large her irises had become, she hauled off and kicked him in the shins.

"And that's for siccing those monsters on me!" she said savagely.

Simon grabbed his shin and danced about on one foot, trying not to burst into tears at the pain. Too late, he remembered reading that a cat's irises expand just before it pounces on its victim.

"Oh, dear!" she said, watching his caperings, "I forgot I had on spike heels! I didn't mean to hurt you that much. Only a little. Let me see how bad it is."

She knelt down and pulled up his trouser leg. Both of them stared in dismay at a walnut-sized bruise with a red bull's eye that was puffing up on his shin.

"That must be agonizing. I'm terribly sorry," she said.

"It's nothing," said Simon, suppressing a moan. "I hardly feel anything in that leg. An old war wound, I'm afraid."

Ms. Ronald looked aghast.

"No, no, I made that up," Simon said hastily. "I do feel it, and it hurts like hell. But it's my fault about the driving and the chickens and not controlling the dogs."

"I have a nasty temper," Ms. Ronald said ruefully, standing up again and brushing off her knees.

"So I see."

19

They both jumped as water drummed on the fenders of the Mercedes. Hilaire was talking rapidly to himself in French and shaking his head as wet feathers and water rained onto the parking area. A line of ducks rocked up from the moat to investigate and stood in the spray, beating their wings in the broken rainbows and quacking excitedly.

"I wish you wouldn't quit right off," said Simon. "I'm too unnerved to face driving you back to the station this minute."

"The idea doesn't enchant me, either," said Ms. Ronald, rumpling her tan and white hair with a long-fingered hand embellished with an immense topaz ring. "I'd be delighted never to get into a car with you for the rest of my life, but I'm not sure what I've gotten myself into here. Your behavior seems bizarre, to say the least."

"I'm not like this," said Simon. "Really, I'm not. I don't know what got into me," he lied, clearly remembering the gap in her blouse. "Then things seemed to—get out of control and gallop away."

"Really," she said dubiously, frowning and studying his face.

"Oh, la-la!" shouted Hilaire. A thin wisp of smoke was curling out of the window on the passenger's side.

"My cigarette!" said Ms. Ronald. "I must have dropped it when I was hanging out the window, unswallowing."

Hilaire opened the car door and doused the interior with the hose.

"I can't ruin your car and then quit too, can I?" she said contritely and bit her lip.

Simon thought to himself that her quitting was a capital idea, but he'd already made an ass of himself, and firing her after having asked her to stay would make him look even more of an idiot. Picking up her bag, he decided that he couldn't give her her walking papers for at least a couple of days now. Even that would be mean, after she'd come all the way from the States.

Jeremy Kirbottle, his publisher, had said Simon was lucky to get her. According to Jeremy, she was top notch, and Simon hadn't even had to pay her way across the Atlantic because she first intended to visit an aunt in Paris, who was dying. Job or no, Ms. Ronald had written him she had to see her aunt (and gave him more gruesome details about her condition than Simon thought was at all necessary) and felt conscience-bound to pay her own way to France. He wished to God, though, that Jeremy had given him a hint of what would be stepping off that train.

Simon gave Ms. Ronald time to look over the foyer, with its life-sized Giacometti nude torso (she seemed to like *that*, anyway), its huge baroque gilded mirror over the table with the tall bronze candlesticks, and the baptismal font that held a pouf of September flowers.

"Charming!" Ms. Ronald said softly, and a small measure of his antagonism toward her ebbed away.

"How is your aunt?" he asked pleasantly, "Well, I hope?"

Ms. Ronald sniffed the flowers, burying her nose in them. "What aunt?" she said absently.

21

CHAPTER TWO

Dear Chris:

Only one day here and already I've blown my cover story! I think I glossed over it fairly well, but Eagleton's expressions are hard to decipher. Once in a while one of his eyebrows goes up and he looks super- cilious, but otherwise he looks as if he's seen everything twice and found it unbear- ably boring the first time round. He's an icy number — completely composed, no matter what happens (he massacred a whole flock of chickens with his car today without flickering an eyelash!). You know cars terrify me after Stephen's accident, and I didn't take it kindly, but E. looked as serene at 90 miles an hour as if he were jogging along in a pony cart.

Oh, Chris, I'm so transparent that anyone can read every thought that goes through my mind. How am I going to be able to carry this off?

E. is one of the most smashing-looking men

I've ever seen, if you like the suave, sophisticated type. One can see why he's cut such a swath all these years through the international set. Those out-of-date photos in the newspaper morgue made his hair look blond, but it's pure silver. Thick. Slight wave in front. Good eyes. Brown. Taller than we thought. About six feet, I'd guess, and slim rather than massive. Very square shoulders but not particularly broad. Actually, he's got a sort of boyish build, with very long legs. The kind clothes look good on. I figured you'd want a complete description, so don't mistake this for wild enthusiasm.

He wears a gold signet ring on his pinkie and has a bad habit of sitting on the end of his spine and looking thoughtful and calculating. I'm sure all those women who surround him in the media pictures find his mouth ravishing, but when he sits there like that and pinches his lower lip, all I can think of is a Stormtrooper wondering if the ovens are hot enough.

You can imagine how I felt at seeing the château. He's got a weird sculpture out front like a gigantic bird dropping, and in back there's a huge sundial with a vane (you know, the things that throws the shadow) that's a reclining woman with breasts like watermelons. Tommy McKenzie, the movie-star-turned-sculptor, did the sundial, he says, but I forgot to ask who's responsible for the bird-shit monstrosity.

23

The interior's decorated beautifully, and why not, with an art critic and dealer to do it? If E. didn't have exquisite taste (despite the two sculptures—maybe he took them as bad debts), I suppose his gallery would have gone bankrupt in two minutes. I'd suspect he was gay, what with the interior decorating and all, except for all those jet-set affairs he's supposed to have had. On the other hand, those women could have kept him around because he was decorative and non-threatening sexually. No, I don't think so. Oh, who knows? Who cares?

Anyway, in the salon (he calls it a sitting-room, which sounds too anatomical for me) there are light green velvet settees and easy chairs covered in buff and an Aubusson carpet and nice things set around. He seems to like green a lot. I can almost stand up in the fireplace. And, of course, there are paintings and prints everywhere. One whole wall in the salon is covered by a huge Moody, in the wild, contradictory colors he's famous for, and you'd think it would clash with the period furniture, but it doesn't.

Anyway, he's never married. So he probably is gay. Still . . . In any case, I don't think I like him, and I'm sure he doesn't like me.

My room's heavenly, with a leather-topped desk and a new electric typewriter and—get this!—a Renoir! Obviously, he expects me to do my work there, which suits me fine. I can nose around as I like without his being aware of it.

The meadow in back is carpeted with tiny white flowers, and the big quince is hung with great golden globes 'that smell like perfume. He's stocked the moat with little fish, and every few minutes one flashes up and plops back in the water. The cuckoos are singing like mad.

Every morning, the cook says, E. rides along the path by the canal, doing the compleat country gentleman bit. I suppose tomorrow he'll stride into breakfast in an impeccable riding kit with his spurs jingling and slapping his thigh with a riding crop and expect me to snap to attention and salute.

The cook-housekeeper is named Mme. Parisi, and she's married to the gardener and has frizzy red hair. She looks like a plump robin. I think we'll get along.

Tonight E. said we'd have our meals together, and after Mme. Parisi brought in a big bowl of salad greens, he rolled up his sleeves and tossed the salad with his bare hands.

"Too theatrical, I know," he said in this marvelous velvety voice (that's what comes of going to school in England, I suppose, and you know what goes on in those boys' public schools). "I must stop, though," he went on, "because once the Snowdons came to dinner after I'd put a bandaid on a finger for a cut, and after I'd tossed the

25

salad this way the bandaid was gone."

I was darned if I'd play straight man for him, so I didn't say anything, and he had to finish the story without my cueing him.

"Luckily," he said, "it turned up on my plate. Had to eat the damned thing, though. Too embarrassed not to."

I wonder if he made that up.

Jet lag is getting to me, so I must close. Maybe I can sleep tonight without having a nightmare, for once. God forbid E. ever catches me walking in my sleep or even screaming! He'd think it was terribly bad form.

Wish me luck!

Kei

CHAPTER THREE

Damn the woman! She was too much of a presence, a personality. Who needed a secretary with *panache*? Disciplining oneself to a writing schedule was hard enough, without having her looking over his shoulder, ready to criticize. Ms. Ronald had the air of a woman who was used to the best of everything, including literary talent, and he could picture her reading the first page of the manuscript, her cat's eyes traveling to the bottom line, and then looking up contemptuously at him, a faint sneer distorting her upper lip.

Something else bothered Simon sorely. When his publisher, Landsend House in London, had said that the public would be expecting his memoirs to be sexy and would scream bloody murder if he disappointed them, Simon had obediently pulled out all the stops without thinking of the consequences. He was going to change the women's names, lest someone have hurt feelings—or sue—but he hadn't thought about a secretary's reading about—and typing, for God's sake!—the details of his discovery of masturbation, the circle jerks in sixth grade back in the States, or his asking Mary Pemberton "Which does it go in?" when they were experimenting on the old couch where the mice nested, up in the attic. Something of a major lapse in thinking ahead. He couldn't very well cross out all the torrid passages now with a Magic Marker. Perhaps an accidental fire . . .

As he bent over the horse's neck to avoid a low-hanging branch, a chilling thought struck him. She wouldn't ask to join in his morning ride, would she, God forbid? Now was the time of day when he most enjoyed solitude, so that he could think his own thoughts and get in tune with the world. His château might be a sort of inn at the crossroads for shoals of friends passing through Europe, but he was fanatical about hoarding a measure of privacy at this hour, and already he resented Ms. Ronald's intrusion into his thoughts on this hazy summer day.

Last night, when he went to bed in his room by the kitchen stairs, she was on his mind for what had seemed hours as he lay awake, listening to see if she had changed the pulse of the house. In his mind's eye he'd seen her, striding about her room three doors down the hall, briskly unpacking her things and putting them decisively in place, knowing instantly where everything would go. Did she, he'd wondered, wear pajamas or a nightgown? Or did she strip and climb naked between the rough-textured linen sheets and fall asleep looking as inscrutable as ever?

When he finally drifted off, he dreamt that

28

a mountain lion was pacing about his room, back and forth, back and forth, its tail whipping from side to side. Then it came and sat by his bedside. Sat down and stretched its paws out in front like a sphinx, and looked at him out of dark hazel eyes through which he could see into infinity.

Simon leaned over and stroked Maeve's neck when they reached his favorite spot above the vineyard. The horse stood still, as if it, too, enjoyed the view. The air smelled of heated dust and drying grass. The landscape rippled away in waves of moss green, yellow, and brown, with spires of churches in surrounding villages riding on them like ships' masts.

This would have been a perfect place for a clutch of children to lie in the vineyard and look up at the shifting clouds through clusters of grapes, to tumble in the hay mow, to fish in the moat with bamboo poles and angleworms. Not having had children was one of the great regrets of Simon's life. By now, he fancied sadly, someone else had fathered the children who had originally been meant for him, and they'd be grown up, and he might pass them in the street without recognizing them. Too late now.

He'd never married. He'd been infatuated, fond, lustful, caring, yes. But never really in love. He hadn't wanted to cheat himself of that consuming experience by marrying without it, but it never came. Now—too suddenly—he was an old bachelor, self-centered and set in his ways.

But that wasn't his public image. He'd been

mythologized all out of recognition for years, just because his business lay with the moneyed set and he happened to be photogenic. By now, he'd come to expect women to treat him with a degree of sexual awareness as a matter of course. Understandably, they weren't throwing themselves at his feet at the rate they did when he was younger, but he wasn't accustomed to being looked at as if he were asexual. The way Ms. Ronald looked at him. It made him feel invisible. Yesterday it had turned him into a little boy jumping up and down, shouting, "Look at me! Look at me!" A fat lot of good that did. Maybe, on the other hand, there was something wrong with *her*. She might prefer women, come to think of it.

It suddenly flashed through his mind that Ms. Ronald was probably wolfing down the broiled kidneys while he was dawdling along here on Maeve, and they'd all be gone when he got back. She looked like a woman who could scarf down a lot of broiled kidneys. And pheasant under glass, too, he thought darkly, remembering her topaz ring and expensively simple clothing.

Mitzi and Bayard met him in the green-smelling meadow and raced him back to the château. The aroma of kidneys was hot on the air when he entered the back door of the foyer, panting. Ms. Ronald was seated at the table, eating a croissant. Not kidneys.

She looked at him coolly. She was wearing chocolate-colored pants and a cream shirt, and a long string of irregularly shaped amber beads looped down her tantalizing front.

"Not having any of the kidneys?" Simon asked in a carefully pleasant voice, sitting down and unfolding his napkin.

"I don't think so," she said, equally pleasantly. Mme. Parisi brought in a sizzling platter and began ladling kidneys onto Simon's plate.

"Don't you like kidneys?" he pursued.

"I don't think so."

"How do you know, if you don't try them?" he persisted, motioning to the cook to serve Ms. Ronald. "Full of vitamins."

"I don't think so," she said, shaking her head at the cook, who shrugged and left through the swinging door without serving her any.

Simon picked up the airmail edition of the *Times* and shook it open with an ostentatious rattle. He sulked behind its pages for a few minutes and then, looking over the top, said, "You could at least *try* them." Getting no response, he hid behind the paper again and silently mouthed, "I don't think so," aping her.

"Joyce's *Ulysses* put me off kidneys," Ms. Ronald said. "The part about their tasting faintly of urine."

Simon looked down at the kidneys and slowly put down the *Times*. Then he picked up his fork and attacked the kidneys heartily. She was not going to ruin his favorite breakfast with literary allusions! "You know," he said through a mouthful, "I ride in the morning. Would you care to join me?" What the blazes was he *doing,* giving his mornings away like that?!

31

"Thank you, I don't ride."

"You don't eat kidneys, and you don't ride," Simon said testily. "Just what *do* you do?"

"I don't read your paper before you've looked at it, and I don't smoke at the table before you do, and if you think that's easy, you're wrong." She was biting off her words the way she had yesterday, just before she kicked him.

"I am now giving the signal to smoke," said Simon, lighting a Players.

"Humble thanks." She lit a Virginia Slim.

"Just don't dump your ashes in the plate. I can't stand that."

"In that case, I'll need an ashtray, won't I?" Fuming, he pushed the ashtray over to her. They sat and smoked rapidly for some seconds, sending up short bursts of smoke and not taking their eyes off one another. Then she glanced down at his hand, and a small smile curled the corners of her lips. Following her glance, Simon saw that he'd been irritably flicking his cigarette over the kidneys and had peppered them with ashes.

Clearing his throat, he said placatingly, "Should I ask Marthe to give you tea and madeleines tomorrow so you can remember things past? I suppose you've read Proust as well as Joyce."

"That would be lovely," she said, and a wide, genuine smile lit her face. A small dent like a dimple appeared on her right cheekbone. A charming irregularity, Simon thought. Her teeth were sharp and very white and made him think of California.

"How does your leg look this morning?" she

asked after they'd shared the paper and had a second cup of coffee.

"Brown and yellow with green around the edges, like a linoleum pattern. However, they've decided not to amputate."

She did not apologize again, but said, "Does it feel well enough for you to show me around the estate before we start work? I'd love to see what you've done with the place."

Simon liked nothing better than showing off the house and grounds to guests. When they got outside, he spoke some stern words to Mitzi and Bayard about their future relationship with Ms. Ronald while they pattered around in apologetic circles on the gravel path. Ms. Ronald knelt down and demonstrated that she was familiar with the itchy spots where dogs like to be scratched. Then the mastiffs bounded ahead, stopping at every rabbit hole to sniff excitedly as Simon and his secretary tramped from one end of the property to the other, having a go on the tractor, saying hello to the horses, and greeting the cow.

In the barn, Simon called out to his hired hand, Fournier, wanting to introduce him so that Ms. Ronald would know the total of the permanent personnel on the estate, but there was no answer.

A new litter of kittens lay on the wood planking of the floor beside the calico cat, in a large circle of tire chains. Bayard leaned his big oblong head down, sniffed the kittens all over, dodged a swipe of the mother's claw, and snuffled out sharply. The runt of the litter sailed along

33

the floor on the current of his exhalation and fetched up against the tire chains. Simon and Ms. Ronald burst into laughter together, and the edginess between them largely evaporated at that moment, Simon felt. Before, she'd seemed to draw back from him, wary and watchful. She remained as taut as a watchspring, but he didn't think he was the cause of her tenseness.

"You've added on a lot of land," she said as they came back to the small oak wood that lay between the farm fields and the meadow by the château.

"How did you know?" asked Simon, surprised.

She was silent and then pointed to the remains of a stone wall that cut the woods off from the fields. "I just supposed that the original estate ended at that wall."

"It did, you're right," he said, leading the way through a gap in the stones. "So much of it has eroded away, you can hardly tell where the wall is now, in some places. Look out." He held back a whip of gooseberry and felt her take the branch from him. "The Americans billeted intelligence staff in the château after World War II. Before they moved in, the Gestapo used it as their headquarters. They put the grand piano outside by the moat, can you imagine it? Just left it to melt, they say. Watch it!"

When she failed to take the branch he was holding, Simon stopped and looked back. It was gloomy here, where the oak trees overhung a large mound of rubble covered with light undergrowth, like a balding head growing out of the earth, but he could see that she'd stopped following and had stayed behind, clutching the trunk of an oak tree, her eyes closed.

"What's the matter?" he asked, returning to her side.

She shook her head and opened her eyes. "Nothing. I just felt strange for a moment. My knees sort of gave way. Leftover jet lag, probably. I'm fine now."

She took a deep breath and expelled it, and then, as if in exhibition of her recovery, broke away and ran through the wood toward the château, lightly dodging around the trees, the mastiffs rocking like hobbyhorses alongside her, until she reached the meadow and stood, hands on hips, calf-deep in white flowers, waiting for him to catch up.

If there was one thing about American culture that Simon missed not one whit, it was the jogging cult, with its frenzy about timing, distance, and muscle tone. If Ms. Ronald was a jogger, he devoutly hoped that she would keep her passion to herself and let him decay away in his own chosen fashion, at his own rate, without making him feel guilty about it.

Their shoes clattered on the marble floor of the foyer, where Marthe had placed a giant copper kettle filled with bright-colored zinnias as a doorstop.

Looking at the flowers, Ms. Ronald said, "If Hilaire does the gardening and takes care of the odd jobs, who farms the acreage? You?"

"Not by myself, surely. I like to stand and

admire fields of grain, but you could put in your eye what I know about agriculture. Fournier does the real work and hires extra hands as he needs them. Once in a while I help out so I can feel picturesque." He opened the doors to the salon. "Fournier has an apartment over the stable, but you're not likely to see him up here. For some reason, he and Hilaire can't abide one another, so Fournier seldom comes as far as the house."

She followed him into the salon and stopped in front of the heroic-sized Moody canvas.

"I thought they'd be too big for anything but a museum," she said. "May I touch it?"

Simon nodded, and she ran her fingertips reverently over the rough painted surface.

"Very tactile, as Berenson would say," she commented. "I *think* he would say. It's futile to pretend to know about art when you're with a world-famous authority, though. You'd know I was faking it. Have you ever seen Moody? I hear he's such a recluse that nobody can get near him."

"He *is* a bit private. But I still see him now and then. In the old days, when I gave him a monthly stipend in exchange for a percentage of his work, he wasn't nearly such a hermit. He's morbidly shy, though. He lives in the village here. I suppose you know."

"He does? Do you think I'll ever see him?"

"Maybe the back of him, scampering away. He's very fleet of foot. From time to time he'll drop off a canvas he wants sold or will leave a religious pamphlet on the kitchen table. Along with the eremite life, he's taken up religion. Several of them, in turns. He seems to change denominations every few weeks." Simon opened the study doors.

Immediately there was a clamor as the brilliantly colored birds in the aviary at the end of the room protested the invasion of their territory. Simon opened the casement windows over the moat to air the room, and the sound of quacking was added to the din.

The study was in one of the turrets that poked up at each corner of the château, so its walls were too curved to hang pictures properly. Instead, tall green plants clambered up the walls or were massed against them, turning the room into a jungle. The resulting humidity had made the ivory-painted walls start flaking up by the ceiling.

In the midst of the greenery sat a leather-topped desk with a tall, very untidy stack of papers in the center. Simon waited until Ms. Ronald had had her fill of the birds in the aviary and then handed her the pile of manuscript.

She settled herself in a nest of pink velvet pillows on the cream-and-gold needlepointed love seat, took Benjamin Franklin reading glasses out of her skirt pocket, and began looking over the pages. As she read, she ran a hand lovingly up and down her arm, as if she liked the feel of her shirt. The sensual movement reminded Simon of something he'd meant to mention to her.

"I think I should tell you that Hilaire and Marthe have their apartment over the garage, so we'll be alone in the château when there aren't guests. I should have told you yesterday," Simon said, sitting down at the desk and tilting back in the Louis XV chair whose back he'd already broken twice. "Will that bother you?"

"Not in the least," she said without looking up. "I'm sure you're perfectly safe."

Simon raised an eyebrow and weighed whether or not there were any implications to be detected in her tone, but she was absorbed in the manuscript, too intent to be playing games with him.

Again he felt that pang in his chest, like bones with shattered edges rubbing together, that came whenever he thought of his humiliating non-performance a year and a half ago, the culmination of a string of failures, and of the weary scorn in the feminine voice that said, "Oh well, that happens when you're getting on a bit, doesn't it?"

"I'm afraid my handwriting's almost illegible," he said edgily. "And how do you pronounce your first name, assuming that I'm to be allowed to use it?"

"Like the letter K." She divided the stack into two manageable piles and tapped one pile on her knees to get the edges straight. "I was born in Kyoto, and my father thought the name Kei would bridge both cultures."

"Call me Simon, if you feel comfortable with it." He picked up the jade-handled letter opener and lightly drew circles with it on the blotter.

"That lot there covers my childhood, nearly. I was a silly little twit," he said, feeling hot around the roots of his hair and regretting his inclusion of the incident with Hannah Hendershot in the fourth grade, after which Hannah's mother had screamed at his mother that Simon was teaching her innocent babe unnatural acts. Which Hannah, an early bloomer, had initiated.

He wished to God he'd omitted the part about what he and his sister Elaine used to do under the porch. Why had he been so idiotic as to open up that can of worms? Ms. Ronald—Kei—would think he'd been a sexual monster. Which he had. Wasn't every kid? What do children know about societal taboos?

If he weren't so vain, he wouldn't be in this spot. Used to good reviews on his books of criticism, he hadn't wanted his memoirs to languish on the back shelves of bookstores, to be remaindered early and pulped after selling badly. The public would, he'd figured, skim right through to his adult life, hoping he'd name names, unless he hotted up the section on his childhood. Ms. Ronald would know that he was trying for a bestseller and find that human, perhaps, and amusing. She might not find his relationship with Elaine so amusing.

"And don't tell me *you* never took your pants down behind the barn!" he said hotly, unaware that he was speaking out loud until the words were out of his mouth.

"Mm?" Kei said abstractedly, pulling up her watchband and scratching under it while he tried to shrink into his chair and be somewhere else. Then he saw his words register in her eyes, and she laughed. "Marvelous! Most people have trouble being open about their sexual lives in their autobiographies — unless they're spiteful and want to get back at somebody. This kind of thing helps sales enormously, though, and people will be expecting it from you. The playboy image, you know."

Simon winced. He detested that stereotype. He could hardly shake hands with a woman without people thinking they'd wind up in bed together. It wasn't necessarily true in the past and assuredly wasn't true now. God dammit!

"This is a big load of work," Kei said, standing up and putting a stack under each arm. "It's going to take at least two or three days. In the meantime, you could be dictating into a cassette so you'd be a tape ahead of me all the time."

"I don't know if I can write that way," Simon said doubtfully.

"Try it. If it doesn't work out, we can go back to the old way. See how it feels. Do you think Marthe could send up lunch so I could type through?"

"There's no need to drive yourself. The world isn't perishing to hear about my career in art."

"Oh, but I am! It's the stuff dreams are made of, for the average reader. Fabulous finds in dusty attics, forgeries, thefts, eccentric artists like Moody, the world's most beautiful women ... I hope you namedrop like mad. That'll guarantee a slot on the talk shows, and that will pump up sales. I can arrange it with . . . " She stopped and then went on in a different, brisk tone. "Besides, you're behind on your deadlines already, aren't you?"

He got her résumé out of his desk, put on his reading glasses, and looked it over again. Not that it disclosed anything about her personal life. Nowadays, with the U.S. regulations regarding discrimination and privacy, résumés seldom did. Unless an applicant volunteered her age or marital status, you didn't even know that. A man could be hiring Typhoid Mary or Jack the Ripper in drag, for all he knew.

Kei Ronald (married? single? separated? divorced? widowed?) had put down her birth date, so he knew she was forty-five. From the back, only her gray hairs gave her away. A teenager might have envied her body. From the front? He supposed she looked forty-five. No adolescent had those lines raying out from the corners of her eyes or the hairline-thin parentheses that enclosed her mouth. But neither did an adolescent have those slumbrous, wise eyes that promised more than youth could know, or the sculptured contours of her face, that looked carved and smoothed by the wind.

She'd taken a bachelor's degree in Japanese (interesting) at a small private school in Illinois (parents had money). Soon after, she'd started working as a secretary to a prestigious company in California (had she had those perfect teeth capped there?). A couple of long tenures at publishing companies in New York, winding up at Bell Tree Press. That was all. No mention of college honors received (surely mediocre students didn't opt for oriental languages?). No societies or organizations. No hobbies. Not even her typing speed.

Simon took off his glasses and chewed their stems thoughtfully. Why would someone who'd majored in Japanese become a secretary? Wouldn't a translator's job or something in that field be more logical? And why was she working at all? Unmistakably, she had that gloss peculiar to someone born to money. Could she maintain that wardrobe on a secretary's salary alone? Probably not. Moreover, there wasn't a trace of that deference he was accustomed to in office workers. Indeed, it was going to be a contest to see who was boss in their employee-employer relationship. You'd think she wasn't a secretary at all, and he could see that the situation was going to be fraught with complications, not the least of which was how his sister Elaine was going to interpret the relationship between him and a strikingly handsome woman who was living in his house.

"I know just the secretary for you," Jeremy had said. "She wants something temporary in France so she can be near her aunt, who's on the verge of expiring, I gather. Anyway, I'll give you her name and address, and you might work something out."

They had, quickly and impersonally, with a brief exchange of letters. In his mind, Simon had

42

been writing to a dumpy dishwater blonde with piano legs, who was going to mouse around and get the typing done without his being bothered to notice her. Sexy elegance he hadn't been prepared for, and that was what had made him so upset at first sight of Kei—the dissonance between what he'd anticipated and what she'd turned out to be. Elaine would surely think Kei had been imported as a sleeping partner as well as an amanuensis. You'd think Jeremy, his publisher, would have foreseen some of the difficulties he was sending to Simon.

Again, Simon remembered lying in the bed in Paris and looking at the ceiling and thinking, "Never again. Never, never again," feeling cold spread through his bones. He rubbed his chest and wondered just how well Jeremy Kirbottle knew Kei Ronald.

He rose and went outside to sit on the bridge over the moat in back. Lighting a cigarette, he looked out over the meadow, crossed his arms, and listened to the cuckoo in the quince tree. This was precisely what he'd worked for all his life: a château in France, enough money to be free, and peace and quiet. The difficulty was that he hadn't found the fulfillment in it that he'd hoped for. Something, he didn't know what, was missing that made all the difference.

Mitzi ambled up and laid her silvery head on Simon's knee, looking up at him with sympathetic eyes (Feeling low, master?). He stroked her silky ears and then stood up and dropped his cigarette over the bridge into the moat. There

43

was a swirl of water, and apricot-colored fish lips nibbled at the paper, shredding it before it sank into the depths. He went into the sitting room again and sat down before the concert grand, took a couple of spins around on the stool, flexed his fingers dramatically over the keyboard, and—by ear—began to play the Mapleleaf Rag very loudly and very badly.

CHAPTER FOUR

Simon pulled on an old Kelly green sweater with sagging pockets, put a large bundle under his arm, and set off over the lichen-patched bridge over the Canal d'Orléans to the village. His new secretary had retired early after a day of industrious typing.

Most of the honey-colored stone houses set along the sidewalks had their shutters closed for the night, but through the chinks he could see a family seated around the table for evening soup, the children with napkins tied like bibs around their necks, and the shoemaker's wife nearsightedly picking over the limp leaves of her African violet collection.

Fay-sur-Loire's one and only plumber was sitting on a doorstep in the twilight, smoking a cigarette stub that threatened to sear his lips, and giving a large section of lead pipe melancholy-sounding whacks with a wooden hammer. Simon wondered what the man was ruining now.

Whatever he called himself, a plumber he was not. Last winter when the sinks froze up, he'd sawed out their elbows and left the sections on the floor and the sinks inoperable for a whole weekend when the château was full of houseguests. This summer, one of the upstairs toilets had clogged up, and the man had shrugged, said there was nothing to be done about it, and left—not forgetting to send a bill later for his expert opinion. In a state of high exasperation, Simon had thumbed through his pocket dictionary to find the term for "plumber's friend," found none, and in halting French had asked the hardware store clerk for a stick with a rubber cup on the end, which produced only a blank stare and a headshake. By placing one fist on top of the other, pumping his arms up and down vigorously, and making obscene honking noises, he'd gotten the message across immediately, but he'd had to stand around and pretend to be interested in the bins of nuts and screws while the conversation and gestures were relayed around the shop and everyone had a good laugh before the clerk recovered himself enough to wrap up the item and hand it over. It was all very irksome, and moreover the plumber had a cocked eye and Simon could never figure out which one to look into. God only knew how many village people had to sneak out to the bushes when their toilets were permanently stopped up because of that cretinous plumber.

Simon looked distastefully at him as he passed by, but the man stood up and pulled at the front of his beret politely—the equivalent of pulling his forelock, Simon supposed—and had to be given a stiff nod of recognition.

The villagers did treat him like the seigneur of the castle, Simon thought, as they probably had every owner of the château since it had been built, although no one had yet offered him a maiden to deflower. He wondered if they really believed a man had walked on the moon. Just the other day he'd overheard the bakery owner direly counseling a young mother to get rid of her cat because everyone knew that cats sat on infants in their cribs and swallowed their breath, killing them. Incredible!

The shops, with signs reading Jardinage, Bricolage, and Droguerie, were shut. The lard sculpture of a pig that stood in the pork butcher's window during business hours had been retired to the cold locker and the red accordion awning above the store was folded back. From the open doors of the Café de la Place came jukebox rock music, and its wire basket of children's soccer balls was still set out on the sidewalk below the newspaper rack riveted on the wall.

By the light of a bare bulb surrounded with a flurry of moths and flying beetles, Simon could make out that continued cattle mutilations in the district had made the headlines of the Orléans paper. He could read French two or three times better than he could speak or understand it and was able to decipher that hearts and other items beyond his vocabulary had been torn out of animals found dead in the fields around Fay. Officials debated whether it was the work of a marauding pack of dogs or—*horreur!*—a Sa-

47

tanic cult might be using the entrails for nefarious purposes. What nonsense! Simon walked on.

Nevertheless, Fay had a goodly share of small-town violence, including a grisly murder nearly every year. Probably the result of tensions seething between the inbred villagers, who wanted to keep things the way they'd always been, and the flamboyant expatriate colony, with their wild parties and drugs, who'd been attracted to the village by its antique quaintness and its beautiful setting in the woods along the Loire River, unmindful that their presence would irrevocably alter and spoil the very thing they'd come for.

This was the season when the town would boil over again, with tires being slashed on the foreign cars and windows being smashed in the tiny business district.

The townspeople were annually outraged by the medieval tournament the expatriates put on at the grounds of the crumbling abbey at the edge of town, and Simon didn't blame them for their annoyance. A bunch of nitwits prancing around in loving-hands-at-home costumes getting drunk and knocking each other off horses in jousting matches or shooting off muskets—eclecticism abounded—while carny types hawked sandwiches and drinks and brawls erupted! Afterwards, the turf would be torn up from the horses' hoofs and the camper vans brought in by spectators, and the town council would levy a charge on the expatriates for the expense of cleaning up the windblown litter and dressing up the grounds again.

48

How the hell they'd talked him into being Tourney Lord this year, Simon couldn't quite remember. He had a vague recollection of the committee's putting pressure on him when he was oiled up and feeling jovial. Not only would he have to make announcements of the matches and lend his name to the tomfoolery, but the Tourney Lord always took the last match himself — a bout with lances. Thank God, it would be dark by then and most of the crowd would be too drunk to see straight, so his ineptitude would not be closely observed by many. Dammit all, anyway! One of these days he'd have to think seriously about going on the wagon.

He walked along in the lavender dusk, out past the last houses, until he came to the old smithy, a small, round building, He knocked on the thick, splintery wooden door.

After a short wait, a glassy-eyed gargoyle looked out. "Did you bring them?" asked Tommy McKenzie, pushing his welder's mask up onto the top of his head. Simon handed him the bundle and went inside the low, dark building.

Tommy set the package carefully on the rim of the hearth that was the center of the room, said, "I'll be just a minute longer," and tipped the mask back into place and lit the acetylene torch he held in a gauntleted hand. "We can't use the stuff until it's dark anyway," he said, raising his voice above the sound of the fizzing gas flame. "Take the throne."

Under a small window near the ceiling loomed a vast black iron sculpture that stood on a pedestal planted on the earthen floor. If one used plenty of imagination and squinted, it could be seen that the work was of a madonna with a child lying in her lap.

Simon had known Tommy for donkey's years and, familiar with his household arrangements, put a foot on an accommodating fold of the madonna's robe and hoisted himself up to sit on the holy child's flat face. Such disrespect always made him feel a little apprehensive, as if he might have to answer for it in the hereafter, but the rest of the baby was swaddled in a metal beehive that imprinted itself achingly on the behind. One mammoth baby hand held an ashtray containing a grubby mound of cigarette butts, most of them Simon's Players. He looked them over to see what brands had been left by other visitors, then lit one of his own and watched Tommy weld.

From this height, he had a panoramic view of the tools and supplies that Tommy had arranged meticulously—in typical compulsive Virgo fashion, his sister Elaine would have said—around the walls of the smithy. Sparks showered as Tommy worked on the jagged lashes of an enormous freestanding metal eye. The scene was medieval, in blacks and grays—the cold hearth carboned by years of fires, a giant bellows overhead, Tommy's black leather apron, the welding mask fitting snugly over his face like a knight's casque.

Under the apron Tommy wore black cords and a white T-shirt. The skin of his arms was smeared with soot and slippery with sweat. As he worked, his large biceps muscles humped and flattened and the cords in his forearms ribbed out sharply and smoothed again in rhythmic succession, accompanied by the clank of his heavy silver chain bracelet.

Not for the first time, Tommy's powerful, dovetailed movements made Simon contemplate what a wonderful machine is man, and he asked himself if his admiration for Tommy's physical symmetry wasn't basically a sexual impulse. On the other hand, he equally enjoyed watching Bayard's and Mitzi's arching movements and the play of their muscles when they ran, and that didn't make him rush to consult Krafft-Ebbing to see if he had deviational tendencies. Regrettably, the question of his own sexuality was immaterial nowadays, and the fact that it was depressed Simon unutterably. He put his chin in his hand and brooded.

Tommy's rugged good looks had been on display in British and American films for a couple of decades, where he played swashbucklers before discovering that he could sculpt and sculpt damned well. He'd told Simon he'd never felt he'd mastered the acting craft and found it exhausting to spend a whole day trying to produce the expression the director needed for a two-second shot. He'd thought it great sport at first, before his privacy vanished, so that he couldn't go out into the street without being mobbed. That the average moviegoer thought that he—or, more likely, she—owned him was part of the profession that he'd resented and never learned to tolerate graciously.

Moreover, when he turned forty, Tommy admitted, he'd begun to worry about the effects of wearing heavy mail that made him sweat like a galley slave and that hurt like hell when he fell off his horse, which he did, frequently. His mother's arthritis had made her walk like a crab in her latter days, and he didn't want to end up like that from leaping into cold water and then standing out in the freezing rain, pretending it was summer. He'd never enjoyed the profession. He was well out of it, he said, and had invested wisely in condominiums on the Algarve.

One of the common bonds between Tommy and Simon was gardening. The château grounds didn't lend themselves to much beyond general landscaping, and Simon worked out his gardening urge in Tommy's yard, consulting the books of Beverley Nichols, the English writer, as he went along. Inspired by Nichols, they planted only white flowers —except for the burning blue of the delphinium spikes that Simon couldn't resist putting in. They were at odds with the monochromatic scheme, but at least he had forgone geraniums—with a struggle. As a child, his favorite poem had been A. A. Milne's one about "delphiniums blue and geraniums red," and sooner or later he was determined to sneak the geraniums in when Tommy wasn't looking.

They'd hidden spotlights amongst the plants to provide for dramatic night displays. All in all, the garden was a whopping success, Simon thought.

Tommy showed a tenderness for his white

roses that none of his fans would have believed, not after seeing him crack heads, carve up torsos, and blast away with every known small arm on the silver screen. He also had an offscreen reputation for punching people out and had left a lot of smashed cameras and noses in his wake. He was one of those people whose personalities change when they get tight, and when some fellow in a pub picked a fight with him to show off for his girlfriend, Tommy had permanently relieved him of the use of a hand and the sight of one eye, with a consequent explosion of publicity that the studio couldn't cover up. After that, he'd sworn off hard liquor. Nowadays, his hostilities were taken out on aphids, black spot, and thrips. But his reputation persisted, and few men wanted to tackle a six-foot-two package of well-conditioned muscle who was known to be touchy about autographs. Here in Fay that reputation, and the fact that the villagers had gotten used to seeing him around, let him live like a normal citizen, and he could go marketing without being stopped every few steps. In this place, in this way, and at this time of his life, Tommy McKenzie at last seemed to be a happy man.

The pop of the acetylene torch signaled that the welding was finished. Tommy took off his mask, hung it with the torch and apron on the wall, and put the long leather gauntlets on the rim of the hearth. "I've made a fresh pot of soup for dinner," he said. "It's only been simmering a day, so I'm afraid it won't have much depth."

"Good!" Simon slid down from the throne. "I well remember the time we emptied the pot you'd kept going on the back of the stove all winter."

"Ah, yes. The tenpenny nail we found at the bottom of the pot." Tommy poured a big dose of salt into a basin of water and began washing his hands.

"And the nylon stocking."

Tommy laughed and dried his hands on an immaculate towel.

"Why do you do that?" asked Simon.

"Because my hands get filthy, what else?"

"No, I mean the salt."

Tommy poured the water into a wall sink and wiped up the splatters with a sponge. "I always wash with salt after working with iron. An allergy. Why don't you go out and have a look at the garden while I get the food together? I just put in some white petunias and some of that furry silvery stuff—dusty miller—where the dill went to seed. Looks quite decent." He thumped the package that Simon had brought and asked, "Good stuff?"

"The best." Simon picked up the package and carried it out to the terrace that lay between the smithy and the farmhouse that Tommy had converted into living quarters.

A semicircular garden joined the two structures. Scattered about the terrace flagstones, whose interstices were planted with thyme, was rustic furniture made from wood with the bark still on.

The spotlights weren't on yet, but splotches of white flowers almost glowed by themselves in the last light of day. Roses shed ivory petals on the ground after a summer of vigorous bloom, and sweet nicotine was opening for the night, mingling its scent with that of the roses and thyme. By the house, huge balls of hydrangea nodded to the ground in masses of greenery. A troop of pink-throated lilies stood in the center of the semi-circle. There was newly-turned earth around the petunias and dusty miller. Tommy was right, the white and silver were elegant together.

After a lifetime of collecting, evaluating, and selling other people's creativity, Simon felt great satisfaction at seeing his own ideas on form and color growing up out of the ground, real and tangible. Even, in the case of the herbs, edible. He squatted down, rolled a sprig of thyme between his fingers to release the pungent odor, and nibbled at it. Did Ms. Ronald garden? Did she feel that delphiniums blue looked lonely without geraniums red?

"The charcuterie finally got in those little pickles they've been out of," said Tommy, all cleaned up in a fresh shirt, bringing out a tray with soup, French bread, paté de campagne, the pickles, red wine, napkins, and all the accoutrements of a meal and setting them on a table beside a red glass windproof candleholder. Simon drew up the chairs while Tommy arranged things on the table with geometric precision.

"Ooooh, that smells good!" A black-haired

girl of about seventeen stood outlined by the lighted windows of the house. Simon hadn't met this one. He seldom knew any of them, because they passed through Tommy's life so quickly and seemed to be interchangeable: the same jouncy breasts, wasp waists, and pear-shaped bottoms. Even their faces looked cast from one mold out of creamy plastic and looked identically vacant. It was hardly worth the effort to learn their names.

"Buzz off, Bridget," said Tommy. "This is man talk. You can bring the dessert out when we're ready." He sat down and tucked a red and white checkered napkin into his shirtfront. The girl pouted and left, her head hanging. Simon sat down at the table.

"Bridget Sunshine," said Tommy. "Nitwit name. Insists on being tied up and spanked. Really a tiresome sort of bird." He ripped off a chunk of bread and spread it thickly with paté.

Simon started on the chicken soup, which had slices of yellow crooked-neck squash and avocado floating on top.

"How's the new secretary?" asked Tommy with a full mouth, the creases running from his cheekbones to his jaws deepening each time he chewed down.

"I don't know. There's something funny there."

"How do you mean?"

"That's just it. I'm not sure what it is." Simon wiped his mouth on his napkin and leaned back in his chair, staring at the flame in the red bottle. "For one thing, although she's spent the day whanging away at the typewriter up in her room and sounds like a wizard typist, I get the feeling that she's not really a secretary at all. Or that she's something *more* than a secretary. It's very odd."

"What's she look like? Anything interesting?"

Simon reflected as he went back to his soup. He'd have to edit out the attractive parts of the description or Tommy would get interested in Kei and have his hands all over her in no time, and she'd probably kick him in the balls. Besides, for some reason, he didn't like the idea of Tommy screwing her. "Not your type. Far too old, for starters."

"Need I remind you that it was laying the sixty-year-old wife of a producer that got me started in films? Older women, as they say, are so grateful. I could use a little rest, too. I'm beginning to feel my age a touch. These young ones are like minks."

"Well," Simon said resignedly, "she's slender. Middle Atlantic drawl. Dark hazel eyes with light flecks in them. Moves nicely, like a cat. Tense. Too tense entirely."

"Perhaps I could relax her, one way and another."

Simon frowned. Tommy pushed away his empty bowl and refilled Simon's glass.

"If she's not a secretary, what would she be?" asked Tommy. "Not having a brush of paranoia, are you?"

"I think not. But I haven't the vaguest notion what she'd be otherwise."

"You don't suppose ... " Tommy began and then stood up and shouted, "Shut up!" very loudly, making Simon miss connections with his spoon.

"Dammit, give me some warning next time," he said, mopping his shirt with his napkin. "I wish we could sit on your terrace just once without you carrying on your private war with the cuckoos!"

"I can't take it, waiting for the other shoe to drop. Sometimes it's two whole fucking minutes between the 'cuck' and the 'oo,' and it makes me want to kill!" Tommy threw down his napkin and jogged off to the house, returning with a box that he put on the table. He took out a wooden slingshot and some ball bearings and drew a bead on an oak tree with a wad of mistletoe the size of a bushel basket growing in its crotch. "I haven't seen Elaine for weeks, and suddenly she drops this off on the doorstep. She even left a note, saying that if she's a dead shot with it, it's conceivable that I might be able to hit the side of a barn with it if I practiced diligently. Your sister is a very odd number." He let fly.

The cuckoo's song stopped dead after one "cuck." The men waited. When the "oo" failed to follow, they looked at one another and back at the tree.

Tommy looked dolefully at the weapon in his hand. "You could kill an ox with this thing, but I didn't really think ... " He got up and went to inspect the ground under the oak trees

58

and came back, walking on the balls of his feet and slightly pigeontoed, like the athlete he was. "Nothing," he grinned and, sitting down again, put the slingshot away and pulled a couple of cigars out of his shirt pocket. He clipped off their ends with a silver cutter and handed one to Simon. "Havanas," he said, bending over the flame in the bottle for a light. "Can't get them in the States now, can you?"

He straightened up as an "oo" floated in from the dark. Simon laughed. For some minutes they sat and smoked, analyzing the flavor of the cigars and comparing them with others they'd had, using a wine connoisseur's terminology facetiously, their arms crossed over their chests. They blew smoke rings into the cooling air.

Tommy tucked his cigar into the corner of his mouth and said, "Now, about this secretary, so-called. Scene I: Mysterious female tries to get into your house by passing herself off as secretary. What comes next? Hm. She's not some art student who fell in love with your picture in the tabloids, is she?"

"Hardly. She's forty-five years old, and I don't think she likes me much." Simon rubbed the sore spot on his shin.

"Well, what could the mysterious stranger be after?" Tommy crossed his arms behind his head and stared up into the darkening sky. "Your collection?"

"Good lord!" She'd certainly recognized the Moody, but considering the space Moody got in the press now with his hermitlike ways and the prices his paintings commanded, she'd have had to be blind or illiterate not to know his style. He was paying off handsomely for Simon's early conviction that the man was a major talent.

Except for his paintings and art objects, Simon couldn't imagine why anyone would bother worming into his house. The doors were unlocked all day. Nothing was insured, of course. Nowadays only the ultra-rich could afford the premiums on such high-value items. The paintings might be appreciating at an insane rate in today's market, but their resale value was theoretical pie in the sky, and the market could turn. The insurance costs, contrariwise, were hard cash—and plenty of it—out of one's pocket, year after year. The only course was to be philosophical about it. If the paintings went, they went. Masterworks never really belonged to an individual, after all, any more than a Mozart concerto did. He would, however, find it considerably vexing to have his things stolen from under his nose by a woman who had irritated him the moment he set eyes on her.

Ms. Ronald didn't look like a thief, but successful ones didn't advertise. Did she have a confederate in the village who was waiting for her to slip him the choicest pieces, to be spirited away to some collector in Paris or Vienna? Did she have forgeries ready to hang in the place of the originals? His collection had been shown in fragmented form often enough and was well enough recorded for copies to have been made.

Oh, the idea was preposterous! But if that

wasn't the answer, what game was she playing? Was she, in fact, the same person that Jeremy had recommended or a substitute? Just what was going on? If anything.

The pattering steps of Tommy's latest girl interrupted Simon's speculations. She set down a pot of coffee, three cups and saucers, three plates of chocolate-frosted cake, and a bottle of Irish Mist and drew up a chair for herself. Tardily, Simon rose and pushed her in to the table. Tommy made a Celtic-sounding noise of disgust in his throat and cleared off the remains of the meal and took them back into the house on the tray, leaving Simon alone with this exquisitely beautiful creature who, he reckoned, would be about a third of his own age and who looked as if she had a howling vacuum between the ears.

"I'm Simon Eagleton."

"I know. I've seen your pictures in the magazines. I'm Bridget Sunshine. I'm going to be a superstar." She looked expectantly at him.

"Well!" said Simon, who was defeated by the blankness of her perfect face. He couldn't think of a bloody thing to say that could possibly interest her. When the silence grew unendurably long, he said, "You're very beautiful."

"Yes, aren't I!"

They sat a few minutes longer.

"You must be very young," Simon said finally to fill the gap.

"I don't tell my age. You never should, you know, or years later they count back and there you are—older than God. Like forty or something horrible." She made a face.

"Horrible!" Simon said faintly, thinking of his own fifty-eight years and wondering if he looked hopelessly decrepit to her. "Ghastly, when you think of it." What would she be like at *his* age?

She nodded, her face very serious.

"You're making a pigsty of this place!" said Tommy, sitting down again and pouring coffee for all. "It's taken exactly three days for you to make the house uninhabitable."

"I'm not your housekeeper!" the girl complained.

"You damn bet you're not, nobody would ever accuse you of that!" said Tommy and took a gargantuan bite of the black walnut cake. The girl tossed her head in a way that Simon thought had gone out with movies in the forties, along with staring out of the window in moments of crisis.

"Tommy made the cake," she said to Simon, turning on a smile as if someone had flipped her switch. "But I put the icing on it."

"That's not the only place she put the icing," said Tommy and licked a gob off the corner of his mouth. "Got it all over the sheets. Chocolate, for lord's sake. I'll never get it out in the wash."

The girl giggled and moved over to kiss Tommy on the ear. She put a hand inside his shirt, and Simon could see it traveling around like a pet hamster. He looked away, asking himself what masochistic streak prompted him to keep up a friendship with a man who could hardly pass

62

a knothole in a fence without straightening his tie and running a hand through his hair.

Trouble was, Simon knew he was saddled with an old-fashioned attitude about friendship that was cumbersome, inconvenient—and completely unshakable. Only once or twice in his life had a friend run him out to the end of his rope and snapped off the relationship by exhausting or outraging him, and the memory of those failed friendships still returned to haunt him quite unjustifiably with a sense of having let someone down. So, although Tommy's love-life was particularly trying for a man in Simon's state, there was nothing to do but bear with Tommy's satyriasis as stoically as he could and think about other things. Why his checkbook never balanced, for instance. Or if Ms. Ronald's nipples were pink or tan. No, no! That wasn't helping at all!

"It's almost dark," he said, hoping to arrest the furtive activity across the table so he could forget how long it had been since he'd had a woman.

"Ah!!" Instantly Tommy brushed the girl away like a pestiferous insect. "Shall we?"

"Would you care to do the honors?" Simon pushed away from the table and fetched the package. Moving the dishes aside, he put the package on the table and broke the string that tied it together. Smoothing down the paper at the sides, he revealed an array of colored cardboard.

"Heh! Heh!" said Tommy, showily rubbing

his hands together in anticipation.

Simon handed him a small replica of a rooster with a fuse sticking out from beneath its tail-feathers. Tommy took it as gingerly as if it had been a Fabergé jeweled egg and bore it off to the farthest edge of the terrace, where he knelt and put it down on a flagstone. With his cigar, he lit the fuse in the tail and jumped back.

Tiny sparks shot out. Then, one after another, minute balls of red fire popped out of the rooster's rear.

"It farts sparks!" Tommy crowed.

Depleted, the rooster emitted a microscopic curl of smoke and toppled over on its side.

"Another!" cried Bridget, clapping her hands with delight.

"No, you've got to ration these things carefully," said Tommy, sticking his cigar back in his mouth. "It's an all-day round trip for Simon to get these beauties." He held out his arms. Simon lofted a column on a wooden base to him, and Tommy caught it and read the label out loud: "Silver Swallows."

One fountain of sparks followed another: A Thousand Flowers, Balls of Snow, Summer Glories, and on and on. Golden showers, zigzagging darts of silver, whirling white flakes, bouncing colored balls, and whirling disks that whooshed up in red fire and turned into spirals like splattering lime sherbet before disintegrating. Simon hoped that some village child lying in his bed and looking out his window was being astonished by the carnival in the sky.

64

He retired to the hammock strung between trees at the edge of the terrace and let Tommy take over the firing, only cautioning him to save the hexagonal box. "I want to keep that for next time," he called to Tommy, and lay back with his glass of Irish Mist propped on his chest. Too bad Kei had to miss this. Next time, he'd play DeFalla and Debussy on a cassette while the skyrockets traced their trajectories in flames across the blackness. It would be perfect then.

When he got home, pleasantly sozzled, Bayard and Mitzi bounded up and knocked him flat. He lay there on the parking area, hugging their huge heads and letting them lick his face while he felt for his key in his pocket. His hand felt abnormally large and didn't fit into his pocket very well, but he finally located the key, which had grown surprisingly small, and got up, teetering a few seconds on his heels. The dogs' joyful dithyrambs kept upsetting his balance and the keyhole on the door wouldn't stay in one place, but he finally got the door unlocked, closed the dogs outside, and put the retied package of fireworks into a cupboard in the foyer.

As he started to close the cupboard door, he found that his little finger was caught in the string around the bundle. Untangling it in this darkness took on the complexity of trying to unknot snarled fishing line. When he got free, he put the package on the shelf inside the cupboard and then discovered that the signet ring on his little finger was inextricably wound up in the string. Reciting obscenities, he got loose by breaking the cord, and the fireworks bounced out of the paper and rolled around on the floor.

Cautiously, mindful of the slipperiness of marble, he got down on his hands and knees and began retrieving them by feel. The light switch was at an impossible height up the wall. If he got up that far, he wasn't sure he could get down again. At least, it didn't seem feasible at the moment.

He crawled around in the dark, gathering them up and then, when he thought he'd got them all, stood up again, stuffed them in the cupboard and slammed the door shut. The foyer echoed with the racket, and he wondered if he'd wakened Kei. Passing the hall table, he joggled it and one of the heavy bronze candlesticks fell off and hit the floor with a metallic "pong!" that surely would have wakened her if the other noise didn't. He disdained to chase after it and pulled himself up the stairs by the bannisters, hand over hand.

The wooden floor upstairs creaked as he wove past Kei's door on the way to his own. He stopped to think and then retraced his steps to listen at her door, hoping for a companion for a midnight snack. No sounds of stirring behind the door, but she must be awake. He tapped. No response. Shit.

Without turning on the light in his room, he undressed in front of the open bay window, enjoying the chill of the air on his bare skin. A new moon hung directly over the tall quince tree, like the topmost decoration on a Christmas tree.

The grove was full of fireflies.

Wait a minute! He closed his eyes and refocused. Shouldn't the fireflies *farthest* away look *smallest*? Why were the ones out in the oak grove, by the bald mound of earth where nothing grew, so large? Were they fireflies at all?

Arguing with himself about the urgency of satisfying his curiosity, he knotted the sash of his cashmere robe while descending the staircase into the foyer.

As he stepped over the threshold of the back door, his foot came down on the bronze candlestick and he shot out the door on it, rolling up to the railing of the bridge over the moat, where he slammed against the side and barked his shin on just the spot where Kei had kicked him.

He limped through the wet grass of the meadow, getting his bare feet cold and feeling extremely drafty around his nether regions. Maybe Kei's confederate was lurking around, waiting for her to hand over the loot. In which case, what was dear old Simon going to do about it, armed as he was with one cashmere bathrobe? Smother him with it while yelling for the gendarmes who were asleep in the stationhouse? What, in fact, was dear old Simon *doing* out here in nothing but a robe, hobbling along to investigate fireflies, for Christ's sake, wounded by every sharp-edged pebble and vulnerable to the smallest biting insect interested in human blood? He'd probably be lumpy with bites tomorrow. He did not, Simon told himself, seem to have a lot of sense.

He hesitated before going into the oak grove,

which always gave him the same feeling at dark that he'd had when his grandmother had asked him to fetch up a jar of preserves from the damp, echoing cellar where nameless monsters lurked and slithered in the corners. The bare mound within the grove was doubtless nothing more than the remains of an outbuilding that had been razed, ringed by outcroppings of foundation stones, but in the moonlight it looked like the bald head of a giant about to burst out of the earth, and the roots of the oak trees at its edge were like gnarled knuckles creeping upward out of the soil. Reminding himself severely that he was now an adult and that the air of evil that seemed to pervade the place was the product of his own mind, Simon clutched his bathrobe about him as low-hanging branches caught at the cashmere and entered the grove.

Around the periphery of the mound, squat candles with brown and red stripes were set in a circle, sending up stinking smoke. Damnfool teenagers, Simon said under his breath, didn't they have anything better to do than mess about on other people's property, setting up practical jokes? He went around the mound, kicking over one candle after another to extinguish them in the wet grass. Some initiation ceremony, maybe. French kids probably had secret clubs with passwords and do-or-die oaths, just like American ones. Or perhaps they were getting the jump on Hallowe'en. Whatever they thought they were doing, Hilaire had better pass the word around the village that they were not welcome.

Ye gods, where had they found candles that reeked so foully? He'd never smelled anything like them.

Having solved the mystery of the screwed-up perspective of the fireflies he'd seen from his window—which hadn't been fireflies at all, of course—Simon hotfooted it back to the house, caroming off the bridge, the door frame, the foyer table, and everything else that lay in his path. Odd, the odor of the candles seemed to be pursuing him. He sniffed at the sleeves of his robe to see if the nauseating smoke had penetrated the material. No, the smell was in the air. Maybe being so murky in the head from drinking was giving him olfactory illusions. Interesting. He turned off the downstairs lights and felt his way up the staircase wall and back along the dark upstairs hallway to his bedroom.

As he reached his room, the door of Kei's bedroom creaked open, and he could make out a figure emerging from the shadows into the moonlight that lay across the floor by the head of the foyer stairs. Well, *that* was no chic outfit, that long black bathrobe with the hood over the head, Simon thought disapprovingly.

"Bathroom's down the other way," he called. The figure joggled and then stood still as a stone. Probably scared her, shouting like that, when she thought she was alone. "If you're looking for a midnight snack, Marthe's got some cold chicken in the fridge," he added. The hood of the robe bobbed, and the figure slipped down the stairway.

Inside his room, he wiped his foot with a towel,

steadying himself with a hand on the black leather chair in the bay window and considered joining her for a drumstick. No, she didn't seem too friendly just now, not even speaking, and perhaps she'd think it was too clubby, sitting around in her night gear with a new employer. He sat down on the bed and wiped the other foot.

Lying on top of the fur coverlet in his bathrobe and feeling the bed rotate slowly, he smelled the candles again. A charnel house odor that made his stomach seem to be sliding back and forth. Just as he was falling asleep, he heard the hallway floor creaking down in the direction of Kei's room, but it often did that when the temperature changed, and it was going to be hot tomorrow, he could tell.

In his sleep, the golden mountain lion paced back and forth again at the foot of his bed. It was wearing a necklace of tiny white flowers, and its eyes looked kind. It raised its head to sniff the smoke swirling around it, shook its sleek head, and he climbed onto its back, and they traveled into dream countries together.

CHAPTER FIVE

Dear Chris:

Another nightmare last night. I'm getting so exhausted from them! If the cause of them doesn't lie here at the château, my last hope is gone. You know how many ways and how long I've tried to break through the wall that closes off their cause (how tired you must be of hearing about it!).

They were bad enough back home, with those shadowy figures crowding about, touching and dragging at me, calling me vile names, pulling me somewhere. But they weren't anywhere near as real as the one last night.

Someone had put a glass of hot milk by my bedside, which was thoughtful, and I drank it down and thought I'd be lucky and sleep through this time. But along about midnight or maybe later I was shocked awake by that feeling that I'd done something terrible that could never be undone — the feeling I always have — and I sat up in the darkness with my heart going like a jackhammer. I could swear there was something in the room with me that smelled like rotting flesh, a sort of bat-shaped blackness that was moving about quietly. Lord, it seemed real! Usually I can tell reality from dreaming when I'm having a nightmare, but this was horrifying. Still, it slipped away through the door and I seemed to lie back and go to sleep again. Maybe it was just a matter of being in a new and unfamiliar place that made the nightmare so vivid this time.

Anyway, I'll work like the devil on E.'s manuscript and perhaps I'll start sleeping better. I wish my trunk would come, because I'm a little uneasy about having my jewelry box sitting around in the trunk while it's at customs.

Thank heaven, when I was having that nightmare, at least I didn't scream or carry on as I sometimes do. Eagleton was the only other person in the house last night, and he said nothing to me this morning at breakfast, so I can be reasonably sure I didn't do the sleepwalking act again. But if I grew fangs and sprouted a tail right before his eyes, he'd probably simply raise an eyebrow, murmur, "Extraordinary!," and keep on eating his stupid broiled kidneys, so who knows?

I know you were against my coming here in the first place and that you had fits about my living in the same house with a man who has his reputation as a womanizer, but there's *no need to worry. Our relationship is strictly businesslike. He keeps his distance and I keep mine. He hasn't made one move toward laying a finger on me, I promise you.*

In fact, he has a way of looking speculatively at me, reaching back to smooth down the hair on the back of his head, and then drumming his fingers on the tabletop that makes me feel like a kid who's been called into the principal's office for wetting her pants in class. When he does that, my teeth seem too big for my mouth, I get all angles and gangly, and my feet become enormous. Even his tailoring intimidates me! My guilt about this masquerade doesn't help, either.

This morning, Marthe put a whole bunch of skyrockets beside his place at the table. He just nodded and kept on reading his newspaper. What do you make of that?

Love,

Kei

CHAPTER SIX

Having shooed Marthe out of the kitchen so he could fix lunch and have a good think by himself, Simon scrubbed the vegetables that Hilaire had brought in from the garden, scrubbing in time to the Bach playing on the cassette.

Perhaps at this very moment Kei was removing the Renoir oil from over the satinwood desk in her room. It was one of the most portable of the valuable pieces he owned — a head of a girl wearing a pink bonnet — and he wasn't likely to miss it from her room. The other really good things were in frequently used rooms, where their absence would be noticed immediately.

So far, nothing was missing that he could detect. She might be biding her time, waiting for the right moment. If she was making off with the Renoir, there was nothing he could do about it now. He couldn't, after all, dash upstairs, fling open her door, and shout "Aha!" She might just be sitting there at the desk, typing away, with theft the furthest thing from her mind. And what if the heat of the day had made her peel off her clothing, so that she was sitting there in the nude? Wouldn't that be a pretty howdydo, with him gawking at her and her wondering if he'd suddenly gone round the bend!

He leaned an elbow on the sink, a glossy purple eggplant in one hand and the scrub brush in the one that propped up his chin, and stared at the whitewashed wall while the tap water coursed down the drain, carrying garden dirt along with it.

Damn it all, it was nasty, keeping a suspicious eye on someone who was practically a guest in the house, watching to see if she was going to sneak away with one of his precious acquisitions. He'd promised to let her use the Mercedes tomorrow to pick up her locker trunk at customs if the seats were dry by then. An ideal opportunity to transport canvases to a waiting contact. Or to disappear with them herself, taking the car along as a bonus. Still, he couldn't bring himself to believe it of her.

He patted the vegetables dry with a towel and arranged them in a wooden bowl on the deal table in the center of the kitchen. Eggplants, tomatoes, green peppers, onions, and zucchini. He added sprays of dill weed for accent and stood back to admire the composition. It looked good enough to paint as a still life. Then he sliced tomatoes into a shallow dish of red wine and oil and sprinkled the sliced tomatoes with chopped green-onion tops, ground black pepper over them, and topped them off with shreds of fresh basil.

After checking to see that the sole was poaching properly, he sat down on one of the rush-bottomed chairs and started shelling peas, relishing the rubbery sound of their hitting the sides of the copper pot.

Actually, she could be just what she purported to be—a secretary. So she carried herself with style. Wasn't that what all this consciousness-raising flurry was about, having a good sense of oneself? Maybe she'd taken courses designed to give her self-assurance or attended group sessions. Just because she had expensive clothes didn't mean she was a thief, either. Executive secretaries made almost as much as junior executives in some companies, and many a vice president paid his secretary's rent and threw in a mink at Christmas in exchange for regular nooners. Maybe—to judge from the private school she'd attended—her parents had left her money, and she'd never lost the patina and arrogance that's the heritage of the privileged class.

"You said lunch at one o'clock," said her voice from the doorway. "May I come in?"

"Mm," said Simon in assent, averting his eyes. He knew they could give him away. They always did, and he didn't want her to know he suspected her of such incredible things. "Have a pea?"

She looked startled and then laughed. "For a moment, I thought you meant something quite else," she said. She sat down and popped a raw pea into her mouth. "They're better this way than cooked, don't you think?"

"Much. Shall I serve them as is?"

"Yes, please." She began helping him shell. He pushed the copper pot closer to her so she wouldn't have to reach and saw that she was looking around at the terra cotta tiles on the floor, the restaurant-sized stove, the rack of shining pots and pans suspended from the ceiling, and the strings of red peppers and garlic, and he felt the pride of ownership and design. "What a marvelous kitchen!" she said. "And what gorgeous vegetables! I suppose you're the one who arranged them?"

He nodded. "The bounty of the earth and all that. I come over all Lord of the Harvest, knowing they were grown on my own land."

"I know. I turn into Mother Earth when I get back from the farmer's market with an armload of fresh-picked vegetables with dirt still clinging to them. Like some mythical being with a cornucopia. Never mind that they cost twice what they would at the supermarket."

For some minutes they shelled peas without speaking, the only sounds in the kitchen the ponk-ponk of the peas and the popping of the gas flame under the fish. Strange how companionable it felt, Simon thought. Especially if Kei really was a professional criminal bent on robbery.

"It's charming and well written," she said without preamble. "Just what I'd expect from reading your books on art criticism. The awakening sex bits liven things up, and that's good, but I have some qualms about the way you handle your relationship with your sister."

He should have known! He was insane to have

77

been so open, but it was, after all, a part of his life and had seemed perfectly natural and guiltless at that age.

"Saying she tried to kill you several times is either libel or slander, I can't remember which," she said, to his surprise. "And I'm sure you put it more strongly than you realized. Children don't have adult standards, and you can't judge them by adult standards."

"You say that because you don't know Elaine." He got up to look at the fish, sniff its herb-laden steam, and turn off the gas. "She was determined to do me in, quite seriously." He leaned back against the sink and wiped his hands on his striped-ticking work apron. "Sibling rivalry can be pretty bitter, you know. She's got a violent temper that hasn't improved with age. So do I, for that matter. But we can cut those episodes out. The one where she stuck the knife in my arm, for one."

He wiped the table with a wet cloth and put out Italian majolica plates bright with flowers and birds. The raw peas went into an earthenware bowl, and he slid the copper pot into the water in the dishpan.

"I'd rather leave out my sexual experimentation with her, too," he said, avoiding her eyes. "I exaggerated considerably for dramatic effect."

Kei looked dubious. "I'm sure there's much more of that going on than people admit. We're not dealing with a puritanical audience nowadays, so I don't see the harm in it."

"Take it out!" he commanded, slapping the

silverware in place. "It will be an embarrassment to both of us."

"All right," Kei said. "I'll excise and retype, no trouble. Maybe it's best."

He brought the food to the table and said, "She's coming to dinner tonight. Lives in the village, surrounded by masses of expatriates who keep her company and out of my hair, for the most part." He poured chilled Vouvray, sat down, and raised his glass toward her.

She echoed the motion solemnly, and then they both tucked into the food.

"Oh, my God, this is good!" said Kei. "I hope you're going to cook the dinner tonight."

"No, Marthe will. I don't cook unless I'm in the mood. The fun goes out of it when you have to do it on a regular basis."

"How well I know!"

Simon congratulated himself for having led her into giving him a clue to her personal life. "Then you've been married," he said smoothly.

"Yes."

He expected that to lead to more revelations, but none come. "Your résumé doesn't tell much about you," he said, miffed at her ability to keep her mouth shut.

"I haven't had a lot of experience in writing résumés. Did I do something wrong?" She turned a level-eyed gaze on him, letting him know that she understood his game plan. He felt shabby for probing, but his curiosity drove him on.

"Ordinarily, I would have interviewed a secretary before hiring her," he said, "but that was impossible this time, of course. Still, I think it's reasonable to want to know something about you if we're going to work together."

She put down her fork and looked at her hands with their unvarnished nails. She fiddled with the big topaz on her ring finger. "I was born in Japan and went to college in Illinois, but you already know that." She sighed and looked across at him. "That isn't what you're getting at, though, is it? You're right, the aunt in Paris was a fiction. I was afraid you'd seen through that. I knew no one in his right mind would fly a secretary from America when he could get a bilingual one here, and I—have you got a cigarette on you?"

He took his pack out of his shirt pocket, shook a cigarette out for her to take, and stuck one in his own mouth. Bending over the lighter he held out, she got her started and then sat back with an arm over the back of her chair and blew a mouthful of smoke at the ceiling.

"I just felt I had to put an ocean between me and the past. I've just gone through a divorce and still am pretty shaky, but it won't affect my work, I promise you. It was final last month, and it seemed the right time to get away. To try to start over again." She held out her glass for a refill and asked, "You're sure you want to hear all this? I don't want to burden you with being my psychoanalyst just because I need some-body to talk to."

"Go on. I'm interested in what makes you tick."

"Really?" She smiled skeptically, then drank down the glass of Vouvray. "I'm warning you, I get high very quickly on alcohol, and then I rattle on."

"I asked, and I'm willing to take the consequences."

"It's a boring story, I'm afraid. Too common to have shock value. Two people who married too young. One son. He was killed in a car crash two years ago."

"I'm sorry," Simon said softly. "It must have been terrible for you the other day, when I was driving so recklessly."

She blinked and looked away. Crossing an arm over her chest, she put a hand on her shoulder and patted it gently, as if comforting herself, and Simon could see her throat working. When she had composed herself, she went on in a husky voice. "My husband was a professor of history, but he had to take over the family business when my father died and nearly ran it into the ground before they threw him out. Professors don't know anything about money and things like that. It hurt his ego, though, and he began fooling around with his graduate students."

She picked up the bottle and poured herself half a glass. "After Stephen's death, there wasn't anything left to hold the marriage together, and the affairs got insultingly blatant. He left me to live with one of his students, and I didn't fight it. I just sort of—ran down, like a watch stopping. Things fell apart. Me included." She finished off her wine and then set the glass away from her at arm's length, very delicately. "See? I told you it was boring. It hurt like hell, though, being thrown away like a piece of trash."

She got up, picked up their plates, and carried them to the sink.

"I've never lived alone before in my life. Not all alone. My parents were always there to fall back on, but they're gone now. And so is Stephen." She rolled up her sleeves and mixed liquid soap and water together in the dishpan. "I'm feeling sorry for myself and scared and sniveling, and I *hate* it! I didn't think I'd be like that. Why is it that the unbearable thing is to find out you're just as vulnerable and incapable of coping as everybody else?"

Simon extinguished his cigarette and the one she'd left smouldering in the ashtray and got up to go over to her.

"But that's not the worst," she said, and he could see her eyes were about to brim over. "There's something else. But it's so horrible . . . "

"There's dessert yet. Pears and a nice, runny Brie," he said, taking her hands out of the dishwater and gently wiping them dry with a towel. "I think you're a little tight. Are you sure you want to tell me this?"

They looked at each other, and some kind of electrical current seemed to run between them.

"Aren't you ever frightened?" she asked, the moisture from her eyes making her eyelashes stick together in starry points.

"All the time," he said softly. For a moment, he felt both their masks slip—the faces they presented, calm and composed, to the world—and he didn't know what to do. One misstep, and she might shatter. He wanted to put his arms around her to comfort her, but he had no idea what her reaction would be. She closed her eyes, and when she opened them again, the shutters were down. The mask had returned. He felt that they had nearly crossed over into a terrible zone where there would have been smoke and screams and sobbing and convulsions.

She took a shuddering breath and said, "You ought to watch those 'quites' and 'rathers.' They weaken your verbs."

It was all right again. At least, for now.

They spoke very little as they finished the meal and had coffee. Kei volunteered to wash if he wiped, and Simon got out a long wine-colored apron from the cupboard and put it around her waist while she held it, as motionless and wary as a rabbit before it breaks and runs, until he'd tied it in back. The top of her head came just to his nose, and her hair smelled of perfume that evoked images of green leaves in sunshine. They didn't look at one another as they did the dishes, but he knew they were monitoring each other's movements through an extra sense in their skins.

To ease the tension, Simon started singing "Cheek to Cheek" in a low voice, and Kei chimed in, husky but hitting the notes right in the middle. They sang through the glassware, the silverware, and even the pots that Marthe had set aside to soak. They both knew all the words from the old Ginger Rogers-Fred Astaire films, a bond

Simon thought more telling than having gone to the same school or coming from the same home town. In general, it was the trivial things that mattered most with people. Probably fewer marriages had foundered on political or religious differences, Simon thought, than on arguments over whether the toilet paper should emerge overhand or underhand from the holder.

When Kei went upstairs to type, Simon went out. Fournier needed to be talked to. The man was lazy and wasn't mucking out the stalls as he should, but he'd come with the place, and—in spite of a heavy accent—he spoke excellent English, so that Simon could understand him without effort. God knows, his own knowledge of farming at this juncture was so minuscule that he had to depend heavily on Fournier's expertise. Too bad the fellow was so unlikable, since there was no choice but to bump along with him.

Where the blazes was he? Simon didn't want to interrupt if he was screwing someone in the barn again. He wished Fournier would remarry if he was going to be in perpetual rut, or have the delicacy to take his women up to his rooms. It galled Simon to think of the brute doing things that he was no longer capable of himself.

Fournier made good wages for the area and had a rent-free place big enough for a family, so there was no reason why he couldn't get married. He was presentable enough—almost as tall as Simon and with much broader shoulders. A heavy beard and long black hair partially concealed his face, but not his large, blue, truculent-looking eyes. On rare occasions, Fournier showed flashes of the charm that seemed to make it easy for him to entice women into a roll in the hay, but it put Simon's back up. It was an appeal that would only attract a woman. Perhaps Fournier felt that the village women weren't his intellectual equals and scorned them except as sexual partners. He was a sharp one and obviously had had more schooling than was usual for one of his station. There was a good story there, Simon was sure, but he wasn't going to waste his time by trying to pry it out of one who was so taciturn and inverted.

There he was, hunkered down behind the tractor and working with a wheel, a rubber-headed mallet beside him on the ground. It took five minutes of a good reaming out before Fournier would admit — grudgingly — that he'd been remiss in caring for the stable. He'd get at it as soon as he was through fixing the wheel, he said.

"I see there is someone at the big house," said Fournier, wiping his hands on a wad of waste.

"Yes, a secretary to help me with a book I'm doing," said Simon, looking up at the sky in hopes of seeing a cloud. A cooling rain would be welcome. "I want you to give her every courtesy if she should want to ride. Though I doubt she will. Her name is Mme. Ronald."

Fournier took out a penknife and began to clean his nails. "American?" he asked.

"Yes."

"She has a first name, perhaps?"

Simon looked at him curiously. "Yes. Kei. Spelled K-E-I, oddly enough. Why on earth do you ask?"

"I like names." Fournier looked him straight in the eye, and there was a flavor of insolence in his glance. "Why not?"

"Why not indeed?" Simon said irritably, obscurely offended by Fournier's question.

"I have work to do before it rains," Fournier said and squatted again beside the tractor. Clearly, the conversation was over.

Why Fournier thought it was going to rain was a puzzle. Not a cloud was in the burnished sky. The dogs were sitting sprawled on the bank of the moat, motionless except for the lolling of their tongues. Their tails thumped politely as Simon passed them on the way to the house, but they didn't stir from their places. The typewriter was stuttering rapidly upstairs.

Guiltily, Simon went up the kitchen staircase so he wouldn't have to pass the room where Kei was working so diligently, stretched out on his bed, and was asleep in a minute.

In the depths of his dream, he became aware that he was no longer alone. Struggling up to the surface of consciousness, he opened his eyes a slit and then gave a massive start. A brown balloon with eyes was not three inches from his face.

"See? I told you he was awake." Tommy McKenzie's voice receded, and the brown balloon turned into a deeply tanned face as Tommy straightened up and Simon focused his eyes. "I knew you were hiding under those eyelids," Tommy said. "Come on down, it's time for drinks."

He had that actress with him. Standing by the emerald velvet of the walls, she looked pre-Raphaelite in a moss green and gold brocade gown that must be too heavy for this heat. Her black hair spread over her shoulders in a cloud. As they left the room, she twiddled her fingers at Simon.

The setting sun struck orange glances off the gold frames of the Russian icons on the wall. It was still hot. Simon sat up and felt his chin to see if he needed a shave. He could, he decided, get away with it if people didn't get too close. He felt worse now, more tired than he had before he lay down.

In the round tower bathroom next to his room, he washed his face and neck with a cold cloth and splashed on some Skye aftershave by Trumper that he took from the small refrigerator by the shower.

He changed into espadrilles and white cotton pants that tied with a drawstring and pulled on a rough brown linen shirt that set off his tan and brushed his white hair with his brushes. His naturally dark skin took a quick, deep tan, and he looked well in the sports clothes that he wore in France. His fingernails looked almost white against the brown of his hands.

Oh Lord, the typewriter was *still* going! He stumped down the hallway on wooden-feeling legs, yawning, and stopped to knock on Kei's door. The typewriter stopped and the door opened a wedge. Kei looked out, holding together at the bosom a kimono striped horizontally in brown, white, and gray.

"Drinks," said Simon. "In the sitting room." She nodded and closed the door, and he went off down the hall, yawning again until his jaws cracked. His tongue felt shrunken and white.

When he got downstairs, everyone already had helped themselves to drinks from the bar by the window. Tommy held out a gin and tonic to him, and Simon downed half of it in one swallow. Giving a strangled cry of relief, he collapsed onto one of the light green velvet settees by the cold fireplace.

"Thanks, you needed that," said Tommy, who was looking obnoxiously cool and energetic in jeans and a coolie jacket open down the front that displayed the golden fur on his chest. As he stood with one arm hooked over the mantelpiece, the actress twined around him like a climbing vine.

Jeanne-Marie LeClair, her white hair screwed so tightly back into a bun that her eyes looked Chinese, was sitting beside Elaine on the other settee and wearing a green gown which looked like a clinical smock that had forgotten to stop until it reached the floor. Jeanne-Marie, whose identification with her profession of obstetrician was so complete that she had de-sexed herself, was scrutinizing her glass of sherry as if it were a test tube containing a culture under question.

Elaine was rolling her glass of grenadine and

gin thoughtfully between her hands, keeping her chin raised and the best side of her profile to the group, but the expression on her face was unpleasant as she studied Tommy and the young girl. She was probably brooding over the gap in years between her and the teenager, feeling over the hill and haggish, which usually meant heavy weather ahead. Simon had hoped this would be one of the evenings when she and Tommy maintained an arctic courtesy toward one another, but if she was in one of her regrets-for-lost-youth moods, the two of them were likely to keep up a running crossfire of sniping remarks, making a battlefield of the dinner table.

Actually, despite being fifty-six, Elaine was still a true beauty. A facelift had erased the traces of age that she complained about so bitterly. Born a brunette, she'd gone titian when she started finding gray hairs. The reddish-gold of her hair suited her cream and pink complexion tones better than its original color. She had a ripe figure just this side of being plump, and her soft, smooth skin looked as if one could poke a finger through it without meeting any resistance.

Her rather decadent sexiness attracted lovers a decade or so younger than she was—of which there'd been a shocking number. Last season's blue-black model couldn't have been a day over thirty. He'd been the most unbearable of the lot, arrogant and with pierced nipples where he wore rings, sometimes stringing chains between the loops. To show off these atrocities, he wore jackets open down the front. He jingled when he walked. Joylessly, Simon recalled dinner parties here at the château with Elaine seated next to that specimen while all the guests' eyes were riveted on the chest jewelry.

It was when the chest fellow was in power that Elaine had started badgering to have her bedroom ceiling mirrored, wrangling about it for a couple of months until, exasperated, Simon threatened to cut back on her allowance. That provoked a lot of stamping around and sulking, and she'd recounted his meanness and miserliness to everyone within earshot. It was beyond credibility that anyone but Elaine would believe that mirrors on the bedroom ceiling were a necessity of life, but Simon disliked being accused of being cheap, and he was always afraid that one day she'd go too far in publicly airing family matters. He wished she'd go to some other corner of the globe and live her own life, but she clung to him like a burr.

"It is too hot," said Jeanne-Marie, pulling out the front of her dress and blowing down it. "I am wet all over."

"Can't keep up much longer," Tommy said. He detached one of Bridget's fingers after the other from his arms and pushed her away gently. "October's just around the corner."

"Rudy's late," said Elaine, rattling the ice at the bottom of her glass.

"Rudy's always late." Tommy stared at himself in the mirror over the fireplace and ran a hand over his chin, inspecting the light stubble that seemed to appear five minutes after he'd shaved.

"I doubt he's got a clock in the house, and if he does, he wouldn't be able to find it in the litter of books and manuscripts. The man's a human pack rat." He turned his profile to the mirror and looked critically at himself.

"Can't you ever say anything nice about anyone? Rudy's a darling," Elaine said. "Everybody adores him. But that's just like you: if a person isn't dipped in Lysol daily and polished to a high shine, he's beyond the pale in your books." Tommy turned his head to look at himself full face in the mirror and the creases along his jaw deepened warningly, but before he could get a retort out, Elaine said to Simon, "Has your secretary arrived?"

"You might say. Definitely."

"Oh, really?" Elaine said slowly and sucked in her lower lip thoughtfully, then asked, "What's she like?"

"Mm. The faintest bit like that American actress, what's her name? Lauren Bacall." Noting Elaine's expression, he backpedalled rapidly. "Except that she's . . . not. Well, higher cheekbones, I don't know. Whatever, she wasn't what I expected. One wouldn't." One of Elaine's eyebrows shot up. "She types *very* fast," he added.

At that, rather than get himself in deeper, he retired from the conversation, leaving Elaine to draw her own conclusions when Kei came down from upstairs. The bar seemed too far off for him to traverse the distance for another drink, so he set his glass down on the small table by his chair and slouched down with his ankles crossed

91

in front of him, feeling out of sorts. He wasn't looking forward to having Kei see Elaine and Tommy at their worst with each other.

He'd been surprised that Elaine had gifted Tommy with the slingshot, but one never knew what whim she'd seize upon. His sister was so different from him in temperament that he had trouble predicting her behavior, even though they'd always been close.

He loved her, he supposed. She was all the family he had left, and people did love their sisters, didn't they? But like her? Not easy. Once, years ago, she'd seemed to soften and he'd thought her prickly personality was changing, but that passed over and she reverted to her usual alternations of sun and shadow. He and she didn't seem to be made of the same cloth at all.

They shared a family resemblance, though. The same well-placed spaniel eyes with slightly upturned outer corners and an identical full mouth that showed no threat of thinning with age. As a youth, Simon had been inordinately pleased with the perfection of his mouth and spent hours posing in front of the mirror, sucking in the corners of his lips slightly and raising one eyebrow in what he considered a killingly sexy expression. Scornfully, Elaine called it his "smartass look" and said it made him look like a sleazy waiter who'd gotten away with padding the bill.

It called forth instant negativity in other people, too. One day he'd been practicing it absentmindedly while passing a gang of street toughs, who'd taken one quick squint at it before being galvanized into piling onto him in a tornado of flying fists and obscenities. They broke his nose and a canine tooth, and his father had been severe about the cost of repairs, especially after Simon had shown him the expression that provoked the attack. "I understand their viewpoint entirely," his father had said, and thereafter Simon confined his use of the look to the bedroom, where it was either gratifyingly successful or prompted tiresome mutual lies about not having done this sort of thing before and respect the morning after.

The group stood or sat silently, in the grip of hot-weather boredom, looking like the cast of a Chekhov play. Jeanne-Marie could have taken the role of the old uncle, and Elaine was eminently suited to play the voice of discontent and *weltschmerz*. Bridget's untouched, virginal air, totally at odds with the trampiness required in members of Tommy's harem, was perfect for the ingenue. Tommy, of course, would be the leading man. He was still almost as fit as he had been when he was on the screen, although his hair was getting thinner on top and the creases running from his cheeks to his jaws were very deep now. He still radiated virility. Which brought up The Subject again. At the reminder of his impotence, Simon felt himself sliding into gloom.

He jumped as a hand came down on his shoulder and a voice with a faint Dutch accent said, "Sorry to be late. I couldn't find the clock."

"Good God, Rudy, do you have to creep up on people like that?" Simon twisted around to take

93

his friend's hand.

"Indian moccasins. Very fine for sneaking up on the unsuspecting," said Rudy van der Zee, a triangular smile spreading between his foxy little cheeks. "I hear you have a new employee." He went over to kiss Elaine's and Jeanne-Marie's hands, nodding at Tommy in passing. "Where is this person?"

"Taking a hellish long time to dress," said Simon. "You know how women are."

"Ah, I wish I did." Rudy poured himself an aperitif and raised his glass to the company before taking a sip. "Unfortunately, God did not see fit to grant me the animal magnetism with which He blessed you and Tommy, alas."

True, Simon thought. Rudy was probably asexual. Tall though his wiry figure was, when Rudy stood still, he blended into the woodwork. There was something faded about his shy personality, like a spray of flowers long pressed between the pages of a book, that yielded up only the dry, brown-edged scent of a forgotten spring. Middle-aged, he still made Simon want to protect him from seeing anything nasty. Rudy's hooded eyes, magnified by his glasses, looked sad even when he was being apologetically witty.

A rapid cascade of heel clicks came down the hallway stairs, crossed the foyer, and Kei appeared in the doorway. She poised there hesitantly until Simon got up and brought her in by the hand for introductions.

Elaine looked her over thoroughly, scrutinizing her skintight black trousers and broadcuffed beige

94

satin shirt, carefully calculating, Simon knew, the cost of each item of her clothing. Elaine was unmistakably hostile, and Kei's compliment on her high-necked caftan of pink and flame silk evoked no reciprocal warmth.

"That's interesting," said Elaine, her eyes resting on a black ball hanging around Kei's neck on a fine gold chain. She reached out a finger to touch it and drew it back again quickly, as if she'd tapped a source of static electricity. "What is *that*?"

Kei drew the ball out on its chain and looked down at it. "I think it's an old pomander ball," she said. "I found it right . . . That's what all those little holes are for, I imagine, to let scent come through." She dropped it back into place between her breasts. "To tell the truth, it smells rather awful close up, but I've never been able to get it open to put perfume in it."

Elaine studied it a moment longer and then transferred her attention to Kei's topaz ring. "If that's your birthstone, you're a Scorpio?"

"It's not. I was born in October."

"A Libra! Oh, no!" A tiny frown flitted across Elaine's immaculate brow. "Simon's an Aries, and that means friction between you. You're polar signs, you know. A Libra weighs her decisions and postpones forever. Simon's all self-centered and impulsive. There's absolutely no hope of anything good between you two. If you had any sense, you'd get out while the going's good. I'd fly if I were in your shoes, but—being a Libra—you'll probably stall around until the roof falls in on you. Don't say I didn't warn you." She took Kei's hand and worked the ring back and forth on her finger, making it catch the light.

"I think Mr. Eagleton and I can work out a comfortable business relationship," Kei said coolly, withdrawing her hand.

"I hope so, for your sake. If the . . . relationship doesn't make you uneasy, this place probably will," said Elaine.

"What do you mean by that?" Simon asked. He didn't like the direction the conversation was taking.

"The château, Simon dearest." Elaine walked over to the bar and looked out into the oak grove. "Rudy's been going over some of the old records, haven't you, Rudy? He's found out some things they didn't tell you when you bought this place."

"Don't spoil Simon's pleasure in his home," said Rudy, taking Elaine's glass away as she started to refill it and setting it down on the bar. "In any case, it's past history. I'm sorry you brought it up. Let's forget it."

"I just thought she ought to know what kind of a place she's staying in," said Elaine, with a little shrug. She looked Rudy in the eye, picked up her glass, and slowly, deliberately poured herself another drink.

"Then let me be the one to tell it," said Rudy. "It's merely that the mound out there in the woods used to be a grotto that the château owner used for certain rites. It's nothing to concern yourself about any longer."

This was news to Simon. He went to the window to take a fresh look at the site. In the slanting evening light, the mound was parchment-colored, like a skull nearly buried in the earth. Rocky rubble ringed it like a stony diadem. He'd tried to plant over the area, but nothing would grow there. "What kind of rites?" he asked. Not good ones, he guessed, or the real estate agent would have used the grotto's history as a selling point.

"Devil worship. Satanism," Elaine said with relish. "The château's owner was the mistress of the cult. She killed her own newborn babies and boiled them down for the fat to make candles for the coven's ceremonies."

"Oh, ick!" said Bridget rapturously.

"They burned human sacrifices in wicker baskets out on the meadow. I hope that thinking about the victims writhing in the flames practically beneath your window doesn't disturb your beauty sleep, Kei," said Elaine, taking her glass over to one of the easy chairs and sitting down with a flourish of her long skirt, obviously pleased at being the focus of all eyes. "There's a local legend that whenever a woman's child is aborted or stillborn, Mistress Sélène has taken the baby's spirit away to the Devil."

"Now, Elaine . . . " Simon began, but she overrode him, raising her voice.

"Just an interesting bit of social history, Simon," Elaine said.

"What happened to her?" breathed Bridget, egging Elaine on.

"Well, they say . . ." Elaine paused dramatically,

took a long swallow of her drink, and then repeated, "They say that the villagers stripped her, tied her up with silken cords, put her in the grotto, and pulled it down about her, sealing her alive inside. If that's true, her body's still in there. That's why nothing will grow there now." She finished off her drink. "They say."

Rudy cleared his throat softly, a forefinger under his lower lip, and said, "This, of course, is not supported by the records, so it shouldn't be taken seriously. Legends grow with time. Europe was overrun with sensation-seekers in the seventeenth century, as was Britain. You'll remember the Hellfire Club? Occultism was an aristocratic amusement, like horse racing."

"Burning people and killing babies was an *amusement*?" Kei looked aghast.

"No, no, I didn't mean that. Elaine is embroidering the facts," said Rudy, looking admonishingly at Elaine. "What really took place, in all probability, was that the local gentry had drunken parties in the grotto in the company of ladies of easy virtue."

Ignoring Rudy's version of the story, Bridget Sunshine clasped her hands together on her bosom, making her breasts bounce, and said, "Oh, how swimmingly divine! Satanists! Devil worshippers!" She shuddered pleasurably. "Oh, and Elaine, in the village they say you're a witch. Are you? *Please say you are!*"

"Don't be silly," Simon snapped, wishing he could get his hands on the realtor's neck. "Elaine fools around with the ouija board and tells the cards, that's all. She got it out of some how-to paperback. And belt up, Elaine. Are you trying to frighten Kei out of her wits?"

Elaine smirked. "Such an idea would never enter my head, darling brother," she said, widening her eyes innocently. "I want her to feel welcome here. I'm sure we're all delighted she came. Particularly you."

"I *told* them they were just being dumb." Bridget said disappointedly and flounced over to sit down on a settee. "Shit, nothing ever turns out to be as interesting as you think it's going to be. They just think all old women are witches."

Elaine seemed to swell slightly, and a flush mottled her neck. She set down her glass on the side table and glanced at her watch. "Give me time, and I'll show you whether or not I'm a witch, my dear," she said to Bridget. "Later in the evening. But first I think I should tell you that it would be wise for you to go back to whatever cathouse you came from before you get into trouble. After a demonstration of my powers, you may want to do just that. And rather rapidly."

"Girls, girls," Tommy said placatingly, bringing Kei a glass of white wine. "I thought this looked like you," he said to her.

Still not over his irritation with the real estate agent, Simon was even more riled to note that his friend was gearing up to add Kei to his collection. It was an old routine, one that he didn't like seeing go into operation. He hoped that Kei would think it beneath her dignity to become just one more subheading in a long list of easy lays. Moreover, he realized unhappily, if things were different, he would have tried to get her into bed himself.

Marthe came to the sitting-room door and raised her eyebrows by way of announcing that dinner was ready. Simon took Rudy's arm as the party went ahead of them through the hallway and detained him to ask in a low voice for details on the château's history, but Rudy shrugged it off, saying the records were vague and fragmented. "You know Elaine's predilection for shocking people," he said. "It seems she's a shade jealous of the new lady, too, wouldn't you say?"

The table was laid with a deep pink damask cloth, and dark red roses on the edge of their prime made a perfumed pillow in a Lalique bowl between candles lit in vermeil candelabra. Although the casement window was open to catch any twilight breeze, the room was heavy with the scent of roses.

Tommy seated Bridget and Jeanne-Marie, while Rudy attended to Elaine at the foot of the table, but Kei was already in her place before Simon could pull her chair out for her, and he was put off a little. He liked the old courtesies between men and women, but the women's movement was making it risky to extend them lately. The last time he'd been in New York, he'd opened a door for a woman and she'd hit him with her umbrella, using language that made him want to scrub out her mouth with kitty litter. Kei's conversation also had a careless scattering of four-letter words that he could have done without, and Elaine's was enough to bake one's scalp upon occasion. Perhaps he'd been born into the wrong century entirely.

Before his place at the head of the table, Marthe had placed a white stoneware tureen. He raised the cover and a delicious aroma of garlic, onions, and tomato floated out. "Gazpacho," he announced, and the guests murmured approval.

The talk languished as everyone got down to the soup but picked up with the ham and asparagus in aspic.

"You've been in France before?" Rudy asked Kei politely.

Her eyes flickered, and she said, "No, I haven't traveled much."

Simon suspected she was lying. The French he'd overheard her using with Marthe in the kitchen wasn't the formal kind taught in classrooms, and she spoke it at a machine-gun clip. Clearly, she was hiding something. Tomorrow he must remember to check on the Renoir above her desk when she was out of her room, just on the off chance.

"Are you married or divorced or what?" asked Bridget, staring with unconcealed cupidity at Kei's ring.

"Divorced. Last month. But it had been over long before that."

"Cheated on you, I'll bet," Bridget said sympathetically. "The bastard, they're all alike."

"Any children?" asked Jeanne-Marie.

Kei opened her mouth to reply, but Bridget interrupted, "If he wasn't fooling around, did

101

he turn out to be gay? There's a lot of that going around. Or maybe *you're* gay?"

"Gay, my ass," said Tommy. "She's got a man waiting in the wings somewhere. I know a lesbian when I see one."

"Who says so?" said Elaine with a sniff. "What kind of a settlement did you get?" she asked Kei.

"*I* say so. She looks about as much like a dike as . . . "

"What's wrong with playing both sides of the street?" said Bridget.

"There is more to life than sex," Jeanne-Marie cut in. "Now, children . . . "

"About the money . . . " said Elaine.

Simon slammed his palms down on the table, making Kei jump and Bridget give a small shriek of surprise. "Will you *please* leave her alone!" he demanded. "You are *not* to cross-examine her this way!"

Kei, whose head had been turning back and forth like a spectator at a tennis match as people spoke, gave him a look of gratitude, and Elaine caught it.

"My, aren't we being protective this evening!" she said. "I'll bet having your . . . associate turn out to be gay wasn't part of your plan."

"Listen, everybody's got a sexual hangup," Bridget rattled on. "Tommy thinks I'm funny because I . . . "

"STOP!" Simon ordered, and everyone fell silent. He shrugged his collar back into place with a twist of his neck and ran a hand over the hair on the back of his head. "Could we all just keep our sex lives to ourselves? As much as possible? Let's change the subject." He buttered a piece of bread furiously. "For Christ's sake!" My God, *could* she be? No, she wouldn't set off that tingle along the nerve ends if she were. At any rate, he'd never find out, not in his condition.

"Dear, dear, we're touchy tonight!" Elaine put down her fork on her plate in the correct four o'clock position. "Something bothering you, Simon, or is the heat getting to you?"

Simon ignored her and, pointing with his chin, said, "Tommy, there's a tray of fans on the sideboard behind you. Would you pass them around? Sorry about no air conditioning, but you know what these old houses are. I had to move heaven and earth to get arrangements made for keeping the third floor at the right temperature for storing paintings."

Tommy took a gentleman's Japanese fan from the tray and passed the others around. Rudy took one the color of a tealeaf and began translating the Japanese calligraphy running down its side under his breath. When the tray came to him, Simon took a black one with a hairline edge of silver. Soon the table was a-flutter, as if butterflies had come to light around the damask cloth.

Bridget tittered. "If you men don't look like a bunch of old aunties!"

"This is getting tiresome," said Tommy, putting the tray back on the sideboard. "You know damned well *I'm* not gay, Bridget, and the trail of broken hearts Simon's left behind him has

103

been documented by the media. Jeanne-Marie's married to her job. I can't speak for Rudy, although I've got an idea he's still attached to his mother."

"What?" said Rudy, startled, looking up from his translation.

"You've got that all wrong," said Elaine, spreading out her gold and red kabuki fan and looking over it coquettishly. "*You're* trying to run away from old age by banging every teenager in sight. Simon's the eternal romantic, always looking for the perfect love. Which he wouldn't recognize if it bit him. The only real stud at the table is Rudy."

All eyes turned to Rudy, who looked ready to wither from embarrassment. Astonished, Simon looked at Rudy with new respect.

"My God, you can't let anything alone that's in trousers, can you?" said Tommy.

"At least I don't go to bed with children," said Elaine, closing her fan with a snap.

"How old was that fellow with jingles on his chest?" said Tommy. "Still on the bottle?" He closed his fan with a louder snap.

"Old enough to know what he was doing, in spades. Rudy's better, though." Elaine opened her fan and began waving it languorously, smiling acidly at Tommy.

Rudy lit a cigarette from the salver in front of him, held it between his thumb and forefinger, cupping his other fingers around it in the Russian fashion, and stared at it as if it were an especially detestable object while he cleared his throat softly several times.

"Don't you think that's enough of that?" said Simon, empathizing with Rudy's discomfiture. "Couldn't we try acting civilized?"

Tommy and Elaine stared at one another across the table, then Elaine asked Kei, "How did Simon get your name so he could hire you?"

"Jeremy Kirbottle," said Simon and then reproached himself for answering for Kei. He was treating her like an emotional cripple without really knowing if she was one.

Kei took over for herself. "Jeremy's the publisher at Landsend House, the one who's doing Mr. Eagleton's book. I'd edited some copy for an American writer he was handling, and Jeremy was kind enough to be impressed. So when Mr. Eagleton needed some help, he thought I'd do, I guess."

"You've met Jeremy, have you?" asked Simon in what he hoped was a casual tone.

"Oh, yes. He comes to the States a couple of times a year to solicit manuscripts from authors."

"I've always wondered what he looked like," lied Simon, hoping to cue her into giving a description. He wanted to find out if Kei really was the secretary Jeremy had intended for him. Did he catch amusement in her eye? She looked down at her rust-colored fan before he could be sure.

"Well, he's built like a stick of chewing gum, the way some Englishmen are. No shoulders and no waist, either. I don't know how he keeps his pants up. And he's got a little moustache that he twiddles like Charlie Chaplin when he gets excited."

That was Jeremy, all right. Simon felt sheepish about trying to trick Kei into giving herself away, but he simply couldn't picture her as an honest-to-God secretary who typed form letters.

"How are you liking the château?" asked Rudy, who looked more comfortable with the conversation now. "I hope you aren't going to let Elaine's remarks make you uneasy here."

"It's a lovely place, so light and airy," said Kei. "You'd think nothing had ever gone wrong here, the atmosphere's so happy and serene. It's hard to believe those things went on out there at the back."

Rudy held his glass out to Simon for a refill and said, "That happened three centuries ago, if at all. You needn't worry that anything like that is going on here now. This is a very peaceful little village."

"I wouldn't be too sure of that," contradicted Jeanne-Marie, putting down her fan and leaning forward with her hands clasped under her chin. "The newspapers tell of male and female cows in the fields with their parts cut out. The heart, the tongue, the penis, or the womb. Cut out while the beasts were still living. And ... *and* ... " She raised a chapped finger in emphasis. "I can tell you from my own experience something else. Never, *never* do the number of stillborns and abortions at the hospital come out correctly. That is to say, one or two are always lacking. Where have they gone? They say that this has gone on for years. Now, what of that?"

"Oh, wow!" said Bridget, her eyes feverish with excitement. "*Ghouls!*"

106

Rudy held a finger in front of his lips and shushed Jeanne-Marie, who pursed her lips and looked huffy. "Surely this is not table conversation? We must remember that the other ladies are not so accustomed to clinical matters. In addition, there is some question. It may be the work of wild dogs, which seems much more reasonable, I would think. We are living in the twentieth century, not the seventeenth."

"With all respect," said Jeanne-Marie, "all the more reason our records at the hospital should be accurate. We have computers, you realize."

"But the human factor, my dear Jeanne-Marie, the human factor." Rudy stroked his ash away on the rim of the silver ashtray before his plate. "We are all subject to error."

"You are altogether too trusting, Rudy." Jeanne-Marie caught up a strand of white hair that had escaped from her bun and ruthlessly tucked it back into place. "You see good in everyone. It is your sweet nature. But doctors see the harsh side of life. Suicide, criminal abortions, incest, murder. Nothing is hidden from the doctor."

"And speaking of murder . . . " Elaine said.

The swinging door banged back against the wall and Marthe sailed in, bearing a crystal bowl of salad.

CHAPTER SEVEN

"Speaking of murder," Elaine repeated as the salad bowl went around the table, "were you aware that one may have taken place right here in the château?"

That Simon *had* heard about, but Elaine was overdoing it. Clearly, she was trying to spook Kei, and he could imagine why.

"That was only a rumor," he said sharply. "There wasn't a shred of evidence of murder. The man went missing, that's all. Probably AWOL."

"Oh, yummy!" Bridget breathed avidly, her cheeks flushed with wine. "Tell us the gory details!"

Elaine posed herself becomingly, three-quarters turned toward the table, her elbow on the damask cloth and one finger by her ear holding up the flesh of her cheek to give herself a good jawline, and proceeded. "He disappeared, that you can't deny, Simon. Vanished without a clue. There was a terrible fuss about it. Sometime after the war. Military police over the house and grounds like ants over an anthill. The Sûreté. Gendarmes.

But just because they never found the body doesn't mean that it isn't still here someplace. Perhaps out in the woods." She smiled at Kei, whose lips had turned white around the edges. "You needn't worry, though. I've done a protective spell on the house, so you're not likely to bump into his ghost. Unless it's especially malevolent. That might be beyond even *my* powers."

"When are you going to leave off with that ridiculous witchcraft nonsense you've picked up, Elaine?" Tommy asked patronizingly. "You're making a bloody great fool of yourself, you know." He stuffed a large piece of avocado into his mouth.

Elaine bridled and her finger slipped out of position, letting a small double chin sag down. "You're a fine one to talk about making a fool of oneself, going around with women who could be your granddaughters! If you were smart, you'd ask me to whip up a rejuvenation potion for you so you wouldn't look like an antique beside those . . . those *popsies* of yours. Who do you think you are? Peter Pan?"

Tommy's Adam's apple went down as he swallowed the avocado quickly and popped up again. "The kettle's calling the pot black," he said and wiped his mouth on his napkin. "How many times do you think you can have your face lifted before your mouth stretches to your ears?"

"You son of a bitch!" Elaine half rose out of her chair and stabbed her fan toward him. "Why don't you get out of my life? Why don't you *die* and leave me alone?!"

Tommy stood up, his face dark red. Simon put a hand on his arm and pulled him back down into his chair. Raising his voice, he said, "There's not going to be any more of this kind of talk! I won't have it in the house."

Tommy and Elaine sat glaring at one another, breathing hard, while Rudy studied his plate and Kei put a hand over her face. Jeanne-Marie looked at the pair with interest, as if she were anticipating a further episode in a Punch and Judy show. Bridget continued to eat her salad, completely unruffled and empty-headedly unaware.

A metallic beeping broke the tension. Heads turned toward Jeanne-Marie, who reached inside the front of her dress to remove a pocket calculator-sized mechanism and shut off the sound.

"I must excuse myself. I have a call," she said and rose and went out into the foyer.

By the time Simon had seen Jeanne-Marie to her car and returned to the table, the conversation had veered back to the occult.

"If we had a seance," Bridget was saying, helping herself to another glass of wine, "maybe we could contact the spirit of the murdered man."

"No seances here." Simon put his napkin back in his lap. "I'm not sure how I stand on an afterlife, but if there *are* spirits, they might not be disposed to going back where they came from afterwards."

"Oh, Elaine could do a spell and send them away. If she really is a witch," Bridget said with

110

a challenging look down the table.

Elaine looked back at her waspishly and glanced down at her watch. "Very well," she said, "I'll let you decide for yourself. It's about time you knew who you're dealing with, and then we'll see if you're still laughing. I shall call up the powers of darkness, and that should squelch any doubts about my credentials as a witch."

Tommy pointedly smothered a laugh by coughing into his napkin, and Elaine sent him a venomous look. Then she closed her eyes and breathed in deeply, as if she were summoning up her powers. She had not been on the summer theater circuit on the Cape for nothing, Simon thought. Bridget lifted the cloud of hair from her shoulders nervously and resettled it. Rudy stubbed out his cigarette and sat back in his chair with a sigh and clasped his hands in his lap.

Abruptly, Elaine rose and strode rapidly into the foyer, her caftan rippling like flames about her legs. Bridget got up and hurried after her, followed by Rudy and Tommy, who paused to pour a Drambuie from the sideboard before taking his glass to join them on the bridge.

"Oh, God," Simon said wearily, watching them go.

"She's not really a witch, is she?" asked Kei with a wobble in her voice.

"She pretends to be. But all she knows how to do is mumble a few spells she got out of some book and make herbal teas. She's perfectly harmless. But I suppose we have to indulge her." He put a hand under Kei's elbow and helped her

111

up out of her chair. A wave of fragrant hair swung back against his cheek and he reached up to touch it but stopped himself before she noticed.

Out on the bridge, Elaine was standing silhouetted against the dark sky at the edge of the steps while the others clustered around the door. A sweet smell of jasmine and greenness came from the meadow.

"I shall raise the wind and bring the rain," said Elaine in a low, chilling voice, sneaking a surreptitious look at her watch. She raised both arms above her head and spread her fingers wide. The loose sleeves of her caftan fell back from her arms like wings. Bridget looked ready to faint from excitement and leaned back against Tommy, who patted her fanny reassuringly. Rudy looked at Simon and shook his head, smiling at Elaine's outrageousness.

Elaine began to chant in an unknown tongue. Unknown to everyone but Simon, who recognized it as a hymn they'd learned as children from a missionary friend of the family.

"Yesu alingee m'toto," Elaine intoned, drawing out the vowels hollowly. "M'toto namo keelee."

Simon's eyes watered with the effort not to laugh. She was reciting "Jesus Loves the Little Children" in an African dialect.

When she finished the ceremony, Elaine lowered her arms slowly, bowed her head, and allowed a long dramatic pause before she turned to the guests and said, "In less than half an hour, the powers of darkness will answer my call with wind and rain, and you . . . " She whirled to

112

point at Bridget, whose eyes rolled up briefly to show their whites. "You will leave, to return nevermore!"

As Bridget's knees sagged, Tommy grabbed her. He dragged her back into the dining room and thumped her back in her chair like a sack of potatoes. The guests returned to their places, and Simon called for the dessert and coffee. Bridget and Kei were as pallid as ivory chess figures. Tommy looked abominably cross and even Rudy looked out of patience, but Elaine resumed fanning herself with a smug smile of self-congratulation.

In silence Simon served the soufflé au Grand Marnier and poured demitasses of coffee. Everyone was listening. The only sound in the dining room was the tick of spoons against glass or the click of cups being set back in saucers until a whisper started across the meadow. Heads went up and necks stretched. Elaine looked triumphantly across at Tommy. The sounds of dining resumed, but no one spoke. The branches of the oak trees creaked.

Suddenly, the window blew open with a slam and the candles went out. Bridget screamed. Rain came down like a truckload of pebbles being dumped out of the sky.

They could hear Marthe racing around overhead, banging windows shut. Simon got up and switched on the chandelier. As the lights came on, Bridget was pawing the air with her eyes closed, trying to locate Tommy, who caught her hands and said sarcastically, "Good show, Elaine!

113

A little early, but well within the half-hour limit."
He hauled Bridget up out of her chair and said,
"I'd better be pushing off. It'll take all night
to calm Bridget down." As he passed Elaine's
chair, he said, "Thanks ever so, Elaine, for the
entertainment."

They heard the car door slam out in front, and
a few seconds later Tommy dashed back in, his
jacket freckled with rain, to hiss in Elaine's ear,
"I heard the weather report on the radio, too,
coming over. But you've got a great sense of
timing, I'll give you that."

Elaine's smile vanished and she bared her teeth
at him. He chuckled and was gone.

Rudy looked amusedly at Elaine, cupping
his fingers around his cigarette, but Kei looked
ashen.

"I don't suppose you'd like to explain that
little act, would you?" Simon said, trying to get
a match flame and the end of Kei's cigarette together as her hand bounced nervously.

"Oh, the son of a bitch is right. I heard on
the car radio that a storm was due about now."
Elaine drained the dregs of her coffee and set
the cup carefully on its saucer. "I couldn't resist.
He flaunts those adolescents of his at me with
so much glee. He loves making me feel like a
hag."

"Nonsense!" said Rudy, "you're a lovely woman. Those young men swarm around you like
flies around a honey pot."

"Pretty soon I'll have to start paying them,"
Elaine said, her large brown eyes melancholy.

Rudy reached across and patted her hand consolingly. Then he put his cigarette out in a silver ashtray and said, "I must also make my goodbyes. I'm doing a chamber piece on commission from the Belgian government. They pay by the length and the density of the musical score, so I have to get up early and put in a lot of little black notes." He made circles with his thumb and forefinger as if he were writing on the air. "If Elaine would be so kind as to take me home, it would save me from a drenching."

Simon packed Rudy and Elaine off in her little Renault and ran back indoors, shaking the wet off the umbrella onto the marble floor. Kei came into the foyer, her cigarette in her hand.

"What you wrote about Elaine's trying to kill you seems a good deal more believable now," she said. "This evening was like a page out of Tennessee Williams."

Simon opened the umbrella and set it to dry on the floor by the door. "So sorry. Tommy sets her off, though at the best of times she's not Rebecca of Sunnybrook Farm. I'm used to her, of course, but she's damned hard to take."

Kei opened the front door, letting in the sound of the storm, and flicked her cigarette out into the rain, where it made a bright arc in the darkness. She looked tired.

Marthe came out from the kitchen to say that she'd lock up the house before leaving. Kei and Simon climbed the stairs together. At her door, he said goodnight and went back to his room by the kitchen stairs, where he stripped

115

quickly and got under the covers.

The rain had slowed to a steady drumming, and the thunder was moving on toward the southeast. The hot spell was over.

What was that? Had he heard something or not? He'd wakened suddenly from a dream about the mountain lion, and a loud sound still seemed to be vibrating in the air, or was that part of the dream? He couldn't remember. His pulse was racing. He sat up groggily and rubbed his eyes with the heels of his palms.

No, something strange was going on. He could hear noises coming from the direction of Kei's room. He got up and threw on his robe, tying the sash as he ran down the hallway.

He put an ear to Kei's door. Nothing. Then a mewing sound. He knocked lightly on the door and called her name. No answer.

Pushing the door open, he whispered "Kei?" into the darkness. Over by the window, where the outside night light cast a very faint illumination, he could make out Kei's figure, her body pressed against the corner as if she were trying to crawl into the plaster.

Bent over at the waist, with her hands buried in her hair, she groaned and ground her teeth. Simon was hesitant to touch her, she seemed so beastlike and inhuman—far removed from the cool, composed woman he knew. He went in and, taking her by the elbows, turned her toward him.

116

Her face was slimy with tears. Someone said that sleepwalkers should not be wakened, but waking her couldn't make her feel worse than she did now, to judge from the animal sounds coming from her throat. Her eyes were open but unseeing.

He shook her gently and called her name. It took some time for the intelligence to come back into her blind eyes. She stared at him and then took his face in her hands and turned it toward the light, looking at him searchingly.

"Simon?" she said.

"It's all right, Kei."

She put her head on his shoulder and rocked back and forth as if she were comforting some-one—him or herself, he couldn't tell. The fabric of her nightgown was satiny under his hands, and he could feel the softness of her breasts against his bare skin, where his robe had come open in front. Gratefully, he felt warmth spreading through his groin. He pulled her hips to him, and she responded, moving rhythmically against him.

It could not be called lovemaking. Rather, they seemed to be trying to tear one another apart, their teeth grating together savagely, their hipbones bruising each other. She raked her fingernails down his back, carrying him back onto the bed on top of her. He pulled up her nightgown and drove himself into her. When she bit him on the chest, he pressed into the pain, welcoming it, and groaned deep in his throat, feeling as if a malignancy had torn loose

117

inside him and was washing away in a joyous flood.

She fell asleep with her head on his shoulder, and he lay awake, looking up into the darkness and feeling surprised. Then he laughed out loud and fell asleep.

CHAPTER EIGHT

Floating in the womb in the amniotic fluid, all needs taken care of, must have felt like this, Simon thought—the golden light behind closed eyelids, the warmth, the lassitude. For a moment longer he savored the deep comfort, treasuring the smarting of the scratches on his back and buttocks, and then slid his hand over beneath the covers to her side of the bed. The hollow was cold.

Disappointed, he opened his eyes and sat up on the edge of the bed. The floor was warm to his feet where the sun streamed across the wood. Maeve would be impatient in her stall.

His lower lip hurt. He felt it delicately and found a smooth raised spot that tasted salty. Kei must have bitten him there, as well as on the chest below his shoulder, where blood had come to the surface in a myriad of tiny red dots. The bruise on his shin had turned to subtle gradations of beige and lavender. Her brand was all over him.

Putting his hands to his face, he inhaled the

female-male odors that had dried on them and felt very fine. He was tempted not to take a shower, to carry the evidence with him through the day, but other people might not enjoy his gaminess as he did. They didn't know the triumph it signified.

He sang in the shower. He pulled on his clothes and then his boots, marveling at the smooth close-grained surface of the leather as if he had never felt it before. This morning, the light seemed brighter, the outlines of objects more distinct, odors more intense. He jounced down the stairs to the hall, reveling in the way the muscles and joints of his body worked together, and went into the dining room.

And there she was.

She was reading a book and eating a madeleine, looking just as she had the morning before, as if nothing earth-shaking, nothing of monumental importance, had changed everything. Somehow, he'd thought it would show in her face.

But she would look up from her book, and then he would see it, and the whole landscape of her world would open out before him, offering itself to him to be traversed. She would take him in and teach him how she thought and what she was and they would lie in each other's arms and make love over and over until she became an extension of his own body, warm and quiet, with nothing left to know.

She was wearing a blouse the color of an autumn leaf and had knotted a bright yellow scarf about her throat. Why had he never realized what a splendid color yellow was? He could almost *hear* it — a bright, singing note of D. The universe could not function without that magnificent color! Everything would collapse without it. Absolutely fucking marvelous, the way everything fit together and everything had its place, including and especially yellow! There had never been such a ravishing color! There had never been such a scarf!

"Good morning," she said, looking at him with the eyes of a stranger. Suddenly he felt as cold and brittle and hollow as an abandoned chrysalis.

"I finished the manuscript last night," she said, businesslike. "I can start on the material you've dictated into the cassette."

Simon stared at the platter of broiled tomatoes and scrambled eggs on the table and felt that he was drowning in a flood of searing rage.

"Fuck the manuscript!" he said. Then he picked up the platter of food and hurled it with all his strength at the kitchen door. The china shattered, sending shards all over the room, and a large clump of eggs clung to the door and slid slowly down to the floor.

Simon turned on his heel and left.

He fled. Rather than face her again, he threw his dinner jacket and the things he usually took to London into his case, called through the outside kitchen door to Marthe that he could be reached at his hotel, and escaped.

Hilaire would have to remove the tarp and the tabby from the Rolls in the garage if the household needed supplies in his absence. Hilaire frequently got carried away with lordly delusions when he drove the Rolls and banged up the fenders, but Simon was in a gloom where such matters seemed trivial. He parked the Mercedes in the lot at the airport and the hell with everything.

On the plane, he ached all over from clenching his jaws and tensing his muscles until he systematically relaxed his rigidity, one joint at a time. Women simply did not reject him once he had screwed them. Not, he allowed, that last night's performance had been stellar. Too fast, too selfish, too brutal. But she'd been as avid as he had. And here he was, having been able to make it with a woman for the first time in a year and a half, and her very look this morning had probably undone him again. He'd felt reborn, miraculous, and then she'd kicked him off the mountain top. He could strangle her! If he was lucky, a day or two in London with some highly-sexed, eager woman might undo the damage Kei had done. He didn't want to lay eyes on her again. By the time he got back to the château, the incidents with the chickens and with the dogs, last night's nightmarish dinner party, and the semi-rape would probably have sent her running off. Jesus, he wanted to wring her neck! He fantasized, looking out on the clouds over the Channel, imagining her clinging to his legs, begging him to make love to her, while he ignored her pleas and turned his attention to a swarm of beckoning women in various states of undress and used them, one after another, while Kei wept and tore her hair. It was a soul-satisfying scenario and did him a world of good.

She meant nothing to him. He was not hurt. She had not dented his ego in the slightest. He did not, did not give a damn about Kei Ronald. He felt sick. What was the matter with him?

Summer had already departed London. The air was crisp and had an edge of dampness that seeped into the bones.

As Simon sat in the cab, watching the familiar streets pass by, he congratulated himself on his timing. He'd been intending anyway to come over in a day or two for Moody's vernissage at the gallery. Although Bony Foxworth had set up arrangements to buy him out in a couple years, he still liked Simon to come around for the shows, to give him reassurance. In any case, Moody was displaying some works he hadn't shown yet to Simon, and he wanted to call Jeremy as well to find out what Kei's story was.

At the suite the hotel kept for him, he had a bath and lay down on the bed to pick up the phone. No use calling Landsend House, it was after business hours. Jeremy's home phone didn't answer. Bloody hell! He rang Bony at the gallery, knowing he'd be spending late hours getting the show ready.

"That idiot new assistant hung two of the big Moodys upside down while I was out for a bite," Bony's voice sputtered. "I can't turn my back on that cretin for a minute!"

"Go home and get some rest. I'll come over to give you a hand in the morning."

"My dear, the hell I go through, you have

123

no idea!" said Bony, and rang off. No wonder male American artists, misled by Bony's shining blond looks and limp-wrist voice, worked themselves into a lather trying to seduce him. His manner was not an unusual one in England and had no relevance to his sexual orientation, which was strictly hetero. He was blindly devoted to his frighteningly ugly wife Margaret and to their two adorable children, Malcolm and Michelle, who were Simon's godchildren. Bony would probably bring the children to the gallery tomorrow to see Uncle Simon, who had better bring gifts. It was getting late, but the owner of the toyshop around the corner could be persuaded to open up in case of emergencies.

He phoned the owner and made the arrangements, then called Mark Bowen, who—with his wife Hilary—could be counted on to make one feel welcomed and cherished. Simon felt he could use a bit of that tonight. Later, he'd call one of the numbers in his book and find just the right woman to repair Kei's depredations.

"Simon!" said Mark's high, light English voice. "So good to hear from you! Sarah's panting to see you. And we've got an extra ticket for the theater tonight, happy day! Misha Damien's into racing cars now and got a bit scorched on the track today. No, nothing serious, but he's somewhat unsightly, with half his hair frizzled off, and doesn't want to go public with a naked scalp. I'm used to nothing on top, of course, but with me it came gradually, one hair at a time. Oh, I think you know the lady he was going to bring along, Missy Hilliard?"

He certainly did. Every time Simon saw Missy, she tried to climb on him, which totally quashed the thrill of the chase, but tonight he was eager to be climbed. It was imperative that he find out whether it was the abnormal circumstances last night that restored his functioning or whether he was really back to normal. It would be one hell of a fix if Kei was the only woman who could get him started! Missy's enthusiasm for him would be a boon, and her magnificent superstructure was celebrated internationally, which didn't hurt.

"Yes, we're old friends, Missy and I," Simon said.

"Splendid! We'll be two happy couples, then. Here's Hilary for you."

"Doesn't it sound fun, Simon love?" said the familiar fluty voice. "I'll call and tell Missy. She'll be so happy. You know how she feels about you. Now, you didn't want me to give out your number, did you? Missy's been wheedling for weeks, and she's not the only one."

"It doesn't matter much. Everyone knows where I am, and I do get overrun sometimes, being on the way to Cannes or Paris, depending. But you and Mark are family, and I've missed you. You haven't been over all year," he said reproachfully.

"We'll get over one of these days, but Mark's got responsibilities to his constituency that just go on endlessly. Darling, I must do things, so I'm going to stop, but we'll be around for you at the appropriate time. And how good it will be to see you, dear heart!"

Now, that was the kind of woman Simon appreciated. Outgoing. Warm-hearted. Hilary did not create hullabaloos in the middle of the night, she did not look at him as if he were unsexed, and he didn't suppose that she pretended she hadn't been fucked when she had been. She was cuddly, buttermilk complexioned, and kissed everybody, having a surplus of affection. After three drinks, she had been known to kiss busboys and doormen.

Mark, on the other hand, pretended to have no emotions at all other than ennui. He could make you laugh your head off with wicked stories about other people, but he was the soul of kindness—as long as you didn't leave the room. Simon was looking forward to the evening. In the meantime, the toyshop.

Buying toys for godchildren was one of Simon's favorite preoccupations. He usually came back from the store with things he really hated to give away. This time he'd bought an entire circus of jointed wooden figures and animals for Michelle, with a gorgeous striped tent to put them in, and for Malcolm he'd gotten a blue and white remote-control airplane that was going to be hard to leave behind without helping give it the maiden run.

Looking in the full-length mirror to check the set of his dinner jacket collar around the neck, Simon pulled his cuffs out to the right length. The jacket, which had been made in London to his recorded measurements by his tailor and shipped to the château, fit superbly. His measurements hadn't changed in years. Never heavy, he'd simply thinned out a little with age. Not being the muscular type was an advantage when it came to wearing clothes well. God knows, it wasn't an advantage in regard to anything else! Because his father punched him hard in the small of the back if he didn't stand up straight, Simon learned early on to carry himself militarily erect. From a distance, he looked much the same as he had thirty years ago. Better tailored now, though, since he could afford the very best. He loved good materials that were well cut and gloried in a whole closet full of boots and shoes, his weakness. One of these days, he really ought to weed some of them out.

Ready too early, he went on down to the bar and asked for an armagnac. The people at the tables in the bar looked exactly like the soft-spoken, well-bred ones who had been here the last time, talking in monotones, listening raptly to each other, laughing softly, nodding, and wreathing themselves in cigar and cigarette smoke. Perhaps, Simon fancied, they were permanent mechanical fixtures that ran down about three in the morning and sat in the bar all night, halted in mid-gesture, until the barkeep came in and wound them up for the next evening.

He took a sip of his drink and looked at himself in the mirror over the bar. So that was what Kei saw across from her at the breakfast table in the mornings. Was it really that bad? He rather liked his good eyes and clearly defined dark brows, but he'd never been fond of his nose. It was straight enough, but there was just something about it . . . He supposed most people didn't like their noses. Could be worse. A trim head on a longish neck. Nothing wrong there. But his hair was pure white now and he was getting crumply around the eyes, where the skin looked pale and delicate. And the lines on his forehead were becoming a complex network, with inverted chevrons running up the center. Could be better. Still. He put on his smartass look to see if it still looked sexy to him. Surprisingly, it did.

"You know, darling," said a heavily made-up woman who had been sitting unnoticed down the bar, "there's a place down the street where you might feel more at home. They have a lot of pretty boys there."

Simon stiffened as if he'd been goosed. Then, drawing his dignity about him as best he could, he tossed a bill on the bar and walked briskly out to the street to hang around until the Bowens showed up with Missy. Not until he was outside did it occur to him that the woman probably thought he was following her suggestion immediately. He had half a mind to go back in and tell her a thing or two, but he overcame the urge.

Not many minutes passed before a long, black limousine slid silkily up to the curb and debouched Mark, whose pink pate was peeling badly and looked sprinkled with soap shavings. The two men seized one another, pummeled each other lightly on the back, and exchanged laughs of greeting. Simon climbed in on one of the jump

128

seats, closed the door on his side, and leaned over to kiss Hilary, who smelled of musk, and Missy, whose perfume smelled urgent. Hilary wore something glittery like shiny chain mail around her forehead and something similarly glittery as a dress. Missy, he noted with a glow of anticipation, appeared to be housing a couple of lively puppies in her bright yellow blouse.

"Simon, you look super," breathed Hilary. "You must have been born in a lounge suit. And you're an American, too. You're not supposed to look impeccable. I can't understand it at all."

"He was English in a former life," said Mark. "No other possible explanation."

"Actually, my tie lights up in the dark and spells out 'Kiss me quick, I'm full of fun'," said Simon. "Lord, what snobs you are!"

"Yes, aren't we?" Hilary said comfortably, fitting a cigarette into a long gold holder. "It's one of the few national virtues we've been able to hold onto, despite the Labor Party and the Communists."

"No politics tonight," cautioned Mark.

"Why don't you ever call me?" asked Missy, taking Simon's hand.

He did not withdraw it, though it made him feel awkward, since that might queer his strategy for the evening. "When I have, you've been rehearsing, taping, or on the road," Simon said, feeling that this was a foolproof evasion. It seemed to placate Missy, who squeezed his hand and raised it to her lips, looking at him hungrily.

"I'm going to kill my maid. She never gives

129

me your messages," she said.

Simon felt a nip of guilt.

"I can make my own way home," said Simon, getting out of the limousine at Missy's mews house.

"Don't be a stranger," said Hilary. Mark, who had sunk down into his collar, muttered something amiable that was half a snore, and the car pulled off along the jewel-lit street.

The show had been untaxing and amusing, but they'd stayed too long at the café, drinking and table-hopping, and Simon was tired. He was, after all, pushing sixty. She unlocked the door, chattering on in a monologue about the theater set, but Simon didn't hear a word, he was so worried about whether or not he was still operative. His temples and upper lip grew moist as he held an interior debate over the advantages and disadvantages of testing himself with Missy. If he failed again, what was he going to *do*? Was Kei the only woman who could arouse him? He tarried so long over his drink as he stood by the side of the bed that Missy lost her temper and tore off his dinner jacket, popping off a button that rolled somewhere and disappeared.

To his vast relief, they had a good time together in bed, although Missy got petulant about the bite bruise on his chest and had to be told flatly to shut up about it. She gushed with compliments about his performance and was comfortingly affectionate and generous with strokings of his ego and other areas. The only thing missing was having Kei sitting in a chair by the bed, writhing with jealousy.

As he dressed, he discovered that Missy had stolen the gold medallion he wore around his neck on a chain. He held out a hand for it, and she retrieved it from under her pillow and gave it to him sulkily, but he was far too sleepy to bother looking for the button from his jacket.

In front of his hotel, he gave the cabbie a kingly tip and whistled all the way to his suite, heedless of the late hour and the sleeping hotel guests. Before he fell asleep, he began a replay of the fantasy scenario, this time with a cast of thousands, while Kei nearly went off her nut with despair at having turned down the chance of her lifetime.

CHAPTER NINE

Dear Chris:

Maybe you were right about its being a lousy idea for me to come here. This place is beginning to spook me, although Marthe's sleeping next door on Eagleton's orders while he's in London. I'll feel safer when he gets back. On the other hand, maybe it's a good thing that he's not here so I can think over— oh, I don't know what I think any more! I'm all mixed up inside.

In the first place, it seems that the château used to belong to a female monster who was the head of a cult of devil-worshipers. Hideous things—killing babies and burning people alive—went on out in the woods, which may explain why I've always felt so queer and sickish out there by the mound. Knowing this hasn't added to my sunny good nature at all, and I'm afraid it's overheating my imagination.

Take what happened this afternoon, for instance. An accident, but my first reaction was that someone was trying to do me in, which is absolute nonsense. Anybody can leave a brake off.

I'd been typing all morning and decided to take a break by going for a walk with the dogs (mastiffs, big as Shetland ponies but gentle as mice). This is a wonderful spot for just mooching around and communing with nature — as long as you avoid that spot in the woods where the grotto was. I lay down in one of the fields to watch the clouds go by, and the sun was hot and the dogs went to sleep by my side, all warm and cozy. Before I knew it, I was dead to the world.

Thank God, one of the dogs woke me with his barking just as a huge farm machine was bearing down on me with horrible sharp discs rotating and flashing in the sun! I barely had time to roll out of its way, about an inch away from the blades. It trundled on by, churning up the ground as it went, and ran up against a tree, where it kept on grinding away. I hadn't had time to get scared, so I ran over and turned off the ignition before the machine dug its way to China.

Then I got scared and had that crazy notion about someone trying to finish me off. As it is, I'm stuck with half a sweater. I was lying on it, and the other part was shredded like confetti. Gives me the shakes to look at it! I'd be mincemeat now if it weren't for the dog. Aside from the sweater, no harm done, and there's no need to say anything to Eagleton. He's got a murderous temper and throws things, and I hate to think what he'd do to the farmer if he knew.

Naturally, after that my legs were like Jello, but I got back to the château and found Rudy van der Zee there, who didn't know E. was gone. His departure was rather sudden. Rudy and I had a much-needed drink together and talked about everything under the sun. He's by far the most brilliant man I've ever met. Makes me feel hideously ignorant and unlettered. When he found out I majored in Japanese, he asked me to look over some poems he's been translating and to play a game of go. I think I will take a peek at the poems for fun, but he'd beat the pants off me at any game. He's got this theory that all of life is a game, which is an intriguing way of looking at things. "You must never neglect a chance to take part in any intellectual exercise," he said, making me feel like I've spent my life using only the south quarter of my brain.

In spite of being so scholarly, he's got the most powerful aura of sexuality you can imagine. (Don't worry, I have no intention of getting involved with him.) Still, you sort of wonder what it would be like to go to bed with a man like that. Presumably, there would be some artistry involved. None of this slam-bang stuff some men engage in. But don't worry, that's one intellectual exercise I'm not going to take on.

Whoa there! I forgot to tell you how I

met him. Chris darling, you wouldn't believe *the dinner party where I met Rudy! Of all people, Tommy McKenzie was there (looks better offscreen than on) with his dopey girlfriend. And there was a lady doctor and E.'s sister Elaine, who could play the former owner of the château—the head of the devil-worship cult—without a change of makeup. She's really beautiful, but she must have seen too many old Charlie Chan movies and thinks she's the Spider Woman. Hated me on sight. I'm not going to let her get under my skin, though.*

Anyway, I've never heard people be so nasty to each other over a dinner table before.

Altogether, this has not been idea of a picnic lately. I should have listened to you, but it's too late now. I'll just have to muddle through somehow. Keep your fingers crossed for me!

Always,

Kei

CHAPTER TEN

Simon started off his next day in London in high spirits, happy to consign Kei to the devil and rejoicing at being normal again. He was so thankful to be back in form that for almost fifteen minutes he considered stopping at a church and lighting a candle of gratitude, but he wasn't Catholic—he didn't know *what* he was—and felt awkward in cathedrals, afraid that a priest might buttonhole him and try to convert him. Simon knew that any religious person with a reasonable philosophical structure to offer could out-argue him on cosmic issues, and then he might be embarrassed into signing up for something like catering the church bazaar. Even Moody's religious fanaticism made Simon feel like a small boy skipping Sunday School, although Moody seemed to be boosting all sects simultaneously and handed out copies of *The Watchtower* and the Baghavad Gita with equal conviction.

Just having thought about lighting a candle was next best to doing it, and Simon felt surrounded by an aura of sanctification until breakfast, when he indulged in unworthy thoughts about British bacon and its conveyors.

Malcolm was at summer camp in Switzerland, but Michelle gave a crow of delight when she saw Uncle Simon and attached herself to his leg and rode along on his foot, according to custom. She was getting too big now for him to carry her around that way without feeling a real strain in his stomach muscles. When she saw that he wasn't as rapid a form of transportation as he used to be, Michelle let go of his leg and stood up, pulled up her pink T-shirt, and showed him that her stomach was still absolutely flawless — a smooth balloon of ivory skin with a round navel, rosy pink, like a delicate coral cameo pushed into her center. She demanded that he kiss her tummy and then settled down on the wheat-colored carpeting with her gift, refusing thenceforth to be distracted from the elephants and tightrope walkers.

Bony leaned Malcolm's present up against an Arp sculpture in the form of a giant egg and said, "Simon love, would you fire my assistant for me? He's a bloody ass, but I hate to dampen his feelings."

"Oh, I'm afraid you're in charge of personnel now, Bony." Simon hung his suit coat on the Arp egg and rolled up his shirtsleeves. "I'm out of that end of it. You'll be putting me to pasture soon. Can't lean on me any more. Your own good."

Bony sighed mournfully. Simon made a tour of the gallery with Bony in his wake and was pleased to see how well things were being handled without him. There were minor errors, but nothing that couldn't be put right. The Persian ivory miniatures were out of chronological order, and the Simmons "Et in Arcadia Ego" canvas was hung an inch too low. Simon adjusted a spotlight that was throwing heat too near an oil and stopped in front of an antique Japanese print in triptych form.

"Where did that come from?" he demanded.

"Lady Sheil asked me to flog it for her," Bony said nervously. A strand of flaxen hair fell over his forehead.

"Well, tell Lady Sheil to take it to Sotheby's and pay the twenty per cent, or I'll tell her if you can't face her. Look at the fogging on the fine strokes around the women's hairlines! You know that doesn't happen until the woodblock's been used too many times."

"But Lady Sheil . . . "

"See here, Bony," Simon said with asperity, "this gallery's reputation was built on my taste. Until you buy me out, nothing's coming in here that isn't first rate. I don't care that it's a genuine Kiyonaga. It's been pulled from an old block, and I don't want it in here!"

Bony looked crestfallen. Simon put an arm around his shoulders.

"Otherwise, everything's smashing, and I'm proud of you. You know what a bastard I am." He cocked his head in front of the black-on-black textured Moody and said, "I don't know, I rather like it this side up."

"Oh, my dear, we can't leave it that way!" said Bony. "Don't you remember that show we had when you were buying aboriginal art in the Outback and Moody thought we'd put too slack a wire on one of his pieces? It only projected just the odd millimeter beyond what he thought it should, but he locked himself in my office for two days and went on a hunger strike! I thought I would *perish*!"

"Why didn't you lock the toilet so he couldn't use it at night? That would have gotten him out instanter. And you're just lucky he didn't nail himself to a cross in front of the gallery. The sales were uncommonly good that month, with cameramen all over the place and the TV picking it up on the news. He couldn't have got us better publicity."

"Oh, but my ulcer!" Bony put his fist to his diaphragm and burped.

They climbed the ladders and turned the canvases around to fit Moody's directions, getting chalky in the process from sizing in the fabric. When they were done, Simon lay down on the floor beside Michelle, who promptly sat on his stomach, and Bony went into his office to bring out glasses and a bottle of wine.

"My lord, Michelle, quit bouncing!" said Simon. "You've gotten so big, you're squashing the stuffings out of me!" Michelle gave two or three bigger, triumphant bounces and then went back to her circus. "What's this?" asked Simon, rolling onto his side and holding out a glass for the wine.

"Well, I think it's called 'pink wine,' " said Bony,

139

squatting beside him and pouring. He looked up at the display and said, "Looks nice, doesn't it? Hate to sell a thing. Pay the tailor, though."

"Life."

"Quite."

"I don't suppose you'd rent that out by the week, would you?" Simon said, motioning with his glass at the small girl on the carpet.

Bony smiled fondly. "Her mother's against it. Oh, we've had offers. Hundreds. Fabulous prices."

Missy burst in through the glass doors, trailing a long, gauzy scarf the color of a stoplight. She had a straw fedora on her head and enormous round sunglasses with yellow lenses that turned her blue pansy eyes a bright green. "Oh, lawsy!" she said, staggering in mock shock. "Simon's got his sleeves rolled up! Has any living Londoner ever seen him in shirtsleeves before?" She came and stood over him. "You know, that way you almost look like you have biceps. Are you trying to fool people into thinking you have muscles?"

"I manage to get along pretty briskly without any," said Simon, refusing to let her get a rise out of him.

"Oh, don't you just!" breathed Missy, rolling her eyes suggestively. She put her hands on her hips. "Listen, you promised to take me to the auction houses today."

"They've just got into gear nearly, and I haven't seen anything exciting scheduled," said Simon, who would rather have taken Michelle to the botanical gardens.

"You promised!"

Reluctantly, he got up, rolled down his shirtsleeves, and put on his suitcoat. He kissed Michelle goodbye and asked Bony to give Malcolm his love along with the airplane. It would have been a perfect cool, windswept day to give it a flight.

Missy clung to his arm like a handcuff, trying to keep up with his stride on her little trotters. As the day wore on and they sat with other bidders, watching ugly china dogs and murky paintings go under the hammer, Simon's morning elation seeped away as if he had sprung a slow leak. All day long, Missy kept catching his eye and giving him just-you-and-me looks meaningfully that made him uneasy.

He didn't want to get involved in her frenetic public life or her elephantine insecurities. She seemed about to bring their relationship to a head, no longer content with his sweet friend role, so successful in keeping his life unencumbered, allowing him to stay just beyond reach, still his own man. He doubted that anyone alive could give Missy the total attention and unconditional love that she thirsted for. Even if he'd been in love with her, which he emphatically was not, the burden of her dependence would have scared the daylights out of him.

She insisted they go back to her place so she could give him a surprise.

"Not on your life!" said Simon. Frankly, he didn't want to test himself so soon again with Missy. Three nights of sex in a row was a bit too ambitious, and he didn't feel athletic enough to

141

frolic with her. Her appetite for varying positions required gymnastics that made him aware of his diminishing elasticity. For the first time, he understood what Bony — an impossible romantic, he'd always thought — meant when he'd said that, without the right chemistry between two people, sex was pretty much of a muchness.

"You *have* to," Missy said. "It's something Tommy and I arranged together."

Warily, Simon accompanied her to her apartment. Missy unlocked the door, pushed it open, flung her gloves down on a chair, and pointed to two fair-sized boxes standing by a wall plastered with enlarged photographs of herself.

Simon looked at the boxes for a moment, then went over and, taking the larger one by the heavy cord about it to pick it up, nearly fell over. "What the hell's *in* this?" It felt like a load of bricks.

"Your armor. It's all telescoped neatly together."

"My armor?"

"For the tournament, don't you remember? Tommy said you needed it. The helmet's in the other box."

"I'm not going to dress up in a suit of armor and charge around on a horse. I'll kill myself!"

"Tommy said you could get hurt without it. Now, don't get stubborn on me. Be a little gentleman and take it with you. Tommy practically had to blackmail the studio to get them to lend it to him, and he had to pay for the insurance. Anyway, you're not going to make me take it back again. You know how much the cab fare is out there?"

Simon shoved his hands in his pockets and glared at the boxes. He'd gotten himself into this fix, no point in taking it out on Missy, but he felt like kicking the furniture. Oh, the curse of John Barleycorn! Get him tight enough, and he'd walk nude down Piccadilly with a peacock feather up his ass!

"It's really marvelous," Missy said encouragingly. "Tommy wore it in that remake of *Alexander Nevsky*. It's Russian armor, and the helmet has wonderful horns, like an elk. You'll look terrific!"

"I'll look like a performing dog dressed up in tin cans," Simon said.

"Don't shout or I'll lose my lease."

"I'm *not shouting!* And Tommy's two inches taller than me. It won't fit."

"He had some links taken out. He and your tailor fixed it up together, and there's padding in the shoulders so you won't rattle around. You just *can't* not wear it after all the trouble Tommy's gone through!"

He had the devil of a time getting the boxes out to the cab and back to the hotel. The only plus was that Missy seemed glad to see him go and take his foul temper along with him. The cost of having the hotel get the armor off via air freight would have cleaned out the cash he had on him, so he charged it to his account and had dinner sent up to his room, where he could grump in peace.

As he closed his eyes that night in his suite,

clean and limp after a hot tub, he was looking forward to getting back to the château. He congratulated himself that he had spent all this time in London without thinking more than a few times about Kei, that he hadn't thought of her twice all evening and, indeed, was not thinking about her now.

CHAPTER ELEVEN

Dear Chris:

As usual, I spoke too soon. Cancel what I said about Elaine. This morning she came over to apologize for her behavior at the dinner party, said she'd been having her pre-menstrual bout of bitchiness, and turned out to be quite charming and fun, although a little too inquisitive. She asked all sorts of questions about my background that required fast thinking on my part (let's hope I can keep the answers that I gave her straight in my head so they don't trip me up later) and grilled me thoroughly on my attitude about remarriage. You know how I feel about that, but she seems to think I have designs on her brother, and nothing I could say would convince her otherwise.

While we were having coffee, Tommy McKenzie dropped by—without his girl-friend, whom Elaine must have scared into skedaddling back to Paris—to set up practice sessions with Simon for some martial arts tournament that's to be held in the village.

I don't know what it is between Tommy and Elaine, but they can't spend two minutes together without getting into a hassle. When they started baiting each other, I went to the kitchen to get fresh coffee so they could have it out alone. They were still at it when I got back, though, and it looked like Tommy was trying to rip Elaine's necklace off. Whatever that was about, she was screaming bloody murder. Thank heaven, they calmed down when they saw me and Tommy excused himself and took off. Separately, they seem like nice people, but together they're crazier than anything I'm up to handling.

I'd just got back to typing when Rudy van der Zee came over to see if I'd come over and work with him on the poems. Now Chris, you know I've never been much of a housekeeper and am not about to faint at the sight of dust, but Rudy's place is the most—well, the only reason I drank coffee over there was because the water had been boiled. Books piled everywhere, sheets of music he's been composing lying around the floor so you have to tippytoe very carefully, half-filled cups of coffee that have dried to brown goo in the bottom, and I don't know what all. To give you some idea, I tried his piano and he warned me that the middle G was off. For a very good reason. I opened up the top and found a chicken drumstick—all green and slimy—stuck to the piano wire. When he went out to the kitchen to make coffee, he said we ought to try something typically Dutch, sugar cubes flavored with anise, and would I please bring him the box with them in it. So I rummaged around a found a box—a big brassbound one filled with red silk cords—and he nearly threw a fit. "Not that box!" he said. "Those went with the curtains I took down." He really was cross. Well, Chris dear, I don't know how he expected me to know that the box he was talking about was under a cushion of the sofa. Honestly!

I hope I'm not slipping back and getting funny in the head, but I could swear that somebody had gone through my things while I was gone. Everything seemed just a little different—something perhaps an inch out of place, my slips and bras in reverse order. But what with all the weirdness of the past few days, I could have done that myself and forgotten about it. Nothing was missing, except that old pomander ball that I found on the château grounds so long ago. It'll probably turn up around the house somewhere. I never did trust the clasp on that chain.

Back up! There was, too, something missing! The Renoir over my desk is gone, but it's probably been taken out to be cleaned or to be used in a show, something mundane like that. I've got to be careful or my imagination will start running away with me!

I'll be all right when Simon gets back and things return to normal—or as normal as they get around here. I feel sort of edgy with him gone. The time seems to be passing awfully slowly. I don't know what's the matter with me. Maybe it's the barometric pressure. The weather should change soon.

As always,

Kei

CHAPTER TWELVE

She was not at the château when Simon returned.

Neither was the Renoir. A faded square on the pale green wallpaper showed where it had been removed from its place over Kei's desk. Simon sat in the leather-backed chair by the desk, and felt abysmally sad and exhausted.

Barely moving his head, he looked about the room. She was gone from the château, but she was still in residence. A shiny brown brassbound locker trunk was at the foot of her bed, and a small lace-trimmed pillow was propped up against the bolster. A bottle of Givenchy III perfume sat on the dressing table in the bay window, where the curtain of crystal prisms caught the sunlight and made it dance in rainbow fragments over the walls and onto the sheepskin throw rugs.

Sighing, he got up and opened the door of the armoire that held her clothing, a spectrum of tawny colors, to see if she'd hidden the painting inside. On the hook on the back of the door was a coffee-colored chiffon nightgown. Not the one she'd worn the other night, which had felt satiny. He picked up a carefully folded square of cream-colored silk that was on the bottom of the armoire to look under it, and it slithered into a long streamer of material that was recognizable as a nightgown. The one she'd worn that night. It looked creased. He held it to his face. It still smelled of him and her. Funny, he would have thought that she couldn't wait to wash it out and get rid of the memory. He folded it again carefully and put it back. He didn't understand *anything* about her.

It had been weeks since he'd been in this room. It was done in tones of light green and cream, with yellow accents, and had been intended for women guests. It looked very feminine, except for the electric typewriter on the satinwood desk. Now, what had happened to the Renoir? He didn't know why the hell it was gone, but he was sure Kei had nothing to do with it. He *thought* he was sure.

The bright blue cornflowers and white carnations that he'd arranged in a white pitcher before she arrived were beginning to look melancholy and needed to be replaced. Only a few days ago, Hilaire had brought them in from his garden. Only a few days. How could a woman get so entrenched in one's thoughts in such a short time? Not that she really meant anything to him. It was only the sensuousness hidden behind her cool exterior that tugged at him, intrigued him, and made him want to explore her further. He wished he'd seen the expression in her eyes when they'd been in bed.

Now that hurt pride wasn't overwhelming his reason and he was certain that his sexual future wasn't dependent on her alone, he could look at her more objectively, and he could see a constellation of reasons for her reserve the morning after her nightmare.

To begin with, he'd taken advantage of her emotional upset, which was dirty pool. His eagerness had permitted no subtlety and, although she'd been just as abandoned, he hadn't been gentle with her. Then, too, middleclass women of her generation still had reservations about sleeping with men they'd just met. In addition, it would be particularly shaming for a woman of Kei's upbringing to let herself be used by her employer. A blank face the next morning and a businesslike impersonality would be her only protection against further abuse. He couldn't expect her to think of him as anything but her boss, and America was a long way away.

His own relief at breaking the eighteen-month dry spell was so great that he'd invested the episode with unwarranted romantic overtones. The best course was to pretend that nothing had happened and to keep his distance. It was not important. It could have meant nothing to her but unpleasantness and was best forgotten.

Attracted by noise from the driveway, he closed the door of Kei's room behind him and went across the hallway to lean out the window. A shiny, low-slung yellow sportscar was newly

151

parked on the gravel below, in front of the giant marshmallow. The entire back seat was crammed with packages.

The front door banged open downstairs, and Elaine, wearing a large pink straw hat and a loose violet shift over orange pants, came out and took a load of the packages into the house. Then a young man dressed in white cotton shirt and pants and with long dark hair emerged from under the glass canopy, was joined by Kei, and together they emptied the back seat of the car.

Simon went halfway down the staircase and leaned on the bannister railing, watching the bustle in the foyer as the three laughing people sorted bags and packages, taking out purchases, stripping wrappings away, and arranging them in piles on the marble floor.

"Is it Christmas?" Simon asked from his perch on the stairs. All three looked up at him and froze. Kei smiled hesitantly, but Elaine looked patently guilt-ridden. Her recovery was swift, and she said gaily, "We've been to Paris to shop! It was all Kei's fault. She had this terrific idea about all of us getting dressed up like Monet in smocks and straw hats and having a painting party." She fanned herself with her pink straw hat. "So I got half a dozen of each and some stools and oil sets and a picnic basket, and while I was at it, I bought a few clothes . . . " She put a hand to her mouth and chewed her fingertips nervously, looking up at him.

"Whose car?" he asked.

Elaine looked wildly about her, as if searching

152

for an escape hatch. Finding none, she looked accusingly at Kei. Finally, in a small, resigned voice, Elaine said, "Mine, if you must know."

Simon said, "Really?" thoughtfully, and came the rest of the way down the staircase, his hands in his pockets.

Elaine threw her straw hat the length of the foyer, and burst into tears. The hat cartwheeled on its brim out the back door and away down the steps of the bridge.

"Where is it?" Simon asked quietly.

"You bastard!" cried Elaine and snatched up one of the heavy bronze candlesticks from the table. She swung it at his head but was grossly wide of the mark. He caught at her hand and took the candlestick from her and set it back on the table. Elaine stood with her fists clenched, a dangerous look in her eye, and then she began yelling at the top of her voice. "Papa shouldn't have done it!" She started crying. "It's all his fault! He shouldn't have left me in this fix, or I wouldn't have to do these things. He knew I couldn't manage money!"

She began swinging at Simon, who held her off with a hand on the top of her head so she couldn't reach him. Kei was wearing a fine mask of disdain, looking at them like two snotty-nosed brats having tantrums on the floor. The young man in white backed up against the wall, covering his ears with his hands. Simon could see them both over the top of Elaine's head as she continued whirlwinding with her fists. Her face was purple. "You'd already made your million when Papa

153

died. You didn't *need* your half of the inheritance, dammit!" Elaine pulled away from Simon and shouted at the ceiling, "Damn you, Papa! Are you listening to me, Papa, you son of a bitch?!"

Simon put a restraining arm around his sister, who made a couple of ineffectual punches at his chest and blubbered. He took out his handkerchief, wiped her tears with it, and put it to her nose, saying, "Blow." She did, like an obedient child. He handed her the handkerchief so she could complete the mopping up.

"I want a drink," she said sulkily, her voice muffled by the cloth.

"First, tell me what you did with it."

She stared saucily at him and said nothing. The young man in white bolted out the door.

Hit by sudden understanding, Simon ran to the front door and shouted at the figure in white that was hotfooting it across the moat bridge, "Get it back! I don't care what it costs, you get it back! Hear?"

The young man paused to look back and then ran toward the gate into the roadway. Simon's long legs carried him rapidly up to the fleeing figure, and just as the young man was about to slip through the gate, Simon's hand came down on his collar, drawing him up short.

"I didn't want to. She talked me into it," said the young man, coughing and rubbing his neck where the collar had been jerked hard against his Adam's apple.

Simon let him go.

"Don't worry. The picture's still at my place. She said if I'd sell it, she'd be nice to me in bed and ..."

"I don't want to hear what she'd do!" Simon roared. "I can imagine it without your help. Just go and undo any deal you made and I'll made it right. Christ, *loyalty* isn't in your vocabulary, is it!"

"But she's so zaftig and does such wonderful things to me ..."

Simon considered decking the fellow, but thought it might jeopardize the arrangement for getting the Renoir back. Instead, he went for where it hurt most: "God is going to take a very dim view of this, you know," he said, and provoked a flood of tears. The young man crossed himself, drew a pentagram in the air with his forefinger, and kissed a Judaic star hanging from a chain on his neck.

Then he knelt down before Simon, took his foot, and – before Simon knew what he was up to – put it on his own neck. "Oh, stop that!" Simon said disgustedly, and stamped back across the gravel to the foyer.

Kei stood by the door. "Who *is* that?" she asked as he came in. "Elaine didn't introduce him, and he never said a word all day. We had to stop at every church along the way and let him run in for a minute. I thought he was either a novice or had weak kidneys. What was he doing with your foot?"

"That was Moody," said Simon, looking around for his sister, "and he was apologizing in his own fashion."

155

Elaine was in the sitting room, pouring herself a gin from the Waterford decanter. At Simon's approach, she put her glass down on the bar and bowed her head coyly, like a little girl caught in doing something naughty. It took all of his strength not to hit her.

"Don't be cross," she said, looking up at him flirtatiously. "Don't be cross, Simon dearest." She pulled his head down and kissed him. Her tongue darted into his mouth before he could draw back. He pushed her away, and she fell back against the bar, knocking her glass onto the floor, where it fell without breaking, spread a fan of colorless liquid onto the parquet, and jittered to a standstill in the yellow square of sunlight below the window. They looked at one another. The cuckoo sang in the woods.

"Go home, Elaine," Simon said wearily at last. "We'll talk about it tomorrow."

He turned away toward the window and poured himself a scotch. As he stood looking out at the meadow, he heard her heels tap once, twice, across the parquet, and then her footsteps were muffled by the carpet. Her heels clicked on the parquet by the door to the foyer and stopped.

"You leave him alone," he heard her say to Kei. "He belongs to me. Yes, *that* way, too."

Simon leaned his forehead against the cool wood of the window frame and felt sick. The scotch didn't help. He put it back on the bar.

The sportscar pulled out of the driveway with a loud splatter of gravel. Afterwards, the room was creakingly silent. The cuckoo had stopped singing.

After a long time, Kei said, "Tell me that what I'm thinking isn't true."

"I can't."

A fish splashed in the moat.

"I don't mean about the picture. I can see that Elaine and Moody took it, and that's why she has the new car."

"You mean what she said just now," Simon said. He took a cigarette from his shirt pocket and managed to light it, in spite of the shaking of his hands. "Yes, it's true," he said hopelessly.

He heard Kei's step on the carpet and then felt her turn him toward her. She looked into his eyes questioningly.

"She's never been this blatant before," Simon said, looking away. "She wanted you to know." He looked back at her, to see if she was recoiling from him.

A flush spread up from Kei's neck. "Then the things you did together as children ... " Her voice dried out, and she swallowed. "They just never stopped."

"Don't make it worse than it is," he said, expelling a gust of smoke. "I stopped it years ago, but she's still very possessive, and the fact that I support her financially is tied in with it. She spent her inheritance and ... "

"How can I make it worse than it is?!" Kei broke in. "My God, you talk about it as calmly as if it were a perfectly normal family relationship, instead of a psychotic aberration! How *can* you?"

"I'm not. But I've lived with this for years.

Do you want me to fall at your feet, sobbing 'Mea culpa, mea culpa'?" You can't imagine how I felt and how I feel now, but it *happened*. It *was*. It's a part of my life, and I can't make it not be!"

She looked at him sadly and said, "It's not really my business how you live your life, is it?" She shivered, put her arms around herself, and turned her back on him.

Wanting to put a hand out to her and not daring to, he turned to look out the window again, to draw in sanity and stability from the pastoral, peaceful scene outside.

As they stood with their backs to one another, he watched the mastiffs romp around the base of the sundial in the meadow and thought how ironic it was that — when he'd bought them from the same litter — the kennel had spayed Mitzi so she wouldn't breed with Bayard, her brother. Their mating would have been thought a natural thing, and no censure would have been laid on them.

He thought he heard Kei crying. "Look," she said, "I can't cast stones. We all have our secrets."

He turned around and looked at her. She put a handkerchief back into the pocket of her skirt.

"My mother used to make a pot of tea when I was feeling rotten," she said, "and right now I feel lousy. Would you happen to have some tea around somewhere?" Her eyelashes were spiky with moisture.

"Shall I be mother?" he asked, with a lame smile.

"It would be a nice switch." She smiled back at him. Her nose was pink.

While Kei got out pottery cups and saucers with blue rings around them and set them on the table by an earthenware bowl of peaches that smelled like perfume, Simon put the water on to boil and got out the green tea.

"I've got crystallized honey, if you like," he said. "The bees gather it from the flowers in the cemetery." He picked up his cigarette from the ashtray and took a deep lungful of smoke.

She did not reply, but took the cigarette from between his fingers and put it between her lips. Arms crossed, she prowled restlessly about the kitchen while the water purred in the kettle. When it came to a boil, Simon rinsed the teapot with the hot water, put in a hefty dose of tea leaves, and filled up the pot.

Kei made a complete circle of the room again, scuffing her feet against the terra cotta tiles, and came to a stop in front of him. "You honestly don't sleep with her any more?"

"No, I promise you." He leaned back against the counter top, crossed his ankles, and looked down at the toes of his handmade loafers. "You wouldn't believe how hard it was to unclasp her hold. Sometimes, even now, she tries to . . . " At the look on her face, his voice trailed off. Then, desperately wanting her to understand how natural it had seemed, he said, "When we were children, we knew it was wrong, but not in any special way. We weren't supposed to do things like that with *anybody*. Kids do, though. Everyone. Then, when we found out it was wrong because it was *us,* it felt too good to stop."

Oh Jesus, was that the wrong thing to say!

"You can't keep doing that to your sister just because it *feels good*!" Kei exploded.

"I thought you said it wasn't a puritanical age any more," he said, picking up a cup and saucer and pouring tea into the cup. The tea overflowed into the shaking saucer, scalding him. Exasperated, and surprised by pain, he threw the cup and saucer across the room, where they shattered on the tiles.

"God, how self-indulgent you are!" she said, indicating the mess with a jab of her cigarette. "There have to be *some* restraints. You're not an animal!"

"The hell I'm not! We all are," he said, enraged. "Even you, you silly bitch!" With one sweep of his arm, he brought everything off the table but a majolica pitcher, and the china crashed on the floor. Peaches bounced into the corners of the room. He looked stupidly at the teapot in his hand and set it down on the table.

"I suppose you mean the other night, you bastard!" she said, flipping her cigarette into the sink, where it died with a sizzle. "Maybe I should call you mother-fucker instead. I don't suppose you drew the line at that, either!"

"Don't tell me you didn't think it felt good! I was *there*!" He grabbed her by the shoulders and shook her until her hair whipped into her eyes. When he let her go, she sagged against the

160

table with her head back and her mouth half open. Tears slid slowly from the corners of her eyes and ran back into her hair.

It was very still.

He put his arms around her and kissed her gently. The soft, moist inner sides of her lips opened out for him. Very slowly, he entered her mouth and tasted the sweetness there.

The nearest bed was in his room at the top of the kitchen stairs. He put her down on the fur coverlet, raising eddies of motes that glittered and swam in the sunlight from the bay window.

They looked at each other like travelers about to set off into unknown territory. As if he were readying a sleepy child for bed, he unbuttoned her dress down to the hem, laid back the sides, and caught his breath. She lifted her hips and then raised one leg and the other afterwards as he slipped her panties off, moving slowly and unashamedly to let him look his fill into her depths.

She was already wet to the touch. His hand left a small snail's trail across her belly as he slid it up to cup her breast, graze her nipple, and come to rest at the back of her neck. Bending over, he ran his tongue lightly over the outline of her lips.

He felt her hands at his belt, "Hurry," she whispered, and moaned and rubbed her legs together.

When his clothes had joined hers on the floor, he lay down beside her, and she got up on one elbow to run her hand lovingly over his body, stopping to squeeze his balls lightly, and then brought her fingers caressingly up the back of his cock. Feeling that he was about to burst through his skin, he caught her hand and held it, reciting aloud the succession of the English kings. She smiled. Then she leaned over and ran her tongue in rapid circles around his nipple and damned near undid him completely.

"I could have herniated myself, carrying you up the stairs. You're heavier than you look," he said to distract himself. "I saw *Gone with the Wind* at an impressionable age."

He rolled over onto her and then ran his medallion around on its chain to the back of his neck and parked the medal on his back so it wouldn't swing in her face. He had only worked up to biting her nipples tenderly when she brought her legs up around his waist and drew him to her. He butted gently at her and slid into the luscious, deep slipperiness inside her body.

She was too aroused to wait and urged him to savage her. Almost immediately, he could feel her tensing, and he drew back to watch her face. She made a growl in her throat like the purr of a giant cat, and he felt a faint fluttering within her. He exploded inside her like a skyrocket.

As his shudders subsided, he heard himself laughing quietly. He suspected that he had said things to her as he came and wondered if they'd had to do with love.

He lay on top of her in warm, blurry comfort,

half asleep, until she said, "I have to have a cigarette. I think it's an obligatory part of the scene."

He rolled off her and felt along the carpet at the side of the bed to locate his shirt, extracted the flattened pack from the pocket, and said, "There's only one left."

"Share."

"There's a lighter on the table by you." He lit the cigarette and motioned to her to pass the ashtray. He put it on the chest, and they handed the cigarette back and forth between them.

She put her palm on his chest and, lightning quick, pulled out one of the few hairs he had there.

"Son of a bitch!" he exclaimed, clapping a hand to his chest in pain. "I haven't any of those to spare, and that *hurt*!"

"I want it for a souvenir," she smiled. "Would you rather I'd taken one from a more sensitive area?" She put the hair carefully on the white base of the bedside lamp, where it was clearly visible.

"Has anyone ever told you how really strange you are?" he asked, putting an arm under his head and blowing smoke up at the ceiling.

"Look who's talking!"

Her hand was doing interesting things at his crotch.

"Do you know how old I am?" he said grabbing her hand. "You'd better not get your expectations too high."

"Don't be silly. You're in fine fettle." She took the cigarette away from him and put the ashtray back on the table. Her lips and tongue proved the validity of her statement, and when he was aching and ready, she knelt over him, stroked herself with the tip of his cock a few times, and impaled herself on it. He pulled her down so his mouth could reach her breasts and moved beneath her, pressing up into her. "Let me do it this time," she said, and as he lay almost passive, she tightened herself around him and squeezed and milked him until he came again, gasping and digging his fingers into her buttocks. At the same time, she straightened up convulsively, looking like a marble caryatid above him, her face beautiful with anguish, and then collapsed into a broken arch with a harsh sob.

She fell asleep smiling, with her face in the hollow of his shoulder. Simon lay wide awake and alarmed, staring at the icons on the wall. This time, he thought, *this* time he was definitively and inescapably in love. Oh, God!

CHAPTER THIRTEEN

In the middle of the night, Simon wakened. Kei was standing naked in the moonlight of the bay window, looking with sightless eyes out into the woods. He got out of bed and woke her from the spasms that shook her.

"Again?" she said, and he nodded, leading her back to the bed.

With his arms around her, he said, "You're safe with me. I'll watch over you so you can sleep," and put his cheek against the top of her head. She fitted herself into the outline of his body with a sinuous wriggle, took his hand, and fell asleep.

The emerald velvet on the opposite wall looked black in the moonlight that picked out the gobs of gold in the antique icons hanging there. Twenty smaller icons surrounded the central painting, a large madonna with dusky skin and compassionate doe eyes. Silently, Simon addressed a petition to her to give some peace to the woman he held in his arms, and closed his eyes.

It was not the sound of the rooster crowing

in Hilaire's chicken run that woke Simon, but the noise of the shower in the circular tower room where he had installed the bath.

He lit a morning cigarette from the inlaid wooden box on the bedside table and lay back, his arm behind his head, feeling surpassing blithe and glad to be alive.

The velvet walls were their normal jewel green now, and the giant madonna seemed to be giving him a look of private rejoicing. Kei opened the bathroom door, revealing a pie slice of white walls and sand-colored tiling, and came out in his cashmere robe, toweling her hair, and sat down on her side of the fur coverlet.

"I think this calls for a little something," said Simon, getting out of bed and going into the bathroom where, among other indulgences, he kept the small, square refrigerator that housed his aftershave and items for midnight snacks. He returned with a long-stemmed wineglass, a tooth glass, and an open bottle of white Beaujolais.

Kei was back on his side of the bed, in the warm impression left by his body, and his robe was on the black leather chair.

"Sorry about not having matched glasses," he said, handing her the crystal one and keeping the squat, thick one for himself. He poured the wine. "I never had a woman in here before."

"Nor man either?" she asked teasingly, touching her glass to his and taking a sip of the wine.

He drew in his chin and looked down at her with mock reproach. She put her glass down on the table and, taking him by the hips, drew

166

him up against her face. "I love the way you smell here," she said, rubbing her cheek against his pubic hair.

"Darling," he said, detaching himself, "You're going to have to go easy, or I'll be worried about not being able to make love to you. I'm frightened to death of not being able to get it up, so let's not tax me too much all of a sudden."

"Ah!" she said, nodding understandingly, and lay back and reached for her glass again.

"However," he said, pulling back the cover and kneeling between her ankles.

Leaving Kei smiling lazily to herself, Simon showered, bellowing the Toreador Song at the top of his voice as he lathered down. When he came out dripping from the stall, he grabbed a king-sized towel and, still singing, made passes with it at an imaginary bull and ended with a superb veronica before drying himself.

He hummed as he put on tan riding breeches and a white shirt, and Kei sighed, pulled the fur coverlet up to her neck, and rubbed her chin sensuously against it. Simon sat down on the black leather chair in the bay window to pull on his boots and stamped his feet to settle them before standing up again. Kei kissed the air at him and closed her eyes.

When Simon finished rubbing Maeve down after a glorious ride, he turned the horse over to Fournier and jogged back to the meadow along the path, made an exuberant circle around Tommy's sundial, and bounded up the steps and over the bridge into the dining room.

He stopped dead at seeing Elaine sitting across the table from Kei, whose poise was marred only by a small, steady tic under her eye. Otherwise, she looked magnificently aristocratic and long-necked, but Simon knew she was as rattled as hell. On his way past her to his place, he put his hand on the side of her neck for a moment.

Elaine caught the gesture and tightened her lips grimly. She poured a cup of coffee with hot milk for Simon, and the cup ticked in its saucer as she handed it to him.

"Moody says he's taken care of everything, and there won't be any trouble from his fence," she said.

"Fine," said Simon, setting the cup down. "But where's the Renoir?" He unfolded his napkin onto his lap and looked around for the newspaper. Kei gave a guilty gasp and handed it meekly across the table. Simon told himself not to be so old-maidish and smiled at her to show that he didn't really —*absolutely* — mind having the purity of the *Times* sullied before he got to it. He put on his reading glasses.

"The picture's in your fucking study," said Elaine, who was looking less flamboyant than she had the day before, in jeans and a sullen red blouse.

"I don't use the study for that. The loveseat's too short," said Simon from behind the paper, unable to forgo at least a look at the headlines.

"Not funny!" said Elaine with a snort.

168

"Okay, okay, I don't consider what you've done very funny, either. I suppose there's no need to tell you that if you pull that again, I'll hang you up by the thumbs," Simon said lightly, feeling too good to come down on her as hard as she deserved.

Marthe came in the door with a platter of bacon and eggs, and the aroma set Simon's stomach growling.

"God dammit to hell, that's torn it!" Simon threw the paper down on the table, took off his glasses, and jammed them in his pocket. Without a break in her stride, Marthe turned smoothly around and exited, removing the platter from the combat zone. "It's one thing to look at the paper first, but doing the puzzle's another! And in ink, without a markover! I can't even finish one of the damned things," he complained to Kei.

"You should have warned me that you had dibs on the puzzle," she said. "I get very crotchety if I don't have my morning crossword fix. It's the least you can allow me if I have to listen to you complain about how the left wing's taking over the world."

Simon could see that they were about to take out their nervousness on each other in a political wrangle if he didn't stop it right there, and said, "You can have the puzzle if you don't touch the editorial page before I see it."

"Done!" said Kci.

Marthe peeked in the door and, seeing that even a minor scuffle looked unlikely, she brought the platter in again and served Simon, who took

five rashers of bacon and three eggs and asked
Marthe to bring in some peaches as well.

"Seriously," he said to Elaine, "I could have
you prosecuted for theft, as you very well know,
and Moody too. Of course, you know I won't,
although this is likely to cost me a good deal
of money, getting things right with Moody's contact — to say nothing of the amount you blew
on bibelots yesterday and the car. Where's what's
left?"

"On your desk." Elaine's dark eyebrows made
matched curves as she frowned at him.

He stuffed himself with bacon and eggs while
Kei and Elaine looked at one another in frozen
silence. Marthe brought in a cobalt blue dish
with peaches in it and freshened everyone's
coffee.

"I think it's about time you cleared out and
moved somewhere where we wouldn't be at
each other's throats constantly, don't you,
Elaine?" Simon said and took a swallow of coffee.
"Like Borneo or Outer Mongolia."

She smiled sourly. "My, you're feeling frisky,
aren't you? Nothing like a good time in the sack
to put you in high spirits, is there?" Out of the
corner of his eye, Simon saw Kei start stirring
her coffee viciously. "I'd need a settlement of
some kind before I could consider a setup like
that."

"What do you mean, a settlement? You had
your half of the inheritance. That's all you had
coming to you."

"I'd need a good deal more. You know that

170

money's gone long since," said Elaine. "It's not my fault that Papa never taught me to handle money. And I'm not as smart as you. You should have gotten me an estate manager. I couldn't possibly afford to move anywhere without either a sizable lump sum or a substantial increase in my allowance." The perfect Eagleton mouth took on an iron set.

"Anyone who could add two and two together could get along splendidly on what I'm already giving you. What's the matter with you, anyway?" Simon said, aggravated. "You could marry and get off my back, you've had enough opportunities. But I suppose a mere husband wouldn't permit those wild spending sprees you treat yourself to. Husbands like budgets. Jesus, Elaine, anyone else would have made you get out on your own and support yourself after you ran through your inheritance!"

"But you're not anyone else, are you, Simon?" Elaine smiled smugly, and Simon's blood pressure rose.

"God dammit, Elaine, you've been blackmailing me for years, and I'd think you'd have enough pride to stop!" he said.

"How do you expect me to support myself?" she retorted. "Doing what? I was just supposed to look decorative until somebody married me, and it's too late for that now. All the good men are taken. I don't know how to do a blessed thing, and you know it!"

Kei intervened. "It's difficult to get into the job market at your—*our* age," she said diplomatically. "but it's possible. Perhaps I could help you find something."

Elaine reared back and looked scornfully at

Kei. "Oh, come on! How could you help me? You're only a secretary. Help yourself!" She narrowed her eyes and leaned toward Kei. "You keep your nose out of this, it's a family matter between my brother and me. Just because you managed to drag him into bed with you, don't get ideas above your station. He's balled some of the most beautiful women in the world. He's out of your class."

Kei squared her jaw and looked consideringly at Elaine, as if she were something she'd stepped into on the sidewalk. "If it were up to me," she said, with admirable control, Simon thought, "I would have thrown you out long ago. You're only helpless because you want to be. I dare say you're Simon's only heir, so you've taken care to scare off every other woman in his life. I know exactly what you're up to." She took up her cup of tea and looked over its rim very collectedly at Elaine before taking a sip.

Elaine's face took on an unbecoming red and white mottling. Seeing that Kei was able to hold her own against Elaine—a phenomenon that he found fascinating—Simon continued to shovel in the bacon and eggs while keeping an eye on the women, ready to step in if Kei needed him.

"You're not really entertaining some wild hair about Simon's marrying you, are you?" Elaine laughed theatrically, and there was a note of fear in the harsh sound. "Better than you have tried that on! You ought to take a good look at yourself, you—you *secretary*!"

"It's an honorable title, and I don't like your

making it sound like a dirty word," Kei said crisply. "Particularly when you're nothing but a leech yourself."

Oh, a hit, a very palpable hit, Simon said under his breath.

"Poor, darling Kei," Elaine drawled in mock pity. "I can see he's won your heart. You've fallen in love with the unattainable. Of course, once you've been fucked by the great lover, you're not going to want to give him up, and I don't blame you. He's one of those rarest of creatures, a man who honestly loves everything about women—the way they act and think and feel and smell and taste." She gave Kei a tiny, tight, vitriolic smile, observing that she was sickening her. "Unfortunately for you, he's mine, and you can't have him. Didn't you realize that there were *three* of us together in bed when he was screwing you? I'll always be there with you. Who do you think taught him those loving, winning ways with his hands and his cock and his tongue . . . "

Kei recoiled as if Elaine had hit her, looked at her for a moment, and then got up and bolted out the door.

Simon jumped up, sank a hand in Elaine's hair, and drew her up by it out of her chair. Then he brought his eyes down level with hers while she held her hands to her head, grimacing, and said, "Get out! I want you out of here and out of the country in a week. I'll keep the money coming, but don't show your face around here again!" Then he let her go.

Elaine ran her fingers through her hair. "It's not going to be that easy, Simon!" she said defiantly and walked out, her head high.

Simon picked up a peach, tossed it in the air, and caught it with a smack of his palm, then bit into it and went out to find Kei, who was sitting on the bridge steps, having a crying jag.

He sat down beside her and held her until her sobs dwindled off into hiccups. "I'm sorry you had to go through that," he said, fighting his own nausea. The impulsion to beat Elaine until she was bloody was still making his stomach churn.

"She's right," said Kei, wiping her eyes on the sleeve of her loose saffron-colored top. "She *was* in bed with us."

"Was your husband?"

Kei looked startled. "No," she said, "of course not."

"I'm not your first lover, and you're not mine. It doesn't matter who the others were, does it? We've both learned from other people, but what we have together belongs to us, and us alone. Please don't let Elaine spoil it. That's exactly what she wants."

Kei took the peach from him and bit into it. Her lips were sweet and wet with juice as he stole the fruit from her mouth with his own. "I can't think straight when you do things like that," she said, and tossed the peach up and over the moat.

"I don't want you to think about that any more," he said, and swallowed the bite. "I told

174

you, that's in the past. Years ago. Elaine wants to dredge it up and ruin things, and it's up to us not to let her get her way." He stroked the long, golden leg next to him.

She slapped at his hand. "Don't touch the merchandise unless you're going to buy it," she said, and he was relieved to see her humor returning. A whinny came from the stable. Kei looked out across the meadow and said, "This place is so beautiful. No one would suspect how much trouble's in it. Are you here for good?"

"That was the idea."

"Are you going to take out papers? Become a French citizen?"

"I don't know, but my position here isn't very satisfactory as it is. I don't feel like an American when I'm living so far away, but I'd make a rotten Frenchman. I don't have much aptitude for languages." He ran a hand up the inside of her thigh and was amused to find that she was wearing nothing under her loose skirt. To his disappointment, she stood up.

"I don't have much aptitude for lying, either," she said. "I'm sick of not being honest with you. Come walk with me and let me set things straight." She put out a hand and pulled him to his feet.

"To the woods?"

"No, not there. I don't like to get near the grotto. Let's go see the kittens." She walked as if she were hurrying down a city street, although the sky was full of popcorn clouds and the cuckoos were having a singing fest. It was a perfect summer's day, and Simon felt Elaine had already be-

175

clouded it enough without his having to face the sordid facts of life that Kei was about to unload, to judge from the stern set of her jaw.

"What I am, really, is . . . " she began. "Well, the reason Jeremy recommended me is that I told him to, I'm his boss. I own Landsend House in London and Bell Tree Press in the States. My father started the business. Then when he died, my husband Robin took it over and nearly bankrupted it." Simon put her arm through his as they walked along. "I didn't have any choice but to take it over after that."

Simon was not inordinately surprised. "Very impressive," he said. "I never thought you were a secretary, not from the moment you stepped off the train."

"I'm not very fond of being a lady executive, either," said Kei, "but I searched out good, strong people who could guide me along, and it's worked out well. Bell Tree Press was a small publishing firm when I got it. My father specialized in oriental material when it began, but we've broadened the scope of the publications since." She stopped and searched his face with her eyes. "Do you mind awfully?"

"You're not the only businesswoman I've ever known. It doesn't defeminize you, if that's what you mean. But I am a little curious about the reason for the charade."

They had reached the barn. It smelled sweet with hay, and the kittens were on display in a nest made from an old sweater of Fournier's. He had moved them away from the circle of tire chains and put them next to a long, flat pile of sacks of grain. Kei sat down on the sacks and watched while Simon stood beside her.

"They're almost ready to leave the mother," he said.

Kei picked up a kitten and held it against her cheek while it made a sound like a creaking door, showing needle teeth and the inside of a baby-pink mouth. She put it down again beside the mother cat.

"Don't think I asked you to do the book so I could get inside the gates," she said. "I'd read your book on hagiology in Italian painting, and thought it was unusually well written. Then in Paris *Match* I saw a picture of you with a bunch of the jet set at Cannes and thought that the whiff of the playboy . . . "

"I'm not really like that," he interposed.

"I hope not." She caught his hand and held it against her neck. "But that, combined with your writing ability and your reputation as an art authority, would be a good gamble, I thought. Not a best seller. The art world's too rarefied an atmosphere for the popular market. All those art terms and all. Still, it should sell well. You've had an exciting life and know a lot of celebrities intimately. Too intimately."

"But the reason you came here," he said, trying to get her off that subject.

"Yes. While I was doing research on you in the library at the press, I ran across a picture of you by the château gate and got the idea of coming over here on some pretext or other to clear up something that's been bothering me more and more."

"Does it have something to do with the nightmares?"

She stopped and swallowed hard, as if her throat hurt. "I wasn't sure." She looked at the back of his hand and worked his gold signet ring back and forth with her thumb. "Maybe it was the trauma of Stephen's death, followed by the divorce, that set those off. I tried psychoanalysis and even hypnotism, but I seem to have buried something in the back of my mind so deeply that nothing could get it out again . . . until the nightmares started. More and more of what caused them has been coming back to me, and I'm scared out of my wits."

He sat down beside her on the sacks and held her head against his chest.

"I worked here as a secretary for intelligence in the early fifties," she said. "That officer that Elaine was talking about, the one who disappeared? His name was Alexis Michaelson, and he was my lover. I think I killed him."

CHAPTER FOURTEEN

"What do you mean, you *think* you killed him?"

"I can't remember," Kei said with quiet anguish. "Something happened out in the oak grove there. I thought it was just the history of the grotto— the devil worship—that made me afraid of the woods, but a wisp of memory came back last night. I can remember burying...No, that's not true. I was there with a spade in my hands, but what went before that is still gone. Maybe forever. I thought that if I came back here, I could fill in the gap that's missing, but I can't."

"Don't be silly," Simon said impatiently. "You couldn't bury a man out there without being noticed. Do you know how long it takes to dig a hole for a body?" He'd supervised burial details occasionally during the war, and he knew.

"I could have done it, over several nights. No one ever went out there then. There weren't any paths."

"But why would you want to kill him?"

"Oh God, I don't know! I have a hazy remem-

179

brance of *wanting* to kill him, but not why. There are still too many blank spaces. But I was there with the spade, and he *did* disappear, that I know. There were M.P.s all over the place, and I was scared to death. And I know I was shipped back to the States on a stretcher because I was terribly sick, but I never found out what happened." She sighed. "I just don't *know*. Who else could have done it but me?"

Simon began slapping his pockets. What a time to forget his cigarettes! Kei lifted the hem of her blouse and took a pack of Virginia Slims from between her belt and her skin and handed it to him. Her gold lighter was stuck into an empty place in the pack.

"It was so long ago. Can't you let it lie?" Simon asked, knowing she could not. "What good would it do now?" He gave her a cigarette, took one himself, and lit both of them. Tobacco had never tasted better.

"The nightmares are getting worse," Kei said. "I could walk off a moving train or out of a hotel window some night! And I'm not sure what I might be capable of doing in that state, either. I haven't much faith that I'm a decent person when I'm out of control, not after killing a man."

"Do you know where the . . . Can you remember what part of the woods you were in? It's not such a very big area, after all."

She shook her head. "And I can't dig the whole place up, can I? Marthe or Hilaire or your hired hand would notice. And maybe they'd remember about Alexis' disappearance, and God only knows

180

what would happen then. The books never close on murder, you know."

"Don't say that," he said sharply. "You can't be sure you killed him."

"What happened to him, then?"

They both fell silent.

"We're in a bit of a mess, aren't we?" Simon said, stroking her hair.

"*I* am."

"Same thing."

The mother cat began washing the kittens. While they'd talked, the kittens' mealtime had come and gone, and their stomachs were tight and round with milk.

"I can hear your heart beating," Kei said after awhile.

He smiled and, taking her chin in his hand, tilted up her face so he could look at it. Her mascara was smudged under her eyes, and tears had made tracks down to the corners of her mouth. "You look awful," he said tenderly.

She pulled away with a little laugh and then looked down at the floor, solemn again. "Simon, do you think you could make love to me?" she said in a low, ashamed voice. "I want you close. I feel so frightened, I want to hold you inside of me, all still and quiet. I need it," she said urgently.

They both moved very slowly, not looking at each other, as if they were in a dream state. She put out her cigarette and lay back on the sacks with her blouse rucked up above her breasts, waiting to be serviced. He ground his cigarette out under his boot and stood up to unzip his fly.

As he lay warm and enclosed in her, he thought that, although he had always enjoyed sex, taking and giving pleasure, he had never felt this way with any other woman. Before Kei, his inner self and body had been separate entities, the one observing the other's actions, so that he could detach himself, analyze the woman's reactions and needs so as to orchestrate his performance and satisfy her skillfully before letting himself plunge into the final spasm. As he'd grown older, he could postpone his orgasms longer and longer, sometimes abandoning them altogether, until he exhausted the woman with pleasure, but there was no clinical detachment when he was with Kei.

He tried valiantly, but finally he said, "I can't . . . I can't hold still much longer." His body began moving of its own accord. "Sweet Jesus!" he said, and came after a few quick, deep lunges and lay panting on top of her, feeling like a heel. "I'm so sorry," he said, his face against her breasts.

"Don't be," she said, stretching under him like a cat. "You comforted me, and that's all I needed." As he pulled out of her, she ran her hand over him to collect the wetness and rubbed it into her breasts. He had never felt so treasured.

He stood up to rearrange his clothing and then sat down again beside her. "I love you, Kei," he said.

"Me, too," she said sadly, sitting up. "Why

182

couldn't we have met years ago, before we got so tangled up?"

He leaned his head against hers, and they sat there together like two rag dolls.

"Oh, shit!" he said.

"Damn," she said.

They came out of the barn into a fresh wind that scooped up dust and bits of straw and sent them swirling skyward. The motor of a tractor started up not fifty feet away.

"Fournier!" Simon shouted, wanting to finish up the introductions on the estate and get that out of the way, but the wind must have carried his words off, for Fournier trundled the machine down the path toward the fields without looking back. Simon shrugged.

Then the short hairs prickled on the back of his neck. Fournier could have been watching them. Simon wouldn't put it past him to make a dirty peepshow out of what had just happened. He rather wished he and Kei could do it in the streets while crowds cheered. But not if Fournier were watching.

"Do you mind if I make some collect overseas calls from the house?" Kei asked. "It's been hard, keeping tabs on the business by running down to the post office in the village to use the telephone. Jeremy's been having some trouble with a press run of a new color process." Her skirt bellied up around her like a lampshade in the wind, and she pulled it down. The clouds had been blown into streaks of carded wool that shredded across the sky. "You know," she said, sounding puzzled, "every time I go into the village, the people down there make me uneasy. Do they treat you that way?"

"What way?"

They turned back to the château. Kei peeled back a strand of hair that had blown into her mouth and said, "If it made any sense, I'd say that they'd sent me to Coventry. No one will talk to me, but I see them in the backs of the stores, whispering, when I come in. And I don't like the looks on their faces. The shopkeepers are always out of the things I ask for, too—just ordinary things like Kleenex or a sewing kit. Not just at one shop, either. All of them."

"That's odd. They're quite friendly to me, probably because the château brings in business, so they can overlook the fact that I'm an American. The French can be pretty dour. None of those automatic American social smiles. You don't suppose they remember you, do you?"

"After all these years?" She took his hand and swung it between them as they walked down the path. "Besides, I did all my shopping at the post exchange in town, where I could get Stateside goods. Maybe once I bought ice cream at the bakery, but that was all." She shivered. "I'd forgotten how chilly it can get here at summer's end when the wind's off the Channel."

He put his arm around her shoulders. "Considering the way you've been upset since you got here, I don't think you're a very objective observer. You're probably misinterpreting the villagers. I wouldn't worry about them."

She thought about it and nodded doubtfully. Bayard and Mitzi came racing up the path, stimulated by the change in the weather, and stopped to paddle their front paws on the gravel, signifying that they were ready to play. Kei paddled her feet back at them, and Bayard gave a delighted bark. Mitzi sat back on her haunches, her mouth open, and looked full of romps. Simon gathered up the loose skin on either side of her neck and wrestled it back and forth, to Mitzi's ecstatic enjoyment.

"Forget the villagers," said Simon. "Let's not borrow trouble. We have plenty of our own."

After Kei made her phone calls, she said that she had to go to London the next day. Appointments had been made for her that she couldn't break. In the meantime, they agreed, they would keep up the fiction that she was his secretary, if only to allay the suspicions of the household staff until more information could be unearthed about what had happened to Alexis Michaelson.

"While I'm gone, I wish you'd do some more dictating so we can meet the printing schedule for your book. You're already two months behind, and it would take too long to get someone else in to do the typing. We've got to hurry," Kei said and went upstairs to get to her typewriter.

Simon closed himself in the study, fed the birds, and called Bony Foxworth about the Rowland print coming up for auction at Sotheby-Park-Bernet.

"Memler's going to bid on it," said Simon, tilting back in his chair, "so get your ass over there Monday and see that he goes to the sale in person. If he phones in his bids, the auctioneer can drag things out long enough to send the price over the top."

He sat up straight, and the chair legs clicked down onto the parquet. "Don't ask me how to get him there, that's something you'll have to figure out. But do it! And report back when you've got it."

He tilted back again, opened the desk drawer, and — cradling the receiver on his shoulder — began making a chain of paperclips, saying "Mmhmm" periodically while Bony heartburned about personnel problems at the gallery. "Another thing, would you get me a pair of tickets for *Sylphides* next month? In the grand tier. I don't want to hear the toe shoes slapping on the boards ... I know, but you and Margaret can use them if we don't make it ... Who? Oh, my secretary and me. By then she'll be ready for a break from the manuscript. How did Malcolm like the plane?" He nodded and smiled. "Good. Give Michelle a kiss from me," he said, and rang off.

Distastefully, he looked at the cassette. He was almost up to the Second World War and didn't look forward to reliving his experiences. Maybe he could skip them and take up the narrative again where he came out of the internment camp, yellow as a lemon from jaundice and about sixty pounds lighter. It had taken years to tamp down those memories so they wouldn't pop out again unexpectedly, and he didn't want them revived. Besides, readers wanted a recounting of a glamorous life, not a catalogue of the misery that had gone on about him in those years. He didn't think Kei would object to the structure he had in mind. Pushing the recording button, he began, "That summer in Cape Cod...," raising his voice above the sound of the birds in the aviary and the rattle of the windows in the wind.

At noon they met in the dining room. On a black lacquer plate, Marthe had arranged sliced tomatoes, green beans, greenish-yellow hearts of lettuce, purple onion rings, artichoke bottoms, and glistening black olives and had strewn all liberally with anchovies. Kei helped herself while Simon poured vin ordinaire into thick glass tumblers.

He had drizzled olive oil and wine vinegar over his salad and eaten half a plateful before he noticed that Kei wasn't touching her food.

"Something wrong?" he asked.

She stopped staring at the red wine in her glass and said, "Simon, I have to stay to find out what happened to Alexis, but what's happening between us frightens me."

He started to speak, but she interrupted. "No, you don't understand," she said. "Any more losses, and I'm not sure I can heal again. After Stephen was killed, I went under for two years while Jeremy and the others carried on. Even now I can't bear it that he's gone. Then I lost my husband. Perhaps he wasn't much to lose, but he made me feel like a piece of garbage he wanted to get rid of. A friend of mine who went through the same kind of divorce is still in the psycho ward. And that was before I had any idea I might have killed Alexis. I don't know if I can come to terms with that."

"But we'll be together now . . . "

"No, that's just it! You're what frightens me most! I'd always be afraid of losing you too. In all your life, you've never been able to commit yourself to a woman, and that's abnormal enough by itself. The only permanent relationship you've had was a sick one with your sister, one that makes my flesh crawl. You're no refuge! You're a disaster, and I don't want to wind up blowing my brains out over you."

The tablecloth, pale yellow linen, had a coarse weave. Some of the strands under his fingers were thick and some as thin as fine wire. There was a spot by the handle of his knife that had not come out in the laundry. The windows shivered. It was getting colder.

Simon got up slowly and left the table. His boots clacked on the marble of the foyer. He opened one of the back doors blindly, went out, and closed it behind him.

Standing in a sheltered pocket where the noise and the sweep of the wind was at his back, he lit a cigarette. It was not the cold that was making him tremble.

The door opened and he felt Kei's hands on his shoulders. He shook them off.

When his voice was under control, he said, "There's nothing I can do about Elaine now, and I'm not proud of my reputation with women. It's been humiliating, having my private life on display, blown out of all proportion. I'm not one of those men who need a new partner every night, no matter how it's looked. I just never happened to fall in love. I don't think that makes me a monster." The silhouettes of the trees blurred and swam in the wind. "I've been lonely all my life, Kei."

A slim hand slid into his, and he turned his hand so he could grip hers. She leaned against his back, warming him.

"How do you think I feel?" he said in a low, tense voice. "I'd like everything to be perfect for you, to make you happy instead of agonizing you. Don't you think I'd give my eyes to undo everything?"

"I couldn't lose you, Simon. I'd want to own you, and you'd hate me for it, sooner or later."

He tossed away his cigarette and turned around to look into her eyes. "Damn you, Kei, I *want* to be owned! I didn't want all those short-term relationships, I just didn't *have* anything else. I don't want to grow old alone."

"I can't believe we're cut out to be the sweet little old couple from down the block who tend their roses and take Sunday walks together, hand in hand."

"Why not?" he pleaded. "If we were lucky enough, that would come in its season."

"But I couldn't share you, Simon. Not with

Elaine, not with anybody. If you had affairs, it would destroy me."

"There wouldn't be any affairs."

"Honestly?" She gave him a sad smile and shook her head, as if it were more than she could imagine.

"On my honor."

She looked at him for a long time, while he waited, almost without breathing, for her reaction.

"Maybe I'm a fool, but I believe you," she said finally. "I want to believe you."

He put his arms around her. "I know I'm asking for a leap of faith, Kei, but I'll never hurt you, I swear."

They kissed with cold, dry lips, and she molded herself against his body. A sudden gust of wind chilled them, but everywhere they touched was warm. The door blew shut with a bang, startling them. Kei looked up, and then said, "Oh, how beautiful!"

Simon turned to see a hot air balloon, red and white, skimming along in the sky, driven by the high winds.

"Let's not waste the wind," Kei said. "I have something marvelous upstairs. Wait!"

She ran inside and Simon followed her into the foyer. He looked around at the painting equipment still stacked around the walls as he waited and wondered what this woman of his had on her mind.

Today was Saturday. He'd never done the view from the vineyard with water colors. Tomorrow would be the perfect day to be, literally, a Sunday

190

painter. Smocks, straw hats, a bird and a bottle . . .
But she'd be in London.

"Where's the highest point of land on the estate now?" Kei called, coming down the stairs
with an armful of colored fabric and short lengths
of bamboo. As Simon watched, she inserted the
sticks in the fabric, and it began to curve and
stretch like a living being, expanding into a butterfly with blue and purple wings that stood as high
as her shoulder. She handed him the kite, keeping
the reel of string, and attached the cord to the
bamboo frame.

The field above the vineyard was high and clear
of trees, bordered at its base by a low stone wall.
The vineyard below, its squat vines heavy with
clusters of grapes ripe for harvesting, ran down
to the road leading into the village. The field had
been reaped, so they could run through the stubble to launch the kite.

As soon as Simon made a pass across the field,
the wind caught the kite and lifted it away. He
worked it up into the sky, loping back and forth
across the field, invigorated by the cold air chilling
his face and back. He let the cord go, and the kite
soared out across the valley.

Holding the reel, Kei turned as the butterfly
flew overhead and braced herself against the pull
of the wind against the stone wall. She fed out
line as the kite climbed up across the road and
the river, bucketing in the air currents, blue and
purple in a vast pale wash of sky. Simon shaded
his eyes with his hand and watched the butterfly

rise and shrink. The wind riffled the hair on the back of his head. A gust lifted Kei's skirt, exposing her smooth ivory buttocks, and Simon felt himself grow hard. Knowing Kei loved and wanted him swept aside the restraints with which he normally guarded himself, throwing him into constant joy and lust, like a ram in spring. He knew he couldn't sustain it forever, but he was going to enjoy it as robustly as he could while it lasted.

Putting his arms around her from the back, he slid his hands under her loose blouse, felt the creaminess of her skin through his fingertips, kneaded her breasts roughly, and nipped their tips with his fingernails. She gasped and pressed back into his crotch, rubbing herself against him and arching her neck, her movements so like those of a female cat being mated that mounting her, here in the wind under the high blue sky, seemed the natural, imperative order of the animal kingdom.

He reached around and manipulated her until she was ready for him to enter her, freed himself from his riding breeches, and bent her over the low wall. While she guided him, he bent his knees and slid up into her. She put her hand over his and moved it against herself to match his rhythm.

He was bucking into her hard, ready to spend himself, when Tommy McKenzie came down the road below on his motorcycle, looked up, and stopped with one foot on the blacktop.

Tommy cupped his hands around his mouth and shouted up the hill, "We'll be over at seven!" When he got no reply, he shrugged and drove off, the sun striking flashes off his shiny black machine and helmet.

"God dammit!" Simon groaned, gritting his teeth and grinding himself into Kei with strong spasms. She shook with laughter. When his heartbeat and breath slowed, Simon said, "Are you all right? Did you come?"

As if in answer, she pointed to the sky, where a tiny blue and purple butterfly, freed from its tether, was floating out to infinity. The reel was empty.

They finished off the salad, down to the last caper, and had grapefruit ice and gaufrettes with powdered sugar besides. When Simon lit a cigar after pouring coffee, Kei asked for one too, and they sat back in their chairs with Cheshire grins as if they were the only people in a blithe and carefree world.

CHAPTER FIFTEEN

The wind died away as if it had never been, and summer returned fullblown for the afternoon. While Marthe did the dishes and got ready to take the rest of the day off, Kei sat down on the bridge in back, sandals off, her bare brown toes curled around the edge of the third step down, and leaned back with her eyes closed, letting the sun bathe her face. Simon stretched out with his head in her lap and demanded her life story.

"The scales have to be balanced," he said. "You're learning every detail of my personal history while you're typing my memoirs, but I don't know enough about you."

"My life's been hideously dull, compared to yours," Kei said, running a hand back through her hair. The big topaz winked in the light. "I'll bore myself as well as you. I've never gotten much thrill out of staring at my own navel."

"How do you expect me to understand you if I don't have all the data?" asked Simon, the sun glowing red through his eyelids.

Kei yawned noisily. "Oh, very well, if you

insist," she said in a sleepy voice. She stroked his hair back from his forehead. "Do you blow dry your hair?" she asked. "It always looks so clean and silvery."

"No, I look like a dandelion gone to seed if I do. Get on with it, Kei."

She yawned again and then told him about growing up in a well-to-do publishing family.

"I wanted to see the world after high school and took a job with intelligence as a civilian secretary, which is how I wound up here for a few months. Broke my parents' hearts by marrying at eighteen, but they paid my way through college while Robin got his Ph.D. and I majored in Japanese. I was a freshman when Stephen was born." She sighed. "He was too young, too, when *he* married—but that's all over now, and coming back to the château brings me full circle."

He heard the dogs' light crunch on the gravel path. A wet nose bumped at his hand and he reached out to tousle a silky ear.

"I roomed up on the third floor, facing the meadow. Well, if you don't blow it dry, what do you do?"

"Towel and brush it dry, and you're changing the subject."

"The other two secretaries, Becky and Sophie, and I used to go into Paris to shop and look around the museums to keep from having to fight off the men in the outfit here on weekends." She scratched his scalp gently. "We used to pretend we were having mad love affairs with mysterious Frenchmen, but the only ones we ever met were bus guides and hotel clerks."

The scratching stopped and Simon looked up at the under side of her chin. There was a mole like a freckle there that he had never noticed before.

"Go on."

She stroked his eyebrows. "You know, these are just like wires," she said.

"Happens when you get older," he said. "Do I have to drag every word out of you?"

"Well, then Alexis was posted here as a translator. He arrived under a cloud because he'd had a mistress connected with the communists in Algeria. The American government was keeping an awfully close eye on him. I thought that was terribly romantic. It was exciting to be pursued by a dangerous man. You see, one of the reasons that the Army was so alarmed by his disappearance was that they thought he might have gone over to the Reds."

"Is it possible that he did?"

"I'm afraid not. Their double agents came up empty on him, I heard later. They couldn't trace him anywhere. No wonder, if he's lying out there in the woods."

The stroking stopped and he could feel her legs start trembling under his head. He opened his eyes, ran a hand up her arm, and said, "Don't think about that, Kei. We'll cross that bridge later. Tell me what he was like." He couldn't resist asking, "Was he good in bed?"

"How was I to know?" Kei looked down at him and smiled, the dent beside her eye deepening.

"I had nothing to compare him to. He was my first." She looked up at the sky as if she were remembering, and Simon wrestled with massive jealousy as his imagination painted a graphic picture of Kei in bed with another man. "He was billeted over in St. Denis at the Poisson d'Or, where I could visit him without anyone here knowing about it."

"I suppose you visited him a lot?" Simon asked crossly.

"Nobody had ever bothered to tell me that sex was fun, and I couldn't get enough of him when I found out."

"I suppose he was all animal magnetism and muscles, too," said Simon, noting that his voice was rising.

"Oh, it was all a long time ago," said Kei, putting a finger softly on his lips. "I've lost his face. But he was big and tall, with dark hair. That's all I remember, except that he was very good to me and treated me like Meissen china."

He caught her hand away and said, "Except when you were in bed, right?"

"Please, Simon. It's all a long time ago, and you surely didn't think I hadn't had any experience before you."

"Do you know your nostrils don't match?" Simon said bitchily.

Kei put her hand over her nose and stared down at him. "It's a deviated septum, and I'm too cowardly to have it fixed. Most people have the courtesy not to mention it." She gave him a push to make him sit up. "I'm not going to tell you

197

any more if you're going to look up my nose."

"I've got two false molars attached in back by a gold prong," Simon said placatingly. "I take them out at night. Is that a fair trade for your deviated septum?"

"I didn't notice you taking them out last night."

"And let you know right off how I'm falling apart? My family doesn't age particularly well, especially me. I'm going on sixty, and my face looks like a road map."

"I adore your wrinkles," Kei said, tracing the ones at his neck with a finger. "They're your history, don't you see? They sort of make my stomach turn over with fondness." She sighed. "I only wish you had a bald spot. They're so endearing. Anyway, I didn't fall in love with your face or body, beautiful though they are."

"Then what did you fall in love with?" He smoothed the hair back from her face and tucked it behind her ears.

She shook it loose irritatedly. "Don't do that. My mother used to do that," she said. "With your faults, I think. I don't think that any woman falls in love with a man's perfections. Who wants to feel inferior?"

"I think matched nostrils are very boring," he said, smiling.

She stood up and stretched. "That's all the talk about noses I can stand. What should I wear tonight?"

"I like those black trousers." He stood up and dusted off the back of his breeches. "They

198

make your legs look miles long."

Up in his bedroom, Simon dug a knuckle into his groin and said, "I think I'd better take my shower alone. All this screwing after a year and a half of not being able to make it is making me itch like blazes."

"Why didn't you tell me that?" Kei asked sympathetically. "You know, I didn't realize we'd made love that many times." She cocked her head thoughtfully, and with a sinking feeling Simon watched her start counting on her fingers.

He took a deep breath and let it out. "Kei, I have to level with you," he said. "While I was in London, I was sleeping with someone else."

She took a step backward. The hurt in her eyes flowed out to him and stuck like something sharp at the base of his throat. He went to her and put his arms around her. "I had to be sure it wasn't just the craziness of that first night with you that made me able to get an erection again, and the next morning you looked as if you didn't want any part of me."

She pushed him away, turned her back on him, and stood silent a moment before facing him again.

She glared at him and wrenched off her blouse. "I am *not* going to cry, you rat!" she said, stepping out of her skirt and kicking it up onto the black leather chair.

"There's no reason for you to. It meant absolutely nothing, and at that point, you and I weren't . . . "

"I know! I know!" She took one of his military brushes from the bureau and stood there naked, giving her hair short, violent strokes with it. "Jesus, you're nothing but an alley cat!"

He sat down on the bed and began working his boots off. "You don't know what it means to a man, not to be able to get it up. For a fucking year and a half! I thought I'd go out of my damned mind!" He stood up to take his pants off, got his leg caught in them, thrashed around, and knocked the telephone and lamp off the bedside table.

Kei picked them up and slammed them back into place, hard. Pushing him back onto the bed, she grabbed his breeches and pulled them the rest of the way off. Then she threw them across the room.

"Who was she?" she demanded.

He sat up and began unbuttoning his shirt, considering lying to her and then deciding to brazen it out. "Missy Hilliard." He put his shirt on the bed and peeled his silk briefs down and off.

"Oh, Christ!" She flung her hands in the air. "It has to be an international star, doesn't it?! How can I compete with that?"

"Do you want me to be honest with you, or don't you?"

"I don't think I can stand this!" she said, and ran out of the room and down the hallway.

He followed her. She slammed the door of her room in his face. He yanked it open again.

"Don't you come in here!" she shouted, snatching up a corner of the bedspread and holding it up to cover her body.

"It's *my* house, dammit!"

They stood staring at one another, breathing hard. Kei's mouth began to twitch. Once they started laughing, they couldn't seem to stop.

"We've got to stop doing this," Simon said, staggering up from the bed, where Kei lay exhausted, her hair in a tangle. "I'll never reach sixty at this rate!"

The body's automatic responses were fascinating, Simon thought as his hands advanced gingerly toward his chest with a bandaid spread out ready for application, and his chest retreated of its own accord at exactly the same rate, goosefleshing, protective of its raw nipples. Determination won over the game between his hands and his chest, and he got the bandaids on and was prepared against the chafing of his shirt.

He didn't like to think how sore Kei must be. Correction. He *did* like to think of it. After a year and a half of feeling like everybody's old maid aunt, it was terrific to feel armed with a deadly weapon.

He picked up the phone and called Tommy.

"McKenzie here," said Tommy, sounding stuffily British.

"Eagleton here," Simon said, equally stuffily. "Tommy, old friend, do you mind if we cancel the restaurant and eat Chinese here? Perhaps play some mah jongg? What with one thing and another," Simon scratched his crotch, "I'm absolutely worn out. Just can't manage it tonight."

"Fine with me, though my date will be pissed off at having got dressed up. I've spent the whole day—well, not the *whole* day—wrestling with a stubborn bit of sheet metal, though, and could do with a quiet evening myself. And what the devil were you two doing up by the vineyard this morning? It looked very peculiar."

"Inspecting the wall," Simon said shortly, then diverted Tommy from that subject by asking, "who's your lady tonight?"

"She'll kill me for telling you. It was supposed to be a surprise. Missy Hilliard." Tommy hung up.

Simon stared at the receiver in his hand. Jesus Christ and all the saints! He slammed down the receiver so hard it hurt his hand. No use to phone back and try to rearrange things. Missy would come, regardless. Wild horses couldn't stop her. She hadn't got where she was in show business without superhuman determination. Shit! *Shit!* Simon scratched his crotch furiously. These were the times that tried men's souls!

He put on a pair of faded blue jeans and a light blue bouclé sweater, pushing up the sleeves, and then sat down and buckled on his sandals. Why had nature wasted hair on his toes instead of putting it on his chest where it would do some good?

Well, no getting around it, Kei would have to be told. Why had he been stupid enough to tell her Missy's name? Because she asked, that's why, and he was cursed with an inability to lie when asked a question point blank. Was there *any* weakness or vice left out of his makeup? What did Kei see in a mess like him? She must have a phenomenally strong stomach. Or rotten taste. Not that lying would have helped, really. Missy would have blurted everything out. She'd never had an unexpressed thought in her life.

He smoothed back his hair with his military brushes and then went down to Kei's room, where she was sitting at the dressing table, topless but wearing the black pants and spike-heeled sandals. She was stroking foundation makeup around her mouth, where his beard had scraped her skin. She looked at him in the mirror as she put on lip gloss and said, "You're not very dressy."

"We're not going out. Too bushed. I'll cook something and we'll play some mah jongg with Tommy and . . . and his friend."

"Good." She went to the armoire to get out a wheat-colored pullover. A gold locket swung between her breasts. Noticing his eyes on it, she held it out to show him, saying, "I put the hair from your chest in here. My version of being pinned." She pulled on the top and went back to the dressing table for a brush. Bending over so that her hair fell over the back of her head onto her face, she brushed it and then straightened up and pushed her hair into place. "Why the long face?"

"Kei, do you love me?"

She put the brush back and said, "I was under that impression, God help me."

"No, really. Do you?"

"Scout's honor." She put her arms around his neck and leaned back to scrutinize his face. "Do you love *me*?"

"I swear."

"Well, then."

"Tommy's bringing Missy Hilliard. There's no keeping her away, so we're in for a very trying evening."

She dropped her arms and gave a gurgle of revulsion. "What a treat!" she said and then looked at him suspiciously. "You're not trying to test me, are you, Simon Eagleton? Was this your idea?"

"Don't be ridiculous!"

"Can't I just stay up here and hide? I'm not sure I can carry off a Noel Coward evening of clever banter with the last woman you had in bed."

"Not the last," he reminded her. "I'd rather not face Missy alone. She's been after me for years, but if she sees you, she should get the message."

"Can't you fight your own battles?" Kei slammed the armoire door shut.

"Of course I can, dammit! But we can't go through life avoiding all my old girlfriends." Kei opened her mouth to protest, but Simon barreled on, not letting her interrupt. "—Any more than I'm going to avoid your old lovers." He looked her in the eye and saw that he had hit the mark.

"Alexis disappeared. You're not likely to

run into him," she said evasively.

"I didn't mean him."

Kei made no retort.

Downstairs in the kitchen, Simon put on a denim work apron, got out the chopping block, and set to work on a pink pork tenderloin with the cleaver while Kei looked on nervously.

"I wish you'd be careful," she said, peering over his shoulder. "Chinese cooking stops being fun when you chop a thumb off."

"Quiet. I'm giving Missy the death of a thousand cuts." He whacked viciously at the tenderloin. "What a foul sense of timing she has!" He looked around at Kei. "Why don't you set up things? The wok's on the ceiling rack, and I'll need a heating dish for the fried rice, and the oven should be turned on to three hundred degrees. Better get out the stockpot for the rice, while you're at it."

"You're very good at giving orders," said Kei and began looking through the cupboards for the things he'd requested.

"I'm not making you cook, am I?" he asked. "Incidentally, can you?"

"After a fashion. I do other things better."

"I'll testify to that."

She abandoned her search for a moment and stood with her fists on her hips. "I didn't mean *that*."

"I did. You must have had plenty of practice to get as good as you are."

She drew in her breath sharply and turned to

the cupboard again to take out the containers, which she banged down noisily on the table, where he could reach them. Without a word, she turned on the oven and set out the wok and the oil and then stood looking at him with her jaw squared, her arms crossed over her chest.

Simon said "Ow!" suddenly and grabbed his hand theatrically. Kei was beside him instantly, reaching for his hand to look at it, her face stricken. "Just kidding," Simon said, stretching out his uninjured hand and wiggling his fingers. "Just wanted to see if you still cared."

Kei's hand shot out and caught him a wallop on the jaw. "What a mean thing to do!"

He laughed and caught her wrists. She lunged at him, trying to get close enough to bite. "I'm sorry, it *was* mean," he said, still laughing and imprisoning her with his arms until she quit struggling and calmed down.

"Of course I've had lovers," she said into his shoulder. "Robin egged me into having affairs so he wouldn't feel guilty about his own. And it used to excite him, knowing I'd just been fucked by another man. That's when he'd consent to make love to me again—after I'd just come from someone else. Don't tell *me* about loneliness!"

"Oh, baby . . . " Simon said compassionately, stroking her hair.

"I don't much like talking about it," she said, extricating herself gently. "I never slept around until Robin did, and I'm not proud of myself." She went back to the cupboard to look for things. Feeling faintly rebuffed, Simon prepared the food.

Mounds of minced shrimps, green onion tops, ginger, shredded pork, black mushrooms, and the other ingredients of the meal grew in the dishes on the table as he chopped away, until he'd assembled a palette of oriental splendor. He fried the rice with eggs, onion tops, and shrimp and set the dish in the oven to keep warm. Then they set the table together, with the antique imari ware he'd sent back from his tour in Burma during the war. The Chinese beer and the honey-dew melons were in the refrigerator, chilling.

Now all they had to do was wait, which they did with increasing restlessness. Kei paced around the salon, picking up things and putting them down again, while Simon slouched on the end of his spine in one of the easy chairs, smoking and tapping his fingers on the top of his glass of scotch. When the knocker clonked on the front door, they both jumped and looked wildly at each other.

They advanced toward the door at a funereal pace. Simon was seized with a hideous desire to giggle but stifled it as Kei shot him a barbed look.

The door banged open before they got there, and Missy burst through in a flurry of chrome yellow chiffon and attached herself to Simon like a starfish sucking an oyster out of its shell. She kissed him so hard she mashed his nose against the side of his face, and he couldn't breathe. Struggling for air, he detached one of her hands and then the other, but as soon as he freed himself of one, it came down and clung somewhere else.

He felt like a lifeguard being drowned by the person he was rescuing, and a bandaid tore loose. Finally Missy let him go and danced back to feast her eyes on him, running smack into Kei.

Missy whipped around, her chiffon swirling round her, and snapped, "Who are *you*?"

"Kei Ronald," Kei gasped, cowed by the whirlwind.

"Charmed, I'm sure," Missy said acidly, making it sound like a curse. "Are you *living* here?"

"I'm Mr. Eagleton's secretary."

"Missy, Kei. Kei, Missy," Simon said superfluously, reaching under his sweater to adjust the bandaid and wincing.

Everyone seemed to be mad at everyone else as they stalked through the salon without speaking and served themselves at the bar. The women looked frostily at one another over the tops of their glasses.

"Some welcome!" said Missy to Simon. "She's no secretary! I can tell something's going on between you two." Putting down her glass, she fished in her mesh evening bag and then held something out to him on the palm of her hand. Looking meaningfully at Kei, she said, "Here's the button you left in my bedroom Wednesday."

Awkwardly, Simon picked it off her outstretched hand and put it in a pants pocket.

"Anyone read any good books lately?" said Tommy, his voice two notes higher than normal as he looked back and forth between Missy and Kei, who were poised like two fighting cocks getting ready to circle each other for the attack.

208

"Kei, go out and start the flame under the wok," Simon said.

Kei looked prepared to argue, but seemed to think better of it and set down her drink and followed orders.

"Well?" said Missy, crossing her arms and tapping her foot.

Simon cleared his throat. Then he cleared it again and said, "Missy, there isn't any graceful way I can handle this, and I don't want to hurt you, but whatever went on between us isn't going to go on any more. I'm in love with Kei, and I won't tolerate your giving her a hard time. If you can behave, I'm going to go ahead with the dinner. Sorry you didn't know about this, Tommy."

Emotions passed over Missy's face like still photographs being flipped rapidly. When a passive expression stabilized on her features, she said, "You could change your mind."

"I don't think so," Simon said quietly, in a tone that brooked no argument. Watching the struggle going on beneath Missy's face, he felt a surge of compassion for her.

Tears stood out in her eyes. "You can't win 'em all," she whispered gamely, and Simon went over and kissed her softly on the forehead.

"I've got to go out to the kitchen," he said. "The oil's probably smoking."

Missy gave a long, shuddering sigh. Simon turned as he left the room and saw that Tommy had his arms around her.

"Don't say anything," he told Kei as he came

209

into the kitchen. "Nothing you could say would make me feel any worse than I do already."

He inspected the wok. The oil was smoking and ready. He picked up the bowl of shredded pork, scattered it in the pan, and stirred it around quickly. Kei brought bowls to him as he cooked and removed them to the table as he passed them back to her. As he was stirring the beef and broccoli, he looked at her out of the side of her eye and was comforted by the smile she gave him.

" 'Oh, for a quiet life,' said the little, small red hen," she said.

At first, no one spoke at the table. Simon thought that, rigid as they all were, they looked like four of those inane toys shaped like birds that keep dipping their beaks into a glass of water. Down the group bent to their chopsticks, and up they sat again to chew, stiff as wood. And down they went again.

Then Simon asked Missy about her next appearance, and the conversation started to flow. To his puzzlement, the two women warmed up to each other, and by the time they were squeezing lime juice onto their melon slices, it was plain that they liked each other.

Simon felt greatly relieved on that score, but what he didn't like was the way Tommy was focusing on Kei. He and Tommy had always made something of a game of stealing women away from each other until Tommy entered his Lolita period, when Simon's interest flagged.

Younger women bored the bejeezus out of

Simon. Half the time, they didn't know
he was talking about and made him feel like an
antique. Most of the rest of the time, they were
over his head, with talk about rock groups, various
forms of meditation and self-realization, and sub-
jects in which he had no interest at all. He hadn't
any taste for the Pygmalion-Galatea game, either.
Serving as a savant or a father figure for some
blank-eyed, beautiful ninny didn't appeal to him
in the least.

Tommy was lighting Kei's cigarettes with an
obtrusive dispatch that Simon could see was
annoying her, and Missy was irked that Tommy
was directing all his conversation at Kei, lacing
it with unsubtle compliments and sexual innu-
endos.

"Tried on the armor yet?" Tommy asked.

"No. Do I *have* to wear it?"

"Don't get peevish on me, old dear. Those
lances are blunt and have pads tied around them,
but they can knock you into next Tuesday. You'll
be glad of the protection. We'd better go out
tomorrow for some practice with the horses.
Handling a lance is pretty tricky."

"How did I get myself into this? If I don't
break my neck, I'm still going to look like a
fucking idiot. Tommy, get me out of this, can't
you?"

"Not a hope. Everything's set, and we didn't
exactly put a gun to your head, either. On second
thought, tomorrow's out. I'm practicing kendo
for my own match. I'll call you later to set up
a time for the horses and lances."

211

endo?" asked Missy.

se thing," Tommy answered. "Masks,
d hoods, and wooden staves. Takes more
nan galumphing around with a lance, make
no mistake."

They all helped clear, and Simon brought in
the coffee and liqueurs to a table near the game
table that he'd set in front of the fireplace, all
the while trying to figure out some emergency
that he could trump up to get out of the tournament. Tommy wouldn't let him get away with
a quick case of the flu, and the fellow he was
supposed to fight, whoever he was, could hardly
be left to hang around without a match, he supposed. There was nothing for him but to go through
with the bloody thing. He brought down the
teak and gilt mah jongg box from its home on
the bookshelf flanking the mantel, and the four
of them hiked their chairs into place around the
game table.

"Now, what is all this?" asked Missy. "I
thought mah jongg went out in the twenties."

"It did," said Tommy, taking a drawer out
of the teakwood box and emptying ivory-faced
tiles onto the tabletop, "but we've been having
a private revival. It's played something like rummy.
You'll catch on in a game or two." He helped
Simon set up the Wall of China in a hollow square
made of the ivory and bamboo tiles, saying, "You
nearly have to inherit a set to get one. I finally
found one in a flea market in Ostend, and it
cost me a pretty penny."

Simon handed around long black lacquer tile

212

holders and distributed ivory counting sticks so they could wager on the game. Giving Tommy the score card, he instructed the women in the rules, telling them about the suits and how to collect winning combinations. "These are the winds and dragons," he said, holding up samples with colored Chinese characters on white backgrounds.

Missy played unenthusiastically, complaining constantly, until she got a winning set of Heavenly Twins and raked in a pile of counting sticks. "God, you can make a lot of money at this crazy thing, can't you?" she said, snapping her fingers for Tommy to hand over some counters he had subtracted from her winnings, hoping she wouldn't notice.

They played for a couple of hours with mounting fervor, slapping the tiles down on the table with loud clacks and swearing at each other for snaffling off coveted numbers in sequence.

"That's fifteen hundred points and I cleared, so that's doubled, and my wind is the south and I have all of them, double and double again," said Kei, counting up her tiles.

"I'll be screwed, blued, and tattooed!" exclaimed Tommy, paying up. "You've cleaned me out. I was going to use that money for some platinum wire. I think I've reached my limit."

"You're no gentleman!" Missy complained. "I've lost twenty pounds, and you're stopping now without letting me recoup?"

"Oh, come on, Missy, you're insatiable," said Tommy, yawning and stetching. His buttonless corduroy jacket fell back, exposing the golden pelt covering his chest. Simon felt a pang of envy.

"Look at that! Isn't it heavenly?" squealed Missy, leaning over to stroke Tommy's fur. "That's the only thing wrong with you, Simon," she said mischievously. "If you were built like Tommy and had a chest wig like his, you could rule the world."

Simon groaned and lit a cigar, then poured himself an armagnac.

"Stop it, Missy," said Tommy, clutching his jacket together in front like a coy model on a Victorian postcard. "Women aren't supposed to be body watchers. That's a man's game."

"Oh, is it?" Missy sniffed. "You men go in for either tits or asses, so why shouldn't women have their preferences, too? We do, don't we, Kei?"

"I'm not sure I want to get into this," said Kei, collecting the tile boards.

"I read a survey they'd taken on it," Missy said, settling back in her chair and letting the others put things in order. "Women didn't rate high on the things men thought they liked. Like bulging biceps or big shoulders."

Tommy looked distressed. He had a whole gymnasium built into his house for his body-building exercises.

"What *did* women prefer?" asked Simon, his curiosity piqued.

"Flat stomachs and beautiful asses!" Missy said with a voluptuous sigh. She patted Simon's hand consolingly. "Don't feel bad about this, Simon, because you're great on those, but hairy chests came in a vigorous third, as I remember."

Tommy's hand stole up under his jacket to stroke his chest. "I'd like to know Kei's preference," he said, and Simon saw signs of a little skirmish under the table as Tommy used his other hand to feel Kei up.

"It's really stupid," said Kei, hitching her chair away from Tommy, who moved his close to hers again. "You don't want to hear."

"All right, Kei," Simon said tartly. "Don't keep us in suspense. I suppose you like a man to look like an ape, too?"

"No, I have a thing about knees."

"Knees!" Missy sat back with a flop, her arms dangling down at the sides of her chair, and rolled her eyes up at the ceiling.

"The way the bones and tendons and muscles work together there," explained Kei. "And there's that smooth curve of muscle that goes upward on the back of the leg." She looked musing, as if she were seeing acres of knees in her mind, and pulled her blouse out. Simon suspected she was easing a pair of hot, sore nipples. "And brown hands, too, with square, pale nails."

Simon looked at his hands and felt smug.

"And forearms with big veins running underneath," Kei added and then looked embarrassed and began putting the drawers back in the teakwood box.

"You mean you women look us up and down like some damned piece of meat you're going to buy at the butcher's?" said Tommy, looking at his hands and finding them wanting. "You make my blood run cold!"

"I don't see why," Missy said contentiously, "when you men have been doing it to *us* forever. I've heard the ghastliest, squint-eyed prawns —creeps I wouldn't go to bed with for millions— rate a woman as a dog and laugh at her. The gall! You men think you're God's gift to women, no matter how ugly you are, just because of that thing between your legs. But let me tell you, you're all pretty much the same in bed, except some of you are worse than others!" She paused for breath. "Present company excepted, of course."

"Physique doesn't really matter if a man can make a woman laugh," said Kei. "That's the one thing that's guaranteed to make a woman fall into bed. I don't see why you're all so confounded serious about sex. Actually, what most women want is a man who can be . . . if they can enjoy themselves together. Every sexual encounter doesn't have to be a test of one's manhood."

"Oh, yes!" breathed Missy, her eyes bright. She squeezed Kei's hand in agreement and sisterhood. "They expect us to treat them like holy relics or something in bed. I can't count the number of times I've had to fake it just to build up some poor boob's ego!"

"This is disgusting," said Tommy, getting up. "I don't think I want to hear any more."

Simon was folding up the game table, laughing quietly to himself.

"Holy Mother of God!" Tommy flung his cigar into the cold fireplace. "I'd better throw out my weight-lifting equipment and get a ball and jacks!"

The women put the chairs back in place. As Kei passed him, Tommy reached out to give her breast a squeeze, and she slapped it away, hard.

"Hey, she's got Simon already, dammit!" said Missy. "Give me a break!" She attached herself to Tommy's arm, looking waiflike.

"Speaking of playing," said Tommy, "got any more fireworks?"

"In the foyer closet," said Simon, putting the black box away and feeling pleased that Kei wasn't falling for Tommy's maneuvers. "If we're going to fire them off, let me get a cassette player so we can have a musical accompaniment. You set things up in the meadow, and I'll get some tapes."

He took Kei's hand and led her into the study as Missy went out to help Tommy. The light made the birds set up a racket. He opened a closet door and ran his fingers over the titles of the cassette tapes on the shelf, saying, "Debussy, Debussy, Debussy,"

"Fauré?" asked Kei.

"*Parfait!*" Simon handed her half a dozen tapes and switched off the light. The birds twittered and called until they got out on the bridge in back.

"Where's the box?" said Simon to Tommy, who had the package of fireworks in his arms.

"I was saving that for Kei."

He put down the cassette player on the top step and took the tapes from Kei to make a pile of them before taking the hexagonal box and going down to place it a few feet away from the group. With his lighter, he lit the fuse at the bottom. White sparks shot out and spun the box around like a catherine wheel, round and round, propelled by the white fire. Then the sparks died, and Missy said, "Oh!" in disappointment. Suddenly the sides of the box popped up and up and up until it became a multi-storied pagoda with red flames glowing behind tiny windows, and the company cheered and clapped.

Tommy went down into the darkness of the meadow with the rest of the pyrotechnics, and Simon sat down on the top step and fed the cassette player with a De Larrocha tape that started with Fauré's *Fantaisie*. Missy sat down beside him, her yellow chiffon luminous in the light from the lamp over the back doors. Kei stood by the entrance, leaning against the jamb with a cigarette in her hand.

"Fire away!" called Simon, pressing the *play* button.

Piano notes cascaded into the blackness like a shower of sleet. A streak of gold shot up beyond the oak trees and flowered into an umbrella of falling sparks. Missy applauded, and Tommy's voice shouted "Bravo!" His lighter flame flared down in the meadow, and another rocket soared up and flung red balls into the sky, popping like a carnival shooting gallery.

Simon half rose, about to join Kei, when there was a loud *splat,* and Kei cried out and sprang away from the door, falling against the railing of the bridge. Magically, with no discernible lapse of time, Simon had her in his arms.

"What happened?" he said. Her mouth opened, but no sound came out. Her hair was flecked with chips of paint. Simon saw that a large leaf of wood had been torn out of the jamb, next to where her head had been. Jammed into the door frame was a large ball bearing, deeply buried in the wood.

"Get inside!" he said, giving her a push. "You too, Missy."

He ran down the steps into the darkness, across the meadow toward Tommy's shadowy bulk.

"What's the matter? Aren't I doing my job right?" asked Tommy, snapping on his lighter and kneeling to plant a rocket stick in the ground by its illumination.

"Where is it?" Simon demanded. "The sling-shot."

"Back home, I guess. I don't know. What do you want it for?"

Simon grabbed Tommy, pulled him to his feet, and began slapping at his pockets like a policeman searching a suspect.

"What the *hell* are you doing?" said Tommy aggrievedly.

"You've got a rotten sense of humor! You could have killed her, shooting a ball bearing at her!" There was nothing shaped like a sling-shot in Tommy's pockets.

"You son of a bitch, I don't shoot ball bearings

219

at women!" Tommy's fist crashed into Simon's jaw, knocking him to the ground. "Don't you mess around with me, accusing me of trying to kill people!"

Simon got up and felt his jaw, probing in his mouth to check his bridgework, which seemed intact. "Oh, shit, I'm sorry, Tommy," he said, working his jaw back and forth to ease the pain. "You were the only one out here, and I thought . . . "

"What were you going to do, beat me up?" Tommy said scornfully.

"If I had to."

"Well, obviously, I am *not* the only one out here. Whoever did it's probably scarpered by now. Anyway, it's too dark to look for anyone." He still sounded angry. "For all I know, you made the whole thing up."

"See for yourself. The ball bearing's embedded in the door."

They used their lighters to gather up the fireworks, and Simon turned off the cassette player and scooped it up with the tapes on his way into the house while Tommy inspected the damage to the door frame.

Simon locked the front and back doors of the foyer after Tommy had satisfied himself that someone had actually shot at Kei, and they both went into the study, where the birds set up their clamor again. Simon dialed Hilaire's number and waited several rings before Hilaire's sleepy voice answered.

"Let the dogs loose," said Simon, "and lock

your doors. There's been some trouble. I'll tell you about it in the morning."

The women were in the kitchen, where Kei was waiting for the tea kettle to boil and looking taut as a bowstring. Missy was perched on a stool in the corner, chiffon drooping about her, looking like a nervous canary in molt. Dirty dishes covered the table and were stacked on the counters. Tommy went about fussily consolidating the dishes into neat stacks and cleared off the tabletop.

Simon leaned back against the cupboard door and lit a cigarette after making sure that Kei was all right. Tommy sat down at the end of the table, but scooted his chair back with alacrity when Simon said that he was in a direct line with the window.

"I don't understand this at all," Missy said bewilderedly. "Maybe it was an accident."

"Brilliant!" said Tommy. "What would anybody be doing out there with a slingshot, shooting ball bearings around, in the first place? Don't be stupid."

"You know there are a lot of acidheads in the village," Missy said, straightening up and looking belligerent. "They could do any crazy thing. Who would want to kill Kei? And who are you calling stupid?"

Simon and Kei exchanged glances. There was only one person he knew who would want to get rid of Kei, and that person was fully capable of pulling a damn fool trick like that to scare her away.

221

"Well, why don't you big, strong men go out and see if you can find who did it?" challenged Missy.

"Too dark," said Tommy. "He wouldn't hang around this long."

The kettle sang, and Kei made tea, but Missy waved hers aside, saying, "Gimme a cigarette, for God's sake, somebody!" Simon supplied her with one and picked up a cup of tea and stood leaning back against the cupboard while Kei poured for Tommy.

"You have any idea who'd do a thing like that to you, Kei?" asked Tommy, loading his tea with sugar and stirring it noisily.

"None at all," she said firmly, looking at Simon.

"Holy mackerel, *I* was out there, too!" said Missy, looking electrified. "Maybe they were trying to hit *me*!"

"Somebody didn't like your last performance?" Tommy said. "There are critics everywhere."

"Oh, screw you, funny man!" said Missy.

"Would you people rather spend the night here?" asked Simon, putting down his tea. "There're masses of bedrooms."

"Not me!" said Missy, sliding off her stool. "The car's right by the door and the gate's open. I'm not staying anywhere that's got a maniac on the loose." She went over to kiss Simon and give him a long, melancholy look and said ruefully, "Better luck next time, hm?" She turned to Tommy and, with a jerk of her head toward

222

the foyer, said, "Let's go. I need a warm body next to me tonight."

Before going upstairs to bed, Simon got his revolver out of the desk and loaded it.

"You wouldn't use that on her," said Kei.

"We don't know it was Elaine."

"No."

They went slowly up the stairs, his arm around her shoulders and hers around his waist.

"I like Missy," said Kei.

"Yes."

They sat down on opposite sides of the bed and undressed without speaking, like an old married couple. Before getting into bed beside him, Kei went into her room and brought back the picture she used—not very successfully—as a talisman against nightmares. Recognizing the frame, Simon reached for it.

"Where did you get this?" he asked.

"It was on the dressing table," said Kei. "I think I fell in love with the boy you were before I fell in love with the man." She took it back and put it on the table at her side of the bed.

"Elaine's in the picture, too," Simon said.

"I know."

He looked at the revolver on the table at his side.

They lay on their backs, looking up at the ceiling. When she felt his tremors and knew that he was crying, Kei gathered him into her arms, and he fell asleep with his head on her breast.

CHAPTER SIXTEEN

The sleek, tawny pelt was dry and scruffy, and the great transparent eyes had gone flat and opaque. The creamy entrails were greasy with blood, hard to drag out of their cavity, and tasted sickeningly of saliva and vomit. A bell was tolling in the dark. Each stroke of sound swelled out into an iridescent bubble that broke softly into soapy fragments before the next one fell.

Simon awoke with a start, his pulse racing. The Sunday church bells were chiming in the village. A rooster crowed in Hilaire's chicken run. Kei lay with her back toward him. This time she'd slept through the night. He could see tiny golden hairs curving upwards on either side of her neck until they reached the brown and silver of her hairline. From across the table, two children with shiny chocolate drop eyes stared guilelessly at him from behind the safety of their glass enclosure in the gold frame.

Simon buried his nose in Kei's neck, snuffing up her sleepy scent, and ran a hand over her belly, tracing the silky striations of her stretch-marks with his fingertips. Here was where she'd held a baby. Not his. Never his, now. How must it feel to lose a child? He could not imagine what she'd gone through. It was beyond his powers of conjuration.

Unattached and uncommitted, he'd only skimmed over the surface of living, like a dry leaf blown across the ice. That was over now. He felt as if all the agony of the human condition was hanging over him, about to seize him and draw and quarter him. If Kei hadn't appeared, he'd still be safe.

He got up and went to the bathroom before his body got a mind of its own. Not that he got those instant erections as regularly in the mornings nowadays, but he didn't want to take any chances. He simply had to give his body a chance to recover. His jaw hurt where Tommy hit him, the scratches on his back itched — nothing like the maddening itch in his penis, though — and his lips were on fire and his nipples felt like hell. One of the bandaids was dangling. Biting his lip as a counter-irritant, he tore it off. Jeeeeezus! Some of the skin came with it, leaving a single red drop behind. His balls felt sore, but at least his leg was back to normal and the bite mark on his chest had faded, be thankful for small favors. Either a feast or a famine, dammit. He felt a hundred years old.

After a shave and a shower, he only felt eighty years old. He tipped up the bottle of Beaujolais that had been in the refrigerator, drained it, and dropped the empty into the wastebasket.

Now he felt a fragile seventy, and that was as far down as he'd come this morning, he figured.

Kei was sitting up in bed, looking radiant, and the very sight of her made him feel fatigued. "Don't touch," he said, leaning over to kiss her. "Want to come for a ride? I can teach you. Barney's as gentle as a maiden's sigh."

"I don't feel up to sitting in that position right now, thank you. Someday. Besides, I have to pack. My plane's this morning. May I take the Mercedes?"

"I'd better drive you," he said, getting his riding clothes out of the closet. "The seats smell mildewy where Hilaire hosed them, and I'd better take the car to the garage Monday, when you're gone."

"Oh dear, I'm sorry about that. I should give up smoking."

"Me, too. My first two fingers are permanently Chinese." He stopped to look in the full-length mirror on the back of the closet door. He did not find his knees inspiring, but women's minds were the enigma of the ages. The world might go unisex in some areas, but the twain were never going to meet on all scores. You could put a woman in an executive position where she could rule an industrial empire, but incontrovertibly she could not grow a beard or pee against a wall.

"Do you think it's safe for you on the path?" Kei asked, sitting up in bed.

"I'm afraid so."

He dressed and pulled on his boots while she went into the bathroom. The revolver went into his pocket so he could return it to the study. He pulled his navy and green soccer shirt down

226

to hide the bulge it made in his pocket, in case Marthe happened by.

On the way back to the château after riding, he stopped to talk — as elliptically as he could — with Hilaire about last night's events, putting the cause to some addict from the village, and telling him to keep it quiet. The last thing Simon wanted was police nosing around the place. Hilaire's doggy eyes bulged, and his French got too fast to follow, but Simon gathered that Hilaire was going to make a circuit of the estate — to what purpose, only Hilaire knew.

A Chopin ballade floated out across the calico meadow, perfectly in tune with the morning's freshness. Something else he hadn't known about Kei. The middle A was a bit off. Better get a tuner in. Simon's own untutored pounding on the concert grand didn't do it any good.

Kei was wearing a silver-beige suit of light suede, and her suitcase was leaning against the legs of the piano. He lifted the hair on the back of her neck and kissed her above the thin gold chain holding her locket.

"Miss you," he said."

"I wish I didn't have to go," she said, turning around on the stool. "Marthe's holding your breakfast. Can you take me now? My plane's due in forty-five minutes."

"Isn't that a little early?"

"I'm always afraid of being late." She took a mirror out of her lizardskin bag and looked at her face. "Please don't wait with me," she said, adding some gloss to her lips. "I'm a sniveling craven about flying, and I want to worry in the waiting area without any distractions."

She brought a towel out with her to lay across the car seat as a protection against the residual dampness from Hilaire's hosing out the interior. "Could you sort of creep along?" she asked, getting in. "Your driving . . . "

"I *told* you I was showing off that day. I never drive like that. Never!" He got in beside her and turned on the ignition.

The green of the French countryside had an intensity he'd never seen in America. Often, when hung over, he'd thought it was *too* green. Sickening. By way of contrast, the farmhouses were a shabby gray. A new one just being built had a flag stuck in the chimney to show it was still under construction. The Loire glinted in the distance, a broad, shallow expanse of brown with sand bars lying in it like submerged whales and trees with feathery moss-green foliage fringing its banks. They passed through small villages on the way to town, where houses sat flush with the sidewalks, as did the shuttered stores. Thin-legged boys with apple cheeks practiced soccer shots in the empty streets.

"Of course, you'd have to give up the business if we got married," Simon said, thinking out loud.

"Is that a proposal, and what the hell do you mean?" Kei sounded angry.

228

"Yes," he said, veering over the center line in surprise for a few seconds. "I mean, yes, I'm asking you to marry me. Is that too old-fashioned for you? I always had this funny notion that if I ever found a woman I loved, I'd rather like to live with her."

They were back in the country now, passing mowed fields and low gray farmhouses.

"Great God, you don't know whether or not I've killed a man! You can't marry a murderess. I don't even know if I'll wind up in prison." Kei said. "And as for selling the family business just to gratify your macho image . . . "

"All right, all right!" His foot came down hard on the accelerator. "I don't believe for a minute that you killed that fellow. And whose side are you arguing on, anyway? Yesterday *I* was the one who wasn't fit for marriage, and now it's you?" Simon said, exasperated. "And I'll concede that your business is as important to you as mine is to me. I'm not dead sure I want to retire, either. But don't you think we've earned a rest?" They were tearing along the highway now. "How many years have we got left? Fifteen? Twenty? How can I carry you off to Samarkand if you're attached to an office by a telephone line?"

"We'd never get along. I'm a liberal, and you're so conservative that your idea of rebelling against your parents was buying Chippendale because they had Queen Anne furniture. I can't imagine myself listening to your reactionary potherings every morning when you read the newspaper."

"What does that have to do with anything? I love you, and you love me. Granted, I'm traditional. In addition, I'm egocentric, set in my ways, and impossibly selfish, and I'd insist on being the center of your attention. I'm a twenty-four-hour proposition, take it or leave it. But you love me, don't deny it!"

"That doesn't mean I've lost my mind! You can't expect me to sell the businesses just because you're a male chauvinist pig!"

"What kind of a home life do you think we'd have, with you running off to America to oversee the presses all the time?" The landscape was whizzing by.

"A home life?" She braced herself against the dashboard. "Is that what you call it, with your friend pinching me under the table and old girlfriends kissing you in front of me and your sister trying to kill me?"

"That's not fair! They're nothing to do with me. I'm not responsible for their behavior."

"I hate your political views!"

"You haven't *got* any!"

"And I'm afraid that I'd *like* it, waiting on you hand and foot, ironing your shirts fondly just because they were going to go on your precious body, bringing you your pipe and slippers. I'd get content and fat and mindless . . . "

"Don't make me laugh! You're about as submissive as Attila the Hun. And Marthe sends out the laundry anyway."

"You're doing it again!" she wailed. "Slow down!" She covered her eyes with her hands.

"My God, look out for that chicken!"

When they both quit panicking and the car settled back to a reasonable speed, he said, "Moreover, you don't know for sure that it was Elaine who shot at you. I'll talk to her today and get this whole thing cleared up. Once she's gone and out of the picture, maybe you can let us both forget the past for a couple of seconds. In the meantime, I'll thank you to remember that she's my sister!"

They were at the edge of town, by the restaurant where they were to have gone to dinner last night. The little wooden booths on the square were closed up for Sunday, and the merry-go-round was wearing a gray tarpaulin. The buildings bordering the river still looked medieval with blue slate roofs, and antique row houses with balconies lined the city streets, but high-rise apartments were mushrooming on the outskirts of town, lending a jarringly American tone that saddened Simon.

"I'm going into London to sell the businesses anyway," Kei said in a low, grumbly voice. "To sign the papers of sale. I'll stay on the boards of both houses, but I decided to hand over the management before I got the divorce."

They drove out the airport road in silence. Simon reflected that there might be times in the years ahead — if they had any — when he'd want to throttle Kei. Why couldn't he have chosen someone more malleable and less complicated to fall in love with?

"It's the principle of the thing," she said stubbornly as they passed a blue and white sign saying *Aeroport*. "You're positively antediluvian!"

Simon pulled into the parking lot, but Kei said, "Don't come in with me. I'd hate for us to be screaming at each other in front of people. You know how to get under my skin more than anybody I've ever met!"

He drove out of the lot and stopped in front of the terminal entrance, then got out, helped her from the car, and gave her her case. She hitched the strap over her shoulder.

That she looked as she had when she came in on the train frightened him. Was she on her way out of his life again? Why should she come back? All he could offer her was shame and sorrow and constant arguments. He was too flawed— a grotesque she should have nothing to do with. If she was smart, she'd run and keep running. He couldn't blame her if she did.

"Come back," he said. "Come back and marry me."

She gave him a peck on the cheek and walked off toward the door.

"Well, yes or no?" he called.

"I'll think about it," she called back. But she blew him a kiss.

Marthe was concerned about how little of the kidneys he ate. She picked up the glass he'd emptied of scotch as if it had held a urine specimen and shook her head at him.

Simon brooded, chin in hand. Marriage! He'd demanded it, and he didn't even know if he was up to it or not. It took a hell of a lot of sexuality to keep one woman satisfied. To say nothing of ingenuity and plain, raw stamina. God knows, Kei wasn't one to close her eyes and think of England. If all this juice and joy didn't wear off pretty promptly, he'd be reduced to a limp rag. He scratched his crotch. She was a decade younger than he was, and if he bored her, Tommy would be lying in wait, ready to drag her off into the bushes.

And perhaps he couldn't adjust to living with someone else. God, she'd rearrange the paintings and leave wet stockings all over the bathroom! She'd make him finish everything he started, too, instead of letting him leave half-finished projects around when his initial enthusiasm wore off. That was a side of him she didn't even know about yet.

And when they were together, all they seemed to do was quarrel. Every headline would be a cause for contention.

He brightened. Maybe she'd decide she didn't want to marry into the jungle he lived in. She might stay in London and send a telegram asking to have her things sent back. He chewed a hangnail. But life without her was more than he could face.

He didn't even like to have her out of his sight. He wasn't happy about her going over to help Rudy with his translations, particularly after what Elaine had said about him. Apparently, there was a tiger hiding under that shy exterior. Kei would be seeing Jeremy Kirbottle in London, too.

But that was all right. Jeremy struck Simon as the kind who only liked young boys with downy behinds. It wasn't all right, though, if Kei didn't know that and took a fancy to him. Jeremy wasn't the only man in London, either. She probably knew plenty of others, who were younger and who had left their sisters alone. Uncomplicated others. They'd be refreshing after being immersed in this poisonous atmosphere. She might be—he looked at his watch—in bed with one of them right now.

He stood up and threw his napkin down on the table. He'd have to stop this or he'd drive himself crazy. He ought to be seeing Elaine and getting something constructive accomplished.

The streets of the village were deserted, except for the forest woodcutter cycling along with his saw strapped to his back. He touched his cap to Simon, who nodded and wondered if Kei's imagination hadn't been working overtime. The villagers seemed as friendly as ever.

As he went by the drygoods store, Simon's eye was caught by a display of wooden slingshots in the window, a couple of dozen of them, exactly like the one Elaine had given to Tommy. A sign advertised that they were useful in eradicating pests. Simon smiled grimly.

Elaine's house on the Rue Orloff had gray spatterdash walls, a mansard roof, and romanesque windows bordered in ugly red and white brickwork.

She was wearing a jade silk kimono embroidered with gold phoenixes and the thin link necklace of iron she'd taken to wearing lately. Her feet were bare. Unsurprised to see him at the door, she stood back to let him in, and he went into the white living room and sat down on the white leather couch without a word.

"I'll get your scotch," she said, and padded away.

Without the warmth of the wood paneling, the white walls, white furniture, and white statuary—mostly of graveyard angels—would have been chilling. Even the pillows scattered on the furniture and the big poufs on the floor by the fireplace were of textured cream or white—linen, corduroy, and velvet. A white porcelain oven seven feet high, an antique from Austria, stood against one wall on curved legs. Over the couch was a large watercolor pentagram. More of Elaine's witchcraft nonsense. Tlingit Indian masks painted in black and primary colors scowled down from the walls.

Simon rubbed his jaw where Tommy had hit him, making it hurt worse. He lit a cigarette on the glowing cone of incense in an iron burner on the coffee table and sneezed.

"It doesn't look like you're getting ready to move," he said as Elaine came in with his drink.

She served him and then sat down in a white wicker peacock chair like a summer throne and said, "I'm not." She held a drink made of grenadine and gin. It looked like a glass of blood.

"I thought I'd made it plain . . . " Simon began.

"Oh, abundantly plain," she interrupted. "But

235

there's a little something I've never told you about." She opened a drawer in the black chest by her chair, took a packet out, tossed it over into his lap, and sat back with a small, self-assured smile.

It was a bundle of letters tied together with a red cord, a photograph on top. Simon took out his reading glasses, untied the cord, looked at the photograph, and felt as if a hammer had come down on his chest.

"Remember about sixteen years ago, when I went to Switzerland for a few months?" said Elaine.

The boy had shiny chocolate drop eyes and a perfect Eagleton mouth.

"That's Simon," Elaine said. "Not Junior, of course, I'm not crazy. But sisters often name their children for their brothers, don't they? No one would think anything of that."

She crossed her legs, showing him the bottom of a dirty foot. The paper fluttered as he read the letters. They were addressed to "Mother" and told of school, of soccer games and girlfriends, and the trivia of adolescent life.

'I told him his father was killed in a car accident before we could get married. Maybe you realize now why I've been so expensive all of these years."

"Where is he?" Simon heard his voice tremble.

"On Cape Cod. You know I always spend the summers and holidays there. I'm surprised you never wondered why."

After looking at it again, Simon put the picture

236

in his shirt pocket, put away his glasses, and re-tied the letters. He placed the packet gently on the glass coffee table and took a long swallow of scotch. An enormous lassitude spread through his limbs. The glass seemed too heavy to hold, and he put it down.

"Now you see why I'm not moving," Elaine went on, sounding confident that she had the whip hand at last. "You aren't going to get involved with Kei. I could see at a glance that your relationship with her was different. I can read you like a book. But you aren't going to get involved with *anybody*. We're going to go along just as we were. Except maybe you're going to be a little more understanding about my expenditures now."

Simon put his elbows on his knees and clasped his hands together to make them stop shaking. "Just one thing. If you had this trump card in your hand, why did you try to kill Kei last night?"

"What are you talking about?" She had him tell her everything and then claimed total innocence. "I don't have to kill anybody," she said, smiling victoriously. "If you don't get rid of her yourself, I'll tell Simon who his father really is. I never knew a man who loved children the way you do, and you wouldn't want to hurt your own son that way. You'd die, rather than do that. I know you."

"I want him."

"I knew you would. That's what makes it so simple." She moved over onto the couch with him. "It's a bit awkward, but between us we can come up with a story that will satisfy everybody, and he won't suspect a thing. He needs a family after being alone so much. I'll bring him here to live with me. You can see him every day. Or we could move into the château with you."

She put a hand on his cheek. He slapped it away.

"I want you to make arrangements to fly him over here," he commanded. "Immediately."

"If you say so. Poor Simon, I know it's a shock now, but you'll be glad. It'll be wonderful, just the three of us. And you and I can go back to being the way we were, years ago."

She took his hand and put it inside her kimono, squeezing it around the breast he knew so well. Simon recoiled as if her flesh had been red-hot metal and, with icy precision, slapped her hard across the face.

Before he knew what was happening, his hands were around her throat, his fingers buried deep. Grinding a knee down on her groin, he throttled her until she choked and retched, her face purpling and her arms flailing at him. Appalled by his own violence, he sat back on his knees, shaking, and then got up and went to the door. Before he left, he looked back and saw that she was sitting up, her hands around her neck, and looking strangely content.

Outside, he leaned against the wall of the house with his face away from the street and waited for the waves of nausea to pass. His trembling was making the change in his pockets jingle. Finally, he felt his shirt pocket to be sure that the photograph was still there and made his way along the street toward Tommy's on unsteady legs, walking like a convalescent after a long illness. He didn't want to be alone.

"Where's Kei? Why isn't she with you?" asked Tommy, secateurs in hand. He was wearing shorts and a T-shirt and his arms were covered with long scratches. A thorny pile of rose canes lay at his feet.

"She's off to London. I took her to the airport an hour or so ago."

The garden looked straggly and the color seemed drained out of it. Everything looked grayish and fuzzy around the edges to Simon. Tommy's voice sounded tinny in his ears.

"Did you see her go?"

"She wouldn't let me. Why?"

"I'd feel better if you called to see she got in all right." Tommy dropped cut stems on the ground and Simon moved back automatically to keep his boots from getting scratched.

"Look, she's a grown woman and won't appreciate my nursemaiding her. What is all this?"

"I'd just feel better about it, that's all." Tommy put the cutters in his pocket and knelt down to gather the cuttings together. "Missy's probably on the same plane. I dropped her out there awhile ago. We must have just missed running into each other." He stuffed the trash into a plastic lawn bag, exclaimed, and stuck a thumb in his mouth.

239

"Teach me to forget to wear gloves," he said to himself and twisted a plastic closer around the mouth of the bag. Looking up at Simon, he said, "Jesus, you didn't look as if you had *that* much to drink last night! That must be some hangover to make you look like that." He hoisted the bag of cuttings onto his shoulder and led the way up to the terrace. "What's Kei going to London for?"

"Business," Simon said shortly, tiring of the conversation and wanting to sit down and think things over quietly.

"What kind of business would a secretary have in London?"

"She's going to see Jeremy Kirbottle. You know he recommended her to me," Simon said evasively. "And what's this sudden interest in Kei? I don't want to play games with you over her."

"Never fear," said Tommy. "You look like you could do with a drink. Scotch?"

"I'd rather have a cold beer."

"Beer it is." Tommy went on into the house and Simon slumped into a chair by the table, as loose-jointed as a marionette with its strings cut. He pulled out the photograph to study it again.

It was eerie to see his own mouth on that young face. The boy was sturdier than he had been at that age, but his forelock fell into his face the way his used to. Still did, when he was disheveled. How could someone that close to him have existed for sixteen years without his being aware of it subliminally somehow, in his cells or nerve ends?

That bitch! He remembered the feel of squeezing Elaine's neck in his hands. The intense pleasure it had given him was shaming, but my God! What must it have been like for the boy, knowing he was a bastard, having an absentee mother, thinking he was fatherless? What could the boy be like, with parents like them?

His stomach turned over as he recalled wakening to find himself humping her after she'd invaded his bed and handled him expertly—not sure he wasn't still asleep and dreaming it, not quite certain who she was, in too deep to stop. Or when he was drunk and she'd argue that it was nothing new, that the damage was already done, and it would all sound so reasonable and harmless. A private matter between dearest friends, consenting adults, *family*.

Kei would leave him now. He could see her in his mind's eye, dwindling in the distance, her figure growing smaller and smaller as she walked away from him, until she disappeared.

"Did I hear marriage bells last night?" Tommy said, setting down a tray with bottles and glasses and joining Simon at the table. "Slap me down if I'm being nosy, but there was something in your eye that looked like you meant business."

Simon put the picture back in his shirt pocket. "I don't think so. I don't think she'd want me."

"Sorry. I know how it is." Tommy tilted up his bottle of beer. His Adam's apple traveled up and down as he swallowed.

"No, you *don't* know how it is," Simon said sourly, pouring himself a glass and then drinking

241

half of it down.

Tommy detached his mouth from the bottle stem with a loud pop and brushed droplets of water off his T-shirt. "Beg to differ, friend. I've never been able to persuade the woman I want to marry me. She won't have me, and the substitutes have been disastrous, as you know. It's foul, being married to one woman and being in love with another." He gave a tremendous sigh and belched.

Simon wondered who the woman had been who had got away but thought it better not to ask and open old wounds. Besides, his own misery was so global that there wasn't room for worry about anyone else's problems.

"*They* think it's a bit of a giggle, having a string of marriages. Very light-hearted and ha-ha," said Tommy, slouching down and looking glum. "But divorces carve you into pieces, to say nothing of the scenes leading up to them. And do *they* let me suffer in peace, in private like ordinary folk? Damned if they do! Just because I was in films, if I fart, it's the shot heard round the world!"

He reached down and savagely wrenched a shepherd's purse plant out from amongst the flagstones by his chair. He deposited it on the drinks trays, to be disposed of later, and said, "Oh, by the way, the slingshot's down there at your feet, right where I left it the night we were shooting off fireworks."

"Tommy . . . " Simon began, but his friend held up a hand.

242

"Say no more about it. I presume you spoke before you thought, and I more than evened the score on your jaw. Find out anything new?"

Simon shook his head. He was having trouble following the conversation. Lord, he wished Tommy would go away, so he could think! He finished off his beer and set the bottle down on the grass.

"Cold," said Tommy and got up and went into the house.

Good. Simon sat and tried to go over the facts in his mind, but his thoughts were sluggish and wouldn't come together sensibly. The inside of his head seemed to be an enormous, aching fog. Monday. He wished it were Monday. Then he could go out and buy something he couldn't afford. That was guaranteed to cheer him up — until the bills came in. Maybe Oedipus Rex could have saved his eyes by going on a grand shopping spree. Their problems, Simon thought bleakly, shared certain elements.

Tommy had changed into a pair of jeans and a red and black plaid lumberjack shirt. He tossed Simon a thick white sweater with a shawl collar, and Simon listlessly fumbled his way into it. Tommy set down glasses on the grass, opened a bottle of aquavit and, when Simon waved away his offer of some, sloshed a hearty dose into his own glass and sat back down.

Simon was aware enough to be surprised. He hadn't seen Tommy take a drink of hard liquor in years, and aquavit could blow the top of your head off. Tommy took a long swallow, coughed, and sat tapping the glass against his lips, staring out at the garden, which was beginning to look seedy.

"I haven't wanted to bring this up," Tommy said finally, "but I haven't any choice. Everybody's going to be hurt badly if I don't."

"What is it now?" What else could happen? No matter what it was, it couldn't reach him now.

"You'd better brace yourself." Tommy took up the glass by Simon's chair, poured him a drink, and handed it to Simon, nodding at him to swallow some. Simon had never seen him look so serious. The liquor went down his throat like flame and spread fiery tendrils out through his chest. "Have you noticed that iron chain Elaine's been wearing around her neck?" Tommy asked.

"Yes. Ugly, isn't it?" Simon took another sip of the aquavit.

"Uglier than you have any idea." Tommy set his empty glass on the table. "It means she's a member of the satanic cult that's been tearing the entrails out of cattle around here." Simon choked on his drink. "They're the ones who've been taking the dead babies from the hospital that Jeanne-Marie told you about."

"Oh, come off it," said Simon huskily, trying to get his breath back. "You're not funny." He set his glass on the table.

Tommy turned and looked at him intensely. "They boil them down to get the fat to make candles for their ceremonies. No, I'm sorry," he said, observing Simon's disbelief, "they do. And when their spells don't work—and of course they don't—they're not above murder to get what they want. If they had even a question about retribution in the afterlife, it might slow them down. But they only believe in one go-around, so there's no payoff like hell to be afraid of, and the local gendarmes are too slow-witted to catch them at anything. Too terrified of them as well." He reached out and grabbed Simon by the collar of his sweater. "God dammit, are you listening to me?"

"Yes, I'm listening, but you really don't expect me to believe that claptrap, do you?" Simon said, pulling back and trying to get his collar out of Tommy's grasp.

Tommy twisted the collar tight in his hand, drawing Simon's face closer and looking at him fiercely. "I know what I'm talking about," he said. "They *are* trying to kill Kei. Why, I don't know. I didn't want to frighten her or Missy, but when Kei gets back, you've got to keep her under lock and key." At that, he let Simon go and sat back to stare at the garden again.

Simon was stunned into silence. The implications were almost more than he could get his mind around.

Not Elaine. Silly Elaine, with her mumbo jumbo, playing at being a witch. Not Elaine.

The rest of them were downstairs, so he could go in and look at it. He went into the little room that had been his and pushed his face against the bars. All squashed up, it looked. Funny.

He reached through the bars and patted the mound in the middle. Soft. Nice. Something twined around his finger and held it fast. Pink. Tiny little fingernails. He pulled his hand back, but it wouldn't let go. It was going to keep him! Frightened, he yanked away and it went off! It screamed.

"What are you doing, Simon?" His mother's voice startled him. "Don't touch her! You'll hurt her, bad boy!"

He blinked. Elaine. His sister. The mother of his child. He ground both fists into his stomach to stop the pain, doubling over.

"Hey there!" Tommy was on his knees, his hands on Simon's shoulders, looking into his face. "Is it your heart? You need a doctor?"

"No," Simon gasped. "Just wait a minute." The spasm passed in a moment. He shot out a hand and caught Tommy by the sleeve. "If you're wrong about this, I'll kill you! I don't want it to be true, but if you're lying, I'll kill you!"

"You sure you're all right?" Tommy's forehead was wrinkled like an accordion, his eyes concerned.

"Yes. Yes." Simon sat back and rubbed his forehead, digging his fingers into his temples. There was nothing wrong with his heart. The muscle in his chest was perfectly sound.

Tommy looked doubtfully at him but got up off his knees and sat down in his chair, still watching him closely.

"How do you know about this?" Simon's throat was so tight it was hard to get the words out.

"We've been watching. We . . . forced an orderly

246

into admitting that he'd passed one of the . . . It was a stillborn, deformed so the doctor didn't want the mother to see it. Elaine took it." Tommy's eyes were bright with tears.

"We?" said Simon after a moment.

"I'm the head of the local Wicca coven. A white witch. As different from a Satanist as night from day, believe me. An entirely different thing. The old earth religion," Tommy said gently. "I was born into it."

"My God, I've never known you!" Simon cried. "All these years, and I've never known you!" He lurched to his feet. "And Elaine—do I know her?" The ground tilted and then righted itself. "But there's one person I *do* know," he said wildly. "I know *myself!* Jesus Christ, *how* I know myself!"

Tommy grabbed him as he started off across the garden and held him to the spot. "You can't go home like this," he said, but Simon wrenched away.

"Yes, I can. Just leave me alone. *Leave me alone!*"

He had no memory of passing through the town, of opening the gate, of coming up the stairs, yet here he was in Kei's bedroom. He flung open the door of her wardrobe and began searching, throwing her clothes on the floor, yanking out the hangers and tossing them behind him, until he found it. The cream-colored nightgown. "Oh, my God, my God, my God!" he whispered, pressing it to his face, inhaling the faint human odors

247

still caught in its fibers. Slowly he closed the door of the wardrobe and leaned his back against it, then let himself slide down onto the floor, where he sat with his knees bent up in front. He spread the nightgown out across his knees and smoothed it with his hand and smoothed it and smoothed it.

He jerked up out of sleep at the sound of the telephone shrilling on the bedside table. Stiffly, he unfolded himself and got up to answer it.

"Are you all right?" asked Tommy's voice.

Simon rubbed his cheek where his knee had pressed against it. It was as hot as if he had a fever. "Yes, I'm okay," he said and ran a hand back through his hair to get it off his forehead.

"You sound odd," Tommy said, sounding dubious.

Simon cleared his throat. "I fell asleep. You woke me up."

"Short sleep. You only left twenty minutes ago. Do you want me to come over and stay with you?"

"No, thanks. I'd rather be alone right now."

It was noon. Simon put the nightgown back in the wardrobe, picked up Kei's clothing, and put it away again.

Down in the kitchen, he stood at the sink and ate a couple of the Hostess Twinkies he had air expressed in every month and drank a bottle of Coke, but he couldn't taste anything. What was he going to do with himself for the rest of the day? If he sat around and thought,

he'd go mad, and dictating the life story of someone he disliked as intensely as himself seemed
insupportable.

Out of desperation, he changed clothes, got
out the car, and went into town to see a movie.
The only one in English was something dreadful
about the Russian Revolution, one of those Souls-
Torn-Asunder affairs with dialogue that made the
hero sound like an escapee from a home for the
feeble-minded. Unbelievingly, Simon watched a
love scene in which the man said, "You make
me feel like a schoolboy," and ground his teeth.
Only popcorn, which the French theaters didn't
sell, could have gotten him through the ordeal.
The French subtitles kept catching his eye, making
him read them so that he couldn't follow the
spoken English, and he couldn't figure out who
was on which side in the war. He left in the middle of the film.

Morbidly curious, he drove over to St. Denis
to see the Poisson d'Or, where Alexis Michaelson had been billeted, and couldn't find any such
place, although the town was too small for him
to have missed the sign. As Kei had said, it was
a long time ago.

He searched out Moody in his jumbled studio
and negotiated for a settlement with the artist's
contact for selling the Renoir. Having some crook
hunting him down to collect money was an ele-
ment Simon didn't want added to the witch's
brew he'd already stirred up. Moody was abjectly
apologetic and pressed a Christian Science *Sentinel*
into Simon's hand when he left.

Back home, he didn't want to go for a walk; it was too early for the television programs, he couldn't concentrate on reading, he didn't want to take Maeve out.

He went into the study and picked up the London telephone book, thinking of calling Kei, and then decided he couldn't risk blurting out the new developments to her. She'd never come back if she knew. Saturated with ennui, his stomach queasy, he went through the A's in the telephone book and circled all the funny names.

It seemed a futile operation to dig the ball bearing out of the door frame, since he couldn't go to the police even if there were fingerprints on it, but he went out and did it doggedly, making a note on a 3 x 5 card that the carpenter should be called in to make repairs. Without much hope, he searched the undergrowth around the meadow for the slingshot and found nothing. There were no clues, either, as to where a body might be buried.

As he sat on the bridge in the twilight, watching the dogs snap at white moths rising out of the damp grass and the mist rolling in across the meadow, the telephone rang. The line was dead when he reached it. He sat at his desk and looked at the phone. He couldn't call Kei. What she knew already about him was more than any woman should be expected to accept, and the illegitimate child of an incestuous union would tear it completely. If, as Tommy said, the Satanists here were trying to kill her, she should stay in London. But how did he know she was safe there? Devil

250

worshippers could buy airline tickets, just as normal people could. At least, if she were here, he could keep an eye on her, protect her.

God dammit, he wanted to hear her voice!

He called her hotel.

"I just tried to reach you," she said, and his spirits lifted. In spite of himself, knowing better, he told her everything.

She didn't respond, and he shouted "Hello?" into the mouthpiece three times before she said, "I'm here. Just give me a moment to recover." He listened to her breathe. "One thing's sure," she said at last, "I'm not going to let you go through this alone. I'll be back on the plane tomorrow. We'll take it from there." She paused. "Missy sends her love. So do I." She rang off.

Simon got up, did a flamenco step, clicking his heels on the parquet, and went whistling out to wrestle with the dogs.

CHAPTER SEVENTEEN

Dear Chris:

Just a note from London, which is about all I can manage after Missy Hilliard's run my feet off all day. I know I'm getting to sound like a namedropper, but that's the kind of people in Simon's circle. People without money don't buy expensive original paintings, you know. Missy is one of his ex-amours and we were on the same plane. To add to the list of names, I spent a day shopping in Paris with Elaine and the elusive artist Moody. A very handsome fellow, but very, very quiet. Like talking to a tree.

Tomorrow I become a free woman, more or less, when Jeremy Kirbottle takes over Landsend House and Michael Dykstra and Taras Mihailoff make Bell Tree Press into a partnership. I always hoped Stephen would carry on, and it isn't easy, seeing everything pass out of the family's hands after all these years, but I'm just lucky that the businesses didn't fall apart completely when I was going to pieces myself. If it hadn't been for the able people who took over then, we could have kissed both presses goodbye. Anyway, all that will be behind me now, and I'm not going to look back or carry around old regrets.

Chris, things are in a terrible mess otherwise, but I'll have to postpone telling you about it until I get back to the château and the typewriter. I'm just too fagged to write a long letter by hand. To give you some idea, though, it's like being in the middle of a particularly bad soap opera. In fact, no writer would have the nerve to write it into a script, because he couldn't sell it. It's too unbelievable. Unfortunately, life doesn't follow the rules of drama.

I'm signing off now to go have a drink with Missy. I need it!

Having a lousy time, but oh how I wish you were here!

Kei

253

CHAPTER EIGHTEEN

There was no salvaging the seats, which smelled like woollen mittens left to dry on a radiator. The imperious mechanic at the garage in Orléans wouldn't deign to estimate how long it would take to get them replaced. He was not in possession of a crystal ball, he said snippily, and couldn't be expected to know whether or not duplicates were readily available from Paris.

Disgruntled, Simon took a cab back to the château. It was a longish ride, about 18 kilometers. The summer colors had left the landscape along the way. Autumn was almost here, with a sky as clear and bright as turquoise enamel and a hint of crispness in the air. He'd been glad of the chamois vest he'd put on over his thick-ribbed gray turtleneck sweater on the way into town, but the sun was baking through the window, and he rolled it down to let the air in.

He felt infinitely better this morning, having figured out at about two o'clock in the morning that Tommy had already boozed up by the time he'd gone over there and had let his actor's sense

254

of drama carry him away. Perhaps Elaine was flirting with a Satanic cult to amuse herself, but Tommy had fallen off the wagon with a crash and blown up the story into a horror tale. It had been about all Simon could manage, when he'd put the pieces together, to keep from going over there, waking Tommy up, and working him over for putting him through the worst day of his life.

Kei would be back on the afternoon plane. Perhaps, when he told her the Satanic cult connection was one of Tommy's theatricalities, it would be enough of a relief to her to take some of the curse off the development about young Simon.

For the first time in his life, Simon was up against a situation that he didn't want to face alone. With Kei by his side, anything was possible, anything might be weathered. If —*if* she really loved him enough to stand by him. To marry him. Anything less would be too impermanent, too easily broken when the going got tough. In any case, he wanted her with him for the rest of his life. Period. Full stop.

He slouched down in the sunlight with the breeze from the window whipping his hair about his face and tried to catch up on his lost sleep. As for Elaine, he had a hunch that, if he and Kei turned up married, she'd back down and accept it. Her threat to tell the boy who his real father was would be useless then. She wouldn't hurt her own child out of sheer bloody-mindedness, surely.

Back at the château, still sleepless, and itchy with waiting for Kei, he set about getting household tasks done. He called the carpenter to ask him to fix the door, but the word for "door" escaped him and he simply said to come over immediately, which should bring the workman around in a week or so. Then he asked Hilaire to take the pink cockatoo to the vet's before it scratched the rest of the feathers off its neck. He went out to the barn and was irked to find that Fournier had already left for the fields—the man was never around when he was wanted lately. Simon made out a long list of directions and questions and wedged it into the side of Fournier's apartment door, then walked back toward the house.

It wouldn't be long now before the woods were auburn, gold, and brown and the paths were squishy underfoot with wet leaves. How expensive would it be to have the stones of the grotto dug out and the whole area bulldozed flat? Prohibitive, probably. Wouldn't it be lovely to tie up the real estate agent and dump him at the grotto to spend the night, maybe showing up at the witching hour in a black robe and moaning to scare the spit out of him? Serve him right!

Back at the château, Tommy was standing in the hallway with a giant wearing jeans and a plaid shirt. The presence of the stranger stifled Simon's impulse to have it out then and there with Tommy about yesterday's drama.

"This is Loquat Halsey," said Tommy. "What's for lunch?"

Mr. Halsey removed his straw cowboy hat, revealing a shoulder-length shock of red-gold hair that looked as if it crackled with electricity, put the hat over his heart, and said, "A pleasure, Mr. Eagleton," in a mellifluous basso. His outsized eyes were gray, piercing as laser beams, and his smile was disarming.

"I don't know what Marthe's fixing," said Simon, unable to take his eyes off Halsey, who gave off so much energy even standing still that he gave the impression of being in motion, about to accomplish something rapid and surprising. "I'd better tell her there will be three of us. Help yourselves to a drink."

Marthe was long inured to having unexpected guests pop up. She only hit the roof when more than a dozen were forced on her. A restaurant-sized refrigerator, always well stocked, and a raid on Hilaire's vegetable garden could handle most emergencies. Two extra guests for lunch were a mere nothing, but she was disturbed that some cups and saucers were missing.

"They went out with the trash," said Simon, getting out a cold beer. "I'm afraid I lost my temper again."

Marthe shook her head and looked long-suffering, having heard that before. "We need a new suite of plates," she said. "One of this, two of this. Not correct. A man should control his temper."

"Later," said Simon, who tended to get testy when mothered. He took the beer into the sitting room, where Loquat Halsey was pacing from corner to corner as if he were measuring the area for a rug.

"What's he doing?" Simon said out of the corner of his mouth to Tommy, who was making lemon zests at the bar.

"Feeling out the atmosphere of the house. He's a sensitive."

Simon poured his beer into a glass and waited. When nothing further was forthcoming, he said, "A sensitive what?"

"You know, a psychic," Tommy answered, putting the zests into a gin and tonic, confirming Simon's suspicions that he was back on the bottle. "Loquat's a high priest of Wicca. A big one, the head of all the white witchcraft covens in Wales."

"And you're the head of the local coven," Simon said ironically, playing into the charade.

Tommy nodded and sipped his drink, then bared his teeth as if he'd been taken aback at its strength. "I'm a hereditary witch. The McKenzies have been Wiccan for generations. Handed down in the family, like Catholics hand down Catholicism. That's all it is, really, a pre-Christian religion. Nothing to get excited about. Sorry I never told you, but witches aren't supposed to identify themselves as such, in the main."

"Don't you mean a warlock?"

"That's a phony term. Male or female, we're witches. And I don't like your tone. I happen to be proud of it."

"Let's drop it, shall we? You completely took me in with your story about Elaine yesterday, and it damned near knocked the spots out of me until I realized you were having me on. We are not amused. I wish you'd lay off the sauce."

Tommy set his glass back down on the sun-warmed bar, rubbed the back of his neck, and looked at him. "I was telling you the truth," he said simply.

Simon stared at him a long time. Then he walked over to a settee, lowered himself into it, and sat with his legs splayed out in front of him, one hand holding his beer and the other over his eyes.

The leather of the easy chair next to him squealed as Tommy sat down by him. "That's why Loquat's here," said Tommy. "I called him in to help us break up the cult if we can. Trouble is, we don't know who the Master is, and he's the one who keeps the cords and the Book of Shadows. We have to get those if the coven's to be dispersed."

"Perhaps some explanation is in order." Loquat's voice approached and the dry wood of the other antique settee protested under the giant's weight as he joined Simon and Tommy. "The cords are the ones with which the cult members are measured when they're initiated. The Book of Shadows is where their secret magical names are written down, and I imagine that in this case they've got hold of the book used by the old Satanists who practiced in the grotto back there. Doubtless, they think it's exceedingly powerful because of the evil magic it's accumulated over the centuries. Now, you and I know, Mr. Eagleton, that they're only silk cords and an old book. Their power lies in the fear they instill in the cult members, who believe they're under the control of the Master so long as he has them."

Simon sat up. "I don't care about that. What I can't bear is the idea that Elaine . . . Are you absolutely positive that she took one of the . . ." He swallowed. "One of the babies from the hospital?"

Tommy nodded, shoved his hands into his pockets, and looked down at his toes. "It would have been her sacrifice at being initiated into the cult," he said in a low voice. He gave himself a shake, as if he suddenly felt cold, and went over to cross his arms on the mantelpiece and look at himself in the mirror. "It would be a good job to get someone in to watch over Kei when you aren't around. We aren't sure what their plans are for her now, and it's a bit dicey. We know that she brought something back with her—she's been here before, you know—something that they would have killed to get. The central talisman of Sélène's cult."

He took out a cigar, lit it, and watched himself smoking. "Yesterday, after you left my place, I found out that they've got their hands on it." He turned to face Simon and, seeing his expression, said, "No, no, she didn't give it to them, they came in here and got it. You never lock the doors during the day, so they had no trouble."

"Then she's out of danger now?" Simon asked.

Loquat steepled his fingers and considered. "Not if they're bent on vengeance because she

260

took it, which is not an improbability. She'll need to have close tabs kept on her in the event, and I doubt that you by yourself would be enough. You can't be by her side every instant, whatever."

"Hilaire and Marthe . . . " Simon began, but Tommy shook his head.

"Someone's got to run things, which cancels out Hilaire, and you'd need a man's strength if they came after her. I'd come over myself, but Loquat and I have to set things up with our coven members, which will take some strategy. How about Rudy? He lives alone."

Simon thought about it. Regardless of what Elaine said — and there was no way to know whether she'd been telling the truth or just trying to annoy Tommy — he couldn't imagine Rudy's trying to put the make on Kei. Or what about Rudy would appeal to her anyway. He didn't look very strong, but he was the only man Simon could think of who could drop things and move over to the house.

"Is this person Rudy reliable?" Loquat asked.

"Oh, quite," said Simon. "He's an old friend."

"Good enough," said Loquat, his cheeks like pink crabapples as he smiled. "Now, I'd like to purify the grotto back there, with your permission. The bad vibrations from it are filtering in here. Can't you feel them?"

Simon got up and went to look out the window. The leaves on the oak trees were rustling. It looked like a peaceful Indian summer day out there, despite the skull-like mound's protrusion in the grove. "I don't know," he said. "I'm not fond of the idea of having witchcraft done on the place. It seems to me there's been too much of that already. Aren't you trying to fight fire with fire?"

Loquat got up and came to put an arm around him, engulfing him so that Simon felt as puny as a ten-year-old, and smiled angelically. "I'm not here to do you any harm, Mr. Eagleton. I couldn't if I wanted to. One of the main canons of Wicca is that whatever evil we do returns on our own heads, so we needs must be more than commonly ethical. We work with good. With the positive energy of the universe, which is the only real power. It's not fighting fire with fire, far from it. Satanists work with evil." He let Simon go and pinched his lower lip thoughtfully. "Evil is a negation, the absence of power, whatever. Their only instruments are the anger in themselves and the fear in their victims." He looked at Simon and his eyes were like stones. "Which can accomplish a deal of harm if one is not mentally alert against them, more's the pity."

Simon withdrew to sit against the windowsill, where Loquat couldn't get at him. That Simon was the one with white hair seemed to have escaped Loquat's notice, and he didn't fancy being bearhugged again. Tommy walked over to the piano and plinked a few keys unmusically.

"We think they're gearing up for some big ceremony, now that they've got the talisman back," said Tommy. "They've been searching for it for years, probably did a drawing-back ceremony on her, that sort of thing. You know that black ball she was wearing around her neck the other night? I think that may have been it. Sélène would have put some magical concoction inside." He looked at the keyboard and tried a chord unsuccessfully. "If they're cooking up as big a bash as we think, I dare say it'll leave a body or two in its wake."

"Undoubtedly," said Loquat.

"Then don't you think the police should be called in?" asked Simon, worrying about Kei's safety.

Loquat smiled at him as if he were a child. "Don't you think it would be a little difficult to convince the police that a Satanic cult came under their jurisdiction? And they can't be expected to deal with murder while it still exists only in the minds of the intended murderers. Would you care to try to explain it to them?"

Simon shook his head. Loquat's eyes followed Tommy's progress across the room to the bar.

Just as the glass of gin and tonic reached Tommy's mouth, Loquat said, "I wouldn't, Tommy. We'll need to purify ourselves and be in tiptop spiritual condition to prepare for what's ahead."

Tommy started to set the gin and tonic down, then pushed open the window and tossed the contents of the glass into the moat. He always had to add a dash of color to things, Simon thought. Live an actor, die an actor.

Marthe came in, wiping her hands on her tablier, and announced that the meal was ready.

"*Ah, Marthe! Comment ça va?*" said Loquat.

"*Assez bien, merci, maître,*" said Marthe, and

made a little bob that was almost a curtsey before retiring through the foyer.

"Fine woman," Loquat said expansively, patting his stomach with both hands. "Good cook, too, I'll be bound."

In the dining room, he put his huge fists on either side of his plate and said, "What have we here? Potage à la bonne femme? Appropriate!"

"You speak French," said Simon, handing him the straw basket of bread. "I thought Tommy said you came from Wales."

"Culture penetrates even into our wild hills, Mr. Eagleton." Loquat took a hunk of bread and tore it daintily in half. "I speak French, Italian, Portuguese, Spanish, Russian, and passable Swedish, but my Sanskrit's regrettably patchy."

"You ought to get together with Rudy, then. He knows Sanskrit and Tibetan and I don't know what-all." Simon took a quick drink of wine. The soup was hotter than he'd expected.

"Loquat has a Ph.D. in anthropology and a master's in botany," Tommy added, noticing that his cigar was smouldering in the ashtray and stamping the ash dead emphatically. "We witches aren't the primitives—the uneducated clods—we're painted. You Christians write the most irritating rot about us. You're the limit! So infuriatingly biased."

"And then, I do a lot of traveling on the astral plane," said Loquat, being noisy with his soup. "One must keep up with developments everywhere."

Simon set his spoon down on his service plate

and lit a cigarette. Thinking about Elaine made eating impossible.

He was accustomed to being in command of his own life, without its being impinged upon by other people's problems or affectional ties. Up to now, Elaine had only been a nagging nuisance, but now the world had been knocked out of kilter and things were out of his control. Having the reins out of his hands was a new, unsettling experience, and he detested the feeling of helplessness it gave him.

"I don't want Elaine hurt in this, whatever you're planning on doing," he said. "Will you promise to look out for her? It may not be evident, but I do care for her, in spite of what she's got herself into."

"I care about her, too," said Tommy. "Otherwise, I'd let the Satanists go to hell in a handbasket until they finally got nailed by the police." He wiped his mouth with his napkin, reached for his wine, and waited for a nod of approval from Loquat before taking a sip. "The complication is that she'll be fighting against us as hard as the other cult members. You've got to watch in particular that she doesn't get near Kei." He reacted to Simon's expression. "I know it's hard, old friend, but she'd be acting under orders. She hasn't any choice, or they'll kill her too, you see. That's one reason we need Rudy in here."

"It would help if we could change her nature by doing a binding ceremony on her," Loquat said, "to keep her out of the thick of it. She's safe enough, so long as she does what they say.

But as Tommy mentioned, she will be opposing us unless we can alter her attitude through such a ritual."

"Actually, that's why we've come round," said Tommy. "For the binding ceremony, we'd need to have something that belongs to her, that she's handled recently. I suppose a lock of hair would be too much to ask?"

"That's right, it would!" Simon said brusquely. "You can fool around with this voodoo all you like, but you're not involving me in it, and I'm not helping you do a job on Elaine!"

Marthe brought in the salad and they all waited until she'd left before resuming the conversation.

"You're under some misapprehension, Mr. Eagleton," Loquat said soothingly. "In the matter of the binding ceremony, it's the evil in Elaine that needs to be exorcised, nothing more. Surely you have no objections to helping the real, original Elaine be released from the malignant influences she's been under?"

Simon humphed a little and began serving the salad.

"When we destroy the measuring cords and the Book of Shadows," Loquat continued, pointing to a prize piece of palm heart to urge Simon to include it in his portion, "that will break her belief in the Master's control over her, but I understand she's been attracted to the lefthanded path—the dark side—for some time now. Apparently, she could use a general sweetening up." He carefully picked the ham and chicken strips out of his salad and put them to one side, explaining that vegetarianism was part of his purification regime when he was facing heavy spiritual work. Tommy followed suit but didn't look happy about it and sneaked a morsel of ham into his mouth when Loquat wasn't looking.

Well, what harm could it do? It would probably be a matter of Loquat prancing around in a sheet in the moonlight, scattering flowers, and if such inane caperings made him and Tommy feel better, why not? Loquat was such a lovable fellow that Simon didn't like to wilt his spirits. It would probably be entertaining anyway. He could use a chuckle or two.

"If you must," he said, and Loquat beamed. "I'll see if I can find something of hers. I'd be happy myself if Elaine would give up playing the Dragon Lady." Wouldn't the picture of young Simon, fresh from her hands, do the trick? She'd probably handled it a lot, and it would be—in Loquat's terms—charged up with psychic energy. Wrapped up and sealed so that no one could see what it was, it would serve nicely.

"Would you have a box of salt in the kitchen, now?" asked Loquat, pushing back from the table. "I'd like to let my stomach settle before dessert, and now's as good a time as any to purify the grotto."

"That's all you need? Table salt?" Simon had supposed that setting up a ritual would be more complicated. When Elaine had played at being a witch, he'd watched her fool around with in- cantations a few times before losing patience with her self-dramatization and telling her to cut it the hell out while he was around. Everything about her ceremonies had to be just so and were undertaken with the greatest solemnity, as if she were tinkering with a bomb about to go off.

Loquat chuckled. "Eye of newt, eh? I hope I don't disappoint you by not slitting a goat's throat." His eyes twinkled. "The last maiden I sacrificed, believe it or not, was my wife on our wedding night. She thought it a capital idea at the time."

Simon went out into the kitchen to look for the salt and had to stand a moment or two to recollect what he'd come out for. The bizarre events of the past couple of days were beginning to addle his brains. Marthe was at the table, sprinkling nuts over crême brulées and looking so everyday that he calmed down. This was only a kind of game they'd be playing. They'd go out to the grotto, act silly for a bit, and that would be the end of it. He found the box of Morton's on the back of the stove.

"Hold the dessert," he said to Marthe. "We're going for a walk in the woods first. We won't be long."

Tommy was standing in the foyer door when he got back. "No dessert for me," he said, patting his flat stomach. "Have to watch the waistline. While you and Loquat take care of the grotto, I'm going home to get the lances. We should have time for a practice bout before you go to pick up Kei at the airport. While I'm at it, I'll pop over to Rudy's and talk to him about moving in."

When he'd left, Loquat took the salt from Simon and, looking at the label, said, "Iodized! Couldn't be better. More like sea salt, which the traditionalists prefer."

He whistled as they walked over the bridge at the back, across the meadow, and into the woods, but as they approached the grotto, he stopped. "Achyfi!" he said, sniffing the air. "Smell that! Really nasty, don't you know."

"Smell what?" asked Simon, who noticed nothing but the natural barnyard odors from the stable and the woodsy fragrance of the plant-life about them.

Loquat looked at him and shook his head. "Then I suppose you can't feel the vibrations, either. Hopeless." He stopped before the mound and put a boot on one of the rocks cropping out of the earth. "There's been a lot of malevolence concentrated in this area, and it's left its residue behind. For one thing, there's a pervading reek of—if you'll excuse the indelicacy—shit. The devil's characteristic odor. It's worse than I thought. You'll probably need a second, more elaborate purification, but I'll do what I can this afternoon."

He stomped around the perimeter of the grotto, dousing the ground with salt and waving his arms majestically while muttering to himself, then walked up the plane of the mound and scattered the rest of the box broadcast over the barren hillock.

"Used up the whole box, I'm afraid," he said, coming back down and handing the empty container to Simon.

"That's all there is to it?" asked Simon. "Not very formal, is it?"

"Oh, we witches improvise like crazy," said Loquat and scratched an armpit, releasing a homey smell of sweat. The sunlight made his reddish hair shine around his head like a nimbus. "It's amazing how well an ashtray, a plastic cup, and a Kleenex can substitute for a thurible, a chalice, and an altarcloth when you've got a deity helping you out. The Satanists are the dogmatists. They don't believe their rituals will work unless they're correct in every detail. They're on their own, you see. Godless. Most of them don't even believe in the devil. He's just a handy device to scare the wits out of folks."

"I thought witches were pagan."

"We are. We are. Look up the meaning, Mr. Eagleton. So are Buddists and Hindus. The main difference between your God and mine is that yours is a male chauvinist. My god is dual, male *and* female. God and goddess. It's more a semantic difference than a philosophical disagreement. Have a Lifesaver?"

Simon accepted one. Wintergreen. Loquat put the roll of candy back in his breast pocket and buttoned the flap. Fluttering his fingers as if he were palpating the air, he walked off a ways and stopped by the only linden tree in the grove and felt its bark.

"Something's amiss around here, too," he said, shifting his Lifesaver into his cheek. "Not evil, precisely. Odd. Terror and sadness, I'd say." He looked toward the barn and crunched the candy

270

up. "I'm catching something from over there, too."

"Probably Fournier," said Simon, humoring him. "He's a rotten apple who's capable of spreading bad vibes for blocks, I'd imagine."

Loquat smiled. "You're being typically thick-headed about witchcraft, my boy," he said affably, "but we're used to it. To each his own."

"Not bad. Not bad at all," said Tommy, standing the lances up against the wall by the back door. "You'll give a very good accounting of yourself. Were you in games at school?"

"Only when forced," Simon replied, puffing and unbuttoning his vest, which had grown far too hot after all the exercise out in the pasture. "Hated every minute of it." He pulled the turtleneck top away from his skin to let the air at it.

"When does Kei's plane get in?"

"About forty-five minutes from now. I've got to rush," said Simon after consulting his watch. "I need a shower."

On his way out, Tommy turned. "Then we're on for tonight?"

"Yes, I'll pick you and Loquat up about seven."

"Don't forget, it'll be a day or two before Rudy moves in, so keep a close eye on Kei."

"Count on it."

The workout had temporarily banished problems from Simon's mind, and as he lathered up, he resolutely concentrated on looking forward to Kei's return. She'd like Loquat. He was the kind of man one would want to be tucked into bed

271

by, who'd tell tales of elves and ogres, cozily assuring one that all was right with the world. He was anticipating listening to him discourse on improbabilities in his marvelous voice and luxuriating in the feeling of security that the giant teddybear-man imparted. A bit of that kind of thing would be just the ticket for tonight, besieged as they were by difficulties on all sides.

But sooner or later they'd have to face the hard realities. Elaine was going to make arrangements for young Simon—it was going to take some getting used to, having someone share his name—to come to France, so Kei had to be braced for his arrival. They might as well tackle the situation immediately, while she was still unsated and not so likely to leave him as she might be when the initial sexual excitement had dissipated. Simon was not above using her appetite for him to shackle her to his side.

But if it came to the point of having to choose between them, his responsibility was clear. His obligation to his son was inescapable, no matter what the cost.

CHAPTER NINETEEN

Dear Chris:

Sitting here on the plane back to the château with warring feelings boiling around in my head is driving me quietly crazy. Maybe if I write it all down it will help. In any case, I owe it to you to let you know what's really been going on. You've always said you wanted us to be honest with each other, even if the truth hurt. So sit down while you read this, because it's going to.

Perhaps I should begin with Simon, since everything revolves around him. To put it bluntly, I love him. It's sudden, yes, but it doesn't take time to recognize what you've been looking for all your life. I know how hard it's going to be for you to accept this, particularly when you hear the rest of the story, but there it is. A fact. God knows, the situation is tearing me to pieces, but I didn't ask for it to happen. It would be better for everyone if it hadn't, but I can't change that any more than I can change the color of my eyes.

There's no way to cushion this—and I'm not going to justify Simon to you—but he and his sister Elaine had an illegitimate son. At least, grant that he didn't conceal that from me and that he has the decency to want to raise his son. Elaine wants to keep her claws in Simon, which means getting rid of me. Which is why I assumed that she was the one who tried to kill me the other night. Three other witnesses can testify that there's a ball bearing sunk into the wood right by where my head was, so I'm not imagining things. Now I wonder if that accident with the farm machinery wasn't another unsuccessful attempt to put me out of the way. Elaine swears she had nothing to do with shooting at me, and because all she has to do to keep Simon and me apart is to threaten to tell their son that Simon's his father, she can make us dance to her tune without resorting to violence. That leaves the question of who tried to kill me. It doesn't make sense. Can you imagine what it feels like, knowing that someone— you don't know who—hates you enough to want you dead? That's something that happens to nameless strangers in ghettos or foreign cities, to people in mystery stories or on TV, isn't it? But it's happening to me, *really happening! It seems so improbable, so outlandish that it really hasn't sunk in yet.*

274

There's more to the story, but the plane will be landing soon, so there isn't time to go into it.

Just one thing more. No matter how dreadful all of this sounds, don't condemn Simon right off. If he weren't a man of honor, he would have hidden the boy away somewhere to protect himself and not told me about him. If you knew his sister, you might understand him a little. He's a wonderful, deeply passionate, funny man, and I can't help loving him, no matter what he's done.

Anyway, now you know.

Forgive me,

Kei

CHAPTER TWENTY

Nothing formal, nothing that made him look authoritarian, able to take care of himself. Something — something vulnerable-looking. God knows, he certainly felt vulnerable! After looking over his wardrobe, Simon chose deck shoes, jeans, and a light blue pullover. No, that brought out his tan, made him look too healthy. He pulled it off and put on a dark brown velour shirt. Better. Made his skin look paler, his eyes dark and rather pathetic. If Kei was half as sorry for him as *he* was, he'd have a better chance of talking her into marrying him. Having her gone for a day in London gave him an inkling of what it would be like without her, and he wasn't having it! Selfish. A noble soul wouldn't drag her into this nightmare, would give her up and tell her never to darken his door again. But he wasn't noble. He was scared. Scared and hopelessly in love. What a combination! Dammit, he *needed* her! He had to be sure she wouldn't leave him, and he fully intended to use every weapon at his disposal to get a commitment out of her. She liked things that felt sensuous, so the velour would help, and he had other things in mind.

Hilaire was polishing the Rolls dotingly when he got to the garage. Simon asked him to cut all of the flowers left in the garden and fill the house with them. Hilaire wagged his head roguishly and kissed the air. Simon was annoyed to find himself blushing.

He drove the Rolls into the airport gate and saw a plane circling overhead, preparing to land. He rushed into the terminal. The plane taxiing across the runway wasn't hers, which was due in fifteen minutes. He sat down in the waiting area and rehearsed arguments why she should marry him. None of them sounded very convincing to his inner ear.

When she landed, they greeted each other with middle-aged dignity at the gate, talked about business affairs in London while waiting for her bag to come down the chute, walked at a leisurely pace out to the car, got in, and fell on each other like ravening beasts. He suspected that she had worn the tawny silk blouse because it had only one button closing it in front, and he did not disappoint her. When a couple got into the car next to them, banging the side of the Rolls with their door, Simon and Kei straightened up and rearranged themselves, faces flushed.

"I think I'd better drive," said Kei, rubbing her chin against the velour of his pullover. They got out and changed places. "Goodness, this car is garish!" she said. "Black and yellow! I'm surprised at you."

"It's a Rolls," said Simon defensively, smarting at her sniffishness.

"It's *still* black and yellow," Kei said implacably, studying the dashboard. After some instructions from Simon, she felt able to handle it and drove the car out of the lot and through the busy downtown, skillfully dodging people who, in the French manner, pulled out of parking spaces without giving warning. The sidewalks of town were crowded with people browsing at tables of goods with signs saying "Solde" and the traffic was thick, but soon they were over the Loire bridge and on the road to the château.

"Let's pretend," she said as the blacktop unrolled before them. "It's such a beautiful day, let's pretend that we're just like anybody else. We can deal with the Sturm and Drang tomorrow, I don't suppose it will evaporate before then."

"Good idea," said Simon, putting his hand up her skirt. A few minutes later, the car ran off the road and bounced on the shoulder, coming to a halt. Under the circumstances, Simon felt it would be unfair to make any smart remarks about her driving.

Crystal bowls set about the bedroom held a confusion of white flowers tinted palest green by the light reflected from the emerald velvet walls. Kei buried her face in the flowers, going from one bouquet to another, exclaiming at their fragrance, and then ate a creamy petal.

"We going to dinner tonight at that restaurant downtown," said Simon, kissing her in the crook of her neck as they stood before the bureau.

"Oh, not tonight," said Kei, reaching back to hold his head close. "I'm still tired from the trip."

"We can't let Tommy down twice in a row," said Simon. "I'll give you a massage. That will revive you."

In the mirror, he saw her raise an eyebrow.

Timing was of primary importance, Simon thought, working warmed lotion into Kei's shoulders as she lay on her back on the fur coverlet. Afterwards, when she was satisfied, she might not find him so difficult to do without.

Kei sighed blissfully as he circled each shoulder and then stroked one arm and then the other all the way down to the hand, between her long, slim fingers. "Kei, do you love me?" he asked.

"I thought we had that all settled," she said dreamily, eyes closed. "Are you going to ask me that on the half hour? You know I do, or I'd still be in London."

He poured more liquid into the palm of his hand and smoothed it on her breasts, kneading them like warm, elastic dough, and her breathing quickened. "You said you'd think about it. Have you?" he asked, running his fingertips around her rosy aureoles and then brushing her nipples with the backs of his nails. She caught her breath.

"I haven't thought of much else," she said and pulled his head down to her open mouth. He sucked her full lower lip and bit it softly before drawing back.

His hands traveled down her belly, making deep, vertical strokes, as he said, "What's your decision?"

"Do I have to make one now?" She ran her hands back through her hair. Her hips were beginning to make small, restless movements. "Why does it have to be marriage?"

"People fall out of love."

"I'm not in love with you," she said, and his heart stopped a split second before she went on. "I love you. They're not the same. But I'm not ready to be rushed into that sort of commitment, not before I know you better. I don't know what your expectations are, for one thing. Do you want a mother or a wife?"

"I don't know, which are you?"

She opened her mouth, looking cross, then closed it again, and a smile crept into her eyes.

Simon opened her legs and massaged the inner sides of her thighs. "Kei," he said, "I'm asking you for the last time, will you marry me or won't you? Living together isn't enough. It has to be legal to get Elaine off our backs. More than that, I want to be absolutely certain that you belong to me."

"No, then," she said angrily, sitting up on her elbows. "I'm not a piece of property that you can buy with a legal document. If that's your idea of marriage, you can stuff it. No!"

He poured a handful of lotion out and began coaxing it up into her with his fingers. She drew up her knees and raised her pelvis toward him. "Is that final?" he asked, inserting his hand and feeling the cone of her womb.

"Yes!" she gasped. He withdrew his hand and fluttered her clitoris lightly with his fingertips, then rubbed it slowly, lingeringly. "No! I don't know what I mean! You're being very unfair," she said, turning her head from side to side on the pillow and rocking her hips. He slid his fingers into her again and worked them in and out, leisurely at first, then faster and faster.

"I want an answer," he said, moving into a different position and bending down to flick her clitoris swiftly with his tongue and then softly sucking the tender button of flesh. He sat back. She arched upward like a bow, her thighs quivering. The sight of her made his breath ragged.

"Oh, please!" she breathed.

"An answer."

"Jesus, yes!" she said, clenching the coverlet at her sides. "Yes, I'll marry you. I'll do anything you want, if you'll just get in me!"

He slid into her like a ship coming into harbor, any feelings of guilt washed away by his relief. "You underhanded bastard, I'll get you for this!" she said, and he put his mouth over hers and rammed himself up her until she threw back her head and gave a sobbing breath as he spurted into her.

Smiling with her eyes closed, holding him against her, she sighed, "Darling idiot, did you think I'd let you get away?"

They slept and lay in bed a long time afterward, smoking and arguing over the lyrics to So Rare, wrangling about politics, disagreeing over the details of the wedding. They did agree on one thing—that one dismal penalty of living in Europe was missing gridiron football in the autumn, but they got into a fearful row over the existence or nonexistence of absolute truth, in the course of which she pulled his hair.

Still in a huff, Kei got up to go to the bathroom and put on his bathrobe without asking first, further annoying him with a preview of what it was going to be like, sharing every god-damned thing in the house with somebody else. His irritation slipped away as he went back over the times they'd made love, remembering the feel of her, the look on her face, the sounds she made, her openness about wanting him. When she came back to sit on his side of the bed, he said, almost afraid to bring up the matter, as if discussing it might magically bring about disaster, "Kei, what's going to happen later, when I can't . . . The whole fucking mechanism copped out on me for a year and a half, without any reason. It could happen again. It'd kill me to disappoint you." He took her hand and pressed his lips on her wrist.

She rubbed his cheek, seeming to consider before she spoke. "Simon," she said, holding his head in her hands and turning it upward so he had to look at her, "you know who you are and what you are. You're a loving man, a real man, not a boy trying to prove himself in bed. I hope we spend the rest of our lives fucking our brains out, but if we can't . . . then we'll just hold each other. I want to find you beside me when I wake up in the morning. The rest is only the icing on the cake." She looked deep into his eyes. "Do you understand me?"

He nodded, his eyes wet. She kissed his eyelids and licked up the moisture, then rose and added, "But don't think I'm your property. I belong to myself," and went into her room, saying that she was going to get dressed for dinner.

As they drove over to Tommy's under a pink evening sky, Simon gave Kei a thumbnail sketch of the man she was about to meet, working up to what he'd learned about the Satanist-Wiccan situation in the calmest, most reasonable manner he could muster, trying not to frighten her with the news that she was the target of a band of bloodthirsty fanatics.

"Well, that's a relief!" she said, and at first he thought he hadn't heard her correctly, but she went on, "Then it's nothing personal."

At that point, Simon relinquished any hope of understanding the female mind, hers in particular.

"I didn't like thinking I'd hurt somebody's feelings enough to make them want to kill me. If they're just sore because I took something of theirs — that pomander ball, must be — it's *their* problem."

"Kei darling, we're not talking ethics here . . . "

"I know, but now I know what I'm dealing with. It was all fuzzy before, and I didn't know where the danger was coming from. A bunch of crackpots, I can deal with."

"No, you can*not*! I'm frightened to death I can't keep you safe here. Tommy and Loquat think they'll try again. I want you to go to London to stay with Missy until . . . until they've taken care of things."

It took some concerted arguing to get her to see reason about the seriousness of the threat against her, and even then, the only concession he could get out of her was a "We'll see."

She stayed in the car—with the doors locked—while he ran in to tell Loquat and Tommy that the car was waiting.

He'd dressed for town in white linen trousers and a beige raw silk jacket, and Kei had picked out his wine silk tie, making him feel tamed and domestic. It was a new role and one he had some qualms about. It could lead to a double chin and paunch if he wasn't careful not to get too husbandly and contented.

Tommy's house had a monastic look, a minimum of furniture, and a depressing atmosphere of fixed order, as if nothing had been moved a quarter of an inch since being set in its original position. A string of housekeepers came in the front door and left by the back, one replacing another, as they got overwhelmed by his pickiness and quit.

Now that he knew about Tommy's religion, some of the furnishings—silver chalices, ornate candlesticks, and the crystal ball Simon had assumed was lifted from the set of The Crystal Quest—took on a new significance. They were not souvenir props from Tommy's films after all, and the evidence of witchery had been right before Simon's nose for years. So much for his keen, discerning eye! The room smelled of stale incense. Simon sneezed.

When they came down from upstairs, freshly combed and still damp from showering, he rushed Tommy and Loquat out to the car, saying they'd have to get a move on or lose their reservation. Kei rolled down the window to accept Loquat's kiss on her hand and was immediately taken with him, as Simon knew she'd be. Loquat said she was a drop of amber on the bosom of night. Coming from him, it sounded no more overblown than if Tommy had said she looked smashing.

"Did I feel a drop?" said Loquat, holding out a hand and looking up at the sky before getting in. Big cabbage roses of clouds were gathering in the east.

Rain came down lightly as they reached town. It was getting ominously dark. They ran from the parking lot to the restaurant, arriving breathless and laughing in a snug room with wood paneling, bentwood chairs, tables devoid of decoration, and a flock of penguinlike waiters who could hardly bear to associate with the masses. The menus were too big to see over, and the ones given to ladies omitted the prices—at which Kei took umbrage. The oysters were delectable, and they all consumed a lot of wine before Tommy's lobster shot off his plate into the lap of a woman at the next table.

Her military-looking escort jumped to his feet, threw his napkin down on the table like a gauntlet, and spat out a stream of French, none of which sounded complimentary. A waiter hurried over to mop at the woman's skirt.

Loquat rose majestically, went over to the man, and spoke in his ear. The man stared icily ahead. Then he wilted before their eyes and sat down again, turned to shake Loquat's hand, and made protesting, deprecatory flourishes with his hands, evidently refusing reparations. He smiled and raised his glass to Loquat's party, and they returned the salute. Simon asked Loquat what he'd said to effect the miraculous transformation.

"I told him Americans were barbarians who didn't know how to handle a lobster, but that you were taking out French citizenship so that you could disassociate yourself from the plastic culture of your native land," said Loquat, appropriating the butter and basket of bread. "But I think it was saying that you'd had to leave the country because you'd insulted the President that did the trick." His gray eyes sparkled with mischief.

After pastries and coffee, they moved out to the cafe's outdoor section, under the striped canopy, to enjoy the rain. Reflections of neon signs across the street jiggled like colored snakes in the wet of the pavement as they listened to the swish of cars passing by. On the square, at the T of the street, the merry-go-round was shrouded in a gray tarpaulin and looked like an elephant with baggy skin. The little booths that sold novelties and carnival favors—magic tricks, dribble glasses, confetti for throwing into the mouths of celebrants, papier mâché butterflies with burrs to stick on clothing, and noisemakers—were shuttered and barred. Across the way, a waiter was cutting up tidbits on a plate for a dog sitting on a chair beside its mistress, a napkin tied around its neck.

Simon ordered four armagnacs. They arrived in saucers, the liquid looking like shiny ink in the dark under the canopy. He sat with his arm over the back of Kei's chair, where he could touch her shoulder from time to time. "Are you warm enough?" he asked, and she nodded and pulled her fur vest closer together in front. The air was fresh and, with the rain running in strings of gray beads from the edge of the canvas and plopping into the gutter, with the ground bass of voices from the cafe's interior mumbling an accompaniment to their own conversation, Simon felt cozy and euphoric.

It was one of those evenings when anything seemed possible. A divine hand might come down through the stormy clouds, wave a wand, and turn the Satanists into chinless bank clerks in pinstripes, make over Elaine into a Girl Guide, and banish famine in India and Africa. He'd keep young Simon, though. He was looking forward to being a father, regardless of how the child had been acquired.

"Supposing you do put down the cult," he said to Loquat, "I've still got Elaine to contend with. She's been getting very difficult. Do you actually think that binding ceremony you talked of would change her nature?"

"I've seen it do wonders," said Loquat. "I shouldn't be drinking like this."

Kei asked for an explanation and then said, "But how can putting something in a box and tying it up make any difference? I do that when I'm fixing Christmas packages, and the only effect that has is on my budget."

"Part of it depends on what you put in the box, of course," Loquat answered after ordering another round. "Everything we do, each smallest action, has some effect on the cosmos, will you concede that point? I thought so." His hair, which had started out being neatly slicked down, had sprung back into a wild gold mane. "Magic is simply a small adjustment of the balance and is no more mystical than anything else in this mystical world." He paid for the drinks as the waiter set them down. "It's a little like playing cat's cradle, if you think of the web of circumstance. We select certain strands in the web, move them into a slightly different configuration, and come up with an altered pattern, while the stuff of the web remains the same."

"I think I've had enough," said Kei, pushing away the armagnac on its saucer with the tips of her fingernails. "You seem to be making sense. I'll probably find holes in your theory tomorrow."

"Is it necessary for Elaine to know you've bound her if the thing's to work?" Simon asked. He didn't want Elaine's fury coming down on his head for that as well.

"No, *our* knowing about it is sufficient," said

Loquat, whose consonants were getting blurry. He hiccuped. "We're not wish—witch doctors trying to frighten Elaine into psychosomatic disorder." He enunciated the last words very cautiously. "But we need something of hers for the box, and that's up to you."

Simon thought again of the picture of young Simon and said, "I've already got it."

"But we still have to get back her cord, or she'll continue to think she's under orders from the Master. That's the tricky bit," said Tommy.

That required a long explanation for Kei, who looked unusually thoughtful afterwards, Simon thought.

"But we're agreed, we will do the binding ceremony?" asked Tommy, who had been keeping up with them, drink for drink, and was now thoroughly smashed and looked as if he had a terminal case of pinkeye.

"Right," said Simon.

"Done and done!" Loquat slapped a hand on the table.

They had another drink on the strength of it. And another. The waiter summoned an accordionist, who began to play "La Vie en Rose," a guaranteed sentimental favorite with Americans.

Simon discovered that he was dancing with Kei's head tucked in his neck, on the sidewalk, and that he seemed to have strayed out from under the canopy, because rain was running off the end of his nose. He steered back under the shelter. Kei's wet hair was making rivulets inside his collar and she was singing the words to the music in French, nibbling his ear between phrases.

"I love you, Kei," Simon said.

"You've said that seven times now," she said. "I was counting."

"My turn," said Tommy, tapping Simon on the shoulder. As Simon turned to protest, Tommy slid into his place and began dancing with Kei. Simon sat down at the table and kept a vigilant eye on them. Sure enough, not two minutes passed before Tommy had his hands on Kei's hips and was moving suggestively against her.

"God dammit, that's private property!" said Simon, shooting to his feet. "Hands off!" He pushed Tommy aside and put his arm possessively around Kei. Tommy, who was almost blind drunk, fell back against one of the poles that supported the canvas awning and knocked it over. The canvas sagged down on him. He batted it away and came out fighting. Simon let Kei go and tried to hold Tommy off and calm him down, but Tommy was too tight and belligerent to listen and landed a fist on the side of Simon's jaw, the one he had hit before. Simon sailed back into the table and fell in a welter of chairs.

Tommy reached down, grabbed him by the lapels, and jerked him to his feet, then retreated to arm's length so he could take another swing at him. Simon, too tight himself to be cautious or worry about his bridgework, cut in under Tommy's arm with a short, sharp punch to the jaw, making his teeth click together audibly.

The waiter got in between them, remonstrating in thunderous French, and caught a haymaker that Tommy intended for Simon. The waiter collapsed with a sigh onto the sidewalk. Tommy stepped over his body, and Simon landed another hit on his eye while Tommy was in mid-stride. Tommy staggered back against Kei, who had been moving around the periphery of the fight, and went down suddenly.

Simon looked down at Tommy, who was lying in a relaxed cross on top of the waiter. "I didn't think I hit him that hard," he said, sucking his sore knuckles.

"I think I helped," Kei said quietly and put the bottle back on the table.

It took generous applications of money to quiet the shrill restaurant owner and to satisfy the waiter, who finally crawled out from under Tommy and looped back and forth across the sidewalk, listing to port. He was, however, sufficiently in control of himself to pocket the francs that Simon pressed upon him. Tommy took longer to recover, but finally sat up, groaning pitiably, and Loquat and Simon helped him to his feet.

"Great goddess!" said Tommy, feeling the side of his head with delicate probings. "I'm never going to lay a finger on you again!" he said to Simon. "Or you, either," he said, looking at Kei. "Ye gods!"

They moved over to the café across the street at the urging of the restaurant owner and were met with resistance by the waiter over there, who had observed the fracas. More francs were applied before the waiter consented to serve them coffee — and only coffee.

291

"Four filtrés," said Loquat, holding up three fingers.

Tommy sat in his chair like a bundle of old laundry, his hands to his head. "I never knew you to be so possessive before," he said and gave a small moan.

"I never was going to marry the girl before," said Simon.

Kei snuggled up against him, and Tommy turned an envious look on him. "So she is, after all," he said. "Christ almighty, you've finally fallen in love, and she's going to marry you. Lucky sod!"

Loquat burst into tears. "A marriage!" he said. "I do love to see people happy. It always makes me cry." He kissed Kei, and then kissed Simon and Tommy for good measure. He got up to have a go at the waiter as well, but the waiter beat a retreat into the café, leaving them there with their coffees.

"Well, best wishes all around," said Tommy, and then leaned over to Kei and said in a stage whisper, "Are you sure you know what you're getting into?"

"Yes," she said, crying and wiping her tears on Simon's tie. "It's all perfectly awful, and I'm so happy!"

Tommy demanded a bottle of champagne, and the waiter came out to argue but was mollified by the fact that they were celebrating a very special romantic occasion—and by a few extra bills on the side.

There was toasting and more kissing, even

292

by Tommy, after Simon made him promise to keep his hands to himself.

"I want to ride on the merry-go-round!" said Tommy. He repeated it several times, louder and more petulantly, banging his fists on the table until the waiter, after extracting more money from Simon, scouted up the operator, who arrived after a few minutes, looking thunderous. His expression sweetened a little when Tommy clapped some bills into his hand. The man removed the tarpaulin from the merry-go-round, getting soaked in the process, and started up the engine.

The calliope hooted mournfully and then began to play "Singing in the Rain" as the carved figures on the platform jerked and started slowly dancing up and down, gathering momentum. The operator crossed his arms and leaned against the central shaft, looking viciously cross.

The party squelched over to the merry-go-round, and Simon boosted Kei up onto a pink horse with a white mane and clambered onto a purple charger beside her. Loquat squeezed into a sleigh drawn by a silver reindeer and sobbed blissfully, crying, "On Comet! On Cupid! On Donner and Blitzen!" Tommy ran around the platform in the opposite direction to its progress, swinging from horse to horse and bellowing "Scots Wha Hae with Wallace Bled" at the top of his lungs. The operator crossed his ankles and looked baleful.

Simon leaned over to kiss Kei, but their horses weren't synchronized, and he nearly fell off his mount. "Got the coordination of a kumquat," he muttered. He felt absolutely marvelous. Kei was marvelous. The world was marvelous.

He jerked up out of a doze, the mane of his horse imprinted on his cheek, when the operator yanked at his sleeve and said something about his wife and children waiting for him. Simon slid off his mount and roused the others.

He drove home very slowly, on the alert for chickens. The dimensions of the road puzzled him. It kept getting narrower and narrower, until there was so little room on either side that he had to drive straddling the central stripe.

"Ahoy there," said Loquat, "that farmhouse with the flag sticking out the chimney is following us! Seen it three times now."

Simon took a different turning, and the passing scenery of the night became more familiar, although the road seemed to have been replaced by a new one in the past few hours. This one was no wider than a bicycle path. Oncoming lights flared, veered to the side, and a horn blasted angrily. By God, they let anyone drive in France, Simon thought. Ought to stay home and leave the road to people who knew what they were doing!

"Missy's coming tomorrow," said Tommy, whistling his esses. "She's got a poe in Sharis— a show in Paris—she's doing. Good old Missy!"

"Good old Missy!" Kei echoed sleepily.

"Biggest boobs on the Continent," said Tommy.

"But not the best," said Simon, putting an arm around Kei and drawing her over so her head was on his shoulder.

Loquat sobbed ecstatically.

294

CHAPTER TWENTY-ONE

Dear Chris:

I've just hung up the receiver, but I'm writing because we weren't communicating very well, with the line crackling and you yelling at me. Simon's out on his morning ride, so I can take time to explain things.

It's really not fair, your saying that I didn't give you any warning before hitting you in the face with the news about Simon. Everything happened too fast for me to lead up to it gradually. And I certainly didn't appreciate that remark about not sparing your feelings. You act as if I'd fallen in love with him just to make you feel awful, and I don't see how you can think I'd want to land myself in this mess for the fun of it. I'm sorry if you're hurt, but from now on this is between Simon and me, and you'll just have to learn to live with it.

Everything you said about his relationship with his sister is true, and so are your snide remarks about his reputation as a womanizer.

I don't deny any of it, but he simply isn't the kind of man you think he is. He is not a monster! Do you think I could love him if he were? Anyway, what's done is done. It's the best thing that ever happened to me. And the worst. He's a terrible man and a wonderful man. He'll be absolute hell to live with, but impossible to live without. I don't expect you to understand.

Please don't worry about the murder attempts. Yes, that's what they seem to have been, but everybody's watching me like a hawk. I can hardly go to the bathroom alone! Simon's insisting on packing me off to London, where I'll be out of harm's way. He wants me out of here when the tournament's on and the village is crowded with people. I'll explain when the whole thing's over. In the meantime, I'm fighting to stay on a few days to get more of the manuscript done so Jeremy will be able to estimate how many pages it'll run.

Things are a nightmare, but you know how I can close off my mind about things that upset me, and that's what I'm doing. I'll worry about it later.

I'm sorry about everything. I hope it doesn't tear things between us. You mean too much to me for that.

Always,

Kei

CHAPTER TWENTY-TWO

On their way back from another practice session next day, their lances under their arms, Simon and Tommy came upon Kei leaning up against the barn, removing mud from her sandals. The rain that had washed and brightened the land had left miry patches on the pathways. She tossed away the piece of bark she'd been using as a scraper and brushed her hands together.

"What are you doing out here?" asked Simon, kissing her on the neck and then stroking back a lock of hair that had fallen over her eye. "You're to keep indoors, you know, until Rudy's here."

"Even on such a nice day? Have a heart, I just wanted a breath of air. Nobody's going to try to kill me in plain daylight."

"You look very thoughtful. Something on your mind?" He put his arm around her.

She squinted up at the fresh blue sky, where a hawk hung suspended in an updraft, its wings spread wide, and said, "A couple of things. You know, it's odd, but when I finally caught a glimpse of . . . oh, I guess I must just be seeing

things. Never mind. I'll worry about that later."
She kissed him on the jaw and rubbed her lips
over his stubble.

He winced. "Take it easy. I'm going to have
to learn to turn the other cheek. That seems to
be Tommy's favorite." He touched his jaw tenderly.

"You're both very brave, going out to jounce
around on horses with the hangovers you must
have," she said as they walked back toward the
château.

"Greater love hath no man and all that."
Tommy's face looked puffy and he had a glorious
shiner. "Little does he care that my brain's oozing
out of my ears! He has to get me out of bed while
I'm lying there praying for a quick death. I've
told him and *told* him he'll do splendidly, but
he wants to look pretty at the tournament, I
suspect. The man's a tower of vanity. I was always
satisfied not to fall off the bloody horse!"

Mitzi came tearing out of the woods and jumped
up on Simon, muddying his shirt with her paws
and whining. Simon took his arm from around
Kei and brushed at his shirtfront, reprimanding
the dog. Mitzi circled him, her rear end down
and her tail tucked under, whimpering. Then
she jumped up at him again. "Down, girl, down!"
Simon said. His white shirt was covered with
brown rosettes. "What's the matter with you?
Go find Bayard, there's a good girl!"

Turning slowly, slowly in one direction until
the rope doubled up on itself, then unwinding

in the other direction, the body stretched down from a branch of the linden tree by the buried grotto. Mitzi whined and danced beneath her mate, leaping up to try to reach him.

Tommy gave him a cognac and water and squeezed his shoulder sympathetically. Simon blew his nose and wiped his eyes. Couldn't cry over ruining his son's life or his sister making candles out of babies, nothing as sensible as that!

"At least they killed him quickly, or we'd have heard," said Tommy. "Usually they tease and torture animals so they'll be aware of their impending death, to stir up as much fear as possible. Gives them power, they think, so they torment their victims into a frenzy before killing them. Bayard was lucky, think of it that way."

The other settee creaked as Tommy sat down, leaned forward with his elbows on his knees, both hands around his drink and a cigar projecting from between his fingers. "I don't see the point, though. What was it for?" he said, putting his thumb on his temple and rubbing his forefinger back and forth over his forehead.

Kei, who had been trembling against Simon's arm, began to shake spasmodically, "I know why," she burst out. She jumped up, went to the fireplace, and pounded her fists against the mantelpiece. "It's the place! They know about it, and they're showing me that they know!"

"Kei . . . " Simon said warningly.

"What's Tommy going to do, turn me in?" She turned and looked at Simon. Fiery patches

299

stood out on her cheeks. "I don't care! I have to know!"

"If this is family business . . . " Tommy began, putting his glass down on the side table and half rising from his seat.

Simon motioned him back in place. "What do you want to do, Kei?" he said quietly.

"See! Go and see, get it over with! For God's sake, I can't have it hanging over me for the rest of my life! *They* know, don't they?"

Simon looked at Kei, who gave a bob of her head to signify that she was braced for the procedure. Tommy put an arm around her, and Simon began to dig. He, too, was dreading what he might find, though decaying bodies were nothing new to him. He'd seen more than enough of them in the war, but there was no way to build up an immunity to their sight and smell, and the presence of this particular corpse would determine the course of his and Kei's lives.

About two feet down, the spade uncovered the remains of a piece of blue figured silk, a scarf stained and darkened from lying in the dampness underground. It didn't look like anything a man would wear. He hesitated to dig further and looked at Kei, who rubbed the back of her hand across her mouth and looked puzzled.

"It's mine," she said slowly. "I remember it, now that I see it, but I don't . . . " She frowned in concentration. "I don't remember what . . . "

Simon scraped at the scarf with the spade, trying to summon the nerve to bite the blade deeper into the clay pan that lay beneath.

"Oh, stop!" Kei cried suddenly and seized his arm, stabbing him with her nails, and dragged him back. "Don't look! Cover it up again!" Red spread across her cheeks like dark birthmarks.

Quickly, Simon shoveled dirt back on the cloth and tamped it down with his boot.

"Oh, not so hard!" She crossed her fists on her chest and began to pant convulsively. "Be gentle with her." She leaned over, shaken with dry retching, a silver string of saliva looping down from her mouth.

Tommy reached out toward her, but she whipped around and ran down the path to the château. Simon handed Tommy the spade and took off after her. She was going so fast that, in spite of his long legs, he could hardly catch up with her. She reached the meadow before him, dropped to her knees, and collapsed face down in the wet grass. Simon threw himself down on the ground beside her, put his arm over her back, and held her hard.

Finally, she rolled over and sat up with her legs angled to one side. Bits of grass stuck to her cheeks and she brushed them away. "She was so little, you can't imagine," she choked, wiping her face on her sleeve. "But perfectly formed. All curled up, so tiny, so tiny."

Bewildered, Simon sat up and got out his handkerchief to wipe her face, but she took it from him and did the job herself, leaning back against his chest. "I couldn't get an abortion here, a Catholic country," she said, gulping,

301

stifling her sobs. "Sweden was the only place then, but where was I to get the money? Not my parents, or they'd have known. Not from him, he'd just gotten married. Someone in the village, I think. I kept on working, getting more and more frightened, knowing I was starting to show."

"Slow down," said Simon, alarmed by her color and her shaking. "Are you saying that it's a baby buried out there? Not him?"

She nodded, beating her fists together with the movement of her head. "We'd stopped seeing each other by then. Finally I panicked and went to see him. He'd always been so wonderful to me. Gentle. Kind. And then . . . " She scrubbed at her eyes with the handkerchief until they were owly with smudged mascara. "I couldn't help screaming at him, I was so desperate. And he turned on me. Changed into some person I'd never seen before, somebody horrible. He beat the hell out of me. Kicked me in the stomach over and over while I rolled back and forth on the floor, trying to cover my belly, trying to cover my face, and his foot kept on smashing into me and smashing and smashing . . . " She went rigid for a moment and then began laughing quietly. She laughed to herself until Simon was thoroughly frightened for her and shook her roughly. She gasped and coughed, and the laughing stopped.

"God knows why I didn't abort then. But I didn't. I bled some, but I didn't lose the baby."

Tommy came and joined them, kneeling down a tactful distance away. Kei was unaware of

302

his presence, staring up at the window where her room had been then, as if she were seeing the scene again through the château walls. "The days went by, and I kept dreaming that a woman was telling me to kill the baby, that it was the only way. So—it was like I was still dreaming, everything in slow motion—and I took a coat hanger . . . " She turned and buried her face against his chest, digging her fingers into his sides but silent.

"Oh, Jesus!" Simon said under his breath, hurting for her.

"I got myself down those long stairs and clear out into the woods," she said, her voice muffled against him. "Blood running down my legs while I dug the hole. I wrapped the baby in my best scarf." She stopped again and Simon held her tight, his face pressed against the top of her head. "I thought I could be prosecuted for concealing a death, just as if I'd murdered someone in cold blood. And I did, didn't I?" She looked up at him.

"It's not the same, Kei," he said. "She wasn't . . . she didn't know. It's not the same."

When she twisted around, took the handkerchief, spat on it, and worked at removing the smeared mascara from under her eyes, Simon knew she was recovering. "I took a few days off from work, told them I had the flu, but the hemorrhaging got worse and worse, until one day there was a whole flood of blood." She gave a long fluttering sigh. "They had to send me home by hospital plane, and the infection

303

nearly killed me. I was in a coma for three days, and when I came out of it, the memory was gone as if it was a word wiped off a blackboard. Until now."

She blew her nose. "But I didn't murder Alexis. And I don't care what happened to the bastard, as long as I didn't kill him." She ran her fingers through her hair to get it back from her face, then said hesitantly, "Simon, do you think we could put her somewhere else? That's no place for a baby to be."

"Of course." He looked across to Tommy, who stood up, the spade still in his hand. Tommy shook his head slowly with a meaningful look.

They both helped Kei to her feet. "I'm all right," she said, shaking off their solicitous arms and walking ahead. "I didn't kill Alexis! You don't know how much better I feel, knowing that."

Tommy caught at Simon's sleeve, holding him back. "It's not there," he whispered, making sure Kei didn't hear him.

"You couldn't be mistaken?" Simon said, keeping his voice low. "After all that time underground . . . "

Tommy shook his head again. "Somebody must have taken it, and I think we both know why."

CHAPTER TWENTY-THREE

Simon clicked off the cassette recorder and planted his elbows on the desk, listening to the birds scrape, twitter, and call in the aviary and the ducks gabble outside in the moat, and marveled that Kei could make out his narrative over the background racket on the tapes. He was trying to dredge up a suitably deceptive alias for a French screen actress. It was about time to turn the manuscript over to a real secretary. This was one tape Kei wasn't going to hear.

He'd given her a tranquilizer and made her lie down upstairs for a rest, and had been dictating for about an hour. Although he was growing to hate his sessions with the recorder, Jeremy Kirbottle's phone call a few minutes ago had prodded him on, and he was feeling buoyed up enough at banishing the chimera of Alexis' corpse to forge ahead.

Yes, it was high time he dealt directly with Jeremy, Landsend's new owner, and shipped the tapes to London instead of having Kei transcribe them. Originally, Jeremy had asked for a spicy, easily-marketable autobiography, saying he wasn't interested in a disquisition on Giotto or Les Fauves—the type of material Simon published through another, scholarly firm. Days ago, Kei had been delighted with his frankness about his childhood sexual experimentations, neither knowing nor caring that the inception of his relationship with Elaine lay there. Kei had been thinking like a publisher then.

Now even the most discreet history of his adult relationships would set her off. He didn't relish trying to convince her that he'd had many platonic relationships with women who were close, dear friends. Fighting it out with her about the women who had been otherwise was altogether too gruesome to contemplate.

He turned at the sound of her footsteps. She stood in the open study door, looking foggy, a red crease down one cheek testifying that she'd slept without changing position. Holding out a box, she said, "I got a present for you in London. What with one thing and another, it sort of slipped my mind." She put the box in front of him on the desk and stood back, her hands clasped together, and waited for his reaction.

He really wished she hadn't. He loved getting presents, loved having friends go to the trouble over him, but he was hopeless at pretending gratitude for an atrocity that he couldn't give house space to. They hadn't known each other long enough for him to predict her taste, and she read him far too easily to be fooled by waffling ploys like "I've never seen anything like it!" or

"Now, that's what I call a gift!" This could be a catastrophe, but he had to open the box, or she'd be hurt.

"You already have everything," she said, "and it's intimidating, trying to find a gift for a man who's an authority on art objects. You're the devil to shop for."

Out of a rustle of pink tissue paper he took a boddhisatva of light wood coated with gesso. The graceful figure wore a silver gilt robe and ropes of golden filigree. One delicate hand held a gilded pomegranate.

"It's twelfth century," Kei said, and held her breath.

Simon turned it around and around in his hands, studying its detail and touching all the surfaces. The wood felt warm, as if a tiny sun were trapped inside. "It's exquisite," he said, awed by its perfection. "Museum quality."

Kei let out her breath and grinned. "Do you really like it?"

"Yes, very much. More than that, by far."

"They said that it was supposed to bring the owner luck, and I thought you needed that more than anything."

"You can't afford this," he said, deeply impressed by the knowledge and discernment that lay behind its selection.

"Yes, I can. I think between us we have rather a lot of money."

Reverently, Simon placed it on a shelf opposite his desk, where he'd see it every time he raised his eyes from work, came back to Kei, cupped

307

her face in his hands, and kissed her. "Thank you," he said. "You're really extraordinary."

After a satisfying minute of looking at each other, Kei said, "I could do with some lunch, couldn't you?"

He put his arm around her as they went into the sitting room. "Feeling better?"

"A thousand per cent! The world has a new shine to it!"

Marthe had set out an herb-roasted chicken on a platter, with vinaigrette vegetables arranged around it. After they'd demolished it, Simon ground fresh coffee and started it in the coffee-maker, then sat down and lit a cigarette. He sat tipped back in his chair, the arm with the cigarette hooked over the back, and looked at Kei, who smiled back at him. Was she beautiful or not? Was it important, either way? He truly could no longer judge what she looked like. She was Kei. Unique. Irreplaceable.

"Do I get to see the picture?" she asked. "I can see its outline through the pocket of your shirt. It's him, isn't it?" She took the cigarette from his mouth and put it in her own, looking edgy, as if she were preparing for an ordeal.

Hesitantly, Simon took out the picture and handed it to her, watching anxiously for her reaction. She looked at it for what seemed a very long time while he waited for her verdict.

"He's beautiful, Simon," she said at last. "He has your mouth and eyes. You must have looked like that when you were young." She propped the photograph against the bowl of yellow chrysanthemums and studied it. "Was your hair that color before it went white?"

"Darker brown. Almost black." He put the metal Italian coffeepot down by the cups and saucers and sat down beside her with his arm along the back of her chair, looking over her shoulder at the picture, trying to see it through her eyes. "I know I'm asking a lot," he said, reaching across for her hand, "wanting you to accept him, but he's . . . he's just a boy. He's innocent, even if Elaine and I aren't."

She laced her fingers with his gently. Then she tightened her grip so hard that it hurt. "I can't help being angry," she said. "He should have been ours instead!"

Simon laid his face against the back of her shoulder and closed his eyes, unable to speak. Kei seemed to be aware of what he was going through, let go of his hand, and ran hers up and down his arm gently, comfortingly. "I can't help loving him if he's yours," she said huskily. "I just need a little time to get over feeling cheated." After a moment, she felt the side of the coffeepot and said, "It's getting cold," and poured out cups for both of them.

Simon took a deep breath, recovered himself, and accepted the cup she gave him. She sipped hers as he picked up the pack of Players he'd left lying on the table, shook out a cigarette, and lit it.

"Now, I want you to think about this," she said, honing the tip of her ash carefully on the side of the ashtray. "What makes you so sure he's your child?" When Simon, surprised into silence, didn't answer, she went on, "He may be the image of you, but you and Elaine share the same genes, don't you? She's slept with a lot of men, I gather, and you aren't the only possible father."

Frankly, that had never occurred to him, probably because his guilt over his relationship with Elaine had made him accept an incestuous son as the logical, foreordained punishment for his sins.

"It would be hard to pin down if she was screwing everything in sight then the way she has for the past few years," he admitted. "I'm not sure about the timetable, wanted to put the whole thing out of my head. I can't remember when we made it last, precisely. I didn't exactly mark it in red on the calendar every time I fucked her."

"Oh, please!" said Kei, looking ill. "Did you have to say it that way?"

"I'm sorry, love. That was tactless. Let's see, she must have been about forty then. But I can't prove that I'm *not* the father, either. In any event, I don't want him in a boarding school in America, living like an orphan."

"I know, but it would make a world of difference if you weren't. To me, at least."

Simon felt strangely reluctant to give up the idea of having a son. He and Kei were too old to start a family, and—stupid though it was—the notion of dying without having had one bothered him. He would have loved to have had a whole raft of children in the house, spread about the breakfast table, playing on the meadow, and demanding bedtime stories when they were tucked in at night. Being everybody's honorary uncle just wasn't enough.

"What's that?" Kei asked.

"Sounds like an owl's got trapped in the hallway," said Simon, stubbing out his cigarette before getting up to look.

It was Missy, hoo-hooing to announce that she and Tommy were in the house. Two travel-worn bags were at Tommy's feet.

"Whoo! It's turned hot again!" said Missy and gave Kei and Simon smacking kisses. She looked very showbiz in white slacks, a white shirt, and giant sunglasses that came halfway up her forehead. "Tommy's brought Rudy's things. Loquat will be along. He hasn't finished meditating."

Simon looked at Tommy's trunks, sandals, and white shirt open down the front and wondered if he'd dressed that way because of the sudden heat or to show off his legs and the mat of fur on his chest.

"We've got two things on the schedule today," said Tommy. "Trying on your armor and doing the binding ceremony. I'll take Rudy's bags up and you start getting on your gear." He started up the stairs with the luggage before Simon could protest.

This must be what it feels like to walk on the surface of Jupiter, squashed down into a mush-

311

room from the gravitational pull, Simon thought, inspecting himself in the mirror on the back of the closet door. A distressed pair of eyes looked back at him through the visor slot. "How am I going to get on a horse in this?" His voice echoed around inside the helmet. "I can hardly move!"

"A couple of us will boost you on," said Tommy, dusting off the round plates at the shoulders with his handkerchief and looking pleased at what he had wrought. "You'll manage. I did, you can." He went out into the hallway and called to Missy and Kei that Simon was now on display. Simon turned to face the door, clanking faintly, as they came in for the viewing.

"Oh, my!" Missy's eyes widened. "You look gorgeous! Simply gorgeous!"

The dent on Kei's cheek was getting a workout as she tried to keep her face straight. "I always did want a knight in shining armor," she said. "But you do look wonderful, seriously."

Damn right he did! Simon pulled the helmet off, wincing as it clutched at his ears, and put it under his arm with a clang.

Tommy backed up from Simon, cocked his head, and surveyed him from head to foot. "Does it fit all right?"

"I guess so. It weighs a ton." He shifted his shoulders trying to adjust the padding that brought him out to Tommy's proportion. It kept catching the hair under his arms. "I feel like the Tin Woodman of Oz. And the legs don't feel quite right. You don't think they'll slip out of the stirrups?"

"You'll be fine," Tommy said confidently,

going around to check the rear view. "Nothing to worry about. I've been through it hundreds of times. The weight slows down the horse and keeps you in the saddle. You'll see." He came around to the front again and nodded, satisfied.

"There's just one small matter," Simon said slowly.

"What's that?"

"How in the hell do I pee?"

Tommy looked exasperated. "You *don't*! Once we get you in, you're in there to stay."

"It's going to be a long evening. How do I know I can hold it until it's over?"

"Maybe you could put a Dixie Cup inside," Missy said helpfully and sat down on the bed, leaning back on her elbows with her legs crossed.

"I'm not wearing the bottom half," Simon said resolutely. "That's final! And knock off the laughing, Kei."

"You *are* going to wear it!" Tommy folded his arms and looked adamant.

"I am *not*!" Simon shouted, setting off an echoing rattle throughout the suit.

"I think he's about to throw a tantrum," said Kei, sobering, "and you know there's nothing to be done when he gets his mind set." She sat down on the leather chair in the bay window. "How about if he just wore the black tights that go underneath? I've seen pictures of knights in half armor, haven't I?"

Tommy put a fist under his chin and considered. "It'd mean wearing a jockstrap," he said grudgingly. "And what about shoes? There

313

are feet in the tights, but he can't walk outside like that. Black boots might do. Not ideal, but . . . " He removed the hand from under his chin and waved it in a lazy circle in the air, expressing the vanity of trying to change Simon's mind.

"I'm dying to see Simon in tights!" said Missy, sitting up eagerly. "I love his legs, don't you, Kei?"

Kei cupped her hand and looked at her fingernails, then turned her hand over and looked at them from the new angle without saying anything. Tommy looked down at his own legs with a puzzled expression, as if he couldn't imagine any woman finding Simon's legs interesting when his own were available. Then he went over to shuck Simon out of the armor, saying, "Loquat should be coming over to do the binding ceremony fairly soon, and I'd like to get a little sun before autumn sets in. Then it's back to the sun lamp. Pull in your chin, Simon, or I'll never get this off."

There was hardly any point in asking the women to leave when he got undressed, since both of them were perfectly aware of how he looked in the buff, but when he got down to his tights, Simon hesitated before untying the knot at the waist and looked at Kei, who took her cue and hustled Missy out of the room tactfully by saying, "Come on, Missy, I've got an idea."

The women were standing in the hallway as Tommy and Simon came down the stairs. The painting equipment Elaine had brought back

314

from Paris was stacked around their feet, and Kei had bottles of wine under her arms and a folded easel in one hand. Missy was holding a picnic basket and a couple of collapsible camp stools.

"We're going to have a painting party in the vineyard!" said Missy, full of gala spirit. "I told Marthe to let Loquat know where we are. Come on, bear a hand and let's get going!"

Simon patted his shirt pocket to be sure he'd remember to put the packet in for the binding ceremony. Just to be on the safe side, he'd added a small picture of Elaine when she was about three to the photograph of young Simon. It was all a futile exercise, of course, but he'd agreed to it last night. He and Tommy divided the remaining equipment between them and started off for the back door.

"Arf a mo," said Tommy, putting his share down again. "Might as well get a good dose of sun while I'm at it." He took off his shirt, laid it on the foyer table, and rolled his trunks down over his hips. They fell into a figure eight around his ankles, and he stepped out of them and picked them up. Missy giggled and Kei gasped, then looked Tommy over with hair-raising thoroughness, pissing the hell out of Simon.

"God dammit, put those back on!" he stormed, feeling jealous and petty and plain mad.

"I just want a bit of sun," Tommy said reasonably, with a twinkle in his eye. "The French aren't narrow-minded about nudity. I'm not ashamed of my body."

That was putting it mildly! "Well, *I* am!" said Simon.

"Narrow-minded or ashamed of your body?" Tommy assumed a body-builder's pose and popped a biceps muscle up and down. Kei's interest in this phenomenon was not only unseemly but infuriating, in Simon's opinion.

"Both!" he said peevishly.

"Oh, very well," Tommy sniffed and put his trunks back on, having accomplished his purpose.

"You have to admit he looks like a Greek god," said Missy, whose breath seemed a little irregular and her eye distinctly lewd.

"I don't have to do anything of the sort," Simon said. "He's a fucking exhibitionist!" He would have added something about men who can't leave other people's women alone, but he didn't want to hurt Missy's feelings. "Let's get on with this," he said, pointing with a palette at the things Tommy had put down.

As they came down the bridge steps, Tommy said, "You go on. Painting isn't my forte. I'll just take a quick dip in the moat. I've always wanted to try it."

Simon almost said something but checked himself. Tommy set down the stools and paint-boxes he was carrying, slipped off his sandals, and dove diagonally off the top step into the moat.

A fountain of brown water rose into the air and fell back. In the middle of the moat, Tommy's legs waved upright and then tumbled back into the water, flailing and thrashing. The ducks set up a hysterical quacking.

Simon had to sit down on the steps, he was laughing so hard. Tommy waded across to the bank, his head and shoulders covered with mud and green slime.

"Great goddess, why didn't you tell me the water's only up to your ass!" Tommy bellowed, digging gobs of mud out of his eyes and looking like the end man in a minstrel show. "I'm going to make your guts into garters!" He started up the bank, but his muddy feet skidded on the grass and he teetered for a moment, his arms windmilling, and fell back into the water with a smacking splash. A fountain of brown water rose into the air and fell back again.

Tommy waded out again, his face a brown mask, and pulled himself up the bank by handfuls of long grass. A troop of ducks waddled up behind him in a line like a pull toy and began pecking at his dirty bare toes. He stalked over to Simon, who was laughing so hard he thought he might do himself a hurt, and leaned over and grabbed him by the front of his shirt.

"Ah-ah!" said Kei warningly, holding up a bottle by its neck.

Tommy looked at her and the bottle consideringly and then dropped Simon, who got out his handkerchief and wiped his nose. Tommy didn't look like a Greek god now. A tar baby, maybe.

"I'm going to take a shower," said Tommy with theatrical dignity and limped back into the house.

"Simon Eagleton, you have a mean streak!" said Missy, who had failed to join in the laughter.

"They're only playing games," said Kei, redistributing the equipment so Tommy would have a full set of his own to carry and the rest of them would be able to start painting without him. They started off for the vineyard. Every few steps, Simon would remember the vision of Tommy's legs waving in the air and snicker.

When they were almost at the stone wall above the vineyard, they heard the sound of a flute. Loquat, wearing a long white robe cinched with a red cord that danced forward with each step, was playing a gigue and following them, his red-gold hair a bright halo in the sunlight.

Kei and Simon painted seriously, conferring over techniques, while Missy dabbled, writing her name over and over with her brush in red and singing aloud in her famous voice as Loquat played the flute. When Tommy joined them, he had changed into Simon's white shorts and favorite monogrammed silk shirt, open to the waist. He had also managed to hit on Simon's favorite gold cufflinks. Tommy pointedly made no reference to the moat incident but instead, with heavy sighs and sweet, sad smiles, handed glasses of wine around subserviently, thereby letting everyone know that he had been badly used.

"Ready to get on with the binding?" asked Loquat after tossing down his wine and wiping his mouth with the back of his hand. "You'll notice that I've dressed for the occasion. I thought Simon would prefer it."

"You know about this, Missy, don't you?" Simon said.

"They told me. I didn't know Tommy was a witch until this morning. Isn't it cute of him?" said Missy, putting her brush back in the painting kit.

They all moved back toward the wall to stand around Loquat, all but Tommy curious to see what he was going to do.

"What'd you bring that belongs to Elaine?" asked Tommy.

Simon handed him the sealed package of photographs and, before he could stop him, Tommy had torn the paper off. "Where did you get this picture of Simon?" Tommy demanded. "Why did she give it to you? I didn't think you knew about him."

"You've got a hell of a nerve! You could see that was sealed," said Simon, snatching at it before the implications of what Tommy had said sank in.

Tommy held the photographs away. "I have a right to see a picture of my own kid," he said challengingly. He looked down at the picture of the boy, and the long creases running down from his cheekbones deepened. "So that's what he looks like now." For a fleeting moment, his face puckered.

Simon felt a few arrhythmic bumps in his chest. He made a couple of false starts before he could get the words out. "Are you sure he's yours?" He took the hand that Kei had suddenly put on his arm and held it tight.

Tommy gave him an ugly smile. "You didn't think he was *yours,* did you? I made sure you were out of the picture before I planted the seed." He ran a finger softly over the photograph and said, "He's mine all right. I was there when he was born. I held him while he was still wet." He looked up at Simon. "There's no use your claiming him. I checked the dates over and over to be sure, and you *couldn't* be his father."

Missy looked thunderstruck and sat down hard on her camp stool as if she'd been cut off at the knees. The stool turned over and dumped her on the ground.

Tommy said viciously, "I'm warning you, Simon, if you ever so much as *look* like you're going to touch her again, I'll slit your fucking throat, you damned pervert! She may not give a damn about me any more, but you keep away from her! Understood?" The dangerous look on his face was not diminished by the black bruise around his right eye. He handed the photographs to Loquat and went to sit on the wall a short distance away, staring morosely out across the valley.

Kei's face was so alight that Simon was ashamed of the quick, sharp pang he felt at losing his son so quickly, so totally. He'd never known that tears could actually jump out of anyone's eyes, but hers did and ran down her cheeks in parallel streaks. He kissed her, realizing now how much her generosity at accepting young Simon had cost her.

"I can't believe this!" said Missy, picking herself up from the ground and setting the stool upright. "What kind of people *are* you, anyway?"

"We can trust your discretion in this, can we not?" Loquat asked her sternly.

"I won't say a word, I promise," said Missy, dusting off the seat of her pants. "But my golly, I'm just a small town girl from Iowa, and it sort of knocked me off my pins." She looked at Simon and said, as if she were talking to herself, "It makes me feel, I don't know, funny about myself. Having slept with a man who . . . " The rest of the sentence died down too low to hear. She looked away, then went to sit on the wall beside Tommy and lean against him.

Simon walked off a few steps from the group and stood alone. He spread out his hands. They *looked* like the hands of a normal man.

"Don't," said Kei's voice softly by his shoulder. She took his hands in hers and kissed them. "Don't."

"Here, here!" said Loquat officiously, "you're forgetting what we're here for. Gather round, please!" He took a flat cardboard box and a red string from the pocket of his trousers, which he wore under the robe, as the four of them walked over to watch. He handed the picture of the boy to Simon. "We can't use this, or he'd be bound, too. I can't imagine that he needs it, at his age." Simon hesitated, then held the photograph out to Tommy, who took it and placed it in the pocket of the borrowed shirt, then put his hand on Simon's arm a brief moment.

"It's fortunate that you brought this picture of your sister as well," said Loquat. He inserted it in the box, tied it up with the cord, and said a few words over it inaudibly. Then he gave the box back to Simon.

"That's it?" asked Simon.

"There you go again!" said Loquat. "You've read too many books written by people who want to make a fast buck by titillating the public's imagination. Wicca is a nature religion, my dear boy, so what we do is only natural." He put his hand paternally on Simon's shoulder. "Always remember, it's *white* magic. Not like this." He took up his flute and began to play That Old Black Magic, and it seemed only natural for Simon to take Kei in his arms and start dancing to the music on the flat ground by the vineyard wall. Which he did.

In bed that night, their faces itchy from sunburn, Kei and Simon opened a freshly chilled bottle of Macon Lugny Blanc and shared laughter over Tommy's dive into the moat.

"Do you think the binding ceremony will really do any good?" asked Kei, putting her empty glass on the bedside table.

Simon put the bottle and his glass on the floor, scrunched down beneath the covers, and said, "Hope on! I'm satisfied as it is. You're home scot free, and so am I. That's more than I dreamed."

Kei snapped out the light.

"Don't touch!" said Simon.

CHAPTER TWENTY-FOUR

Dear Chris:

I feel so much better since talking to you again! You're such a love, sticking by me the way you are, in spite of everything. We have something very special between us, I think — and no other relationships can change that.

At last some good news! If I were a Victorian lady, I'd be swooning away with delight! Tommy McKenzie is the father of Elaine's son! That snake of a woman lied to Simon about it, and of course he was going to do the honorable thing. He's very exasperating that way. It doesn't change the past, but for a long time Simon and Elaine haven't . . . well, it was over years and years ago. Simon doesn't need to be punished for it any more than he has been already, so it's a closed topic from now on, as far as I'm concerned.

Another great relief is that the gap in my memory has been filled in. It's a long and unpleasant story that I don't want to talk about except to say that everything's all right. I began to get some inklings about those events after that nasty dinner party, but there was no point in bothering you with the details. If you postpone telling people about difficult things, they have a way of working themselves out. I know my habit of putting off telling you things has always driven you up the wall, but this time you would have gotten awfully upset for nothing.

Darling Chris, considering how you feel about everything, this may be very hard for you to take, but Simon and I are going to be married. I can't help it. I love him. Please try to be happy for me.

Since I won't be coming back, there's an enormous favor I have to ask of you, and you might call in my lawyer to help. Could you sell my apartment and put the furniture up for auction? I hate to burden you with this, but there's no one else who knows me and my arrangements as intimately as you do. Simon's place can hardly take another stick of furniture, and my modern pieces would look out of place here. Besides, I bought all of them with Robin and don't want to remember him when I see them.

Please choose whatever you'd like to have. There are only a few things I want to keep, like the photograph albums with pictures of Stephen, my Japanese koto (you remember, the long stringed instrument with the brocade at either end and the moveable ivory bridges), and the things on the list I've appended. If this is too tough for you to handle, I'll understand. But if you can take care of it, thanks a million.

Rudy's moving in today to keep an eye on me until I go to London to stay with Missy (she's leaving today), so I'd better scurry around and see that Marthe's got his room ready.

Dearest love,

Kei

CHAPTER TWENTY-FIVE

"How did Marthe prepare those oysters on the half shell?" Rudy asked. "They were extraordinarily delicious."

"Just grilled them lightly in Chateauneuf-du-Pape. Easy to do. I taught her," said Simon, looking at his new houseguest over the tip of his cigarette and wondering. *Had* Rudy and Elaine, or hadn't they? He'd never noticed it before, but Rudy had a muscular chest there under the ivory turtleneck he wore with his dark blue blazer, to judge from the way the material swelled out and then creased below the pectorals. Maybe Rudy *was* attractive to women. Maybe his shy exterior looked like a challenge. Simon glanced at Kei to see if she was looking at Rudy. She was. At his thighs. And Rudy was looking at her looking at his thighs and smiling in a way that made Simon's blood boil.

"Why don't you play the piano?" Simon said. It came out more brusquely than he'd intended.

Rudy got up, saying, "Any requests?"

"Whatever you like," Simon answered, and

Rudy sat down and attacked the piano in the Germanic style that Simon hated, pounding at it like a mad chiropractor trying to work out a devil of a kinked muscle, making the music ring around the sitting room. Liszt, wouldn't you know it, so he could show off his hands with all those crossovers!

Simon asked himself what kind of a Trojan horse he'd let into the house, asking Rudy to help him protect Kei while Loquat and Tommy set about breaking up the Satanic coven. And face it, Kei was one horny lady. Be reasonable, though. Since men routinely gave women the once-over, women had the right to do the same, as Kei had been doing with Rudy. Simon reminded himself that if he'd put into action all the things he'd thought about while looking, he would have died an early death. Anyway, he trusted her, didn't he? Of course. She loved him. She *said* she loved him.

Look at her, would you? Transported by the music. Rapt. She didn't look like that when *he* played the Mapleleaf Rag! By sheer willpower he made her turn to look at him, and he crooked a finger at her. She came over to snuggle up against him on the settee as Rudy's piece drew to a close. So it wouldn't hurt to let Rudy see how things stood. Simon kissed her as the last notes died away, making sure that Rudy wouldn't miss what was going on.

A few gentle throat clearings came from the direction of the piano bench. Mission accomplished. Simon let Kei go. Both he and Kei complimented Rudy on his performance, which was a tactical mistake. Rudy tore off into Beethoven so vigorously that the whole piano shook.

If Rudy was going to concertize every night, Simon thought as he sat with one arm around Kei and his other hand drumming irritably on his knee, it was going to be an ordeal. He calculated that he could stand exactly two nights of it before starting to foam at the mouth. Kei was doing it again — that stare of enchantment, of going off into a private world of her own, where he couldn't get at her and where she was doing God knows what in her imagination.

"Should I . . . " he began in a subdued voice, about to ask her if he should bring in the coffee, but she shushed him. Rudy hit a clinker, and Simon rejoiced.

When Rudy had finished showing off, Simon brought in the coffee and set it down on the side table.

"Since exact terminology seems to be a vital part of being able to think accurately about any subject, I have never understood the paucity of color words in Japanese," Rudy was saying, and Kei was hanging on his words. "They're the race most noted for subtle use of color, yet there is no exact word for blue. *Aoi,* as you know, means either blue or green, and one must resort to added descriptive words, such as *mizu no iro,* the color of water, to make oneself perfectly clear."

It was not a conversation that Simon had anything to contribute to, and he felt shut out. "Black or white?" he said to Rudy, interrupting.

328

"Black, please."

Simon handed Kei her coffee and Rudy his. As he passed the cup to Rudy, he sensed that something was off key. The smile Rudy gave him was not reflected in the eyes behind the glasses, but the diamond-hard glint vanished immediately, and Rudy said, "I feel like an intruder here. You two should be alone." His eyes twinkled again in the customary manner. "Surely Tommy is overdramatizing."

"The only thing I have to go on is the fact that Bayard was killed," Simon said, taking a sip of coffee and noting that Marthe had made it with cardamom. "That's quite convincing, though. Anyone capable of doing that must be dangerously warped." He picked up the stub of his cigarette from the ashtray and took one miserly puff before extinguishing it. "Rudy, do you think there's a Satanic cult operating in the village?"

Rudy leaned back in his chair and crossed his legs. "There will always be a lunatic fringe." He cleared his throat and took on a professorial air. "They will have been encouraged by the upsurge in interest in the occult in the past few years. There have been publications documenting remarkable occurrences—afterdeath experiences, ghost sightings—that seem unarguable. Indeed, at times—against my better judgment—I myself have intimations that there may be forces out there of which we are only beginning to learn."

"Such as?"

"Well, undoubtedly when you were a child, you saw sinister shapes in the shadows when you went to bed at night and were convinced that evil lurked about you. We dismiss this as childish fancy. Our western, scientific society does not accommodate the idea that there is fragmented evil in a freefloating form. But what if the children are right?"

He set his cup down on the table beside him and fished in his pockets, one after the other, until Simon handed him a cigarette and lit it for him. Rudy leaned back in his chair again.

"It may well be that the child mind is sensitive to something quite real that we blind ourselves to," he continued. "More primitive peoples, who do not educate their young in the same way, retain that sensitivity and believe devoutly in those forces. Who are we to say they are wrong?"

"But there's no evidence," said Simon.

"That, too, is disputable." Rudy tapped his upper lip with a long, artistic forefinger. "When I was doing research on the Navaho language, I encountered a Ph.D. who had gone back to the blanket—returned to the reservation—who had a curious story to tell. One night, he said, his house was attacked by elementals, disembodied spirits of evil, who howled about the windows like wild animals and clawed at the house, pelting it with blows until the walls shook."

He paused to remove some loose tobacco from his lips and took a drink of coffee.

"Of course, I was dubious," he went on. "But he took me to his house, and there were the slashes on the outside walls. It was covered from roof to ground with long gouges . . . though whether he put them there himself to back up his story or there was some other, natural cause, I couldn't say."

"Oh, poppycock!" said Simon.

Rudy's eyes lit up. "Now, *there's* a word that's misused." He leaned forward. "Do you realize that it's not the inconsequential euphemism that you think? Dear little grandmothers who say it in place of something more emphatic do not realize that in Dutch it means the equivalent of—excuse me, may I say it?" He looked at Kei for permission. "Soft shit."

Rudy could discourse endlessly on comparative philology and exotic languages, and Simon didn't want to let him start rambling on a subject where only Kei understood him. "If they were disembodied spirits, how could they have claws?" he said.

"It was his story, not mine." Rudy chuckled. "I did not say *I* believed in elementals, although they may exist. If they do, the disturbing thing is that there's no protection against them. Locked doors would not keep them out, and neither could you nor I if the Satanists evoked them against Kei in some mysterious manner. But if Elaine is involved with the cult—and that's hard to believe—she would hardly allow them to unleash them on this house. As they say in Bulgarian, 'Garvan garvanu oko ne vadî.'"

Simon waited while Rudy did his little act of pretending that they were all fluent in Bulgarian, remembering that they weren't, and then translating.

"The raven plucketh not the raven's eye, that

is to say," he said. "They're not controllable, the elementals, once they've been evoked, you understand."

Simon put his arm around Kei. "Is that part of the Satanists' rigmarole, calling up these elementals?"

"I believe they try to release them by provoking the fear of animals, which attracts them in some mysterious manner. That may be the reason for the cattle mutilations hereabouts." He finished off his coffee and set the cup back on the tray.

Kei got out of her chair and sat down by Simon's feet, tucking her skirt around her. "Then couldn't they just torture the animals?" she asked, leaning back against Simon's legs. "Why do they need to cut out their hearts and those . . . those other things?"

"To cut them out when they're still living would be the height of torment, draining them of the last drop of fear, one supposes," Rudy said blandly.

"What do they do with the parts after they're cut out?" Kei asked.

"Eat them, I imagine," Rudy said, and Simon saw the hardness come into his eyes again.

After a shocked silence, Kei said, "Hearts, perhaps. But not wombs and penises?"

"Magical thinking," Rudy said with a shrug. "One takes on the power of the thing eaten. In cannibalistic societies, one gains the courage of the enemy by eating his heart, his intelligence by eating his brain. Therefore, from the organs of reproduction, fertility and sexual power."

"Now I know we're dealing with madmen," Simon said. "Anyone who can swallow down a penis has to be insane."

Kei chuckled.

"Oh, shut up," said Simon, bumping his leg against her. "You know what I mean."

"You locked all the doors, didn't you?" asked Kei, standing by the window in her nightgown and looking out the window at the oak grove. "I'm beginning to get jumpy. I keep thinking about Sélène sealed up in that grotto out there." She got in on her side of the bed. "No, to tell the truth, I'm scared stiff, Simon."

"*Now* will you listen to me?" he said, standing at the door of the bathroom, his mouth full of dentifrice foam. "I can manage on my own with the manuscript," he said indistinctly. "That damned tournament's tomorrow night and the town will be full of strangers. I'd like to get you off on the afternoon plane to London if you'd just listen to reason." He went to the basin and rinsed out his mouth and put the toothbrush on the rack beside hers. "What?" he said at Kei's saying something he didn't catch.

"I said 'I will,' " she said, raising her voice.

"Thank God, now you're showing some sense!" He picked his bridge up off the sink edge and put it in the cabinet. He had Rudy to thank for her change of mind. They'd talked of elementals, ghosts, witch doctors, and all the shuddery things of the occult until Kei'd got the wind up. If he hadn't known Rudy better, he'd have sworn the whole conversation had been directed to scaring the liver and lights out of Kei, rather than simply being a vehicle for Rudy to show off his abstruse knowledge. In any case, it had had the effect that Simon might have wished for—convincing her that the château was a dangerous place for her to be.

"I don't like leaving you behind here," she said as he got in beside her.

"It's not me they're after, love" He kissed her goodnight lightly, not wanting to start anything up when he was healing so well. "Elaine would see to that, and they haven't any grudge against *me.*"

"Just the same." She pounded at her pillow and then settled back against it. "They did kill Bayard and they have mutilated cattle in this district. I get the cold collywobbles, thinking they may have unloosed those elemental things."

"No such thing," said Simon. "That Indian must have taken a garden hoe to his house when he was smashed. Nothing like that's going to happen here."

Simon awoke with a start. All along her body where they touched, he could feel Kei's tension.

"There's someone in the house," she said in a low voice.

He heard nothing but the whirring of the electric clock by her side of the bed. Over her shoulder he could see moonlight silvering the floor. A serene waxing moon hung low on the horizon.

"It's probably Rudy raiding the fridge," he

said, putting an arm around her waist to draw her close against him.

"No." She sat up, clutching the covers to her chest.

Then he heard it, a slow shuffling and scratching along the floorboards of the corridor outside, a secret sound. Simon sat up and listened. A sound like dragging claws was scuttling closer and closer.

Quickly, he threw back the covers, swung his legs over the side of the bed, and reached for his robe lying at the foot of the coverlet. As he watched, the brass acanthus leaf on the surface of the doorknob, outlined by the bright moonlight, turned on its side with a grate of metal, and the lock clicked.

"What the hell?" he said under his breath and got up to try the door. It was locked fast. He seized the knob and pulled at it with all his strength, but it was useless, it wouldn't budge.

Just then a bawling sound came from outdoors and spiraled up into a strangling scream. Simon whirled and was at the window in two strides. Out in the pasture, an animal was dying in pain and terror, its shrilling bellows tearing across the night air, as the moon calmly floated into a nest of gray clouds rimmed with gold.

Suddenly the door shook as heavy strokes screeched down the light wood, battering against it. And now the screams were outside in the hall, louder than the ones from the pasture, an abrupt tidal wave of noise that pierced the eardrums. The assault of sound from both directions paralyzed Simon, freezing him to the spot and making his flesh crawl, until he heard Kei whimper. She was backed up against the headboard, rigid with fright, a long strand of hair hanging down over one eye.

Without thinking, he grabbed the leather chair in the window, but it was too heavy to lift, so he swept the things off the table beside it and picked the table up by the top.

"Don't!" Kei cried. "You don't know what's out there!"

The shrieking bellows from the corridor thundered into a storm of noise, slashing across the nerves like strokes of a razor. The light panels of the door shuddered and bulged inward as thudding blows continued to rain down on them from outside. Simon swung the table, driving its legs against a panel, and one slipped through. When he drew it back, a long gouge ran down it, as if a wild beast had ripped a claw along its length.

Then it stopped. The sounds from the corridor cut off, leaving his ears ringing, and something scuffled and scraped away from outside the door and off down the hall. Still the animal screamed in the pasture, long shredding sounds as if its life were being torn out through its throat. Simon lifted the table again and heaved it against the door. The wood splintered outward. He pounded at it over and over until he could get his hand through to turn the key in the lock and push the door open.

The corridor was empty.

Someone was calling his name. He ran down to Rudy's room and unlocked the door. Rudy, his glasses askew on his nose, rushed out in his bathrobe and said, "You take the kitchen stairs. I'll go down the ones into the foyer."

Simon charged along the hall and down the steps into the kitchen with Kei flying along by his side, putting on her kimono as she went. As he reached the bottom of the stairs, he heard the front door bang open, but he found no one in the rooms below and went into the study to get his revolver from the desk. As he, Rudy, and Kei met in the foyer, they looked at one another, wordless and panting.

"There's no one out front, either," Rudy gasped.

Simon took off through the door, over the bridge, and out across the meadow. He started to call back to Kei to return to the house, but decided she'd be safer with him and motioned her to catch up with a wave of his arm. A long, despairing wail quivered across the night air, and then all was still again, except for the thud of their feet along the pathway.

Fournier was standing by the carcass, wearing pajama pants, his arms and hands white in the moonlight, his bare chest dark with hair. His hair was standing up around his head in tousled spikes, and his feet were stained with the blood that pooled around the bull's body and streamed across the grass. The bull was a black splotch on the pasture, with white ribbons and pink loops of intestines raveling across the swamp of blood spreading out around it. The body heaved, and a hind leg gave a final convulsive kick.

"Don't look," Simon said to Kei, but it was too late. She staggered away a few paces, leaned over, and there was a splashing of vomit. While Rudy went over to attend to her, Simon asked Fournier if he had seen anything.

Fournier combed his hair with his fingers and shook his head. "They locked my door from the outside. It was like this when I got here." There was no blood on him, except for his feet.

"Better call the police, not that they can do any good now," said Simon. "And in the morning, call the knackers to haul the body away." He went to Kei and put his arm around her. "Pack your things," he said.

CHAPTER TWENTY-SIX

Dear Chris:

I've been up half the night but can't get back to sleep—too scared to close my eyes, so I might as well send you my address in London where I'll be staying with Missy. I'll paperclip it to this letter on a card you can carry in your pocket, just in case.

Simon's right in the next room, but he's one of those indestructible people who sleep like the dead in the midst of catastrophe, so I've got my door locked and the bureau pushed against it.

This will sound outlandish, but some Satanists in the village are out for my blood just because of that stupid pomander ball I found here on the estate. Apparently it belonged to the mistress of the château who was the head of the devil-worship cult in the 17th century, and they're really pissed at me for taking it—to the point of trying to cut me up with that farm machine and shooting at me with the ball bearing. They've killed one of Simon's dogs, and last night they tore apart a bull in the pasture while it was still alive, and I'm so frightened I can't see straight. After it happened, the gendarmes came over to interview us about it, and now I'm so full of coffee I probably couldn't sleep even if I could stop shaking. Rudy's on guard while Simon's sleeping, and he's going to drive me out to the airport this afternoon while Simon gets ready for the tournament, so I'll be perfectly safe, don't worry.

Hold on, Simon's shouting and barging around in the hall. Back in a minute.

Here I am again. It was nothing. Just Simon getting hysterical because he couldn't find me.

No time to say more except for one thing. When the bull was killed in the pasture, I got a good look at Simon's hired hand, Fournier. Chris, his name isn't Fournier at all! It's Alexis Michaelson!

Hastily,

Kei

CHAPTER TWENTY-SEVEN

"How did you get in here?"

"Now, don't get yourself in an uproar," said Elaine, looking up from putting jam on a croissant. At the throat of her blouse Simon could see the fine iron chain. "Marthe let me in. How come you've got this place locked up tight this morning?"

"I don't want you here with Kei," Simon said from the doorway. "In short, I don't want you here at all."

Elaine put the croissant down on her butter plate and began nipping bits of crust off it with her fingernails, looking nervous. "I have to talk to you, Simon. Please sit down."

Warily, Simon went to his place, sat down, and poured himself some coffee. She couldn't do anything to Kei in his presence, and if she had her say, she might go away without causing trouble.

Elaine put her elbows on the table, rested her mouth against her clasped hands, and worked them back and forth against her lips before speaking. "I've done something very stupid, Simon. You would have found out about it sooner or later, but I want you to hear it first from me."

"Yes?" he said impatiently.

"I don't know how I got it into my head that I could get away with it when Tommy's around. One day he would have told you." She rested her forehead on her knuckles and took a deep breath. "I lied to you about the boy. The truth is . . ."

"That he's not my child," Simon said coldly. He took a drink of coffee, keeping his eyes on her over the rim.

She looked up, surprised. "Tommy told you?"

"Yes." He put the cup down onto the saucer with a click.

She nodded and sighed. "Of course. I must have been crazy to try to get away with it." She unclasped her hands and rolled the edge of the tablecloth between her fingers. "It's too late to make excuses, but you don't understand what it's been like, being dependent on you for every penny." Her mouth sagged down at the corners, like a clown's. "Every woman you had was a threat. I never knew when you'd throw me out in the cold."

"I wouldn't have done that," he said, refusing to let her move him.

"But even if I could have gone it alone, I wouldn't have been able to support myself. His schools were so expensive." She looked up pleadingly. "I've felt so helpless! And it's gotten worse as I've grown older. I'm so alone, Simon."

342

"We're all getting older," he said implacably. "And you have your son. He should have been with you."

Her shoulders drooped. She nibbled the nail on her little finger, and her eyes glazed over with tears. "All right. I didn't expect you to forgive me." She ran a finger under each eye to catch the tears, careful not to disturb her eye makeup. "That isn't the only reason I came over, though. About the tournament tonight. You've got to be careful, Simon. I know you'll go, no matter what I say, but you've got to be careful."

He lit the first cigarette of the morning and let the smoke drift across the table. "Tommy and I have been practicing. You needn't worry. Besides, you're in my will. I haven't changed it yet."

"For God's sake, Simon, will you take me seriously for once?" She pounded both fists on the table edge. "You don't realize what you're ... " She stopped at the sound of footsteps in the hall.

"Good morning, everyone," Rudy said cheerily, coming in to take a place next to Elaine at the table. He was wearing the ivory turtleneck without a jacket and looked as chipper as if he hadn't been up half the night. "Don't let me interrupt, Elaine," he said, putting his napkin in his lap and reaching for the coffee. "What was that you were saying as I came down the hall?"

"Nothing. I wasn't saying anything." Elaine dropped her eyes to her lap.

"Oh, now. Wasn't it something about the tournament tonight?" Rudy said pleasantly, pouring more coffee for her and then helping himself.

"No, I . . . I was just asking Simon if Kei would be there."

"Were you now?" He smiled at her and put two spoonfuls of sugar in her cup and stirred it with his spoon. "I'm afraid neither Kei nor I will be there. I'm going to Belgium to hand over the chamber piece I've done for the government after I take Kei to the airport. She's leaving for London this afternoon."

"You're taking her to the airport?" Elaine seemed surprised.

"Yes, to help out Simon. Too bad we will miss the festivities. They would have been amusing."

Elaine pushed her coffee away. Noting it, Rudy smiled. "Too much sugar?" he asked.

"Yes. No. I just don't want any," said Elaine.

"But you'll be there, won't you, Elaine? You wouldn't want to disappoint your friends," said Rudy, reaching for a croissant and taking one to butter.

"I'll be there," she said in a small voice.

Kei came in the swinging door with a platter of broiled kidneys, stiffened momentarily at the sight of Elaine, but covered it up and brought the dish over to Simon and ladled some onto his plate.

"Anybody else want some of these?" she asked. Her face was scrubbed bare of makeup until it shone and there were blue shadows under her eyes. She'd swept her hair into a ponytail and

344

was wearing jeans. Having no takers, she carried the platter to the other end of the table near the door, sat down, and put some of the kidneys on her own plate, saying, "I'll try anything once." She took a bite, froze, struggled the mouthful down, and took a long drink of water. "Oh, Simon, how *can* you?" she said and coughed.

"Did you bring your car, Elaine?" Rudy asked.

"Yes, but . . . "

"I'll need to pick up my musical scores for the trip. Would you run me over to my place?" Without waiting for her reply, he wiped his mouth with his napkin and got up. "Will you excuse me, Kei, Simon? I'll be back in a bit," he said.

As he and Elaine left, Kei said, "He didn't touch his croissant," and appropriated it.

Just as she bit into it, there was a scuffle out in the hallway and Elaine cried out. Kei put down the croissant and got up to look into the foyer. When she returned to her place, her expression of shock took Simon by surprise. The front door slammed, and soon afterwards there was the sound of a motor starting up.

"What happened out there?" Simon asked.

"Either a lover's quarrel, or Elaine's a masochist," said Kei. "Could you slide the coffee down? Rudy gave her an awful slap and knocked her clear across the hall, but she didn't seem to object. I guess that must be the way they carry on together. You aren't given to that sort of thing, are you, Simon?"

"Masochism?" Well, it was another side of Elaine's love life that he'd rather not have known about, but it answered one question. Elaine and Rudy *had*.

"No, slapping women around."

"I should hope not!" Not more than a couple of times at the outside, and then only with severe provocation. He put on his reading glasses, shook out the paper, and tossed the puzzle section down to Kei. "Rudy hasn't tried anything on with you, has he?"

She took out her reading glasses. "No, and I find that vaguely insulting. Have you got a pen?"

He felt his breast pocket. It was empty, so he put down his cigarette and got up to go to the study for one. Through the windows of the front doors he saw Tommy and Loquat walking across the parking area. He nipped in, got a pen, and was back in the hallway as they came in.

"Bit of excitement last night, I hear," said Tommy, whose black eye was fading to a sedate color. "It's all over the village."

"Achyfi! A nasty bit of work! I can't say I'm surprised, though," said Loquat, hugging Simon, who endured it.

"Kei's leaving on the afternoon plane. Had breakfast?" asked Simon, leading the way to the dining room.

"We've been up hours, getting the tournament set," said Tommy, bussing Kei on the cheek as Loquat took her hand and kissed it. "I'm ready for another cup of coffee, what about you, Loquat?"

Simon gave Kei the pen and went out to the kitchen to ask Marthe to freshen the pot, and when he got back the men were seated at the table, prodding Kei to go over the events of the night.

"It's wise that you're leaving town before the tournament," said Loquat, polishing the silver absent-mindedly on his napkin. "The old abbey's the site of the Satanic rites, so they'll be out in force tonight."

"How did you find that out?" asked Simon, sitting down and resuming his breakfast.

"We have double agents." Loquat set down the silver and arranged it neatly by his plate again. "Not that we need them to tell us that. Satanists are perishingly trite. Naturally, that's the place they'd choose. Bats. Rotting stones. An altar to desecrate. One wonders if any of them have a sense of humor. I'd have a deal of difficulty not tittering during their ceremonies. Moreover, the place reeks. Speaking of which, who's been here this morning?"

"Rudy and Elaine," said Kei, looking up from filling in the first horizontal blank.

"Ah!" Loquat nodded sagely. "I take it nothing untoward occurred."

Marthe came in with the coffee, filled the cups, and made a little bob when she came to Loquat, who beamed benevolently at her.

"Oh, Marthe, there's something I want to talk to you about," said Kei, rising. "Will you gentlemen excuse me for a moment?"

"Something you might like to know," said Simon as the women left. "Elaine confessed all. About young Simon. You don't suppose that the binding ceremony had anything to do with that?"

Loquat put three spoonfuls of sugar in his coffee and took two croissants. "It could be the beginning."

Tommy looked wistful as he stirred his coffee. "I wish she'd let me see him. Except for that picture, I wouldn't recognize him now. She's never let me get near him, and of course he doesn't know . . ." He sat with his cup held in both hands, staring out the window.

"Be patient," Loquat said sympathetically, scattering crumbs as he spoke. "Amor vincit omnia."

"Love conquers all?" Simon translated, remembering the phrase from the Nun's Tale in Chaucer. "Then you're still in . . ." he said to Tommy and stopped at his stricken look.

"I'd rather not talk about it." Tommy set down his cup, took out one of his Havanas, and bit the end off savagely before lighting it.

Kei came back and slipped into her chair, looking thoughtful.

"Looks like good weather for the doings tonight," said Simon. Pillow-sized clouds were scudding across the pale sky, drawing after them a crisp breeze that would keep him from sweating under his armor. "Are you coming over to get me into the rig? I can't do it myself."

"Right-oh," said Tommy. "I'll have to drive you over and Loquat and I will boost you onto the horse. You'll be using Maeve, I take it?"

Simon nodded. "Hilaire will take her over this afternoon so she can get used to the crowds and the noise."

"It's a madhouse already. Camper vans. They've filled the grounds with cars and are backed down the side of the road for about a kilometer. The flics have had to break up one dust-up so far, so it promises to be lively. Here's the roster." He pulled a folded sheet of paper out of his breast pocket and handed it to Simon, who unfolded it and was surprised at the eclecticism of the activities.

"There's hardly anything medieval here," he said disapprovingly. "Civil war muskets?"

"Next year I'm seeing to it we have a screening committee," Tommy said around the cigar clamped in his teeth. "It's gotten to be general fun and games. Next thing, we'll wind up with the yodeling and bell-ringing contingent from Wisconsin if we're not more selective."

"Tommy said you had a hand gun of some kind," said Loquat, and Kei was instantly diverted from her puzzle, looking worried. "I'd advise you to bring it with you."

Simon patted the air in a calming gesture to Kei, who looked panicky. "That serious?" he asked offhandedly.

"We think this is the night." Loquat brushed crumbs off the front of his plaid shirt. "And, as you know, these people play for keeps, whatever."

"And where do you propose I carry a gun in that armor?" asked Simon.

"Stuff it in the waistband of your tights, since you're too stubborn to wear the bottom half," said Tommy and carved off the excess ash of his cigar onto the edge of the ashtray. "Be sure the safety's on. We don't want you shooting off the family jewels."

"I *have* handled a gun once or twice before," said Simon.

"Sorry, forgot you were the big war hero," said Tommy. "Loquat's taking his athame — his ceremonial dagger, you know — and so am I, though my kendo staff could crack skulls like eggshells." He looked at Kei. "Simon can handle himself, never fear. It's too dangerous for you to be there, though, if the crowd's full of the local satanists and imported ones as well. You might come over to have a gawk with us this morning if you'd like."

"Better not," said Simon. There would just be time for a bit of dalliance before lunch — itching be damned — and then Rudy would drive her out to the airport.

"I only wish our operatives had come up with the identity of the Master of the cult," Loquat said regretfully. "Unless the cords and the Book of Shadows are there in the abbey somewhere, he will be the only one who knows where they are, and we've got to have them. Destroy them."

"If you knew where they were and destroyed them before the tournament, would that take care of things?" asked Kei.

"Pretty nearly," Loquat answered. "But we don't know where they are. Nobody knows."

"I appreciate your doing this, Rudy," said

Simon, putting Kei's bag in the back of Rudy's MG. "Take good care of her."

"She won't be out of my sight." Rudy got into the driver's seat.

Kei was wearing the silvery-beige suit she'd worn to London before and her cheeks were flushed red. The excitement, Simon supposed, or her blood pressure was still up from their lovemaking. In any case, she looked beautiful and he was reluctant to let her go.

"Take care of yourself," he said, and kissed her soundly. "Say hello to Missy for me."

She got in the car and shut the door. Simon leaned down to the window. "Have a good time in Belgium," he said to Rudy.

"I intend to have a *very* good time," Rudy said, giving him a wave.

The car scrunched around the circle and through the gate. Simon kicked at the pebbles as he walked back to the house. He stopped. Had he stepped in something? He looked at the bottoms of his shoes. No. Funny, he could smell something foul. Well, forget that. He went to the study to get the gun out of his desk.

The barrel of the revolver dug into his hip-bone as Tommy lifted him down from the back of his pickup truck, where Simon had been riding like a discarded potbelly stove on its way to the garbage dump. There hadn't been room in the cab for his helmet's branching antlers, and being wedged between the seat and the dashboard would have given him a fine case of claustrophobia.

351

"Much as I hate to concede the point," said Tommy with a grunt, setting him down in the tall, dry grass, "you probably had the right idea, refusing to wear the bottom half of this outfit. You're unwieldy enough as it is." He handed Simon his helmet and got his own mesh-fronted kendo helmet from the flatbed of the truck. "It used to take half a dozen prop men to guide me around in full armor, and if I toppled over, I could lie there until doomsday unless someone set me up again and got me going." He picked up Simon's blunt, padded lance, gave it to him and put his own kendo stave under his other arm.

They threaded their way toward the announcement stand through the knee-high grasses, between cars with foreign license plates, vans, people getting on their costumes, souvenir hawkers, and refreshment tables, Tommy's black kendo robes picking up burrs and weeds on their skirts along the route.

It was twilight, almost time for the matches to start. The setting looked like bad theater — overdramatic, stereotyped. The abbey was Lugosiesque in the shadows, its windows gaping like empty eyesockets, bats skittering around its ruined crenellations. A hunchbacked Igor might have been on the roof, squinting one eye and hissing through rotted teeth, "Master, the villagers have come to destroy the monster!" Torches set in iron brackets on the bunting-trimmed announcement platform and at its base sent serpentine wreaths of kerosene-scented smoke coiling around the bright banner stretched between poles that blazoned the tournament's name. A low mist was rolling in across the ground from the Forêt d'Orléans crouching behind the abbey.

"Would you look at the mess!" Tommy said, nodding at the papers and rubbish littering the scene. "Every year someone drops a cigarette butt in this wallow, and they've had to dig fire-breaks all around this area. All of it unnecessary if people would only learn to pick up after themselves!"

Simon didn't see Loquat until he was upon them. In his simple red-sashed robe, he looked almost underdressed in this motley crowd, where ladies in robes and wimples, fools in cap and bells, Robin's merry men, Americans in Johnny Reb uniforms, harlequins, and one adventuresome type teetering on stilts were drinking, eating, and rushing about excitedly. As they watched, the man on stilts fell down on a refreshment table, which collapsed in a crash of bottles and sandwiches.

Paying no heed to the fooferaw, Loquat said, "It doesn't look good." He put his hand on the athame stuck in his sash. "There's a camper van full of them up by the announcement stand, wearing iron chains around their necks. We may be badly outnumbered if it comes to a clash."

"Haven't our people come in from Paris yet?" asked Tommy. He went up to the announcement stand, put the lance, the stave, and his helmet on it and from his sleeve drew out a large black scarf and wrapped it around his head, knotting it above his forehead.

353

"Not that I've seen," Loquat replied. "There's a traffic pileup on the route they were to take. Some truck carrying industrial ammonia turned over across the highway."

Tommy consulted his watch and motioned Simon over. "It's five minutes until the appointed hour," he said, taking Simon's helmet from him. "Time for you to get up on the stand and do your duty." He put the helmet on Simon, nearly skinning his ears as he did so.

"Don't you look grand!" said Loquat with a gasp of approval. "The full flower of knighthood! You make a very pretty figure, my boy."

"Is Maeve all right?" Simon asked, pushing up the visor so he could see.

"Fine-oh. I checked on her earlier." Tommy took the folded list of events out of his sleeve, as well as Simon's reading glasses. "You'll need these, I dare say. What would you do without me?" He put on his own hooded helmet and flipped the long tab in front over his collar. "I've written a welcoming speech for you on the list. The kendo match comes first, so I'll have plenty of time afterwards to see to Maeve and get her palfrey on for your match. There's a mounting block for you, and Loquat and I will heave you on." He looked like a praying mantis, with the screened facepiece of his helmet dark and insect-like and his height elongating the slim silhouette of his robes.

Loquat, on the other hand, looked more like the Spirit of Christmas Present, but his face was anything but jolly. "I've looked over the abbey

minutely," he said. "There's not a trace of anything. If the Book of Shadows and the cords
aren't there, which they aren't, they must be
in the Master's keeping. Whoever he is. I don't
feel we have the upper hand in this, not knowing
who he is. He's hidden himself very well indeed."
He scratched his fiery head and clucked his tongue.

"We'll just have to muddle through," said
Tommy through his mask.

Simon took off his gauntlets and stored them
under his arm, since he couldn't handle anything
delicate like glasses and papers with them on.

"Simon!" Elaine hissed at his elbow. He turned
with a clank to see her pushing her way between
a man in a crown and robe trimmed with fake
ermine and a woman in gypsy costume. She was
got up in a gold brocade gown and a long cone-
shaped pointed cap held under her chin with a
gauzy green scarf. "Simon, you've got to be
careful!" she said. "Watch the lance . . . "

Two men in black appeared by her side, took
her arms, and hustled her away and up the steps
of the platform to one of the highbacked throne-
like chairs, sat her down between them and
took stations on either side of her, their robes
falling down at their sides like ravens' wings.

Loquat looked meaningfully at Tommy and
Simon. "She's trying," he said. "She's not fighting against us now, but they've got her under
guard, as you can see."

"What did she mean about the lance?" Tommy
asked himself aloud and felt along its length
and saw to it that the padding at the end was

355

secure. "Looks ship-shape to me."

It was getting dark, and the shadows were growing longer and blacker. Men in Civil War uniforms cleared the crowd away from in front of the stand, shouting orders in military fashion, and one screamed, "Get the hell away from the front if you don't want your tails shot off! *Faites* some room, *vous là-bas!*" When everything was in order, a dozen men in Rebel gray lined up, primed their muskets, knelt in a row, and let off a volley of shots to announce the tourney's opening. Puffs of acrid yellow smoke drifted up from the barrels as Simon climbed the steps to the stand. Applause and whoops broke out, and a streamer of confetti landed on the stage.

The light was terrible. The flames of the torches flickered, throwing shadows across the list, so that he couldn't have read the list even if his arm had been long enough for him to make out the print. He retreated until he was nearly under one of the flambeaux and tried to wedge his reading glasses into his helmet, but they wouldn't fit inside. Then he couldn't get them out again. They were caught on the under side of the visor, and he had to wrestle the helmet off with the glasses still dangling from it. Ears smarting, he handed the helmet by an antler to an official standing beside him, put on the glasses, and read out the welcome Tommy had prepared. There was a scatter of clapping. Then he announced the kendo match and sat down on one of the ornate chairs, feeling his dignity had been publicly tattered around the edges.

Tommy and another masked figure in kendo robes stepped out from the crowd and took up stances in the clearing, holding their staves out at arm's length, right-angled to their bodies. They paced slowly around each other until the other man called out an unintelligible word and took a swipe at Tommy's neck. Tommy dodged, and the pacing started again. It was a graceful, stylized performance, punctuated by shouts preceding blows, and Simon couldn't figure out who had won when they stopped, bowing low to each other. The crowd cheered, and a voice screeched, "Banzai!"

A duel with sabers followed; then a ring dance by women in medieval costume who held their robes forward, making themselves appear to be in the last stages of pregnancy; and then the horses came out stamping and snorting for a rush with their mailed riders at a spiked ball that swung back and smacked the slow lancers off their steeds. Simon had a brief struggle with panic at how it was going to feel going down in armor if he lost his seat during his bout.

The morris dancers came next and were embarrassing, skipping around with bells on their sleeves and legs, tapping short sticks together as the loudspeaker played a cloyingly merrie-olde-England tune. Simon averted his eyes.

It was getting hard to see the crowd from the light stand, but he could make out Tommy and Loquat on the sidelines, keeping an eye on the crowd and conferring with people in colored robes who came and went like messengers. Tommy

357

had his helmet under his arm and his head was still tied up in the knotted scarf, while Loquat was doing a clog to the music. He turned as someone pressed through the surrounding bodies and tugged at his sleeve. It was Marthe, red-faced, her plump breasts heaving. She spoke animatedly with Loquat. Tommy grabbed her by the shoulders and talked at her earnestly. Then Loquat motioned toward the direction of the château and she pushed into the crowd again. A minute later, Simon saw her travel from one patch of light to another across the field in the direction of the house until she disappeared in the darkness.

Simon didn't like the look of it, but it was time to announce the jugglers. When he looked up from the list, Tommy and Loquat were gone. Something was wrong, he was sure.

Now it was his turn. While extra flambeaux were put about the field, he retrieved his helmet from the official and started off across the platform. As he passed Elaine, she half rose from her seat, but her black-robed guards pulled her back into place.

"Just keep your bum in the saddle and you'll be right as rain," Tommy said, steadying Simon as he stepped up on the mounting block. He nearly slipped over Maeve's side from the unaccustomed weight of his armor as they pushed him up, and his hands skidded on the gray satin of her palfrey, but Loquat caught him by the leg and he settled himself in the saddle. He would have felt safer riding Western style, but the skirt of

358

his mail wouldn't go behind the pommel.

Tommy handed up his helmet, and Simon squeezed it on. Although the additional weight of the antlers made it uncomfortably heavy, they were adroitly balanced so that he didn't veer to one side when he turned his head. His range of vision was restricted by metal, but he wouldn't need peripheral sight if his opponent was to come straight at him down the field. He was beginning to sweat, and Maeve was dancing nervously beneath him, excited by the noise, the light of the flares, and the seething mass of people.

As Tommy handed him his gauntlets, Simon said, "You might as well tell me now what Marthe came to say," and drew them on and flexed his fingers in the metal casings.

"Now's no time for that," said Tommy and handed him the reins.

"It's about Kei, isn't it?"

Tommy looked at Loquat, who sighed and scratched his jaw ruefully.

"Marthe got a long distance call from Missy," Tommy admitted, handing Simon his lance. "Kei wasn't on the plane or any since."

Simon hefted the lance thoughtfully, finding its balance. Had she decided to come to the tourney anyway to watch over him? He searched the crowd for her face, but it was getting too dark to see individuals. From his position on Maeve, the heads of the onlookers were only a moving conglomeration of colored balls, drab now in the fading light.

"We'll look into it," Loquat said reassuringly,

"but you keep your mind on what you're about, son."

Simon lowered his visor and nudged Maeve along toward the clearing, which had been widened by self-appointed onlookers taking on crowd-control duties. Amongst them were gendarmes from the local installation.

Down in the shadows at the other end of the field towered a coal-black horse, standing stock still, in perfect control of its rider, who urged it forward into the light of tall, hand-held torches carried by his attendants.

"Holy mother of God!" Simon breathed. The figure on the back of the horse looked as large as a carnival effigy, magnified by Simon's apprehension and the distortion of the light. It was a samurai warrior in full-skirted armor of small lacquer platelets the color of dark tea, threaded with multi-colored and gold silk cords. On his head he wore a brimmed helmet with gold horns curving up from a central boss on the front, and over his face was a contorted mask carved into a frenzied, demoniacal grimace. The figure looked inhuman, like a giant god of war.

A man in a half red, half yellow suit of tights came to the sidelines with a red flag on a stick and announced first in French, then in English, that at the count of three, he would lower the flag and the match would begin.

A bead of sweat crawled through an eyebrow and down into Simon's eye. He shook his head to clear his sight, and the flag came down. He jammed his heels into Maeve's sides.

Maeve, bless her, took off like a lightning bolt in a straight charge down the field toward the towering manikin in the saddle. Simon tightened his lance against his side with his elbow, but both riders misjudged the distance between them and passed each other in a rush of speed. At the end of the course, they wheeled to come back again.

As Maeve whirled, Simon saw he'd caught something white that fluttered at the end of his lance — a flimsy piece of cloth that had hidden the tip of the samurai's weapon. He shook his lance to dislodge it and looked up to see the other rider bearing down on him with an unshielded, sharply pointed lance. He was dimly conscious of the shouts from the crowd and Tommy's voice crying, "Stop the match!" but it was too late. The point of the lance caught him on the side of his helmet, wrenching his neck and shattering an antler, nearly knocking him out of his seat. Maeve reared, her hooves slicing the air, as the samurai sped down past them to the end of the course and pivoted for another pass.

Half-blinded by his helmet, which had been turned askew, Simon whipped Maeve's neck around to reverse direction and reached up to right his helmet as the samurai skimmed by, jabbing his lance viciously at Simon and narrowly missing him.

Still in the center of the field, Simon desperately jerked at the reins to face Maeve toward the next charge, but she was only half turned as the warrior thundered toward them, and she received the brunt of his thrust, the pointed lance sinking deep into the horse's chest. The impact of the blow was like running into a stone wall.

Simon felt himself floating above the saddle, being tossed against the side of Maeve's neck, then falling back and tightening his thigh muscles instinctively to keep his seat as a plume of blood washed upward with glistening beads, separate and distinct, fringing its top. They moved up into a leisurely arch and showered down on him in a spray that spattered the metal on his arms with a rain of flat red circlets ringed with tiny droplets.

The samurai's arm drifted forward, the gilded leather gleaming, and his gauntleted hand opened out and came down on the shaft of his lance. As he dragged out his weapon, the heavy gold cloth at the crook of his elbow fanned out into rounded creases, and the point of the lance slipped out and back, dyed with red. A fresh spurt of blood fountained up and back onto Simon in a lacy web.

Maeve sank backward, and Simon's eyes traveled down a torch at the edge of the field, from the tapering trident of flame at the top to the red and yellow tulip of fire, the rounded cup below, the whole long length of the staff, to the grass, where a ball of crumpled cellophane glinted like a ball of ice crazed over with yellow cracks. His shoulders rolled back onto the ground and his head came forward as Maeve's glossy body floated down onto his leg. His arm glided up and into an arc as his lance sailed like a javelin toward the maniacal mask hovering in the air and slivered away into the darkness. The sound of its clatter as it struck the ground seemed to take endless minutes to reach him.

The black horse was hanging above him, gigantic, inky against the paler sky, its hooves poised over his head. He closed his eyes and curved himself against the warmth of Maeve's body, waiting for the hooves to descend.

There was a crashing thud that jarred the ground, and Simon opened his eyes again. The black horse lay on its back, its legs thrashing in the air. The samurai had fallen clear, the skirt of his armor by Simon's elbow. He could have reached out and touched the heavy brown cording that ran in woven horizontal rows across the skirt flaps and terminated in raised clumps of gold thread. He thought Kei's lizardskin sandals were by his head, each enameled lozenge clearly picked out by the light from the torches. A black boot with stitches of brown thread running around the top of the sole passed by, showing five raised circles as the rubber heel lifted up. The hem of a purple robe swirled and rippled at the edge of his vision.

Suddenly the pressure on his leg stopped as Maeve jerked away, screaming, her hooves tattooing the ground. His leg contracted. Someone pulled him to his feet. The black horse lunged, got to its feet, and a black robe led it away. In the dark pool, Maeve convulsed, the huge hole in her chest spouting rhythmically, her hooves beating the blood and earth into a sticky morass.

The samurai lay beside her, immobile, his neck awry.

"Kei?" Simon called, taking off his helmet and tossing it on the ground. She was in his arms, asking him if he was all right, her suit splattered with blood, her blouse torn out of her skirt, her hair hanging wildly about her face. Simon bent his head into her neck, still stunned, but Maeve's shrills of pain were corkscrewing into his ears. He let Kei go, took the revolver from his tights, went over to Maeve, put the barrel against the side of her head, and pulled the trigger.

Simon groaned as he knelt down by the samurai to undo the clasps of the grotesque mask. In the shadows cast by the torches, its ferocious features seemed to move into a menacing lacquered smile.

"Careful, please," said a voice behind the mask. "I think my neck is broken."

Gingerly, Simon removed the false face and looked down into the dark cavity of the helmet.

Rudy smiled up at him one eye unfocused and veering unnaturally to one side. "My apologies," he said faintly.

Simon sat back on his heels. "Oh, my God!" he said under his breath.

Silk smelling of Havana tobacco brushed against Simon's cheek as Tommy leaned down to look at Rudy. "So it's you," he said. He lowered himself into a crouch beside Simon, and they were silent together, each dealing with the shock and the sadness in his own way. Finally, Tommy said, "You're the Master, aren't you, Rudy?"

Rudy closed his eyes. His face was pasty white.

"Answer me, Rudy," Tommy said.

When Rudy opened his eyes again, the one eye still canted off from the true. "Of course, my friend," he said softly. The muscles of his face tightened in agony.

"But why, Rudy?" Simon asked gently. He reached out to straighten the poor, crooked neck, but stopped, afraid of hurting him.

Rudy smiled sweetly up at him. "It was the challenge of it, Simon, don't you see? The intellectual exercise."

"And how many people are dead because of your bloody intellectual exercise?" Tommy said between his teeth, stood up abruptly, and kicked at the bloody lance, which rolled off into the robes surrounding them.

White and colored robes gave way as black pushed forward to circle around the fallen figure. One of them knocked Simon off balance, and he staggered to his feet.

"Don't touch him!" Tommy cried. "Look at his neck, you can see . . . "

But the black robes swept around Rudy and lifted him up. His helmet dropped to the ground by Simon's boots as they bore him away, and his head rolled back limply from the neck of the lacquered armor.

"They've killed him, picking him up like that!" Tommy said. "Purposely. Because he's no more use to them, now that we know he's the Master."

The crowd jostled closer to get a look, closing in on them. Simon put up an elbow and cleared a tunnel through the bodies, pulling Kei along behind until they were outside the hysterical

365

throng. Looking back, he saw Loquat and Tommy squeezing out between a morris dancer in puce shorts and a man in mail made of yarn sprayed with silver paint.

At the pickup, Tommy threw the weapons and the helmet and broken antler on the flatbed and carefully placed his kendo helmet on the seat of the cab. The four of them stood there, not speaking, for some minutes. Then Tommy helped Simon out of his armor and put it with the rest of the things. Simon pulled his sweater back down over his stomach and ran a hand through his hair, his thoughts and emotions in a turmoil and his body losing its numbness. He felt his knee to see if it was swelling.

"You were magnificent, my lady," said Loquat. "Simon owes his life to you."

"What do you mean?" asked Simon, testing the tendon running from his groin, where he was sorest.

"Who do you think pulled Rudy off his horse?" Tommy lit a cigar. "I don't know how she went away safe from all those hooves and lances, but if she hadn't grabbed Rudy's leg and hung on while the horse dragged her until he plummeted down, you'd be skewered like a chicken on a spit." He took off his head scarf and handed it to Kei, who wiped at the blood on herself and then started on Simon.

"I didn't have time to think," she said. "I didn't realize what I was doing until it was all over." She watched the black robes carry Rudy's body into the camper by the announcement stand and burst into tears, holding her hand over her eyes. "It's all my fault! Rudy's dead and Maeve's dead, and I knew all the time he had those cords in his house, but I wasn't sure they were what you were looking for."

Tommy took the cigar out of his mouth and roared, "You *what?*" and snatched back the scarf.

"I thought I could handle it myself." Kei took down her hand and looked defiantly at Tommy. "I've always had to handle everything myself. What if I'd told you and they *hadn't* been the cords? What would have happened to your friendship with Rudy?"

It suddenly occurred to Simon that she was supposed to be in London right now. "Where have you been?" he asked.

She tucked the tail of her blouse back in her skirt. "Well, I asked Rudy if we could stop at his house for an aspirin on the way to the airport. So I could get another look at what was in that box. He'd never intended to take me to the plane, and it only played into his hand. He had a fellow waiting there who grabbed me and tied me up with those confounded cords of yours like a roast he was going to put in the oven, and Rudy left me with him while he came here."

"Rudy *kidnapped* you?" Simon yelled at her, furious with her for taking such risks without telling him.

"Yes, well, you could call it that." She sniffled.

"For Christ's sake, Kei, why didn't you tell me what was going on?"

"Simon, I can't tell you everything, you get so excited. Look at you now! If I told you every single, little thing . . . "

"Now listen here, in the future . . . "

Loquat interrupted, saying soothingly, "Now, now, children. Let her tell us the full particulars, would you?" and gave Kei a handkerchief.

Simon stood with his fists digging into his hips, staring angrily at her as she blew her nose and continued, "Luckily, silk knots don't hold very well, so I could work them loose while that guy had his back turned, playing solitaire and regaling me with the details of what they were going to do with me after the tournament, practically rubbing his hands together and gloating, and . . . "

"What *were* they going to do?" Simon asked, thinking that what she deserved was a good spanking and, by God, one day it might come to that.

"Well, rape me on the altar and . . . oh, you don't want to know. I can't understand why they left me with only one guard, unless they needed everyone here at the tournament. Or maybe it was that old business that men think all women can do is stand in a corner and whimper. You know, I think I could give nearly as good an accounting of myself in a fight as a man, so . . . "

"Don't string it out, Kei," said Simon.

"So when I got loose, there was a full pot of hot coffee right by my hand, and I brained him with it. He went out like a light, sort of surprising me, but a full pot of coffee is heavy. I'll bet it weighed . . . "

"Get on with it!" said Simon.

"And then I poured the hot coffee on him."
She paused and looked at the men, as if expecting to be reprimanded for overdoing things. "While he was lying there, I searched around and got the box of cords, which had the pomander ball in it, and found the Book of Shadows in the desk. And I ran all the way here with them and there you were on the ground and Rudy had his lance up, ready to drive it into you, and I sort of went crazy." She gave Loquat back his handkerchief, raised her arms out from her sides and flopped them down again. "That's it."

Simon grabbed her and kissed her, working out his anger on her mouth. He was beginning to forget where they were when Loquat laid a hand on his shoulder and said, "Enough! Enough! Where are the things now, Kei?"

"What? Oh, under the t-t-truck," she said.

Loquat dove under the pickup, then wriggled out again, his bottom like a rising moon in the darkness. "Here they are!" he grunted, standing up. "Thank Cernunnos!" He did a little dance, holding the book and box over his head, and said, "Follow me!"

He pranced away to the announcement stand, skipped up the steps, put the box and book down on one of the chairs, and searched around for the microphone to the loudspeaker. Finding it, he held it to his lips. "Attention! Attention, please!" the speakers blared.

Simon stood leaning with his arm on Kei's shoulder by the foot of the stand while Tommy took up position by them and flicked his cigar ash into the grass. It burned a black circle in the weeds, and he stamped it out. It took some minutes to quiet the crowd, who were still in a milling uproar from the jousting match. When a measure of order was restored, Loquat held the Book of Shadows over his head, open for the people to see.

"Be ye hereby notified," he bellowed, "that I hold the Book of Shadows of the Satanic cult who have mutilated cattle in your district, performed vile rites, and committed murder in the name of the Devil!"

The level of noise in the throng grew higher at the news, and a man in a black robe started to clamber onto the platform by Loquat's feet, but Loquat's foot shot out and caught him on the jaw. He slumped down into the grass, and gendarmes filtered through the crowd to stand with crossed arms along the front of the stage.

"Here, too, I have the measuring cords that bound the cult members to Satan, and the talisman of Sélène!" Loquat put down the book and took up the red cords and pomander ball to flourish them over his head. "As I destroy them," he boomed, "I destroy the hold of evil over every member of the cult, setting them free from the clutches of the Devil!" He put down the microphone, but a whisper of "That oughta hold 'em!" carried out across the field.

Men in black started up the stairs at either end of the stage. White robes jumped them, pulling them back, and more black robes appeared around the platform. Fists and weapons swung, and women began shrieking as the gendarmes waded in with nightsticks. A hand reached across the stage toward Loquat's ankles, and he stamped on it.

"Hear me, oh slaves of Satan!" he shouted, backing up to a safer spot while chaos broke out at his feet. The loudspeaker squealed. "You are henceforth free, and your souls are restored to you!" He put the brass box down at his feet, placed the cords, the Book of Shadows, and the pomander ball in it, then ripped up bunting from the front of the stand, hitting off hostile hands as he did so, and stuffed the bunting down on top of the other things. "Herewith I burn the measuring cords, the Book of Shadows, and the talisman of the accursed Sélène, wiping out her influence and memory and obliterating the Satanic cult!" He seized a torch from a bracket and set fire to the lot.

It went up with a whoosh. A black robe leaped onto the stage and grabbed up the burning box, but flames flared up toward his hood and he dropped the box and the relics into the long grass, catching it instantly. The crowd took to their heels in screaming panic as a carpet of red undulated slowly toward them. One after the other, Satanists vacated the van by the announcement stand and ran toward the road, holding their skirts up from the weeds. Knots of black robes and white robes tangled together in combat, then separated, abandoning hostilities to save their lives, and fled before the advancing flames.

Cars and trucks began backing and filling, grinding their gears, denting fenders, churning up the soft ground as campers lumbered awkwardly behind them. Horses stamped and reared at the smell of smoke, swelling the jumble of noise with their whinnies. The white paint on the poles holding up the banner announcing the tournament turned to sludgy brown blisters as fire flashed up them and across the heavy paper strip, and for a moment the print showed satiny black upon a dimpled charcoal background before falling in tatters to the ground.

Tommy was already in the pickup when Loquat, Kei, and Simon reached it. They piled in the back just as Elaine ran up, her gown flapping about her legs. "Wait for me!" she cried, hoarse from the smoke, and tore off her conical cap and threw it behind her as she climbed onto the flatbed. Tommy maneuvered his way through the confusion and the truck shot across the road and turned again to face it. Tommy cut the motor, and they all climbed out to watch from their safe vantage post as gendarmes directed human, animal, and vehicular traffic and a patch of black robes paused at the highway's edge to see the announcement platform flump to the ground, burying the brass box. Dejectedly, they started back toward the village, looking like nuns going single file on their way to mass.

Flames licked high up the stone walls of the abbey, echoed by shadows that flamed higher still. A canvas tent turned black and curtsied to the ashes as the last straggler—a witch carrying a picnic basket—left the scene to follow a line of horses now haunching quietly along the parking.

"His body's still in the van," Loquat said, leaning back against the pickup fender. His robe was streaked with smoke, and he had a smut under one fierce eye. Simon stood in front of the truck with one arm around Kei and the other around Elaine while Tommy added his cigar smoke to the ashes flittering down around them.

The camper van exploded in an orange ball of flame.

"Goodbye, Rudy," Simon said softly.

A siren yodeled in the distance as the wind turned, blowing choking smoke toward them. Loquat, Kei, and Simon got in back, and Elaine got in the cab with Tommy. The truck bumped slowly onto the highway and, as they passed along the edge of the dying fire, Simon saw Tommy's arm reach out of the cab window, a fine iron chain dangling from his fingers. The chain whipped in an arc into the air, soared above the flames, and fell, lost in the ashes.

CHAPTER TWENTY-EIGHT

Dear Chris:

Day before yesterday was the tournament. Rudy van der Zee and Maeve were killed, I'm sad to say, and there was a big grass fire that burned itself out quickly, thanks to the firebreaks all around. It was a horrifying time, but one good thing came out of it — the Satanic cult is gone. Next time we're together, I'll make a big pot of coffee and tell you all about it.

I did find out some interesting things about Alexis Michaelson, whom I knew when I was here before and who has been masquerading all these years as a Frenchman. He went to Algeria, joined the Reds there, and — when things cooled down — came back to this village. His wife was the daughter of the mayor, so it must have been fairly easy for him to get false papers, and he was already fluent in the language. The villagers closed around him to protect the mayor's daughter, and that's doubtless why they were so hostile when I appeared, since I'm the only one from outside who knows about it. And I'm certainly not going to tell! After all, he was a deserter and a counterspy, and I think the penalty for that's death, isn't it? It was all so long ago. What difference can it make now? And you know how I feel about the death penalty. Leave the man in peace, I say.

Simon's feeling pretty stiff after having his horse fall on him, but the doctor says no damage is done. The way he's been knocked around lately, you'd think he'd be lying around and moaning, but he seems to be made of some strange, undamagable material. And at his age, too! Thank God, in him I seem to have gotten a superior product who should be around for years and years yet. And he's gorgeous besides. Lucky me!

Now we can settle down to finishing off the memoirs and calm down. I do love happy endings, don't you?

Much love,

Kei

CHAPTER TWENTY-NINE

"I think we're due for a storm," said Simon, coming into the dining room in his riding gear and seating himself at the breakfast table. "Thunderheads building up in the west."

The Florentine brown dress Kei was wearing set off his mother's necklace to perfection, he thought. He'd given her the long string of small gold nuggets from the Yukon that his uncle had panned, to celebrate everything in general.

"Have a good ride? You smell rather barnyard." She pushed the puzzle aside, looking up at him after taking off her reading glasses.

"Barney's just not the same as Maeve."

"I know," she said sympathetically. She handed him the editorial page, saying, "Now, be good and don't get started on the Russians again."

Marthe came in with a plate of buttery-smelling crepes and, as she was leaving, Kei asked her a question in French. Marthe launched into a long diatribe, to which Kei kept replying, *"Non, non, et encore non!"*

"What was that all about?" he asked after

Marthe had left the room. "Did I catch Fournier's name in that?"

Kei was about to answer when they heard footsteps in the hall and Elaine came in.

"Surprise!" said Elaine, making a half bow and spreading her arms theatrically. "Simon's here! Do you want to see your nephew?"

Simon dashed out into the hallway, where the boy was standing by the front doors, his arms crossed protectively across his T-shirt. He looked at Simon and the whites of his eyes showed around his pupils like those of a frightened horse. Finally, he stuck out his hand and said, "Uncle Simon?"

Simon went up and put his hands on the boy's shoulders, fought off wanting to kiss him welcome, and instead gave him a brief, hard hug and held him away at arm's length so he could get a good, long look at his nephew.

Young Simon's hair was lighter than the photograph had indicated, a dark blond. His eyes and mouth were strictly Eagleton, but the shape of his face and nose had been outlined by someone else's genes. Tommy's influence had produced those broad shoulders and shorter, thicker neck, Simon thought. Or was he seeing what he wanted to see? Had Tommy really checked the calendar?

"Welcome home," Simon said. "We're terribly glad you're here."

Kei came up behind him, and he turned to take her hand and put it in the boy's. "This is Kei," he said.

Young Simon shook her hand solemnly. "Mother said she thought you'd be getting married to her, so . . . so hello, Aunt Kei." He made a dart at her cheek, drew back a split second, then resolutely kissed her.

Kei's dent deepened. She took his face in her hands and kissed him on the lips. "Do you mind if I call you by your middle name? With two Simons, it's going to be confusing," she said.

"I've sort of got used to having the guys call me Eagle. For Eagleton, you know, ma'am. But if you'd rather . . . "

"Eagle's a splendid name," said Simon, thinking it wasn't, and put his arm around the boy's shoulders to lead him back to the dining room. "We have plenty of room here, if you'd like to stay with us. There are horses to ride and . . . "

"Oh, no you don't! I heard that!" said Elaine as they seated themselves around the table. "He's staying with me, no two ways about it. We have a lot of catching up to do."

Friendly relations still hadn't been restored with Elaine, who had gone home after the tournament and holed up, refusing to see anybody.

"Marthe!" Simon called. When her head popped in at the door, he gave orders for more crepes. "Will you be going to the lycée in town?" Simon asked, freshening his and Kei's coffee and pouring some for Elaine.

"We thought I'd be going to the American school in Paris," said Eagle. "The one for the diplomats' kids."

"Home for the weekends, I hope?" Simon shot a suspicious look at Elaine.

378

"It didn't ruin you when you were in prep school," Elaine said defensively. "I never heard you say you felt like an orphan because of it. Eagle's French is good, but not quite good enough for the lycée."

Marthe brought in settings for Elaine and Eagle, returned to the kitchen, and then sailed back with a stacked plate for Eagle and a sedate one for Elaine.

When Simon introduced the boy to Marthe, she ruffled his hair with her hand. He smoothed it back down again crossly.

"Mother says it's just a short trip on the commuter train," Eagle said, frowning as the destroyer of his dignity went back into the kitchen. "I think I'd have a better chance of making friends with guys who can speak English."

"It must have been hard, leaving all your friends behind," Kei said.

"Yeah." Eagle poured half a pitcher of raspberry syrup on his crepes and set about demolishing them at phenomenal speed.

"Maybe we can bring a couple of them over for the holidays," said Simon. "We'd have a real Christmas then, all of us. Bony and Margaret could bring the children over from London, and we'd have a houseful."

Kei opened her mouth and then closed it again. Eagle, his eyes bright, said, "Gee, would you really do that? Pay their fares and everything?"

"I think we can manage." Simon lit a cigar, feeling vastly uncle-ish and benevolent.

Marthe, who must have known about boys'

379

appetites, soon brought in more crepes for Eagle, who thanked her politely in French, winning her heart completely.

"Eat up," said Simon, enjoying playing uncle to the hilt. "That'll put hair on your chest!" Immediately, he was appalled by his flow of heartiness. He coughed into his fist, embarrassed. Where had he picked up that disgusting phrase? Damn, he hadn't suspected he was capable of being so trite!

"Oh, no problem," said the boy, looking around the table with a hint of swagger in his glance that reminded Simon sharply of Tommy. "The guys say I've got so much hair on my chest already, I'm going to turn out like King Kong."

True, a very fine tendril of blondness was peeping out of the neck of his T-shirt.

"Is that rain I hear?" said Elaine, looking out the window.

"I think it's the sound of my cup running over," said Simon, reaching for Kei's hand.

Next week, Jeremy Kirbottle turned up on the doorstep, suitcase in hand, saying he had business in Paris. The perpetual houseguest, he made no apologies for dropping in unexpectedly. Before explanations could be offered, he spotted the relationship between Kei and Simon and demanded to know why Kei had used him to flimflam her way into the château.

"I saw his picture in the papers," Kei said airily. "Naturally, I had to track him to his lair."

"Hmph!" said Jeremy. "Don't believe a word

of it. You're always hiding something, Kei, it's part of your charm."

Simon made phone calls to set up the obligatory dinner for Jeremy and then went into the kitchen. "Let's see, Marthe, there will be Kei and me and Eagle and Elaine and Tommy, and Missy's back," he said, counting on his fingers. "That's six. And Jeremy makes seven. Oh, and Loquat. Eight. Have to put an extension in the table. Don't fix anything fancy. Duck à l'orange, I think, with wild rice and petits pois. A salad, and fruit and cheese for after. See if you can get some of that cheese covered in grape seeds, forget its name. How's the champagne holding out?"

In the afternoon, he and Jeremy settled down to go over the manuscript while Kei and Missy went into town to shop and pick up the Mercedes at the garage.

Kei was right, Simon thought, looking across the piles of typescript: Jeremy did look like a well tailored stick of Wrigley's. Or a twelve-year-old with a Dutch bob dressed up in his father's cut-down suit. He must get ingrown eyelashes, with those curly fringes rubbing against his glasses all the time. Eagle would be just about Jeremy's cup of tea, better keep an eye on things.

They wrangled over the organization of the memoirs, Jeremy grousing about Simon's omission of his war experiences, saying that they'd been dashing and romantic—which was just the kind of tripe that put Simon's teeth on edge. Obviously, the man had never been in uniform (did they make them that small?), and it was useless to try to get him to understand that half of what showed up so bravely on Simon's war record was the result of trying not to look like a fool. The rest was simply a diligent effort to remain in the land of the living. Dashing and romantic, indeed! Jeremy might be a giant in the publishing world, but Simon privately thought he was an intellectual cockroach.

Elaine was not at all gracious when she discovered that Missy and Tommy had been invited. She arrived early and, looking stormy, sent Eagle off to see the horses and kittens.

"You just want to get rid of me so you can talk without me hearing you," said Eagle, "but that's okay. I'd rather see the horses anyway."

"This is very awkward, Simon," Elaine said severely, going to the bar to make one of her grenadine concoctions and watching Eagle's progress across the meadow through the window. "Tommy hasn't seen Eagle since he was a baby." She stirred the scarlet mixture with a glass rod, rattling it irritably. "Tommy would have interfered with my plans for Eagle if he could have gotten his hands on him. I didn't want a kid hanging around my neck." She sat down on one of the velvet settees, crossed her legs, and tapped the air with her foot. "I don't like growing old in front of him, and I wish you'd have some sensitivity about that. Where is everybody?"

"Dressing." Simon's concession to formality, such as it was, was a Donegal tweed vest and jacket, now that the evenings were getting cooler.

He was wearing a Hong King shirt and regretting it. The collar didn't fit right. He always had a devil of a time getting collars that set right, unless he had them made in London, which was a pain in the ass. He stirred the ice in his scotch with a finger. "Whatever happened between you two? To break you up, that is?"

"Oh, he got wrapped up in his acting career— and very full of himself, too—and was all over the globe on location." She shrugged. "I got tired of waiting around for him. Sleeping alone. And there was another man. You know." She held her glass up to the light to observe its color and then took a sip.

"He's still in love with you."

"I don't believe that!" she said shortly. "He's not interested in an old woman. You know he likes young flesh. My God, the roots don't come in black under this dye job, they're white! See?" She put down her glass and parted her hair in front. "Laugh that off! I can't."

"You seem to like younger men yourself."

"Maybe. But young lovers know how to take care of you. They don't cry on your shoulder, like middle-aged men. Men my age think they're doing you a favor if they bring over a bottle for a bit of slap and tickle. They make me sick."

Simon sat down on the other settee, ran a finger around the rim of his glass, and came to the point. "I wish you'd find someone to take your mind off me. Whether Tommy or not. Kei's more than a little upset about us—understandably—and I know she'd feel better if you were focused on some other man."

Elaine leaned forward with her elbows on her knees and her hands clasped around her glass, looking at him earnestly. "I don't know if you'll believe this, Simon, but it's true," she said. "I've always loved you best, you know that, and I never got over wanting you, either." She looked up at the ceiling and her mouth quivered as she spoke. "Sometimes I thought I'd die from it, especially in the last years, when you wouldn't let me touch you! I counted myself lucky if you gave me a kiss on the cheek. You don't know what it's like, wanting someone so badly. I used to put my arms around myself at night, and I'd try to pretend it was your arms. But just before the tournament, something happened." She looked into her glass, then tipped it up and emptied it, and her eyes glinted with tears when she looked back at him. "It was like a fever breaking. I just . . . didn't feel that way any more." She looked down again at her glass and tilted it back and forth, watching the red liquid moving. "You can't imagine the peace, having that awful hunger stop!" She ran her finger under each eye, then said, "I'm so sorry, Simon. It must have been tough for you with me *at* you all the time, giving you so much trouble. And the thing about Eagle. I don't deserve to be forgiven, but I really am sorry."

She got up and went over to kiss him. A light peck on the lips. Then she sat back on the settee. "Just testing," she said mischievously. "I wanted to be sure. My first truly sisterly kiss. Not great, but not bad, either." She laughed softly. "Now I *know* I'm getting old."

Simon was feeling a little misty around the eyes himself. "I don't know what to say. I love you, Elaine. It may not have been the kind of love you wanted, but it was always there."

"I know. And I thank you."

They sat in comfortable silence. He'd forgotten what it was like to be with Elaine without the tension and—to be honest—the fear between them. Was it Loquat's magic that had rooted out the sickness between them? Probably not, but maybe there *was* magic in the world.

"I'm still teed off that you invited Tommy, though," she said in a more familiar tone. "I'm feeling good about things for the first time in years, and then you throw me a left hook like this, when Tommy and Eagle haven't even met yet."

"I'm sorry, Elaine. I would have thought you'd get them together before now."

"And let Eagle guess Tommy's his father? Don't make me laugh!" She went to the bar and made another drink as Kei came in the door, wearing a long honey-colored dress of some material that molded itself to her body, showing every long curve.

Elaine turned and looked up and down as Simon stood up. When Kei turned sideways to greet Elaine, he saw the curve of her bare breasts at the deep opening in the front of her dress.

"Go back upstairs and take that thing off!" he said. "It's cut down to your navel, and everybody at the table will be able to see . . . You might as well be naked!"

Kei looked at him frostily, very tall, very regal, and said, "I *beg* your pardon?"

"It makes you look cheap. You might as well put your tits on a platter!"

"Nothing this expensive can look *cheap*," said Kei, gritting her words between her teeth. "And as for your dictator act . . . "

"Look, I don't want you to wear that!"

Elaine left the bar to stand between them, crossing her arms over her ample bosom. "Oh, come off it, Simon," she said. "Don't be so bourgeois."

"Bourgeois?" People had called him a lot of things, but never that!

Elaine threw back her head and gave a full-throated laugh. "Papa made his money in hardware, love. And I think *his* father was a butcher, wasn't he?" She went back to the bar to pour a sherry for Kei. "He's got delusions of grandeur," she said, handing the glass to her. "Don't let Mr. God Almighty push you around."

Kei took the glass and smiled over it at Elaine. "The trouble is, he's got me convinced that he's just that: God Almighty. I'm going to have a hard time holding my own."

"I think you'll manage," said Elaine conspiratorially.

"Well, will you . . . will you sit up straight at the table, then?" Simon said lamely, knowing he was outnumbered. He sat down in an easy chair, bemused to realize that the two women, who

386

had been so hostile to each other, seemed to be ganging up on him. Loquat's magic—if the cause of the rapprochement was that—was more effective than he'd hoped. When women presented a united front, a man hadn't a chance.

Jeremy bounded into the room, looking for a drink, his eyeglasses slightly askew. When he'd located the bar and splashed some whiskey into a glass, he went straight to Elaine and said, "My dear, your dress is heaven!" admiring Elaine's orange gown and the gold dragon swirling down around her body. "I gather you're Elaine?"

"You don't think it's too gaudy?" She stood back and took a fashion model's turn around, holding in her stomach.

"Oh, heaven forfend! Not with your hair. Your eyes! That ripe figure! You look good enough to eat!" said Jeremy and then twiddled his drink. "In a manner of speaking, of course." He buried his nose in his glass, discomfited.

Missy hoo-hooed from the hallway and flew into the room streaming banners of pink chiffon. She threw her arms about Simon's neck but didn't kiss him, wrinkled her nose at seeing Elaine, and swooped down on Jeremy, demanding to know who he was.

"Jeremy Kirbottle, and you're Missy Hilliard, oh, it is to *die*!" Jeremy kissed her hand dramatically. "They nearly had to carry me out of that benefit you did last December for Oxfam . . ." And Missy was lost to the rest of the company, lapping up his compliments like a starved cat.

Tommy was standing in the doorway, looking like a stray. Simon buttonholed him before he came into the room, warning him in a low voice, "Eagle's here tonight. I thought you ought to know so you could get the right face on."

Tommy stretched up his neck to search for the boy amongst the guests. Not seeing him, his face fell. "He doesn't know about me, you know," he said, "and I guess he never will, if Elaine has her way. I'm getting a drink."

He poured himself a double and stood looking into it without drinking it.

"It's all your fault if this dinner is a disaster," Elaine hissed in Simon's ear. "Tommy's a soggy mass of self-righteousness about the cult to begin with, and now he'll be looking like a bloodhound who's lost his bone about Eagle. Why do you *do* these things?"

Eagle slouched in from outdoors. His white jacket had a smear on a lapel, there was a straw sticking in his dress pants leg, and his tennis shoes were covered with manure. "I've seen the horses, and I've *seen* the horses, and I don't want to see the horses any more," he announced sulkily to his mother.

"Don't track that filth in here!" squalled Elaine. "You reek! Go into the kitchen and clean yourself up. And put on a pair of Simon's shoes or the table will smell like someone died."

"Jeez, did you have to say that in front of everybody?" Eagle looked pained. "Don't you think I have any feelings?"

Tommy put down his drink. "I'll show you where the kitchen is and help you find some

388

shoes," he said quickly and led Eagle into the foyer before Elaine could stop him. She put out a hand in protest and then dropped it, sighing.

When Loquat arrived, Simon didn't recognize him immediately. He was wearing a handsome, conservatively cut white dinner jacket and black trousers and had his hair slicked down and darkened with pomade. But a large peony bloomed in his lapel. "I trust all is well with everyone," he said to the general air and then went up to Elaine. "You're Elaine Eagleton and I'm Loquat Halsey," he said to her, raising her knuckles to his lips. Her nose came to the second stud down his shirt. "Would you make me one of whatever it is that you're drinking? It looks pretty."

Watching her glide over to the bar, he asked Simon, "How are things going vis-à-vis Elaine?"

"Marvelously well. You've almost made a believer out of me, though I suppose her change of heart could be put down to her guilt about the Satanism thing." He smoothed the hair on the back of his neck. "It really does seem an abrupt turnabout."

Loquat chuckled. "Your mind's going to be busier with that than a fart in a colander, going in and out of the holes, isn't it? Why can't you simply accept the evidence?"

"Because it just doesn't seem natural."

"Ah, but that's exactly what it is, you see. Natural! Malice is not man's natural turn of mind." Loquat accepted the bloody-looking drink that Elaine handed him and thanked her with courtly grace. "I think you should be alerted, however, to the fact that I had a very distressing reading of the tarot this afternoon, and it may be in connection with this house. There seems to be a cloud hanging over it."

Simon mentally discounted Loquat's report. Not only was it inconceivable that inanimate bits of cardboard could foresee the future, but there wasn't anything left that could go wrong. They'd already covered the field in disasters, and thank God that was all over!

"What cards did you turn up?" Elaine asked, who had implicit faith in the tarot.

"The tower crossed by the moon. Dreadful!" Loquat inhaled his drink in one long swallow and smothered a belch in his fist. "On the other hand, in the row pertinent to the future—I use the Celtic cross, of course—there were the two of cups, Death, and the Sun, so that's heartening."

"Oh, Lord, Death!" Elaine looked worried.

"No, no, don't look like that," Loquat said reassuringly. "It means new beginnings, throwing off the old and outworn. Not bodily death. It's the tower and the moon that are catastrophic."

"Now, don't dampen things with your card shuffling, Loquat," said Simon. "We've come out safe from hell and high water, and tonight I feel as blessed as if I'd won the national lottery."

Loquat broke into a sunny smile. "And well you should, thank Cernnunos! Bring out the minstrels! Let there be mirth!"

"Let there be dinner!" said Missy, putting

her arm through Jeremy's and snuggling against him. "I'm famished!"

"And just what is it that you said you do, Mr. Halsey?" Jeremy asked, bowing out of the verbal minuet he'd been dancing with Missy, tantalizing her with talk about expanding herself with serious drama in a new play he was backing and then mincing back from promising to boost her for the lead.

"I didn't, but I'm a high priest of Wicca," Loquat said genially and put three heaping spoonfuls of sugar in his coffee. "A witch, that is."

Jeremy laughed politely. "Very amusing. But what is it you really do?"

"That."

Jeremy ran a finger under either side of his moustache and coughed. "But you can't make a living at . . . at that sort of thing, surely?"

Loquat blew on his coffee. "No, because we don't take payment for our services. A love offering is appreciated, but not necessary." In two swallows he emptied his cup, then pushed it toward Kei and raised his chin to indicate that a refilling was requested. "I have a little shop called Imagenesis where I sell the very best hand craftsmanship that brings in a shilling or two. And my wants are simple."

Eagle broke off his conversation about soccer with Tommy, whom Simon had seated next to him, across the table from Elaine so she couldn't interfere. "Can you put curses on people, sir?" he asked.

Eagle got a full rundown on the differences between white and black witchcraft, and Simon's attention wandered. He blew smoke rings, trying to waft one smoke ring through another and succeeding most of the time. People's confusion about witchcraft was getting tiresome. It was all so simple, really, and the only thing strange about it was that Wicca seemed to work. Take Elaine's charge of heart. Maybe she was just making the best of what she found on her plate, nevertheless . . . Simon tuned out of the conversation and finally rose and went to Kei. "Let's have champagne in the sitting room when they're done with coffee," he said, looking down the front of her dress and enjoying it. At the same time that he wanted to cover her up, he wanted to expose her to the company, saying, "Look what I've got!" Love could be very confusing. He sat down again to muddle around in his own thoughts as the occult discussion went on and on.

The events of the past couple of weeks were enough to throw anyone into a mental morass. He'd given up hope of ever falling in love, and now he and Kei were to marry. He'd become a father and and then turned into an uncle. Tommy had come out of the broom closet and Rudy had turned out to be a Jekyll and Hyde. Elaine had finally let him loose. So had Missy. Kei hadn't killed Alexis Michaelson. The Satanic cult had been destroyed. It was all grand and glorious, if one could survive it.

"We have a handfasting coming up on the

schedule," Loquat said, having straightened the party out on the issue of good vs. bad magic.

"What's a handfasting?" asked Eagle, and Tommy smiled paternally at his endless curiosity.

"A Wiccan marriage ceremony. Usually they're for a year, occasionally for six months, sometimes for eternity. I think this one might be one of the biggies," said Loquat, polishing his mouth with his napkin. "The couple pledges to help each other in future lives and to love each other, whether or not as lovers on this plane."

"That's not a legal ceremony, is it?" said Kei and, noticing that Simon was raising an eyebrow, sat up very straight.

"Oh, yes. I'm an ordained minister of the Church of Wicca. One has to have a marriage license if it's to be legal, like any other wedding, but I'm empowered to perform the ceremony, just like your local vicar."

"Who's being handfasted? You didn't tell me about it. You're as tight as a fish's ass when it comes to passing along information, Loquat," said Tommy.

"I don't know yet." Loquat half closed his eyes as if he were looking into the distance. "I just know it's to be very soon. It came to me."

Jeremy goggled. "Do you hear voices telling you the future?"

"Please, Mr. Kirbottle," Loquat said reprovingly. "I am *not* Joan of Arc!" He sounded quite offended.

"Maybe it's Kei and Simon," said Missy. "Can I come?"

"You could if we were," Simon answered, putting out his cigarette in the silver ashtray, "but I think we'll do the traditional thing and have the civil ceremony at the *mairie* in town and the wedding here. You're all invited, of course."

Missy clapped her hands, and a patter of applause ran around the table. He sent a glance of appreciation to Elaine for joining in.

"Can you tell the future? For sure?" asked Eagle. "Do you use a crystal ball?"

"My dear boy, does everything you say have a question mark on the end?" Loquat chuckled. "No, a crystal ball's not needed. And I don't always get clear pictures of the future. It's unpredictable, clairvoyance. Sometimes I just get impressions. Like a dark, foreboding feeling, for example." His expression clouded over. "Let's talk of other things. And remember, son, if you're psychic, it comes looking for you. You shouldn't try to invite it in or fiddle around with your mind at your age. People can get in deep waters when they get embroiled in the occult—usually when they want to control others." Loquat looked straight at Elaine, who dropped her eyes.

"Where are you going on your honeymoon?" Missy asked Simon, leaning forward and showing more bosom than Kei could possibly have offered to view.

"It's up to Kei." Out of the corner of his eye, Simon was observing Jeremy's reaction to Missy's bountifulness. Surprisingly, he looked as if he'd like to sink his teeth into those creamy globes. His moustache twitched passionately. Another one who wasn't what he seemed to be, Simon thought.

Missy pressed Kei for an answer.

"Simon's probably done this already—what hasn't he done?" Kei said. "But I'd like to go on safari in Africa. I've always wanted to see lions in their natural environment. Lots and lots of lions."

"And then perhaps Katmandu," added Simon. "I'd like to take a look at the temple carvings there."

"They're magnificent," said Loquat. "I've been there scores of times. On the other plane."

Reasonably sure that Loquat wasn't talking about an airline, Simon suggested that they adjourn to the salon for champagne before the discussion turned to astral travel. Missy squealed predictably. Champagne infected guests with a festive spirit, but Simon thought it a little overrated.

A fresh breeze was coming in at the salon's open windows. At Missy's request, Simon sat down at the piano and took orders for a singsong. The company leaned on the closed top of the concert grand with their glasses in hand. They'd covered half a dozen football fight songs before Simon realized that Tommy, Loquat, and Jeremy were being left out, and switched to show tunes.

Missy began belting out, and the others dropped

out of the singing to give her the floor. She did a whole routine—which Simon had a hell of a time keeping up with, resorting to plunking along with one finger in some places—that would have cost a producer and arm and a leg if she'd been doing it on the stage.

"Where's Kei?" he asked Elaine, who was standing at his elbow.

"She went out to get a kitten for Eagle. I sent him on home, and a kitten'll be a nice surprise for him in the morning."

Simon's hands kept playing automatically, but he began to feel uneasy. Kei had been gone a long time. He heard Elaine draw her breath in sharply. "Oh my God!" she said, "I didn't *think* . . . !"

CHAPTER THIRTY

Suddenly Loquat's head went up as if he'd heard a call inaudible to the other guests. "The barn!" he said, and Simon sprinted out of the room, abandoning Missy in the middle of her performance, and tore across the meadow as fast as his long legs could take him.

At the barn, he leaned a hand against the door, gasping for breath. Inside, by the light of a kerosene lamp, Fournier was humped over Kei on the pile of sacks where she and Simon had lain together. Blind with rage at seeing them coupling, he rushed in and grabbed Fournier by the back of his shirt, dragging him off her. Kei's face was congested with blood and her eyes had rolled back in her head.

Fournier came off her body in a crouch, his fingers still crooked in the position of the stranglehold he'd had on her neck, and said, "Get back!" Keeping his eyes on Simon, he reached down and snatched up the tire chains that had been the kittens' nest. Hunched over, Fournier began to circle Simon as he wrapped the chains around one hand, leaving the looped ends dangling free like a whip. His giant shadow crept along the walls, and pinpoints of light glinted in the caverns of his eye sockets.

Simon pivoted, watching the chains in Fournier's fist. Abruptly, Fournier swung the chains and caught him around the back, nearly knocking him off his feet. Doubled over with pain, Simon backed away. The end of the chains snapped under his chin, carrying him against the wall.

As he slid down the rough wood, he felt a long handle and seized it, using it like a scythe against Fournier's legs. It made a horizontal, slashing arc, and he could see he'd gotten hold of the rubber-headed mallet. Fournier grunted and stumbled. Recovering his balance, he retreated a step. The two men stared at each other, waiting for a twitch of a muscle that would telegraph the other's next move.

Fournier reared up like a stallion, and his huge shadow shot up to the barn's rafters. The chains looped and descended with a crashing rattle to the floor as Simon dodged and struck out with the mallet. It caught Fournier on the side of the jaw with the sound of a melon splitting.

He swayed sideways and went down like a toppling tower of blocks, knees hitting the boards first, then his torso, and finally his head, as his arm curved forward and bounced on the floor, coming to rest palm upwards. Instantly, Simon was over Fournier's body, straddling it, and swinging the mallet up and downward with all his strength, but someone struck it aside before it smashed onto Fournier's face.

"You'll kill him!" said Tommy, catching the mallet away with one hand and steadying Simon with the other. "He's had enough!"

Simon stood panting, staring down at the body between his ankles, and then remembered Kei.

Loquat was already with her. "Her heart's stopped!" he said, bent over her, holding the lamp over his head.

Simon fell to his knees, Fournier's waist between his thighs.

The party closed around Loquat. The shadow of his fist reached up the wall above the frieze of black shadow heads and then went down again, and Simon heard a thump. He got up and pushed his way between Missy and Tommy just as Loquat brought his fist down again like a hammer on Kei's chest.

"Let her alone!" He caught at Loquat's arm, but the giant shook him off.

"Let go!" Loquat commanded. "We haven't any time to lose." With the heels of his palms, he pushed on Kei's ribs, and her legs rose and flopped like the limbs of a lifeless straw dummy.

As he stood watching helplessly, Simon felt pain spreading through his back and knew that some ribs were broken. His jaw and neck were on fire where the chains had caught him, but it didn't matter. All that mattered was Kei.

"Call an ambulance!" said Tommy, pushing

at Elaine. She took a last look and ran into the darkness outside.

There was a cough, and Kei drew in breath with an ugly strangling sound. Simon had never heard anything so beautiful in his life.

Simon sat with her a few minutes in the observation room before the doctor hauled him off to be X-rayed and to have his ribs taped. Miraculously, her larynx had not been broken, but they wanted to keep her overnight to see that she was out of harm's way. Simon refused to be talked into the pain-killing suppositories the doctor tried to give him. He wasn't about to cater to the French obsession with putting medications up one's ass and demanded a bottle of capsules instead.

"They'll hold Fournier here and treat his jaw before they hand him over to the American authorities," said Tommy on the road back home. "While they were putting Kei in the ambulance, I heard Marthe tell Missy that he's a deserter and counterspy, so they'll probably take him back to the U. S. A. for prosecution. Any road, your place is going to be overrun by officials tomorrow."

"I can't tell them anything," said Simon, sinking into a drugged haze. "I don't *know* anything."

In the kitchen, Marthe was the star, serving up facts about Fournier-Michaelson with crepes for those whose appetites had been roused a second time by the excitement. Hilaire kissed Simon on both cheeks, apologized for making him moan when he squeezed him, clucked ruefully at the black and blue stains spreading over his throat and up his chin, and congratulated him on his courage in vanquishing Fournier.

"That was just me getting bloody mad," Simon said exhaustedly, taking off the gold medallion from about his neck where it was chafing him and slipping it in a pocket. "I didn't know what was going on." Kei might have told him. She *should* have told him. He poured himself a cognac and had the glass to his mouth when Loquat took it away.

"Have you had medication?" Loquat asked. He confiscated the drink when Simon nodded. "It might be a fatal combination, pills and liquor," he said, and handed the glass to Jeremy to drink instead.

"For a witch, you seem to know a lot about medical things," said Elaine, accepting a plate of crepes from Marthe.

"Nurse's training," said Loquat. "A backup system when I do healings. One mustn't risk a patient's life. I'm not an amateur tickling my fancy by posing as a guru, you know."

Simon's head seemed to be stuffed with smelly gray cotton, and the kitchen walls were curving inwards on him. "I've got a hell of a lot to thank you for, Loquat," he said in a voice that sounded as if it originated outside his head. "Kei would be dead now, if it weren't for that CPR you used on her."

"My pleasure," Loquat said modestly and blushed. Simon wished Loquat would pick him up, carry him up to bed, and tuck him in. He was so tired he felt like crying.

"You ought to be in bed," said Tommy. "The doctor must have used all the sticking plaster in the hospital on you. King Tut from armpit to belly button. Eagle, will you help me get him upstairs?"

"I don't need any assistance," Simon said stubbornly. "And I don't want anyone touching my back." Tommy and Eagle steered him toward the kitchen stairs. Simon put a hand on the door frame and called back, "Jeremy, you can have the bedroom next to mine."

Missy got up from her crepes and called up the stairs after the three men, "He's not staying. We're leaving for Paris tonight." Simon looked down at her over Eagle's shoulder. She gave him *her* version of the smartass look and said, "You're not the only pebble on the beach, honey lamb!"

While Tommy helped Simon undress, Eagle inspected the icons on the wall facing the bed and whistled. "Real velvet!" he said, stroking the material.

"Nothing but the best for dear old Simon," said Tommy, hanging the tweed jacket and vest neatly in the closet. He folded up Simon's trousers along the creases and put them in a trouser press. "Simon never does things by halves." After pulling out one bureau drawer after another, he turned around and asked, "Where do you keep your pajamas?"

"I don't know." Simon sat down on the bed

with infinite care, lowered himself to the pillow, and moved his hips over in micro-inches. Tommy lifted his legs onto the bed. "I had a pair once," Simon said vaguely. "God knows where they've got to."

"I might have known." Tommy covered him up. "How you can sleep in the buff in the winter in this drafty old place is beyond me." He adjusted the pillow under Simon's head. "Eagle wants to fool around with a soccer ball tomorrow, and I may do if you don't need me. You don't? Fine. But I'll see to getting Kei home tomorrow from hospital. Don't think of stirring."

"Who was?" said Simon before the gray cotton closed around him.

Kei lay on top of the covers in her striped kimono, grousing about the police questioning her when she could hardly talk. The ten deep bruises on her throat were so clear that the gendarmes might also have used them to take Fournier's fingerprints.

Simon put the three goosedown pillows that Marthe had lent him one on top of the other, sat down, and settled back on them cautiously with E. Nesbit's *The Story of the Amulet* in his hand. "Ouch, ouch, ouch!" he said under his breath.

"Poor lamb," said Kei.

He started to read aloud to her, using a creaky, grumpy voice for the Psammead, the sand fairy. Just once he tried a falsetto for one of the girls in the story but stopped immediately. Not only did he sound too flitty for his own taste, but it hurt his throat, which was already sore with sympathy pain because of Kei's condition. He'd just come to the part where the children wished to be beautiful as the day and then couldn't recognize each other as the Psammead granted the wish, when the phone rang.

"You up to dinner at Elaine's tonight?" he asked, putting the mouthpiece against his chest to muffle Kei's answer. "She's asked Tommy over, and I think something interesting's about to develop. She says she'd like to have the family there to give her support."

"I'm part of Elaine's family?" Kei asked hoarsely. "*I* guess I *will* be, though, won't I? I don't mind trying to supply some solidarity, now that she's quit being so nasty. But the doctor said I should stick to soft foods for a day or two."

Simon relayed her answer to Elaine, who said she'd fix a salmon mousse but not to count on its jelling. Then he took up the book again.

"You ought to have been an actor," Kei interrupted in a whisper. "Your voice practically oozes. You make the Psammead sound like Richard Burton."

Simon, who had been trying for Gabby Hayes, wondered if there was any kinship between the voice on the inside of his head to the voice that others heard.

"You know," she went on, "with all our differences, I'd be worried about our chances of a happy marriage, except that we read the same books as children. Robin hated *Winnie the Pooh,* said A. A. Milne wrote upchuck stuff. I'd never have married him if I'd known that, and would have saved myself a lot of agony."

"What flowers would you plant with delphiniums?"

She looked at him quizzically. "Geraniums red, of course."

The hell with her political views, Simon thought. First things first!

Elaine was in a snit when they arrived. "Simon," she said, wringing her hands, "you've got to unmold the mousse for me. I just know I'll ruin it. My nerves are all a-jangle."

After coping successfully in the kitchen, he returned to the living room to find Eagle seated on the couch in his shorts and soccer shirt, looking stunned. The women sat staring at the boy, with glasses of sherry in their hands. Elaine was on her peacock throne and Kei was holding Eagle's limp hand while he stared off into space.

"Did I miss something?" asked Simon, noting that the pentagram had been removed from above the couch and replaced by a tacky abstract. He sat down in a leather coachman's chair and lit a Players.

"I just told Eagle about Tommy and me," said Elaine. "I couldn't get myself up for it before now, and Kei helped me along. God, I feel like the wreck of the Hesperus!"

"How do you feel about it?" Simon said kindly to Eagle, who was beginning to come out of his daze.

"I don't know," Eagle said slowly, thoughtfully. "I'd sort of got used to the way things were, but I'd rather it was him than anybody else, I guess." He looked up at Simon shyly from under thick, curly lashes. "Do you think he likes me?"

"More than that, you ass!" Simon laughed. "I thought he'd break down and blub when he saw your photograph the other day."

"You did?" Eagle withdrew into his thoughts and stayed in them until Tommy arrived, bearing a big bouquet of flowers from the garden. Holding them out awkwardly to Elaine, he said, "Only chrysanthemums from now on. The garden's about piddled out."

Elaine put the flowers in a vase on the dining room table and came back to offer Tommy a cold beer.

Eagle looked uncomfortable and kept scratching the mosquito bites on his legs while shooting furtive glances at his father. Tommy sat down beside him and gave Eagle's knee a pat before asking Kei, "How's the throat?"

In answer, she unwound the tobacco-colored scarf from her neck and turned so that everyone could see the bruises before rearranging the scarf.

"Great Aradia!" Tommy exclaimed. "You nearly bought it that time!"

"It wouldn't have happened if I'd had the sense to tell Simon that Alexis was on the estate," said Kei. "But I knew he'd feel compelled to do something about him, and I wasn't keen on sending someone to the gas chamber, if that's what they do. I kept weighing one thing against another and wound up not doing anything at all."

"Typical Libra," Elaine said. "They put off and put off."

"I don't believe in the death penalty, you see," said Kei.

Simon was about to argue the point, but he remembered delphiniums blue and geraniums red and poured himself a scotch instead.

Elaine cleared her throat. "Tommy . . . " She knotted her hands together on her lap and took a deep breath before spilling out, "Tommy, I've told Eagle you're his father."

Tommy sat back as though the breath had been knocked out of him. He leaned forward with his hands clasped around his glass, elbows on his knees, and his Adam's apple went up and down twice. After a moment, he sat back again, wiped his nose across the back of his hand, and said to Eagle, "Think you can put up with me?"

"Yeah." It was only one syllable, but Eagle's voice managed to break on it. He coughed and looked cross with himself.

Tommy smiled and took out his handkerchief to wipe his forehead. "Damned hot day," he said and turned his head to one side to doctor his eyes surreptitiously.

Kei put an arm around Eagle, squeezed him, put her chin on the top of his head, and cried. Eagle scowled blackly.

"Oh. Ooh," said Elaine, breaking into tears. Pulling up one tissue after another from the box at her side, she applied them to her nose. Simon blinked rapidly and swallowed.

"You sure are a lot of emotional people," Eagle said disgustedly.

The flowers on the table, Tommy's flowers, were so high that the party had to crane their necks to see each other. The table was set nicely but, Simon decided, Elaine would never be a gourmet cook. She'd done her best, though, tarting everything up with lemon slices, parsley, and regrettably—Simon removed his distastefully from the crest of his mashed potatoes—maraschino cherries.

"This *is* a family dinner, after all, isn't it?" said Kei. "We're all related now—or will be, when Simon and I are married."

Unbelievingly, Simon watched her eat her cherry as if it were a natural accompaniment to mashed potatoes.

"Not enough," said Tommy.

"What? I don't follow," said Simon.

"Not enough," Tommy repeated. "I don't like Eagle being a . . . he ought to have my *name*. I think we ought to regularize things." He looked down at his plate and made whorls in his potatoes with his fork. "I think Elaine and I should be married so Eagle can have his rightful name," he mumbled.

"What did you say?" asked Elaine, peering around the flowers.

"I think we ought to get married," said Tommy, getting red and still messing with his potatoes.

"Do you *mind*?" Simon said crossly, getting up to remove the flowers to the sideboard.

Tommy was still fussing with his potato artwork. "Yes," he said, not meeting Elaine's eyes. "Married."

"What would we do that for?" Elaine asked suspiciously. "Eagle's gotten along pretty well so far."

"You're not making this easy for Tommy," said Simon, on the verge of losing his temper.

Tommy put both fists on the table and said, "Stay out of this, Simon. Do you think you have to do everything for everybody forever?" He looked across at Elaine, then lowered his eyes. "There's the matter of my being in love with you, Elaine. I can't help it, you see. I've never been able to help it."

Elaine's eyes flew wide open. She said, "Oh!" and got up and dashed into the kitchen.

Tommy looked crushed. "A man can't help some things," he muttered to the general air.

"You could quit sitting there looking like an idiot and get your ass out there to the kitchen," Simon said.

Tommy rose and looked around the room disorientedly. Then he looked at Simon for encouragement and, having gotten an emphatic nod, went into the kitchen, his napkin dangling from his belt.

Simon, Kei, and Eagle sat in silence, handing dishes back and forth and pretending not to be trying to overhear what was going on in the other room. The dent on Kei's cheekbone deepened as she gave Simon a plate of pickles he didn't want and smiled to herself. Simon ate one pickle, then another, without tasting either. Eagle looked cross and stuffed mashed potatoes in his mouth.

The silence lengthened, and Simon nervously lit a cigarette before remembering to offer one to Kei. She took one, and he absentmindedly held out the package to Eagle.

"No, thanks. I'm not polluting *my* body!" said the boy.

Simon lit Kei's and his cigarette. More silent minutes went by.

"I'll bet they're kissing," growled Eagle, looking revolted.

"Well, if they're in love, and I think they are . . . " said Simon, thinking that they *were* rather long at it out there, and wondering if there was hope of dessert to take the taste of the mousse away.

"Yes, but she's my *mother*!"

"And he's your father! Did you think you were an immaculate conception, you nit?" said Simon, amused. "You'd better get used to it."

"I'm having to get used to too many new things, and I wish it would stop," Eagle sighed. He reached out his fork. "You want that cherry on your plate?"

"Elaine doesn't seem very comfortable in the mother role, do you think?" said Simon, watching Kei plump up the goosedown pillows before helping him get into bed. The evening at Elaine's had tired him, and now even taking a breath

410

made him feel as if knives were sticking all over him like porcupine quills.

"Maybe it's hard to feel motherly if you had a late baby like Eagle," said Kei, lifting his legs onto the bed and covering him up. "I had a friend who'd been a corporate executive twenty years when she got a surprise baby. She was forty-nine and fit to be tied." She climbed in on her side of the bed. "I think she thought she ought to take the baby out for a walk around the block like a poodle instead of changing diapers. Do you feel like reading out loud?"

"The book's on the bureau. Could you?" Kei got out of bed and brought *The Story of the Amulet* to him. "Wasn't forty-five dangerously old to have a baby?"

"Not the best age, I guess," said Kei, snuggling down under the coverlet, "but they've got a way now of keeping an eye on the baby *in utero*, so it can be aborted if anything goes wrong. Sounds pretty icky to me. Pregnancy can be bad enough without that, if you whoops eternally the way I did."

"Do you do that *all nine months*?"

"I didn't. Just a couple. But I started two weeks after getting pregnant and got to know the basins and toilet bowls in every restaurant in town. My mother said it was a familial pattern —two weeks and you throw up your toenails." She leaned over and kissed him, and a breast popped out of her nightgown. Simon looked at it hungrily and sighed. She popped it back in place and lay back on her pillow, closing her

411

eyes and tapping her finger on the book. "Read," she said.

Simon began, but after a few pages he laid the book aside. "I can't keep my mind on this. Dammit, seeing those two all over each other after dinner's made me so horny I could screw the cow." He turned toward her and then lay back against the pillow again, holding his side and groaning.

"How long since you had your capsules?"

He looked at his watch. "I'm ready for another couple."

She got up and went into the bathroom to return with the pills and a tooth glass of water. Simon took the medication and felt better immediately, being the suggestible type.

Kei got back in bed and laid her hand on his crotch. "Would you like me to . . . ?"

"Jesus, yes! But it would hurt too much." He took up the book and began to read. His hand crept over toward Kei and back again. He concentrated harder on the story, which seemed to have erotic overtones he'd never noticed when he was a child. God knows, he would have been looking then. The words "breast of chicken" on a menu would have sent a delicious, debilitating rush of blood to his head at that age. Kei rubbed her foot along his leg, then flopped over on her side with a sigh. He laid his hand on her hip. In another paragraph, he found he had pulled up her nightgown and was stroking the silky flesh of her buttock. The cover above his crotch began to rise.

Kei pulled down her nightgown and moved away. "You'd better stop that," she said.

He read on. Kei sat up, pounded her pillow savagely, rearranged its position, and lay down again. After a little while, Simon felt her hand on him. He paused in mid-sentence as she burrowed between his thighs. The quickening of his breath sent stabbing pains through his torso.

"What are you trying to do, kill me?" he said frustratedly. "I'll bust out of my tape if you keep that up."

"Sorry, love. I can't seem to keep my hands off you," she said, withdrawing and sighing once more.

He turned the page, but Kei kept changing her position restlessly, making her breasts bounce enticingly.

"I can't stand this," he said, pouncing on one with his hand and rolling over toward her. The pain made him howl. "Oh, my God, my God!" he cried, rolling back. "Will you go away? Just please *go away!*"

"When you're old enough, you're supposed to reach 'the age of serenity,' Colette said." She got up and put on her kimono. "With you, I think that will come five minutes before you die."

She called goodnight from the other room and Simon finally fell asleep with the light on and did obscene things with her in his dreams.

CHAPTER THIRTY-ONE

Dear Chris:

Thank you for being willing to take care of the apartment-selling and the furniture. Be sure to keep anything you want, and save out enough for a four-bedroom house, because I have something in mind. More of that later.

Everybody seems to be getting married lately. Tommy and Simon's sister Elaine are getting handfasted, and Simon and I are planning on next month. From what I hear, even Missy and Jeremy Kirbottle look altar-bound, but I wouldn't make any bets on that. Oh, yes, a handfasting is a Wiccan marriage ceremony, but it's perfectly legal, so Eagle will be legitimized and have a real family at last.

We all feel better about that, but I think Simon's envious of Tommy's having a son. Simon's unbelievably sentimental about children and has always yearned for some of his own. So I asked him if—since he doesn't have any—he would mind being a grandfather instead. If I'd given him the moon, he couldn't have been happier!

And what a relief! Listen, when you're having a grand, passionate love affair, you don't want even to think of yourself as a grandmother. I know it was vain and silly of me, and I knew I'd have to get around to confessing it sooner or later, but one does have doubts about a man's reaction to finding out he's making love to a grandmother! I should have known better.

Now, you've always wanted to finish your degree in French. Why not do it at the Sorbonne? You could live in the village and go in by train. Stephen's insurance must be about gone, and that secretarial job you have pays miserably. We'd be happy to support you through your studies—and on for a master's, if you'd like. That way, you could teach French and have a real career and some solid support for the children (although you know we're always here to help if you need us). Or a Ph.D., if you've got the patience and stamina.

I even know a perfect house for you. Elaine's will soon be vacant, when she goes to live with Tommy. If you accept the offer (and of course I'll pay the transportation and for moving your household goods), you'll have to resign yourself to having Sunday dinner with us. Simon will play grandfather until you're ready to scream, but don't worry, I can argue him into reason. He's already talking about getting a pony.

415

Please write as soon as you can to let me know your decision, or Simon will keep asking me until I blow up. He can't wait to get his hands on the twins. They'll love him, and you will, too. I don't see how anyone could help it.

Oh, one warning: if you come, you'd better skirt talking politics with him.

Whatever you decide to do, please plan on coming for our wedding!

Give my love to Dirk and Gino. Hope they liked the bobby helmets Simon sent from London. He had the dickens of a time getting the right sizes.

Do say yes!

Kei

CHAPTER THIRTY-TWO

"This is the only time I've been glad I don't have hair on my chest," Simon grunted, tight-lipped. Kei tore off the last strip of tape and began daubing alcohol gently on the gray lines of adhesive left behind while Simon tried to be stoical.

"We've got to shake a leg," said Kei. "You don't want to be late for the handfasting. Our guests are already whooping it up on the meadow and getting half lit."

She was wearing a long white robe held in with a gold mesh belt and had a crown of white flowers on her head.

There was a racket of running footsteps outside in the hallway. The house was full with the over-flow from Tommy's place, and Jeremy and Missy had taken over Kei's bedroom. Marthe had had to get in two girls from the village to help with the vegetarian meals that were clogging up Simon's system and upsetting Kei's stomach. That made three new helpers on the place, now that Hilaire's young nephew had taken over Fournier's chores.

The kitchen help would be staying on a week or two after the guests left, to feed the workers when they arrived for the grape harvest.

The witches had been a merry lot at table, surprisingly prudish about anything but wine-drinking and sex. They'd made Simon quit smoking during meals, and he'd taken to sneaking out of the house for a cigarette, rather than face some self-righteous witch staring him down for giving in to a pernicious habit. One tracked him down to his study when she smelled cigarette smoke leaking out the room and rapped on the door to give him a lecture.

The vegetarian diet, loaded with rice and whole grains, which squeaked between the teeth because of the eternal sesame seeds, was playing hob with Kei's digestion, and Simon had read *Out of the Century* — a good, thick book — on the john since the witches had arrived. In spite of the general jollity, he'd be glad to see them go. Another day, and he'd be saying "Blessed be!" compulsively himself.

As sponsor of the day's festivities, Simon had been briefed by Loquat on the rites and their meaning and had supplied everything — down to the sage, rosemary, and thyme for the incense — except for the heaps of moonshaped whole-grain sabbat cakes that had been baked by members of the local coven.

Kei helped him into his robe and tied his gold sash and stood back to admire him. "Don't you look handsome!" she said. "Look at yourself." She opened the closet door so he could see him-himself in the mirror.

"Looks like I'm going to a party in my bathrobe," he said, searching the robe for pockets. There were none. Where did monks keep their billfolds? "Where did you get your penchant for costumes? I feel ridiculous."

"You don't look it. Anyway, everyone else is wearing one, and you don't want to be a party pooper, do you?"

The crowd was getting noisy outside. Looking out the window, Simon saw that the guests were clustered around the refreshment table set on the meadow and were emptying the wine bottles at a prodigious speed. The full moon silvered the scene with bright light. In the meadow, the faded white flowers had been replaced by a carpet of blue with a random pattern traced by the footprints of the revelers.

"Don't you just want to squeeze him, the little bunnykins?" said Missy, spiffy in an orange robe. She looked proprietarily at Jeremy, whose powder blue robe trailed on the ground and made him look like one of the seven dwarfs.

"Not awfully much," said Simon. "Are they about to begin?"

From his station in a large circle of string that marked the ground at the ceremonial site, Loquat waved. He was wearing a white robe and a fillet around his hair that had a silver pentagram in the center. Simon was staggered to see Marthe standing beside Loquat, holding a gnarled, thick stick taller than herself.

"Marthe's the high priestess!" said Kei in as-

419

tonishment. "I had no idea!"

Eagle threaded his way through the multicolored robes and came over to stand beside Kei and Simon on the bridge. He looked almost like an adult in his yellow robe, and very handsome indeed. The light over the doorway made the light golden fuzz peeping out of the deep V of his robe shine. "I feel like a creep in this," he said in a voice that was turning baritone, "and they won't let you eat the cookies until this thing's over. Bunch of weirdos!"

Beyond the meadow, the woods were inky, but the tops of the trees looked like silver lace and a full moon stood over the quince tree. Someone was plinking on a zither, and some of the guests had formed a ring and were dancing slowly to the music, their long robes making stately swirls around their ankles. People began to gather around the outside of the string that set off the ritual area, and the music stopped and the dancers left off to join the others.

Simon took Kei by the hand and Eagle by the elbow and started off for the bottom of the circle, followed by Jeremy and Missy. Along the way, they encountered Ron Moody, who looked like a double for Jesus Christ in his sand-colored robe and was carrying a bouquet of sunflowers whose brown centers looked as if they had been cross-stitched in yellow thread.

"I think I'll go Wicca," he said to Simon. "They give such good parties!" Kei took Moody's arm and drew him into their group.

On an altar behind Loquat stood two white

candles in silver candlesticks and bunches of red and white flowers. On the white tablecloth was a silver chalice, a round silver plate inscribed with a pentagram, a censer, and other witchy gear. Marthe leaned the tall staff against the altar.

The crowd quieted as Elaine, wearing a silver mantle over her white robe and white flowers in her hair, came from the woods and joined Tommy, whose mantle was gold. Loquat cut an imaginary door in the air with sweeps of a long, double-bladed knife to admit them to the ritual circle. Simon was puzzled by the unfamiliar expression on Elaine's face. Then he understood. She looked happy for the first time. Unqualifiedly happy and beautiful.

After lighting the candles on the altar, Loquat took salt from a bowl with the tip of his knife and sprinkled it on the silver dish, intoning an incantation to purify the salt. His voice sounded like tones from an organ. With almost the same words, he purified the water of the chalice, dipping his knife into it. Then with both hands he raised the chalice toward the moon, put it down again on the altar, scooped up three pinches of salt from the plate on the end of his knife, stirred it clockwise into the water three times, and laid the knife across the chalice, chanting

> Water and salt, this charge I lay:
> Let no phantom in thy presence stay.
> So mote it be!

More ritual followed, all possessed of an antique

grace. Simon's eyes traveled up to the mistletoe glimmering in the fork of an oak tree and wondered what other rites had been performed in the meadow, centuries ago. Kei put her arm through his, raptly watching the ceremony.

Loquat walked around the inside of the string circle with the chalice, sprinkling briny water on the ground and reciting a spell of purification and protection while Marthe followed, holding the smoking censer of incense. Simon sneezed, and bystanders shushed him. Again the high priest and priestess went around the circle, this time with Loquat holding out the long knife at shoulder height with both hands and Marthe tracing the circle with the giant wand. At each cardinal point, Loquat stopped to light a candle that had been placed on the ground and pronounced an invocation to the archangel of that direction. As he spoke, he traced a pentagram in the air.

When the rituals were completed, Loquat addressed the guests. "This rite of Wicca joins two souls in karmic union, that they may bless one another and comfort one another as they follow their spiritual paths in this life and in lives to come, throughout eternity. May they cherish one another unreservedly, without shame, with heart, mind, and body. So mote it be!"

In a surprisingly mellow voice, Marthe joined Loquat in singing a rejoicing, and sniffles began to break out amongst the onlookers. Tommy placed a silver pendant around Elaine's neck as she bowed her head, saying, "With this symbol colored as the moon, I pledge myself to thee,

Elaine, to share love and laughter from this time forth."

Elaine placed a gold pendant over Tommy's head and then said, "With this symbol colored as the sun, I pledge myself to thee, Thomas, that we may walk in love and cherish one another forever." Simon's sniffles joined with those of the sentimentalists in the group. He wished he had a pocket with a handkerchief in it. Without taking her eyes from the circle, Kei took a tissue out of the bosom of her robe and handed it to him.

Loquat removed the cords tied about Elaine's and Tommy's waists and knotted the ends together to make a circle. With the double cord, he bound their wrists together, singing a basso blessing, and said, "These two are then joined henceforth in love and laughter."

Marthe placed a broom on the ground. Tommy and Elaine looked at each other as if reciting their vows again silently, then joined hands and jumped over the broom.

The crowd went wild, laughing and clapping and jumping up and down.

"That's it, isn't it?" whispered Eagle. Simon shook his head and put a finger to his lips.

The crowd was growing impatient for the grand exit. Loquat and Marthe opened the circle by trotting rapidly around it in the opposite direction with the chalice and the censer. At almost a gallop, they retraced the circle, holding the wand and the knife, Loquat chanting thanks to the archangel at each cardinal point so fast that the words ran together. Then he tore over to the eastern candle to salute it with his knife as Marthe doused the candles on the altar, and shouted, "This rite is ended! So mote it be!"

A great cry of "Blessed be!" went up from everyone, including Simon, who was struggling with a lump in his throat the size of a boulder. A cheer swelled up, while Moody began sobbing out loud, burying his face in his sunflowers.

Tommy and Elaine bolted from the circle and ran into the dark woods as the throng cried out blessings, threw flowers, and hugged each other. Loquat picked up his flute and played, joined by bongos, recorders, guitars, and the zither, while the guests sang and drank and got happily crazy.

"What're Mother and Tommy doing in the woods?" asked Eagle, craning around a man doing a hornpipe. "What did they go in there for?"

"Would you mind bringing out some more wine?" Kei asked the boy quickly. "I think we're running low."

"Okay, but what are they doing in there?"

"Eagle!" said Simon, giving him a look.

The boy looked back at him, waiting for an answer. Then realization spread through his face. "Oh, fuck!" he said, deeply repelled, and stamped off for the house to get the wine, kicking every object in his path.

Kei and Simon walked around the moonlit meadow hand in hand, mingling with the guests and drinking wine while waiting for Elaine and Tommy to come back from the woods. They wound up over by the towering quince tree and stood and looked at the moon, enjoying the music coming from the meadow.

"You're sure you don't want a handfasting?" asked Kei. "Nothing could look happier than that."

"Mm," said Simon, shaking his head. "I'd hate to have to explain it to my relatives. They'll be shocked enough, my getting married after all these years." Kei looked magical in the silver light, he thought, with her white robe spreading out around her like a moonflower. If a unicorn stepped out from behind the quince tree, she could mount its back and fly away across the sky without its seeming unnatural. Nothing, he mused, could surprise him any more. "I've been thinking, perhaps it would be better to postpone our wedding until Christmas, when it would be more convenient for all the clan to gather."

"I don't think I can wait until then," Kei said firmly. "*Definitely* not!"

Spotting something at the base of the quince tree, she walked over to it. A small white marble marker—a lacy carving of a lily of the valley, just right for a baby—grew up out of the grass. There was nothing beneath it, but Simon couldn't bear to let Kei know what the Satanists had done with her child.

"It was so dark there in the woods," he said, wending his way carefully around the truth. "No place for a baby to be. And you always loved the quince tree." He took her hand and pulled her to her feet.

"You did that for me?" She kissed his cheek softly. "Who could help loving a man like you?"

Simon looked sadly at the marker. A child wasted, never to be loved. What would it have been like to have one of his own?

From the meadow rose a roar as the newly-married couple came back from the woods. The music picked up tempo and swelled louder. Simon leaned down to pick up a discarded wine bottle.

"This place is going to look like Coney Island after the Fourth tomorrow," he said. "Maybe when the witches leave, we can get some peace. Would you ask Marthe to broil some steaks for breakfast? I don't want to see another sesame seed or slice of whole-grain bread for the rest of my life! And have her serve prune juice, too, dammit! Maybe when we get back on a decent diet, you can quit getting sick in the bathroom every morning. You couldn't have caught the flu, could you? Are you sure you're all right?"

"I've been meaning to speak to you about that," said Kei, and smiled.

TERROR LIVES!

THE SHADOW MAN   (1946, $3.95)
by Stephen Gresham
The Shadow Man could hide anywhere—under the bed, in the closet, behind the mirror . . . even in the sophisticated circuitry of little Joey's computer. And the Shadow Man could make Joey do things that no little boy should ever do!

SIGHT UNSEEN   (2038, $3.95)
by Andrew Neiderman
David was always right. Always. But now that he was growing up, his gift was turning into a power. The power to know things—terrible things—that he didn't want to know. Like who would live . . . and who would die!

MIDNIGHT BOY   (2065, $3.95)
by Stephen Gresham
Something horrible is stalking the town's children. For one of its most trusted citizens possesses the twisted need and cunning of a psychopathic killer. Now Town Creek's only hope lies in the horrific, blood-soaked visions of the MIDNIGHT BOY!

TEACHER'S PET   (1927, $3.95)
by Andrew Neiderman
All the children loved their teacher Mr. Lucy. It was astonishing to see how they all seemed to begin to resemble Mr. Lucy. And act like Mr. Lucy. And kill like Mr. Lucy!

Available wherever paperbacks are sold, or order direct from the Publisher. Send cover price plus 50¢ per copy for mailing and handling to Zebra Books, Dept. 2657, 475 Park Avenue South, New York, N.Y. 10016. Residents of New York, New Jersey and Pennsylvania must include sales tax. DO NOT SEND CASH.